The
Rail Kings

*Also by Jim Walker
in Large Print:*

The Dreamgivers
The Nightriders

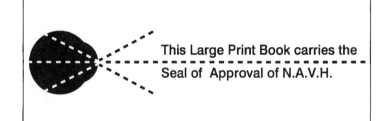

This Large Print Book carries the
Seal of Approval of N.A.V.H.

THE
RAIL KINGS

JIM WALKER

Thorndike Press • Thorndike, Maine

Published in 1998 by arrangement with
Bethany House Publishers.

Thorndike Large Print ® Christian Fiction Series.

The tree indicium is a trademark of Thorndike Press.

The text of this Large Print edition is unabridged.
Other aspects of the book may vary from the original edition.

Set in 16 pt. Plantin by Juanita Macdonald.

Printed in the United States on permanent paper.

Library of Congress Cataloging in Publication Data

Walker, James, 1948–
    The rail kings / Jim Walker.
      p.   cm.
    ISBN 0-7862-1277-2 (lg. print : hc : alk. paper)
    1. Railroads — West (U.S.) — History — 19th century
— Fiction. 2. Frontier and pioneer life — West (U.S.)
— Fiction. I. Title.
    [PS3573.A425334R35   1998]
    813'.54—dc21   97-38614

*To a man who
worked on the rails
and labored to guide his
daughters into adulthood —
my father-in-law,
Orrel.*

JIM WALKER is a staff member with the Navigators and has written *Husbands Who Won't Lead and Wives Who Won't Follow*. He received an M.Div. from Talbot Theological Seminary and has been a pastor with an Evangelical Free Church. He was a survival training instructor in the United States Air Force and is a member of the Western Writers of America and the Western Outlaw-Lawman History Association. Jim, his wife, Joyce, and their three children, Joel, Jennifer, and Julie, live in Colorado Springs, Colorado.

PART I

THE CHASE

Chapter 1

Standing between the cars of the rapidly moving train, the young detective was thinking about his future. It was the thing he did best and the thing he did worst. The wind whistling through the breezeway of the cars made the cold Kansas air even more rousing to his blood. He turned his collar up, then buried his left hand deep in his overcoat pocket. Sucking deeply on his cigarette, he gaped off at the prairie, the monotonous clicking of the rails lulling him deeper into thought. He barely acknowledged the man who came out to stand on the platform with him, a scruffy-looking sort he had seen in the car earlier.

The detective had thought he would be the only man lightheaded enough to stand in the wind to smoke. He always liked being alone. He especially liked the feeling of the prairie, the sense of being alone on the earth's open sea of grass. His irritation grew as the stranger inched closer, standing far too close for Ed's comfort. Refusing to acknowledge the intruder, he looked off into the grasslands. The brief lack of attention was costly. He didn't see the knife.

The railcar was nearly empty. One of the two men who sat near the door had gone outside shortly after the young detective had left the car. The other man sat near the window, his hat pulled down over his eyes.

A small family huddled near the iron-grated stove, bracing themselves on the polished oak seats against the movement of the train. The young father held the little girl's hands toward the flaming grate of the coal-burning stove. "It's warm, Nikki." He leaned down and spoke loudly into the girl's ear. "The fire is warm."

"Warm." The little girl pressed her lips together and looked up toward her father's face. Her eyes flashed. "Warm," she said slowly and smiled. "The fire is warm."

"Yes, Nikki. The fire is warm." Her father spoke loudly and directly into her ear. His hands squeezed hers in approval and then held them once again toward the glowing stove.

Across from them, Sam Fisher, a large-framed, gray-haired man with a snow white walrus mustache, sat stone still, watching silently. His hands were pushed into the pockets of his black overcoat. His derby hat was pushed back, exposing his balding forehead. He clinched an unlit cigar between his teeth and chewed it ever so slightly.

The young father noticed Sam studying his daughter. "She's not feebleminded," he said. "She's blind, and she has a profound hearing loss, but she thinks well." Bruce Elliott was overprotective. At the college where he taught, their family was accepted and Nikki's blindness was not an oddity, but in the community at large, he still felt the need to fight for a normal life for his daughter. "She's only five, however," he went on, "and with the poor hearing, she needs practice."

The wind rattled the windows on the train and the swaying movement of the coach gently rocked the glowing green-shaded brass lamps. The movement of the train lent itself to sleep, and the lone man at the rear of the car seemed to be taking advantage of it. He had slumped his large frame in his seat with his head resting on the window. Sam watched as the man's dingy companion reentered the car, closed the door, and seated himself on the opposite side of the aisle, lacing his legs across the narrow walkway. He pulled a dark plainsman hat down over his eyes.

Sam frowned. The man's legs made it impossible for anyone to leave without waking him up. *Not smart*, Sam thought. He continued to look past the man and out at the small window that peered onto the platform. *Ed ought to be back,* he thought. *How long can it take to smoke one cigarette?*

The woman's attention had been fixed on Sam. Her blue eyes twinkled as she scooted across and sat beside him. She reached out and patted his hand. "It's so good to see you again, Sam. I haven't seen you since my wedding, and I've missed you. You always seemed more like an uncle to me, never like someone who just worked for my father."

"Thank ya, Miss Irene. I've known your daddy a long time, served with the general all during the war, but I wouldn't exactly call that working for him. I was working for the United States Army then."

"Daddy always said you ran the outfit in anything that truly mattered. I've seen pictures of you in your Sergeant Major's uniform. You were splendid!"

His chest swelled and he sat straighter, lifting his chin.

"Do you still enjoy building railroads, Sam?"

"Sort of, I suppose." He scratched the back of his head. "The general builds the railroads. I've always been in the railroad detective side of things. I don't know the first thing about surveying and my back's too bad to drive spikes like a gandy dancer." He patted the revolver in the shoulder holster under his coat. "I work with firearms and muscle."

"And Daddy trusts you, he always has." She squeezed his arm. "But tell me, why did he have to send you to bring us back to Colorado? If he wanted us to visit, why didn't he just wire us and ask us to come?"

"I suppose he was just hoping that you'd trust me too, Miss Irene." He looked at the man and his daughter still warming their hands near the stove. "You and your husband, that is. He don't seem too partial to me."

"Oh, don't mind Bruce. He just hates to leave his work at the college. He's quite taken with teaching, you know. He loves his study time and he loves his books."

"I can believe that."

She laughed. "That's right, you handled the bags. Well, he does love them, and he loves our daughter, too. But you haven't answered my question. Why send you, Sam? Is there some kind of trouble?"

"Miss Irene, he just wanted to be sure you came home, no matter what. The general wants you at the Red Rocks as quickly as I can get you there. I really can't tell you much more than that."

"He's all right, isn't he? I know Mother's death was hard on him. I had hoped that his shopping trip in Europe with my sisters would bring him out of it, but I know he must be lonely there in the castle."

"Well, he's lonely on the inside, I s'pose. Got over seventy servants in that place, so he can't be very lonely on the outside. Hell, I'm —" He stopped midsentence. " 'Scuse me, ma'am. My tongue gets away with me and I forget who I'm with."

She laughed. "Thanks, Sam. It's the army still in you."

"Ought to know better anyway, the general being a Quaker and all, a body can't use coarse language around him. Given all the time I spend round the man, you'd think I'da laid aside the habit afore now."

He shook his head and continued. "Well, what I'm trying to say is, I'm bunkin' in that there place myself lately. Hate it, too. Makes me feel like another blame suit of armor just standing around for decoration. Can't get myself used to it, nohow." He curled his lip as he drawled out the phrase.

"I thought you had a place of your own in Colorado Springs. What do they call it now, Little London?"

"Oh, I still got it. Downtown, by the tracks. All the travel I do in this job behooves

14

me to live pretty near the rails."

He took the cigar out from his mouth and turned it over. Then replacing it under his mustache, he bit down. A grin came over his face. "Yeah, you know how the general is so all-fired smitten with them English people and all their highfalutin, English ways. Never had much use for 'em my ownself. Thought it was good riddance when old Andy Jackson peppered their behinds down in New Orleans. I'da thunk that woulda been enough for 'em."

"Daddy likes the culture found on the Continent."

"Don't know nothin' 'bout culture, but with all of them hoity-toity types struttin' around, I'd just as soon stay to my ownself and in my own place." He paused and, lifting the back of his derby, scratched his gray hair. "It's just that right now, I got to be up at the Red Rocks. The general's done hired a right smart larger batch of new detectives and said with all them new faces around, he'd feel a lot better seein' mine more often."

"Why all the new men?"

Sam looked toward the two sleeping men at the end of the car and frowned. He opened up the gold watch he carried on a chain attached to his pocket. He seemed distracted for a moment. "How Ed can stand outside in that wind and smoke is beyond me. He didn't want to offend you with the smoke, Miss Irene. I do fine just chewing on my cigar here," he took the soaked stub out of his mouth and held it out, then replaced it between his lips, "but Ed needs to light up his makings."

"Sam" — she crossed her arms — "you're not answering me."

"Sorry, didn't want to worry you none. We've gotten ourselves into a patch of war with the Chicago Pacific. There ain't but a few choke points outta them mountains and both the general and Jim Ruby want 'em."

"Can't Daddy work out some sort of compromise? Has he gone to the courts?"

"Humph. Compromises are for losers. We lost Raton Pass in the courts already. CP got there the night before our surveyors were due to arrive. I 'speck the way the courts see things, possession is — what do they say? — nine points of the law. Now the race is for the Royal Gorge and the general is determined he ain't gonna lose again."

Irene shifted in her seat. "Has there been trouble?"

"Yes'm, I'm afraid there has. We've had bridges blown up and track destroyed." He dropped his eyes slightly. "Also, there's been six men killed."

16

"Sounds dangerous," she said. "Why would Daddy send for us?"

Sam glanced once again at the two sleeping men and lowered his voice. "Well, Miss Irene, there's been threats against the general's family."

Irene quickly put her hand to her mouth.

"Them threats is serious," Sam said. "The general's keeping your sisters at the Red Rocks and has guards all along Razorback Ridge. I guess he was kinda afraid that them boys from the Chicago Pacific might try to get his only grandchild." He glanced over at the girl. "Even if —"

Irene tightened her lips and finished his sentence. "Even if she's blind and feeble."

He hung his head. "Yes, ma'am. The general sets a lot of store by the child, no matter what."

Irene sat tall in her seat and looked him in the eye. "Sam, you're a good friend. I know you have a soldierly disregard for weakness of any kind."

He looked at her and blinked. He had watched her grow up, ridden with her on the front of his saddle. Now he braced himself to take whatever medicine she was ready to deliver.

"Sam, you need to understand, Nikki may not be strong, but she makes us strong. She has made Bruce and me stronger people for knowing her. God made her just like she is. Bruce and I would never change her, even if we could."

Irene looked at the little girl, laughing now in her father's arms. She slipped her arm around the arm of the gruff detective and motioned with her chin toward the child. "We might change her for her own sake and for her future but never for ours. Nikki brings out the best in us. She's God's special gift to us, to make us better people. We wouldn't change her, Sam, and," she added, smiling, "we'd never try to change you."

Miles away in a railroad restaurant, Zac pushed back the uneaten pie and wrapped his fingers around an empty coffee cup. An attractive dark-haired woman, coffeepot in hand, wove among the tables toward him, her starched white dress and apron rustling as she walked. With a bright smile, she poured more coffee into his cup. She moved away and stopped to pour coffee for other diners, but smiled warmly back at him.

The Harvey Houses had made quite a difference in the way people ate when they rode the Chicago Pacific Line. Zac remembered when a meal used to be a ten-minute stop, when people paid before they ate and left uneaten food for the next diner. The new eating places, however, served good fare, and the railroad allowed a stop that was long enough to eat one's meal. A second cup of coffee was no longer an impossible luxury.

Zac kept the locked pouch next to him. He didn't know what it contained, but he had a few guesses. Often companies in Chicago shipped jewelry west by special Wells Fargo courier, and Zac Cobb was a very special courier. He'd unload the shipment in Denver, pick up his pay, and make his way back to California. He missed Jenny and the boy something powerful. Meanwhile, he'd keep his eyes open.

He took out his pipe and thumbed his special whiskey-soaked mixture into the black briar's bowl. Two men sitting beside the door had caught his attention. Each time he looked up from his coffee or from loading the pipe, he saw them watching him. One of the men was tall and wore a flat white hat. They leaned close and talked to each other when they spotted his glance, and he'd be willing to bet that he was the subject of their conversation.

Zac raked his match across the table and poked it into the bowl, puffing the pipe to life. He looked through the rising smoke and thought he recognized one of the men. Zac made it a point to recognize the known men in the territory, and he'd heard of the man with the flat white hat. If the man stood up and Zac could see where his pistols sat, he'd know his identity for sure.

The shorter of the two men rose from the table and made his way to the door while the man in the white hat kept his attention on Zac. After watching the shorter man pass by the front windows, Zac took out his pocket watch. His westbound train wasn't due for another hour and fifteen minutes. Until then he'd have to content himself with his pipe and the small book of Tennyson's poetry that he'd brought along to read.

More than a refill and a half later, Zac saw the man who had left return. He wasn't alone, however. A thin man in a black suit stood with him, talking to the man in the white hat.

Suddenly the man with the white hat pushed back his chair and stood up. Now Zac knew it was Jake Rice. Rice always carried pearl-handled revolvers fixed for cross draw. The butts of the revolvers lay at a forty-five degree angle, pointing toward the man's midsection. As the three men strutted toward Zac, he braced himself. He knew he had to be a very inhospitable man when carrying the company's property.

The thin man in the black suit, flanked by the two gunmen, stopped in front of Zac. "I say, pardon me, sir. My name is Peter Williams. I'm chief of detectives for the railroad. My companions here tell me that you are Mr. Zachary Cobb. Is that correct?"

Zac dropped his left hand under the table to the butt of the sawed-off shotgun he liked to carry. It was a great equalizer. He eyeballed the three men and blew smoke from his pipe. Finally he spoke in a passive baritone. "That's right."

"Well, I daresay, Mr. Cobb, after all I've heard about you, it's a pleasure to finally make your acquaintance." The thin man stuck out his hand. Zac ignored it. Instead, he used his free right hand to pull the pipe out of his mouth.

The dark-suited man was persistent, however. He dropped his hand but smiled, showing a golden front tooth. "Might we join you for tea, or whatever it is you are drinking?"

"You English?" Zac asked.

"Why, yes, Mr. Cobb, I am. I — let's see, how do you say it? — hail from Manchester, England."

"Well, Mr. Williams, I'm a little particular about the company I keep, and while I'm working I'm downright partial to my own company."

The man's golden smile disappeared and he leaned forward toward Zac, placing his hands on the table. "Mr. Cobb, you do appear somewhat unfriendly . . . to a man you do not even know."

"I know of your friend here" — Zac looked hard at the man in the white hat — "by reputation. None of it good."

The man in the white hat stepped forward, but the dark-suited Englishman swept his right hand back to restrain him.

"And I don't know you, Mr. Williams," Zac went on, "but I've seen your type before."

"And what would my type be?"

"The type of man who leaves his own country when the law is onto him and plies his trade as a thief and a killer in another country."

The man's jaws snapped shut. He spoke through his teeth. "Mr. Cobb, your own reputation as a killer is well known."

Zac replaced the pipe in his mouth and picked up the book of poetry. "I ain't killed nobody that didn't need killin' real bad. Now, this conversation is beginning to bore me, so if you don't mind, I'd like to get back to my friend Tennyson, one of the few Englishmen who prods my mind."

The man in the white hat placed his hands

on the butts of his pistols. "We ain't here for no tea party, Cobb," he said. "We got business. Now you get up from there and come with us."

Zac picked up a match and popped it to life on the edge of his thumbnail. He allowed it to burn above the bowl of his pipe before he spoke to the man. "I'd ease your hands to your side if I was you. See, Rice, I know who you are and I only go up against gunslingers with an edge. I got myself a ten-gauge cocked under this table and one twitch of my finger will just about saw you in half."

Zac touched the match down into the pipe and watched the man freeze.

The third gunman spoke up. "He's bluffing, Jake. We can take him."

Chapter 2

Zac watched Jake Rice begin to sweat. The man's posture stiffened and he seemed to search the air for Zac's mind, trying to penetrate the blank expression that Zac had perfected for times such as these. Slowly, Rice dropped his hands back down to his side, away from the cross-draw, pearl-handled revolvers.

Williams smiled, breaking the tension. Once again, the Englishman's tooth blinked in the sunlight. "This is unnecessary, Mr. Cobb. These gentlemen informed the man I work for of your presence here today, and Mr. James Ruby, the railroad superintendent, asked me to invite you to his private car for a taste of his excellent liquor. He wants to speak to you about a business proposition that might interest you."

Leaving his left hand on the shotgun under the table, Zac took out his watch and snapped it open. All the interest shown in him made him curious — not tempted to take an offer, just curious. He puffed smoke at the men. "All right, gentlemen, I've got fifty minutes I can give to your Mr. Ruby. I'll go with you, but your guns stay right here."

"We're detectives for the CP, Mr. Cobb." Williams continued to smile. "We'd feel naked without our side arms. You can trust us."

Zac pulled the shotgun up from under the table and puffed on his pipe. He looked the three men in the eye, one by one. "Trust you? I wouldn't trust you three to watch a mule of mine for five minutes. Your choice," Zac said. "I go with you while them guns of yours stay here, or I just wait for my train and you can go back to Mr. Ruby alone. Wells Fargo pays me to be careful and to be very good at what I do, and right now I'm on Wells Fargo time."

The Elliott family walked the aisle toward the Pullman lounge. Sam Fisher walked in front of them and paused in front of the outstretched legs of the gangly man who had positioned himself across their passageway. " 'Scuse me," he said.

Remaining outstretched, the man pushed his hat up. His craggy face was unshaven and a long scar meandered down the length of his left cheek. Dirt was caked beneath his long fingernails. "You got yerself a difficulty?" he asked.

"No difficulty," Sam said. "This family just wants by."

"Well, pardon the fire outta me." The man sat up and put his legs under the seat in front of him.

Sam stepped forward and pushed open the connecting door to the next car. Irene walked by the men and Bruce followed with his hands on Nikki's shoulders, guiding her up the aisle.

The man with the scar watched the little girl in her pretty blue dress. His gaze settled on the small, dark glasses that covered the girl's eyes. "Looky here, Wooley. The little girl's blind."

"Believe yer right, Renfro."

Bruce stopped as Renfro leaned into the face of the child. "You blind, little girl?"

Nikki stuttered a greeting. "Hell . . . oo." She smiled.

Renfro looked up at Bruce. "She don't talk so good, either, for a gal as old as she is. What else's wrong with her?"

Bruce didn't respond at first. He gently pushed Nikki toward Irene in the open door before pivoting to face the two men, still slouched in their seats. Bruce's gaze pierced into Renfro's bloodshot eyes.

"Sir, you don't — how did you put it? —

26

talk so good, either. Your language and your manner I find offensive, and in the presence of a woman and child, I find them downright reprehensible."

Sam pushed Irene and Nikki through the connecting door of the car and watched the dirty man who had blocked their exit get to his feet. "What'd ya call me? Rep — what?"

"Reprehensible, sir, and I didn't call you that. I used the term to describe your language and your despicable behavior, a distinction which I'm sure you couldn't possibly understand."

Renfro moved closer to Bruce, and Wooley, the larger man who had been seated across from him, rose to his feet. "Where do you come off talking to me like that? You strut awful bold fer someone who sounds like a preacher."

Bruce stood ramrod straight. "I am a Christian gentleman, but I am not a member of the clergy. I teach at a university, and my duties there include training and supervising the boxing team."

Renfro's scar angled as he smiled, then he bent over and began to laugh. He slapped his knee. "A fighter, that's a hot one. You . . . a fighter."

He swiveled his head around. "You hear that, Wooley? We done gone and riled up a

27

mean fightin' man."

With that, Renfro moved with great speed. He swerved on his heels and swung a round-house at Bruce, who was firmly planted in the center of the aisle. Bruce ducked under the would-be blow and came up into Renfro's midsection with surprising force, stunning the man and knocking the wind out of him.

While Renfro held his stomach Bruce sent three rapid, left-handed jabs into his jaw. He then stepped forward and unleashed a final right to the tip of Renfro's chin, one that sent him sprawling to the floor.

Wooley reached for his side arm, but Sam stepped forward, his own revolver leveled. He cocked the six-gun. "I wouldn't," he said. "You just relax and let your friend here learn his lesson from the professor."

Both Sam and Bruce backed out of the car, closing the door. Bruce looked up at Sam. "Unpleasant people," he said.

"This is the Chicago Pacific Line. It's full of what a body might call unpleasant people."

Sam and the Elliott family moved through the sleeping car and into the parlor where they all sat in the overstuffed sofas and sipped coffee. A waiter in a white waistcoat poured the coffee from a silver pot. "We'ze gonna be in for a stop in little over an hour, I reckon," the waiter offered. "There's one a them Harvey Houses there. Serves good grub. We'ze only gonna stop fer 'bout half an hour, but that be plenty a time to eat, or to have 'em build ye a box lunch."

"Thank you," Bruce said. "I think we'll do that. It's getting warmer. It's amazing the changes in prairie temperature when the sun gets high."

"Yessir, it'll shore be a gettin' warm pretty directly now, I reckon."

The two ruffians entered the parlor car and cast glances in the direction of the family. Without saying a word, the man with the scar looked at his large companion and motioned him on. They both left through the opposite door in the direction of the second sleeping car.

Sam looked over at Irene. "Don't know where Ed went off to. I'da thought he'd have been here. He was looking kinda peeked, though. Maybe he went on back to the sleeping car to lie down."

"Sam," she said, "don't trouble with those men. I don't like them, don't like them in the least."

Sam pushed his chair back. "Oh, don't worry about me, ma'am. I've had fellers like that for breakfast. Besides, that husband of

29

yours" — he pointed his chin at Bruce — "has already taken more than a little starch out of them boys. I don't 'speck we'll see much of them two for quite a while."

He stood up and tipped his derby. "If you'll excuse me, I'm getting a little tired of chewing on this cigar. I think I'll go out between the cars and light it up, then I'll check on Ed."

"Sam," Irene spoke up. "You don't have to worry about offending me with that cigar of yours. I've smelled plenty in my day."

"Oh no, ma'am, I wasn't worried about you. I figured the child might have a sensitive nose."

He produced a match from his vest pocket and got up from the couch to leave. Irene put her hand on his sleeve. "Sam, please be careful. I'm feeling a little frightened." She paused. "There, I've said it."

"Miss Irene, from what I just saw of that man of yours, you've got nothing to worry about." He smiled at her. "I know enough not to light these things up in the presence of women and children. I may have only been a noncommissioned officer, but that don't mean I can't be a gentleman. Congress don't have to name you one to be one."

Sam's frame filled the doorway as he left the car to stand in the vestibule between the parlor car and the sleeper. He put his back to the wind and struck the match. Cupping his hand over the end of his cigar, he sucked the flame into the tobacco and sent the smoke out into the prairie air.

Riding on the Chicago Pacific worried him a mite. He'd been careful with the tickets and tried to keep a low profile, but something told him that Jim Ruby knew exactly where they were and would pick his own time and place. He knew that if it came down to it, he'd be more than willing to put his own life on the line for Miss Irene and her family. He'd come close enough to dying before, and for things he cared about a lot less.

He puffed on the cigar. He suspected the general knew how he felt and that was the reason he'd sent him cross-country on this errand. Roberts could have picked a younger man, he knew that. He smiled and puffed another cloud of smoke. He could have sent a younger man, but not a better man.

He mashed out the fire on the end of the cigar and flicked it out onto the passing track. He had to look in on Ed. For all he knew, he'd probably find the dreamy-eyed fella buried in a book.

Shoving open the door to the sleeping car, he watched the curtains fly. The gust of wind from the open door pushed the heavy fabric out. The curtains hung back down when he closed the door. "Ed." Sam croaked out the man's name in little more than a whisper. "Let's get back to the Elliotts. We'll be pullin' in for lunch directly."

He raked his hand over the top of Ed's compartment curtain, drawing the fabric to one side. He wasn't there. Sam stood upright and scratched his head. It was mighty peculiar; the bunk hadn't even been slept in. *Maybe Ed got into the wrong bunk by mistake,* Sam thought.

He began to lift each curtain one by one and whisper, "Ed, Ed, time to get up, Ed. Where are you?"

When he lifted the curtain on 3-G, he could see Ed's boots with holes in the bottoms he had urged the man to get fixed. He grabbed his foot, shook it, and then raked back the curtain that hung on the wire.

Sam blinked. It took him a moment to register what he saw. Ed's eyes were open, staring up at the bottom of 4-G, and a pool of blood soaked his shirt and the bunk. Sam could see the man was dead.

The next thing Sam heard or felt was the sound of something hard against his own skull. A thousand cannons exploded in his head, and then all was black.

★ ★ ★

"Mr. Cobb, how nice of you to join us."
The man rose from behind his desk in the private car and extended his hand. His green eyes sparkled above a black full beard. He was a large-framed man, wearing striped trousers and a white shirt with ruffled lapels. He also sported a bright red vest. "I'm Jim Ruby and I run this railroad."

Zac merely nodded, tightening his hold on the shotgun under his arm. Zac's refusal to shake his hand didn't alter the smile on Ruby's face. He extended the intended handshake with an open hand and motioned toward the overstuffed red couch. "Please take a seat, Mr. Cobb. I have an offer I'd like to make to you."

Zac sat deeply into the too-soft couch and looked around the ornately designed car. Red carpet and drapes, red upholstery, and red glass shades on the hanging brass lamps made it easy to see that Mr. James Ruby wanted everything he came into contact with to bear the appearance of his name.

Ruby picked up the ornate brass humidor from his desk, decorated with red velvet. "Try one of these, Mr. Cobb. The finest panatelas found anywhere in the world."

Zac leaned forward and chose one of the fine cigars. He bit off one end and smelled

33

it. Then he put it in his mouth and took one of the matches from the side of the elegant box. Striking it against the box, he puffed the cigar to life.

"Allow me to pour you some fine Napoleon brandy." Ruby picked up a red cut-glass container and began to pour, but Zac held up his hand.

"Thanks, but no. I'm working."

Ruby put the glass back and looked around the room at the assembled disarmed gunmen. "You see, boys, our Mr. Cobb here is a man who puts his duty first." He looked back at Zac. "I admire that in a man, I surely do." He smiled at Zac. "I'm happy to see my men were able to convince you to come and pay me a visit, and when I've made you my offer I think you'll be glad too."

Zac puffed on the cigar and looked at the henchmen around the room. "Ruby," he said, "I came to satisfy my own curiosity. These gunnies of yours didn't have the first blamed thing to do with it." Fire flashed in Peter Williams' eyes, and Jake Rice flinched at the bold statement.

"I can see you managed to take their guns away," Ruby smiled.

Zac puffed on the cigar and took yet another opportunity to grate on the nerves of the CP gunslingers. "That was their own decision, but when a body walks another man's dogs, it always pays to pull their teeth."

Seeing that the remark put fire in the men's eyes, Ruby smiled, then changed the subject. "Cobb, I'll get right to the point. I want you working for me, nobody else but me. I've heard of your reputation, but everybody in the express business has reason to admire the work you do. You keep yourself out of the papers and dime novels and such, but nobody in the industry can hide the results you deliver."

"Save yer air, Ruby. I work for Wells Fargo and they do right well by me."

"Well, hear me out, Cobb. I know you're not allergic to money, and I can promise you more money in the next six months than you could make by working for Wells Fargo in the next five years." He leaned forward across his desk. "You could pay off that place on the California coast you've got and add some more to your spread to boot."

Zac watched the man sip from his glass. Obviously Ruby was a man who did his homework, and the fact that he knew about where he lived and what he needed made Zac uneasy and a mite riled at being snooped on. "I can see your men do their work well," he said.

Ruby grinned. "Shoot fire, I already got some known Kansas gunmen working for me — Doc Holliday and Bat Masterson, to name two of them. You see, I got this man with an empty-headed dream. He wants a family-owned-and-operated railroad enterprise. He wants what he wants, but he's in my way."

Zac flicked the ash from the end of his cigar into a cut-glass ashtray. "Mr. Ruby, if this don't concern Wells Fargo, then it ain't no concern a mine."

"But you see, Cobb," the man said, scooting forward, "I want you working for me, and then it *will* be your concern."

Zac stood up and crushed the cigar into the ashtray. He looked around at Williams and Jake Rice, who dutifully sat by in silence. "Seems to me, Ruby, you've got all the guns you're gonna need to do whatever it is you want to do. I think I'd just get in your way." Zac dropped his chin and added softly, "At least my scruples would." He looked Ruby in the eye. "You may know what I need and what I do with my pay, but you don't know me. I'm not about money. I'm about what's right and what's wrong."

"If you won't become part of the Chicago Pacific operation," Peter Williams interjected, "then just make sure you don't be-

36

come involved with the Denver and Rio Grande."

"Or what?" Zac shot back.

"Just a polite warning, Cobb."

"I don't take too well to warnings, Englishman." Zac knew he lost no love on the English. There was something about the mask of properness they wore that grated on him. It might have also had something to do with his Scottish Highland ancestry and the stories he heard at family gatherings.

Ruby had stood when Zac got to his feet and now walked around his desk. "Peter, don't upset our guest. Mr. Cobb is a very smart man. He recognizes a stacked deck when he sees one."

The big man took out his gold watch and sprung open the lid. Snapping it shut again, he placed his hands on the edge of the desk and leaned back. "And, Cobb, this deck is getting more and more one-sided by the minute."

Chapter 3

Bruce shifted nervously when he saw the two men returning from the direction of the sleeper car without Sam or Ed close behind them.

"Well, looky here, Wooley, it's that sweet family we met earlier." Renfro smiled and tipped his hat to Irene. "Very nice to see you, ma'am; believe you and me is gonna be very good friends."

The remark brought Bruce to his feet, his eyes lighting up as he stepped forward, but the man backed away and drew his revolver. "You just stay back there where you are. Asa Renfro only needs to learn his lessons once. You might look like a preacher, but you shore 'nuff fights like a teamster." He waggled the revolver. "I'm a gonna keep you at a distance, but I'd just as soon put some hot lead through you."

Bruce Elliott stood his ground, not moving an inch. "Sir, my companions will be all too happy to dispatch you when they join us, and nothing would bring me greater joy and pleasure."

A smile spread across the man's face. "I'm afraid you done got your horse hitched to the wrong wagon. Them fellers have done skipped out on you. They ain't gonna be joining us." He pointed the pistol toward the sofa. "Now, if'n you don't back up and set yerself down, you just might be joining them."

Stunned, Bruce backed up slowly and sat down on the sofa beside Irene and Nikki. Taking Irene's hand in his own and patting it reassuringly, he said, "It will be all right, dear, we're on a public conveyance. They can't harm us here."

The two men sat on either side of the family and stared at them. The larger man spoke for the first time. "We ain't gonna hurt you none." He smiled slightly. "You all is jes' gonna get to ride in a private railroad car, and it's real nice, too. Mr. Ruby of the railroad owns it." His eyes widened and he nodded. "A course, he owns prac'ly ever'thin' on the Chicago Pacific."

Ruby smiled at the lanky Englishman. "Peter, show Mr. Cobb our hospitality, won't you? Pick up his bill at the restaurant and see that he gets on his train." He put his hand on Zac's shoulder as he walked him to the door. The heaviness of the man's hand

39

made Zac feel uncomfortable. Patting Zac's shoulder, he commented, "Peter, Mr. Cobb minds his own affairs. He's a company man through and through, I can see that now." He looked Zac in the eye. "I only wish the company you worked for was the Chicago Pacific."

Zac stepped out the door first, followed by the unarmed detectives. He could see the westbound train pulling into the station.

"Those chaps will not be leaving for another thirty minutes. They've been allotted lunchtime at the Harvey House, so you have plenty of time for some more coffee, if you choose."

Zac walked on in silence, his short-barreled shotgun curled under his arm. Right now, he just wanted to get on that train and hightail it. The sooner he got to Denver and dropped off his pouch, the sooner he could head back to Jenny and Skip. They weren't exactly his, but they were all he had.

The steam was rising from the engine and men were loading coal onto the tender. As Zac watched the passengers get down from the cars and make their way toward the restaurant something caught his eye.

"Over here, Mr. Cobb." The men had stopped and Williams was pointing toward the restaurant. "Mr. Ruby asked us to pay your bill, and you have time."

Zac continued walking toward the train in silence, his eyes riveted on a drawn nickel-plated revolver that glinted in the sun. The couple and their little girl were being assisted off the train by two men. Neither of the men appeared to be cut from the same cloth as the family, and one carried the drawn pistol. Zac was trained to look for things that were out of place, and these men were definitely out of place. Even at a distance Zac could read the fear on the woman's face. He quickened his pace and dropped the shotgun into his right hand.

The little girl began to wander off, and the larger of the two rough-looking men reached out and picked her up. Panic spread across the mother's face.

Williams and one of the detectives who had remained standing on the platform near the restaurant hurried to catch up with Zac.

"Mr. Cobb, Mr. Cobb. Back this way, please."

Zac continued to ignore the Englishman and walked up to the family. Tipping his hat, he said politely, " 'Scuse me, folks. Name's Zachary Cobb. Hope you've had a pleasant trip."

The tall man with the drawn revolver re-placed it in his holster and stepped up close behind the frightened woman. Placing the little girl on the ground, the large man spoke up. "Yeah, we all has jest about had the best train travel a body could have. Ain't that right, folks?"

Zac looked at him and squinted his eyes slightly. "Don't believe I was talking to you, bud. I was talking to these nice people."

"Well they're with us. Any talking you do, you can do to us."

Zac looked at the couple and spoke. "Is that right, folks? Does this feller speak for y'all?"

"Not exactly," mumbled the well-dressed man with the dark eyes.

Zac stooped to the ground and looked at the little girl with the dark glasses. Putting his hand up to her face, he touched it lightly and asked, "How about you, angel? Have you had a nice trip?"

"She's slightly deaf," the woman said. "You'll have to speak a little louder."

Zac looked up and then turned back to the child. "Have you had a good trip, honey?"

"Yes," the girl nodded. "I had a fine ride on the t-t-t-train."

The mother looked down at Zac. "Her speech is deficient because of the hearing problem, but her mind is good."

Zac lifted the little girl's chin. "I'm sure it is. I got a little boy that has a talkin' problem, too. He's not actually mine; his folks are both dead, though, and I'm watching him for a spell. He has trouble with words, but I think his brain runs too fast for his mouth." Zac grinned. "Sometimes my problem is just the opposite."

"Mister, I'd sure say that was your problem right now," the tall man said as Williams and his fellow detectives arrived. "Come on, folks, we gotta go, and we gotta go now."

"Excuse me," Williams said. "If there's a problem, I can handle it. I work for the railroad."

"No problem, limey," Zac said, getting to his feet. "Just talking to these folks, and the feller here has some mighty bad manners. It seems these people aren't as anxious to go wherever it is this boy's got in mind."

Irene spoke up. "We are the Elliotts. My father is General Sydney Roberts, the president of the Denver and Rio Grande Railroad. My husband and I were traveling to meet him in Colorado. We had two traveling companions who worked for my father, and I'm afraid they have met with foul play at the hands of these two men."

Peter Williams spoke firmly. "Cobb, you're working for Wells Fargo, and this situation is something that I need to handle in my capacity. I would suggest you just board the train and permit me to do my job."

Zac looked at the couple. "Folks, I'm on my way to Denver myself. I'd be right happy if you'd join me. I'm sorta missing little Skip, and your girl here, even though she's younger than Skipper, puts me in mind of him. It would be pure pleasure for me to have her along for the ride."

"That will not be possible, Cobb," Williams interrupted. "These people will have to remain here to give us the details of their trouble, and I know you have to be on your way."

"You know, Englishman, you really get under my hide. I was talking to these good people and not to you. Now, it seems to me that if you were interested in doing your job, then you'd be arresting these two men here and not bothering the good people and their little girl."

"I'm afraid we don't have the means to do that just now," Williams said, opening his coat to show that he was still unarmed.

"Yeah, we got some business," the tall man standing behind the mother said. "You just butt yourself out of what don't concern you." He grabbed the woman's arm, and she winced at his touch.

Like the tongue of a serpent, Zac rammed the barrels of the shotgun into the man's forehead with a loud crack, dropping him instantly to the ground. Zac then stepped forward and sent the butt of the gun into the jaw of the oversized man standing beside the woman's husband, following the blow with a hard kick to his groin.

He cocked the shotgun and stepped aside, looking Williams in the face. "There you are, limey. Even *you* have the means to arrest these men now. They won't be putting up much of a fight at the moment."

Obviously caught off guard by the suddenness of Zac's action, everyone stood suspended, listening to the men wallowing on the platform in pain. Jake Rice walked out of the Harvey House, his pearl-handled guns in place, and stood there joined by more than a dozen equally unsavory-looking men, which Zac could only guess belonged to the railroad.

"Folks," Zac said as he turned to the still-stunned family, "I'd suggest you get back on the train so we can go on to Denver." The couple turned, picked up their daughter, and made their way back to the steps of the railcar.

"You'll never get away with this, Cobb," Williams said.

Zac pulled out his travel voucher. "Shore I will. I got me a ticket!"

He watched over Williams' shoulder as the men assembled, then motioned with the shotgun. "Limey, you and I are going to take a train ride. Get up in that cab."

The engineer and the fireman were directing the loading of the coal when Williams and Zac swung their way up the ladder. "Here now, who in the blazes are you two fellers? We can't be taking any passengers up here."

"Just relax," Zac said. "We're pulling out right now. I just brought you one more man to shovel coal."

The engineer looked at his watch. "I can't be leaving for another twenty-six minutes yet. Sure'n you want to get me fired?" He gulped. "There's signs all over, 'Irish need not apply,' and mister, I want to keep this job."

Zac pointed the shotgun at him. "There's worse things than unemployment. You'll leave when I tell you to."

The redheaded engineer blinked at the sight of the gun's muzzle. "I see your point." He turned to throttle up the engine. Motioning to the fireman, he said, "Let's get up some steam." He looked back at Zac and the shotgun. "You can bet your life I will," the

46

engineer said, nodding. "I'm going to do just that. I'm going to leave on your say-so, just like you was Mr. Jim Ruby himself."

A shot exploded, making a ringing sound as it glanced off the side of the steel locomotive. "Here, Englishman. Get over here and stand in the door. You better hope them detectives of yours are as bad at shooting as they are at detecting."

Zac backed away and pointed at the open door with the shotgun. Williams stood at the door, waving his arms over his head. "Cease fire!" he yelled. "Cease fire!"

The big locomotive rolled out of the platform as numerous passengers came out of the restaurant. Some were still wearing napkins tied around their necks, watching their train pull out without them.

"Cobb, you will not get away with this. You are stealing a Chicago Pacific train!"

Zac laughed. "How does a body steal a train? I'm just making sure it gets to where it's supposed to get, with that family back there on board." He scratched his chin and smiled. "Come to think of it, I think I'd love to see you take me to court on that charge. Train stealing! Just imagine it!"

The train rolled past the sidetrack and Ruby's private car. Jim Ruby stood on the top step, watching helplessly as the train rolled by, his detective chief acting as a shield.

Williams stood staring at the passing view of his boss. "Mr. Ruby will have another locomotive on these tracks in an hour, with a hundred men chasing you, Cobb."

"Limey, I don't like you; don't like you and don't like your kind. It's gonna grieve me some to have to put up with listening to you squall this whole durn trip." Zac lifted his boot and, placing it on the Englishman's backside, gave a sharp push, sending the sandy-haired foreigner vaulting to the ground below.

He turned back to face the startled engineer and fireman. "Never liked them English, no ways."

"Well, mister, you won't get much of a disagreement from the Irish."

Zac reached into his holster and took out his Colt Peacemaker. Carefully, he took aim at the telegraph pole they were approaching. He cocked the trigger and fired off a round, shattering the glass insulator that held the wire in place and dropping the line near the ground. "Speed up a mite," he said.

"We're just headed up this hill, mister. Don't rightly have enough steam up to roar on up 'er."

Zac reached around and took out the knife

he carried between his shoulder blades. He jumped to the ground and ran to the tele-graph line. Grabbing a fistful of wire, he sliced it clean. Replacing the knife, he ran back to the cab and jumped for the ladder.

"Well, help the man." The engineer's Irish brogue rang out over the boiler, and the young fireman stuck out a hand.

Scrambling aboard, Zac let out a puff. "Thanks, but why the help?"

The Irishman pulled out a pipe and knocked the bowl clean. "Well, I saw what you did on the platform out there. Sure and I don't miss much from up here. Besides," he smiled. "Saw the pipe in your pocket and I figured maybe you had something fresher."

Chapter 4

"Thing's dead!"

Williams leaned over the telegraph operator. "Are you sure of that? It's imperative that we reach Newton without delay."

The man with the green shade over his eyes leaned on the key and once again began to clatter a staccato of words on the wire. He stopped and waited for a reply. None came.

The Englishman grabbed a piece of paper and wrote a message, then handed it to two of the men who stood nearby. "Take this and one of those portable key boxes. Get on a handcar and go on up the line until you find a place to send this message. Talk to whoever will answer. That train must be stopped at all cost. If you can reach El Morro or Pueblo, tell them to start a trainful of detectives this way. We will pin that man in between us."

He looked back at the operator. "Send a message to Wichita and tell them to bring an engine up track and any men they might have. Tell them to bring some track equipment with them too, and horses. I do not want to be surprised by that man again."

Jake Rice had been sitting on the counter smoking a black cigar. Williams caught his eye and stopped. From around the edges of the cigar, Rice spoke. "Shoulda let me kill him at the table. People like that are a lot of trouble."

"Next time, Rice. Next time. The only thing is you'll have to wait your turn to try. Some people just can't be stopped by threats . . . or by Mr. Ruby's money. Something else drives Zac Cobb."

"Don't matter what it is," Rice replied. "Lead is gonna stop him."

When Jim Ruby walked into the telegraph office everyone fell silent. His face was almost as red as his vest. He was obviously very angry. "That train is carrying my payroll; $88,000 in cash money," he said.

Eyes widened all around.

"Now I don't care what you have to do, but just remember this — if you lose one dollar of that payroll you will answer to me. Is that understood?"

Williams nodded.

"You sent men who were amateurs to do that job. I had hoped to delay Cobb in my car until those people were out of sight, but he decided to leave on his own. I talked to the men outside and they tell me your men had guns drawn on the platform. That was what brought all of this on — men who couldn't or wouldn't think about their actions."

"We are taking steps, sir. We'll have a chase train with horses here in an hour, and I'm getting word down the line to send men this way. We will stop him and we will get Roberts's grandchild. I can promise you that, sir."

Ruby crossed his arms on his chest. "Peter, don't wreck my trains, don't kill my men, and don't lose my payroll. You may have men working for you who make mistakes, but that man you are chasing doesn't. Your men may not think, but Cobb does."

Jake Rice grunted and let out a cloud of smoke. "A thinker or not, bullets kill smart men same as dumb ones."

Bruce had situated Irene and Nikki back in the parlor car. "I'll get you both some water, darling."

"Thank you, that would be wonderful."

"Keep your head down, sweetheart," he warned. "There might be more shooting."

After the brief slowdown outside of town, Bruce skirted around inside the parlor car, in a low crouch, taking care to keep his head

52

below the windows. The train was moving faster now, and he rounded the bar and saw the steward huddled behind the heavy mahogany barricade. "Are you all right?" Elliott asked.

"Yessir, I is. Whaz happening out there? Whaz all the trouble about?"

"Some men were trying to kidnap my family, enemies of my father-in-law, I fear."

"Lawsey," the man grimaced. "My wife's daddy's got some men that I 'speck want to kill him, but it ain't as bad as all dat." Bruce could tell by the man's rapid speech that he was very nervous. "Yo' wife's daddy musta took somebody in a card game."

"No, I'm afraid it's much more serious than that. Do you have some water? I'd like to take some to my wife and daughter."

"Where I comes from, dere ain't nuthin' more serious den takin' somebody in a card game."

The man scooted over and reached behind the bar. "Here y'all is." He handed a pottery jar of water to Bruce and two glasses. "Y'all take dis. I ain't a gonna come out from behind dis thing till I'ze plumb shore all dat shootin' is done stopped."

The train was picking up speed when Bruce came out from behind the bar. He peeked over the windowsill and could see the rail yard in the distance. "I think we're all right now, Irene. You can be a little more comfortable."

Irene was a strong woman. She was not one to panic, and the few times Bruce had seen her frightened she had kept her fears inside. He could see the concern she had for Nikki, and he felt a fresh respect for her strength.

Irene bit her bottom lip. "What will happen to us now?"

"I don't know," Bruce answered. He knew better than to try to fool her. She had always been able to see right through him. And to conceal a matter from Irene went against everything he stood for. He knew that secret thoughts between a husband and wife became the building blocks of a wall.

He reached out and touched her cheek. "I don't know, darling, but I do know we're better off right now trusting the stranger who's controlling this thing than we would have been with those two men."

She silently nodded and held the cup to Nikki's lips.

"I've got to go back to the sleeper car. You stay here with Nikki; no need to spoil your good memory of Sam."

She blinked back tears.

The fresh breeze ripped past Bruce as he

opened the connecting door to the sleeper. The curtains were blowing with the wind. He stood at the door for a moment. He had liked the old man, too. He liked him and he trusted him.

He moved down the line and pushed each curtain aside, knowing what he would find but not knowing where he would find it. He pushed aside the curtain marked 3-G and saw Ed again. Ed had always struck him as a dreamer, a quality very unusual for a hard-working man of the West. Now, as he looked into Ed's lifeless eyes, Bruce thought about the fact that Ed's dreams would never be realized.

"Aww . . . hunn . . ."

Bruce heard the moan from below. Stooping down, he raked aside the curtain on the bottom marked 1-G. Sam Fisher rolled off the short ledge and onto the floor of the car.

"Sam . . . Sam, it's me, Bruce Elliott." Bruce started looking the rotund man over for blood, but Sam was dry as a bone.

"Awwww . . ." The low moan was followed by a whispered guttural curse.

"Where are you hurt?"

The older man put his hands on his head. "My head, they done split open my head."

Bruce felt the man's disheveled gray hair. "You do have a knot back there. It feels like the size of a goose egg. Here, put your arm around my shoulders. I know one woman who's going to be very happy to see you."

"You boys just hold her steady." Zac turned and began to climb the tender.

"We aren't going to move a muscle, mister," the engineer answered. "Whatever happens on these tracks will be your affair, and all the saints in glory won't be able to prod us to interfere. We are going to have to stop to take on water, though, sure'n the day is long."

Zac stood on the coal. "All right. Just make sure everything is clear when you do. Anybody in the express car?"

"Well to be sure there is. Crabbtree is holed up in there. He'll know something is wrong. He's of the conscientious variety. He might give you a bit of a struggle."

Zac turned and climbed up on top of the moving train. The sound of the wheels on the track rumbled beneath the cars. The train swayed beneath him as he steadied himself and moved toward the rear. He knew what he was doing was risky. He knew if he'd taken the time to think about what might happen, he might not have put himself in such a spot. But some men see risk in walking across a street, and to a precious few the

56

real risk is to stand still and do nothing, be nothing. Zac was one of those few.

Reaching the top of the express car, he reached around and drew out the long Green River knife between his shoulder blades. He began to pry at the top of the hatch. Seeing a crack in the seal, he lifted it and shoved it aside. Down below, in the car, he saw a man scrambling for cover. Zac swung his body through the opening and dropped to the floor of the moving car. He tumbled sideways as he hit the deck.

Several shots belched out of the darkness. "Stop there. Who are you? This is my charge here and I'll protect it."

"Crabbtree?" Zac asked. "Is that you back there, Crabbtree?"

"Yes, and who, might I ask, are you?"

"I'm Zachary Cobb, agent for Wells Fargo."

The man hesitated before he spoke. "How do I know that, you coming down on me like a snake out of a hole?"

"Well, if you'll just light one of those lamps you blew out, I'll be all too happy to show you my badge and travel vouchers."

Seconds passed. Zac could tell this was a cautious man.

"You light one," the man said. "I won't shoot."

"All right. But if you let loose with that shooter of yours, you better make sure you kill me outright. I don't take kindly to being shot by a mail clerk."

Zac looked around and caught the glint of sunlight from the open hatch against a glass globe that swung near him.

He reached up and steadied the lamp, removing the globe. Taking out a match, he popped a flame to life and stuck it to the wick. Zac replaced the globe and stepped aside.

He could see the man in a white shirt, huddled in the far corner. Reaching into his pocket, Zac took out his badge and the travel vouchers and pinned the badge to the papers. "Here," he said, "take a look at these." He slid them across the waxed floor.

The man in the corner lit his own lamp; after taking note of the brass badge, he unfolded and read the vouchers.

"All right. I guess you are who you say you are. But what do you want here? I don't work for Wells Fargo. I work for the Chicago Pacific Railroad, and I am charged with the defense and disposition of this property until relieved."

Zac walked toward the man and, replacing his knife behind his back, held out his hands. "I respect that, Crabbtree. I've just come to get Wells Fargo property. I might have to leave suddenlike, and I don't want anything I'm supposed to carry left on the train. I also had my rifle shipped, and I think it's here too."

The thin, bespectacled man began to light other lamps. "I think we do have something here that belongs to you." He handed the papers and badge back to Zac and began to rummage in the corner of the car.

Zac could see several boxes of dynamite along the wall. He took his knife out again and began to pry open the lid of one of the boxes.

"Here's your rifle, and a bag addressed to you. Hey! What are you doing there?"

"I don't have time to argue with you, Crabbtree. I may need some of this before I'm through today." He took fuse cord and stuffed several coils into his buckskin jacket pockets, along with about a dozen sticks of the blasting powder.

The man handed Zac the buckskin rifle bag, and Zac opened the end and slid out the long gun to inspect it for damage.

"That thing is heavy. What is it?"

Zac looked it over, sliding his hand over the finish. Breaking it open, he held the barrel up toward the light. "This is a Sharps Creedmore, 44–90 caliber. When I use the rear sight, it'll reach to upwards of 1300 yards, almost three-quarters of a mile."

"And you use that thing in your job?"

"I've had more than one occasion to. I always have equalizers on the job because the people I go up against seem to have more resources in people and time." He pulled out the bandoleer laced with the 44–90 ammunition.

"How'd you get into this kind of work?"

Zac slung the bandoleer over his shoulder and grinned. "My mother would say it was a lack of prayer that got me into it, and I suppose it will be the use of it that gets me out. Now, do you have a Wells Fargo package in that there safe of yours?"

"That safe is not to be opened until we get to Denver."

"Well, Crabbtree, you may be going to Denver, but I doubt if I get that far, and I'll need to take that package with me. Been carrying one from Chicago" — he slapped the security belt around his waist — "but I'll need to take that one, too."

"That's against regulations."

Zac smiled. "Crabbtree, my only regulation is the one that says I get my job done. When my regulation goes up against yours, then there ain't no regulation in my book that says I can't use some of that dynamite to open that safe of yours."

The man blinked. "You'd do that?"

"Quicker than a duck on a June bug," Zac shot back.

The man turned to the safe and began twisting the dials. "Okay, I'll get your property, but you'll have to sign for them." He looked back at Zac. "You can write, can't you?"

"Real pretty like," Zac said.

When the man swung open the heavy doors, Zac saw the stacks of bills on the upper shelves of the safe. "Holy smokes!" He let out a loud whistle. "I guess I can understand why you didn't want to open that up, Crabbtree."

The clerk found the security package stamped Wells Fargo and handed it to Zac. Suddenly they were both bolted up against the open safe. The train had braked without warning.

Chapter 5

The sudden stop launched Nikki onto the floor and she began to cry. Irene scooped the little girl up into her arms. "It's okay, sweetheart. Go ahead and cry." She rocked the child in her arms and held her tight, listening to her sobs.

"Is she going to be okay?" Bruce asked.

"I think so." Irene gently rubbed Nikki's forehead as the girl continued to sob. "It's okay, honey. We all got a little jolt."

The men had moved to the door to look out and see what the trouble was. "Sam, sit down and watch the girls," Bruce said. "I'll go find out what's happening. Your head's still not in the best of shape, and I'd hate to see you agitate your condition."

The older man nodded, and Bruce took a long look at Irene before heading out the door.

Zac heaved on the heavy door of the express car and slid it open. The wind continued to blow, but sunlight streamed into the darkened car. Zac and Crabbtree blinked into the bright light.

Zac saw the fireman pulling at the line on the water tower and lowering the spout that would fill the locomotive's tank. He broke open the Sharps, extracted a shell from the bandoleer, slid it home, and closed the firearm. Lifting the gun, he squinted down the barrel and fired.

The glass insulator that stood on a pole above the tower shattered into a thousand pieces and sent the telegraph wire to the ground in two separate sections. The fireman jumped back and his hands shot up, sending the water spout back up into the air.

"Sorry!" Zac shouted. "Didn't mean to scare you none."

"Well, you did!" the man screeched.

Zac jumped down from the express car and saw Bruce Elliott climbing down from the parlor car. "How's everything in there?" he asked.

"Fine. Nikki was a little roughed up by the sudden stop, but she'll be okay. And I found Sam Fisher alive! What a relief. He's one of Irene's father's railroad detectives, but he's been a friend of the family for years."

"Good," Zac said. "Before all this is over, we'll need an extra gun. Can you shoot?"

Elliott stiffened. "Sir, I served in the 5th New York Artillery during the war. I can shoot." He dropped his head slightly and a smile crossed his lips. "Of course, I'm far better with a cannon like the one you're carrying there."

Zac smiled and slapped the butt of the Creedmore. "Well, Mr. New York Artillery man, we'll have to see about that."

Elliott swiveled his head back, as if to reassure himself that there was no train coming up the tracks. "How long do you think it will take them to come for us?"

"Can't say for sure. Some men move off before they're ready. They're in such a blamed hurry to get there they can't do the job when they arrive. Other people are preparers. I 'speck the Englishman who's in charge of that outfit is one of those. His type like to feel in control even when they aren't, and preparation is one way to feel you've got the situation in hand. 'Course both types are dangerous in their own way."

Zac smiled. "Your General George McClelland was a preparer — but most of the time he was preparing to lose."

Elliott ignored the jab and Zac's obvious amusement at the analogy. "You do seem pretty cool about all of this," he said.

"Mister, keeping your head is the only way to survive when you're outgunned. If you can't shoot more guns, you gotta make more sense."

"Do you think they'll be waiting for us in Denver?"

"We won't stay on these tracks all the way to Denver. Somewhere behind us those folks are gonna pull aside and be able to telegraph up ahead. They'll have a gang barreling right down on us, and we want to be off of this train before that happens."

"When will we have to leave the train? I'll have to get Irene and Nikki ready."

"Well, I don't rightly know how long we can keep this up before we have to light out, but we're gonna make it a little difficult for them to follow us too closely." Zac glanced aside at the car couplings. "You know how to uncouple these cars when I tell you to?"

"Why, yes. Irene's father has shown me a great deal about trains."

"Well, you best get back on now. Be ready to uncouple that last car back there when the whistle blows. I'll send out five short blasts."

As Elliott retreated to the parlor car Zac sauntered over to the tower. Removing two sticks of dynamite, he uncurled a loop of fuse, preparing a charge.

"Here now!" the engineer shouted. "Don't be a bringing that thing down on this poor mick's head."

Zac ignored the man and tied the charge to the base of the water tower. He pulled out a match and looked up at the Irishman. "I'd take some pains to fire that thing up and get outta here if I was you."

The man focused on the unlit match and said, "Can't be a leaving fast enough to suit me, mister. Just hold off on that thing and I'll be lumbering old nine outta here."

Zac watched the Irishman pull the throttle and the train began its movement out from under the tower. He struck the match on the side of the tower and lit the fuse. Watching the sparks fly, he slung the Creedmore over his shoulder and ran toward the engine, grabbing the gangway rail.

Hefting himself into the engine, he turned around to watch. The explosion rocked the tower and sent shards of lumber flying in all directions. The rear car was barely clear, and many of its windows shattered. Zac watched as the tower came crashing to the tracks, water flying up in all directions.

"Wheeeew . . . wee," the old Irish engineer let out a gasp. "Mister, sure'n you leave a trail wherever you go."

"Thomas . . ." The fireman, standing beside the small pile of coal, got the Irishman's attention. Their eyes met.

"Mister," the engineer spoke to Zac. "My

fireman over there's standing by all the coal we've got. You had us leaving Newton a bit early. Now unless you plan to stop up ahead at Hutchinson, we'd better be content with holding our speed down a mite."

Zac rubbed his chin. "Problem is," he said, "it's only a matter of time before those boys coming up behind us find a good connection on the wires. For all I know they already have. When that happens, they'll have sharpshooters ready and waiting for us. I don't want to get anyone killed on this thing. I'm just trying to get Wells Fargo property to where it belongs and to keep that family back there from being taken somewheres against their will."

"I know," the Irishman said. "Aye, and I can't figure out why you'd bother."

Zac saw the steep rise looming ahead. "Just keep the steam up until we get to the top of that hill and then stop. I got a few things in mind to slow those people down back there."

The fireman shoveled in more coal, and the big locomotive continued its ascent to the foot of the hill. When they reached it, the train started its slow climb to the top. The engineer opened up the throttle, but the grade slowed the big locomotive to a crawl.

Zac turned to the fireman. "Better shovel in some more and then you and I are gonna walk a mite."

"Walk!"

"Well, I got work for us to do on this grade and I'd like to pick the steepest part. So let's build up some fire and then you grab one of those grease buckets."

The man began to furiously spade into the coal bin and throw the black rock into the firebox. It roared as he swung the shovel back and forth. There was a rhythm to his work, a rhythm that showed he knew what he was doing. When the flame was roaring sufficiently to maintain steam to the top of the grade, he closed the door on the box and, laying aside the shovel, wiped his face with his red bandanna. "All right, what we gonna do now?"

"Just pick up one of them grease buckets, partner. We're gettin' off for a spell. We'll grease these tracks real good. If those boys behind us are havin' trouble with their steam, makin' their wheels spin on this uphill grade is gonna just give 'em fits."

The engineer laughed. "Captain, you are a pure well of caution."

"Just make sure you're waiting for us at the top of the hill," Zac said.

"Leave you? I wouldn't think of such a

thing. This is the most fun I've had in all me born days."

Zac and the fireman jumped down on either side of the slow-moving train and stood aside as the cars passed them. Zac could see the perplexed look on Bruce Elliott's face in the railcar window as the professor spotted Zac standing alongside the track. Zac smiled back at him.

When the last car passed, Zac tossed the fireman an old pair of gloves he had taken from the engine and donned another pair himself. "Let's rub this stuff on thick."

The two of them pulled grease out of the cans by the handful and slopped it onto the rails. Sliding their hands along the tracks, they smoothed the coating onto the hot surface. When the cans were empty, Zac and the fireman stood upright and surveyed their work. The fireman wiped his brow again and said, "Well, I guess they won't be getting up the track here very fast."

They dropped the cans and their greasy gloves beside the tracks and scampered toward the top of the slope where old Number 9 stood puffing smoke. Running past the last car, Zac caught Bruce Elliott's attention and signaled him to move forward. Reaching the top of the hill, they climbed aboard the engine.

"Did you get her done?"

Zac nodded. He looked back down the track and could see the smoke from the on-coming train in the distance.

"Those fellers will have to stop and clear what remains of the water tower, I'd reckon," said the engineer as he looked over Zac's shoulder at the distant smoke.

"And when they do," Zac added, "they're gonna get another surprise."

Zac reached up to the lanyard that oper-ated the whistle and sent out five short blasts. He waited for Elliott to follow his instruc-tions, waited and watched. Suddenly, the three of them could see the last car rolling back down the hill. It began to pick up speed just over the crest of the rise.

The Irishman let out a whistle. "Wheeeew! Saint's a'mighty! I figure that car and that train got themselves a good chance of reach-ing that water tower at just about the same time."

Zac nodded. He reached into his pocket and pulled out his briar pipe. Loading it with his special mixture, he looked up to see the engineer eyeing the tobacco. Zac offered it to him. The man took it as Zac lit the pipe.

"One thing" — the big Irishman cocked his head and fished for Zac's mind — "you never did answer me down there. Why are you doing this? Why go to troubling yourself? Isn't life dangerous enough on its own steam without a man placing himself in the path of someone else's bullet?"

Zac smiled and puffed his pipe to life. "If a man knew all the reasons why he did the things he did, it would take all the humanity out of being a man."

Peter Williams watched the two firemen manning his own train. The men had stripped off their shirts and were shoveling coal repeatedly into the open firebox. Their engine was highballing, and with any luck at all, Williams knew they'd catch the Number 9.

"We're gonna have to slow down and take on some water, Mr. Williams. There's a tower around the curve up ahead; we'd better start slacking up on the throttle."

Williams only nodded and the engineer began to pull on the throttle, slowing their speed. When they rounded the curve, the man blinked. All over the track lay what was left of the water tower.

"Mr. Williams, we got trouble."

Williams leaned forward to see over the engineer's shoulder.

"We'll have to stop to clear that," the engineer said. "They done gone and blew up the tower."

Williams pushed forward on the man's shoulder. "Increase your speed," he said. "We're going through it."

The engineer turned around with a startled expression.

"Do exactly as I direct you. I will take complete responsibility."

"Mr. Williams, with limited water we'll have to slow down our speed sure enough."

"You do as you see best. But I don't want to stop here and spend time clearing track. Just go on through."

The engineer pulled the throttle open, and the train picked up speed. It hit the first batch of track-side debris, and the cowcatcher on the front of the locomotive bucked the lumber into the air. Crash after crash sounded as the engine roared through the debris. Williams stuck his head out of the cab of the locomotive and watched several pieces fly by him. It was then that he spotted the downed telegraph wire. It hung beside the tracks like a lifeless snake.

He stared at the wires as the engineer roared out, "Holy mother . . ." He hit the brakes. They could all see it now — the empty car barreling down the hill, right toward them.

Chapter 6

Sparks flew as the chase train ground to a halt.

"What are you doing?" Williams screamed into the engineer's ear.

"I'm backing this thing up — fast." The engineer hoisted the Johnson bar to reverse and slowly the train started to lurch backward. The men in the engine watched as the oncoming car approached at a faster and faster speed. The engine slowly began to pick up speed as it backed up through the water tower debris.

The engineer threw open the door to the firebox. "Here, give me more steam," he yelled. The firemen once again began to shovel coal, at the same time keeping a watch on the speeding car.

Finally, unable to avoid a collision, they all held on to the sides of the engine cab.

The car hit the front of the chase engine and shook it, but the backward momentum of the train held it steady on the tracks. Adjusting the throttle, the engineer slowed the train with its attached missile.

Peter Williams jumped down from the engine and began to beat on the windows with the whip he carried. Several men poked their heads out the windows. "Get out of there," he said, waving his arms wildly. "We must clear the track." Williams shoved several of the men who stepped down from the stairs. "Get down there. You've got to push that car off of the tracks."

When the telegraph operator came down the stairway, Williams screamed at him. "Pick up that key of yours and get up the track. There is a downed wire up there, and I want a message sent to El Morro before that madman can cut more wire."

The man scrambled back up the steps to the car and shortly emerged with the wooden box containing the portable telegraph key, along with a spool of fresh wire. Williams' glare made him run toward where he'd been told the downed wire lay. The Englishman briskly followed him down the tracks, stopping to watch the men strain at the car lodged against the front of the engine. "Put your backs to the one side of it and shove it off the tracks," he snapped.

Williams continued down the line, following the operator with the portable key. He stood beside the man as he spliced the line together and connected it to the portable box. Sitting down on the ground beside the wooden box, the man began tapping on the keys.

"I've got 'em!" he yelled. "I've got Hutchinson!"

"Ask them if the Number Nine has passed there yet."

The man began clicking on the keys and then paused for a response. Taking his pad and pencil, he wrote it down. "No, they say it's overdue."

"They will need to take on coal and water. Tell them to stop the train — to make sure they don't take anything on."

The man began clicking the keys as Williams continued to talk. "Tell them to wire ahead to El Morro that the Number Nine has been stolen. Tell them that if they can't stop the train, men from El Morro will have to come east and stop it. Make sure they realize these are my orders — that everything else on the road must be set aside until these people are delivered into my custody."

The man at the key paused for a response. "I've lost them, Mr. Williams."

"Well, did they get my message or not?"

The man looked up at him and shrugged his shoulders. "Ain't no way to tell. Ain't no way to tell when we lost 'em either."

The Number 9 wasn't exactly roaring down the track, but it was maintaining a steady pace. Already, the fireman had to slide the shovel way back in the tender to bring up a spadeful of coal. Zac put the rifle down. Moving at this speed, it had been easy to take down telegraph lines with the Sharps. He had cut this one clean.

Zac gazed at the locket on his watch. He had it open and was studying a picture, not just checking the time. Suddenly he was aware of the Irishman looking at him, and then back up the rail. "You got a wife up ahead somewheres?"

Zac snapped the locket shut and dropped the watch back into his pocket. "No," he said, "I'm a bachelor, by choice."

"Oh, now is that so? By choice, is it?" The man smiled. "Out here in the West, most men are bachelors by location. Aside from hurdy-gurdy gals, there just isn't a terrible lot of choice." He puffed on his pipe. "But you saying you're one by choice must mean there's a woman who wants you."

Zac said nothing. Like the engineer, he puffed on his pipe and kept looking at the road ahead.

"Is she far?" the man asked.

Zac nodded silently.

"My missus is back in Kansas City. Kansas City is a fine town, and she has a husband who has a job." He turned around and grinned. "I suppose that makes her something special, to have an Irishman who has a job for a husband."

He turned back to look at the rail. "Yes, sir, she's just about the finest and fattest woman in all of Kansas City. It shows how prosperous she is. Is this woman of yours prosperous, Mr. Cobb?"

Zac gave a soft smile. "Not quite. She owns her own restaurant back in California, and I suppose that makes her prosperous in her own way."

"Well now, I'd say you were seriously sick in the head there, me bucko. If my woman had means of her own, you'd be hard-pressed to find me here. Not that I mind it, you see. I like driving this huge contraption. Still, being beside the fire with a woman of means, well, that would be the life for this boy. You think about this woman something considerable, do you?"

"Yes, I do."

"Me bucko, when a woman loves you" — he turned around once again to face Zac — "I mean, really loves you, that is the most powerful force the good Lord has put on this earth." He turned back around and looked off, not at the rails, but at the sky. "I sorta believe that a woman like that, God gives her a love for a man to remind the dunderhead how much it is that God loves him. Me mother in County Cork used to say that all love is God's love, and that the love He gave us poor folks down here on this earth for each other is nothing but a poor reflection of it."

"Sounds like your mother and mine were a lot alike," Zac said.

The engineer looked back. "I think all mothers are alike. They got young'uns to love and that kinda shapes 'em. Makes 'em natural lovers, it does." The man tapped out his pipe. "So, me bucko, you gonna marry that girl?"

Zac looked off to the stretched-out prairie. "I reckon not," he said. "Least not yet."

The man looked long and hard at Zac. "Change is a mighty fearful thing, isn't it?" He blew out the pipe stem. "Women all the time want to change a man." He tugged on his red suspenders. "I was very much afeared of that myself. But the way I figure it, God didn't put a man on this earth just to leave him be. He put him here to make changes in him, not just to watch him grow old and die. The animals, they stay like they are. They get older and can't fend for themselves, and then, if there's a mercy" — he leaned forward — "some other critter kills them and eats them." He waved his hand around. "In all of God's own blessed earth, only man changes on the inside, changes down deep in his soul."

He looked at Zac and pointed to the gold watch and locket. "Boy, it is a foolish thing to put off the thing that will make your life a life and not just a job."

Zac grunted. "It's my job that's keeping me from her. This is what I am and this is what I do best, and she hates it."

"Well, it seems to me a man can find another job a far sight better than he can find another woman."

"That just about sums it up," Zac said. "I don't want another woman; Jenny's the best there is. And I don't want another job, because I'm the best there is."

"If that Jenny of yours is the best there is, then a purpose-minded thinking man like yourself ought to act on it, because other men who are more convenient to her just might. Women are scarce and good women are like hen's teeth."

He scratched his stubby red whiskers and looked Zac up and down. "A course maybe what you need is another woman, someone who just might test that steely resolve of yours, someone who might peel back the curtains to your soul a bit and show you just how needy you are."

"There are folks who would say I've got one too many women right now."

The engineer chuckled. "Me bucko, I swear, how you can be so content with such tiny thinking is baffling to the mind. Fact is, you've not met all the women — you might find one that wants to wait for you to die. And it's for durn sure you ain't tried all the jobs. You might find one you're much better at than the one you got. No" — he shook his head — "you remind me of the little boy who fell into a ditch. He stayed there for his whole boyhood 'cause he didn't want any help. Friends brought him things to eat to keep him from starving. Well, he'd just been in that ditch for such a long time thinking that he couldn't get out that he'd forgotten that he was all growed up."

The engineer looked over at the fireman. "We'll be pulling up into Hutchinson." He stuck his head out of the cab and pulled it back in. "Wonder why all them men are out by the tracks? Looks like a wagon across it, too."

Zac peered out the window. He could see the men beside the tracks and two men on the roof of the station, one that shadowed the tracks. "They must have gotten the line repaired. Move on through."

"We won't be exactly going lickety-split when we hit that station."

"Just do your best to open her up, and keep your head down to boot."

The engineer opened up the throttle and gave out several warning blasts of the whistle. He squatted down beneath the window opening. "Don't worry about me, I'm the soul of caution."

Several shots were fired, and Zac reached back and kicked the fireman's legs out from under him, sending him down fast. Bullets ripped through the cab, and Zac stared hard at the man on the floor. "You stay down," he growled. "I don't want anybody getting killed."

"You don't?" The man's look showed shock mixed with disbelief.

"No! I don't. Now, just keep hugging this iron floor till we get by."

Zac looked up in time to see the two men from the roof of the station drop onto the top of one of the cars behind them. The engine hit the wagon that had been placed over the track and pieces of it caught on the cowcatcher and flew past the cab. Gunfire continued to pop, and Zac could hear some return fire coming from the train. He figured it must be the detective Elliott had told him about. As long as the man could keep these people from scrambling on board the train as they were picking up speed, Zac knew it would be his job to take care of the men on the top.

"Keep it steady and keep the steam up," he said. "I'm gonna make sure those fellas up there landed all right." He scrambled up what was left of the coal and made his way to the top of the tender.

Taking off his buckskin jacket, he laid it on top of the coal. "Whatever you do," he said, "don't spade my jacket to your boiler by mistake. There's dynamite in the pocket!"

The two men on top of the train had steadied themselves and were walking gingerly to the front of the train toward Zac. Their guns were in their hands and their legs were spread apart to keep their balance. Zac could see that one of the men was a wiry man with height, while the other was stocky with a powerful build. *Well, whoever they are,* Zac thought, *they got grit.*

He pulled out the long-barreled Peacemaker and took a careful aim. His shot roared out and took the tall man's hat right off, jerking it into the air and away with the breeze. The men froze and then dropped belly-down onto the moving train.

Zac climbed up the rocking car, carefully maintaining a bead on the two men. He moved toward the frozen figures, quickly but cautiously. "All right, get to your feet."

The stocky man slowly rose, Zac's gun pointed at his midsection. He had a black beard that offset his sparkling white teeth. He held his hands up and smiled. "Don't get excited," he said. "We're just doing our job."

Just as Zac started to speak the taller man swiped at his legs, catching his cuff and jerking him to the deck of the train. Zac's Peacemaker flew from his hand and slid along the top of the car, lodging in an overhead bin.

The stocky man jumped for him and Zac swiftly rolled away, allowing the man to land on the deck, but without Zac underneath him.

Zac scrambled to his feet. The two men stood on either side of him. He had the Shopkeeper Special behind his back. It was his hideout weapon, but he had no desire to shoot these men. The man who spoke had been right; they were just doing their job. They were taking orders from that Englishman and Mr. James Ruby. Zac signaled the stocky man forward with his fingers.

The man surprised him — he landed in

front of him with a full body block and knocked Zac once again to the deck of the moving train. This time, however, Zac slid to the iron rail on the sides of the car.

The taller of the two men moved like a cat's paw. He rushed Zac and, taking his feet, threw him over the rail. Zac hung for a moment with his hands clutching the iron. He lifted himself and wedged his elbow into the rail. The wiry man worked to loosen Zac's white-knuckle grip, and the stocky man, who had now gotten to his feet, moved in to help.

I've never been thrown off of a train quite this way before, Zac thought. *Other ways maybe, but not this way.* He surprised himself at how his mind worked. Maybe humor was a way of clearing his head when other people's thinking became muddled.

He hung on tightly and began to search for a foothold on the window of the car below him — something, anything, to give him leverage.

Chapter 7

"Are you all right?" Bruce shouted across the car. The sound of the gunfire and the fact that they were no longer slowing down had sent everyone to the floor. The sides of the train were of wood, not steel, and bullets penetrated it as easily as a cheese box.

"I'm fine." Irene breathed a relaxed sigh at the sound of her husband's voice.

"I'ze jes' fine backa here." The steward had found the one safe place in the car to position himself, right behind the solid mahogany bar.

Suddenly Irene looked to the rear of the car and put her hand to her mouth. Bruce swiveled his head around. A man had swung himself onto the rear of the platform as they rolled through the station, and now he made his way toward the door of their car. He had a pistol in hand as he pushed open the door.

Pointing the gun at Sam, the stranger growled, "All right, get up. Get up and move back there." The man waggled the barrel of the gun toward the rear of the car where Irene and Nikki were seated. Sam looked startled. He obviously hadn't seen the man coming, and Bruce wondered how anyone could have gotten on board, given the speed at which the train passed through the station.

The man pointed the gun at the steward. "You get back there too."

"I can't do that, mister. I works for this railroad and this here is my post. 'Sides, I'd feel a mite safer backa this here thick wooden bar."

Sam moved slowly toward the rear of the car and joined the Elliotts, who sat staring passively at the sandy-haired man in a dark coat. Sam pressed his arm up against the shoulder holster he carried.

"Now, you folks just sit quietly," the intruder said. "I ain't rightly sure what's happening here. I'm a railroad detective and just following orders. I don't mean to get anybody hurt. Whatever it is that's happening, we're gonna stop it, and stop this train to boot. So if you good folks and the old gentleman here will just sit still, then we can get this thing under control."

"We'll sit here," Sam spoke up, "but why don't you put that shooter away?"

The man looked at them and then down at the gun in his hand. Suddenly the sound of the men wrestling on top of the train could be heard, and every eye was on the roof of the car. A man fell and gripped the sides of the car, his legs dangling. Bruce recognized Zac and watched as he tried to position his feet alongside the window next to them.

The sandy-haired man kept the pistol tight in his grip and moved toward the window. He cocked the pistol and moved closer for an aim.

Sam was up in a flash. He jerked the revolver out of his shoulder holster and brought it down hard on the back of the man's head. There was a loud crack and the sound of the man's loss of breath as he fell to the floor in a ruined heap.

"Old gentleman, my eye," Sam said. "I ain't old, and sure as the world turns, I ain't no gentleman."

Then he turned to watch Zac struggling outside the window. The toe of Zac's boot gained a grip as he squirmed to keep his balance.

Zac wrapped his hands around the iron rail that ran along the sides of the top of the car and strained to hold on while the wiry man continued to pry at his fingers. The stocky man scrambled to the edge of the car to lend a hand to his partner. Zac knew that if he was going to do something, he had to put maximum effort into action, and right now!

He released his right hand from his death grip on the iron rail and, reaching up, grabbed the stocky man who was bending down toward him. Tightening a firm grip on the man's shirt and pulling down, Zac launched the man over the side of the train and tumbled him to the passing ground below.

Swiftly Zac swung his leg up and caught the thin man on the head with his knee. The hard rap struck the man on the temple, jolting his head sideways.

Zac followed the kick by punching the man hard in the face and launched another flying kick. The blow loosened the man's grip on him and with a final kick, Zac sent him sprawling back across the top of the car.

Zac strained and hoisted himself up and onto the top of the car, then shook his limbs to put the blood back into his arms. The man picked himself up from the deck of the moving train and extracted a knife from his belt. Zac reached behind his back and pulled the Green River blade out from the sheath he had strapped to his back. The two men began to circle each other as the train continued to pick up speed.

"Whatever it is they're paying you," Zac said, "it ain't enough."

The man stepped closer to him and lashed

out with his blade. He had a longer reach, and Zac jumped back to avoid the knife. "They're paying me enough," the man growled. He flashed a smile. "I'd do this for nothing. I'm a scrapper, always was and always will be."

The man tossed the knife back and forth between his hands and looked for an opportunity to strike. He flicked the blade at Zac several times as the two of them continued to circle.

The men focused on each other, and Zac blocked out the movement of the train, not allowing any other thought to come into his mind. Hand-to-hand combat was not new to Zac Cobb, and he was sure it was a skill that wasn't unknown to the man he faced.

The man continued to toss the blade back and forth, and Zac knew he was trying to get him to watch his hands instead of his eyes. Zac's eyes, however, drilled into the man, never allowing his gaze to drift. Zac had always prided himself on being able to see into an opponent's mind before the thought reached the hand. He had a sixth sense about who meant business and who was simply bluffing.

The man shot out his knife and Zac parried it away with his Green River. Again the man quickly stabbed out at Zac, only this time with a slashing motion. With a catlike move, Zac leapt back and pulled his stomach into his spine.

The man lunged at him, his knife flashing, and Zac stepped aside and ripped at him with his Green River. He could tell that he'd caught some flesh before the man dropped his knife and grabbed on to his arm. He grimaced at Zac and looked down at the fresh flow of blood on his arm. Turning his head, he spotted the revolver that had lodged in the bin on the top of the car and smiled. Keeping his eyes on Zac, he bent down to retrieve the gun.

"Stop right there," Zac said. "Just keep that hand empty."

The man ignored him and reached for the gun.

Zac flipped the knife in his hand over and flung it at the man. It sailed through the air and plunged into the man's upper arm, stopping him cold. He froze in place and grabbed his arm.

Zac moved quickly to his opponent and, grabbing his shirt, pulled him to his feet. The man's eyes glazed over as Zac walked him to the edge of the car.

As blood flowed down the man's arm, Zac held him steady and looked him in the eye. "Well, I hope whatever it was you got for this, they paid you in gold." With that, Zac pulled his knife from the man's arm and wiped the blade on the wiry man's shirt. Spinning him around, Zac pushed him off the train.

Zac watched the man roll along the ground until he lay still at the side of the rails. He shook his head and replaced the blade in the sheath between his shoulder blades. Stooping to pick up the revolver, he started back toward the engine.

"Don't know how far this will take us," the fireman said as Zac climbed down over the dwindling pile of coal.

Zac dusted off his khaki jeans, smeared with coal dust, beating on them till some of the color came back.

"Fer a fella who lives a mite on the rough side, I'd say you were a bit perticular about yourself."

Zac pulled off his gray hat, which he had squashed tightly down around his head. He wiped his forehead, leaving a black, streaky smear. "My daddy used to do a little mine work. He dug coal for some time before he lost a leg in Mexico. Never liked the stuff myself, but selling it up north brought in some cash money." He smiled. "Now, though, I'd just as soon let the Yankees freeze in the dark."

He dusted off the last of the black streaks, fading them to a series of gray stripes. " 'Course, a body can't never tell who he's going to meet on one of these trips."

The engineer let out a laugh.

Zac picked up the jacket and patted the pockets. "Gotta make sure it's all here. Wouldn't want one of those stray sticks of blasting powder mixed in with what's left of the coal."

"Well, mister, I surely hope you don't think I'm full a the blarney now, but we just might be needing that, if we don't find somewheres to get more coal. My fireman here's kinda nursing what we got left, but that pile back there won't be lasting us for very long now."

Zac watched the wires pass by the outside of the train. "I don't reckon it'll do much good to shoot any more of those wires down," he said. "They must have got the word down the line. I'm afraid any edge we had is gone, and I don't suppose we can pull into anywhere and get more coal, leastways not without a fight."

The engineer frowned for a moment and then spoke up. "Aye, there might be another way," he said. "Mind you, I'm not making any promises to you now, and I can't even rightly say why I'm bothering with you at all." He arched his eyebrows and stared at Zac. "You did take my train! And I'm greatly afeared you aren't about to let it go until it's a wreck o' twisted metal beside the tracks."

"I can't make you any promises," Zac said.

"Oh, I'm aknowin' that. Can't say as I'd take a promise from a Rebel nohow. Seems to me you boys broke your promises when you left the Union."

Zac started to speak, but the Irishman held out his hand. "No need for that," he said. "Got no inclination to talk politics. We already jawed about women and such. Next thing you know, we'll be talking religion, and I'm a good Irish Catholic. I don't think about that and I don't talk about it, I just do it."

Zac sloughed the coat over his arms. "Look, say what you're going to say. I have a feeling that whatever it is, you just can't bring yourself to spit it out. You got the look of a man trying to draw into a full house. He ain't got the cards in hand, but he suspects he will."

"All right, all right, there's an old wreck up ahead a piece. It sits on a sidetrack. Now, I can't say for sure that it has coal on board, but it hasn't been there long, and I'd reckon the tender behind it to still have some. 'Course if we were to stop alongside and all of us took turns shoveling the stuff, we'd give those folks a chance to catch up to us, but at least we'd have power underneath us."

"Somehow," Zac mused, "I knew I could count on all that wisdom of yours."

The man wagged his head and then scratched his red beard. "You read people pretty well, Mr. Wells Fargo agent, and you're right to boot. I guess I just feel a mite disloyal to my employer. I should be trying to stop you, not help you."

"Well, I'm not the problem here." He looked back at the cars attached to the train. "The problem is those nice people back there, people who are being threatened. I don't like to see that happen to anybody."

"You sure you aren't the problem, just a wee bit now?" The old engineer cocked his head at him and smiled.

Zac thought for a moment. "Well, I don't much like people thinking they can buy me off, and I don't take well to being threatened or bullied." He took his hat off and ran his fingers straight back through his hair. "And I never cared much for the English."

The big 440 left El Morro with all the men the Chicago Pacific could scrape together. Most of them they had to find in the bars. The railroad practically owned the town.

They could get whatever they wanted, and usually at the drop of a hat. Today they wanted men, men who could and would use a gun. They offered them all twenty dollars a day and food, provided they bring their own weapons. After the first twenty-five signed up, the rest were turned away.

Coruthers was at the throttle, and along with the fireman, there was Frank Maxwell, the local detective in charge who came along to make CP decisions, if needed.

"We're all ready to roll out of the yard," the brakeman shouted at Coruthers from the ground below.

"Good, then get yourself back there. No telling where we're a gonna meet Number Nine. If I gotta stop and blow the steam, I want them brakes down real good back there."

The brakeman waved his stubby right hand at him and ran to the back. Coruthers nodded and spoke to Maxwell. "A body can always tell how long a brakeman's been working by the number of fingers he's got missing. That job's hard on fingers, it is."

"Don't reckon we'd find many ex-brakemen as gunslingers," Maxwell said.

"Reckon not."

"Who's the engineer on Number Nine?" Maxwell asked. "Is he loyal?"

The engineer cut off a slice of tobacco, popped it into his mouth, and began to chew. "That would be Dolin O'Connor. That mick's loyal to nothing but the Virgin Mary." He spit out a stream.

"Then I take it he ain't too popular," Maxwell remarked.

The engineer laughed. "He don't have to be popular, he's good. But he ain't no loyal company man, if that's what you mean. 'Course, I ain't got much agin him. He does his job same as anybody else."

"You people sure do stick together."

Coruthers leaned over and spat out another stream of tobacco juice into the yard. He jerked the throttle open. "Engineerin' is a dangerous business, mighty dangerous. All that hot water up there — if it goes, you're cooked back here, literally cooked."

"When do you reckon we'll get to 'em?"

The engineer looked up, as if he were ciphering. "Near as I can figure, I 'speck we'll get to Number Nine headed our way a couple of hours after sunset. So when that there sun goes down, we'd best keep a sharp eye out, and then just hope that old mick stops. Otherwise you and me is gonna get a lapful of the hottest water on the face of this earth."

96

Chapter 8

"Father, I have something that could be important."

The older man sat in his overstuffed chair, staring into the fire. He was tall and slim, an appearance that the two Great Danes by his side complemented. His hair was neatly combed and his mustache trimmed. The polished boots he wore were English riding boots, unlike the usual western-style boots men of the West wore. The fireplace was his favorite, in spite of the some forty-odd others that occupied the castle. Its structure of rugged broken rock contrasted sharply with the others constructed of antique oak and adorned with English armor pieces.

"Here, Elizabeth, I'll take it," he said, sounding like a man awakened from a deep sleep. Looking at the fire and his wife's photograph had been almost his constant leisure occupation since her death.

His daughter approached him, still clutching the telegram to her breast. She gave him a stern look. "I don't expect you to do anything about this. There's nothing you can do, nothing except wait."

He held out his hand.

She continued to hold back the telegram, thinking she hadn't made her point clear. "We don't even know if this involves them. They are most likely safe on another train, and Sam and his man are with them."

He looked up at her, the pain of grief evident as he held out his hand.

The young woman surrendered the telegram, then stepped closer, laying her hand on his shoulder and watching him as he read.

"Train carrying Elliotts seized at Newton KansasSTOP No report on whereabouts of trainSTOP Chicago Pacific in pursuit-STOP"

The general neatly folded the telegram and stood up. "This doesn't make sense," he said.

"I know, Daddy, it doesn't. Why would they commandeer their own train? What could they hope to gain from that?"

Walking toward the fire he placed his hand on the mantel and continued to gaze at the flames. The Great Danes stood. They responded to the general's every move. He loved the breed and had six of them on the estate, but these two were his favorites, his constant companions. Part of the reason he loved them was because of their enormous size. Everything about Sydney Roberts was larger than life itself. In spite of his stature, however, or perhaps because of it, he maintained a soft-spoken manner and seldom betrayed his self-control, even when he felt panic or anger. "Have you —"

"I've already made preparations to send twenty men to Las Animas to try to intercept whoever has the train, and I've put out a $10,000 reward for their safe return."

"I don't know what I'd do without you, Elizabeth. You're always ahead of me at least one step, sometimes two or three."

The young woman smiled as she watched her father. It was her habit to study the men she came in contact with. Whether she liked it or not, it was still a man's world. She knew that if she planned to be a successful businesswoman, it would take more than her status as the daughter of General Sydney Roberts. She'd have to know what the men around her were thinking. The art of reading men began with her father, and now she'd become quite good at understanding almost any man.

"I've got to go with those men to Las Animas," he spoke matter-of-factly.

Putting her hand on her father's shoulder, she said, "Daddy, you can't do that." She'd learned the power of touch, that any disagreement was better solved with it. "We need you to raise capital and only you can do that. You know investors don't look favorably on a woman. And our litigation is at a critical stage in court. Whatever else happens, we need to establish our legal rights to the Royal Gorge. Besides, if decisions need to be made I don't want to have to go looking for you to make them."

"Elizabeth, you haven't needed me to make decisions since your mother died." He shook his head. "I'm not even sure I've been very capable of making them."

"Daddy, you know you are making all the important decisions about the Denver and Rio Grande. If it hadn't been for you, this town would still belong to the Arapaho and the railroad would be nothing but a ditch."

He turned his back to her and looked out the window in the direction of the carriage house below the castle hill. "You are effective, my dear." He looked back at her. "I fear sometimes too effective."

"If you're talking about the decision to build through the gorge, that was your decision, not mine. And if we don't build there, we'll be all bottled up here and never reach the mining towns or collect all that freight business. It would gall me to see the Chicago Pacific get control of those markets."

"I'm not talking about that, Elizabeth. I'm talking about how competent you are. Your mother was so frail, so gentle, always such a look of kindness on her face. It made me want to . . . protect her. I would have done anything for her."

"You did protect her, Daddy."

"But, you, sweetheart," he spoke as he stepped closer to her, "you don't want a man to protect you. You keep any man that would like to at arm's length." He looked wistful. "I should have insisted you spend more time with your mother . . . and your friends at school, instead of allowing you to be with me all the time . . . and the gandy dancers at the end of track."

She dropped her eyes. He spoke the truth. She knew she was a highly capable woman, and men regularly took orders from her as if she were the general. She wondered if her height and figure was a factor. Male heads from miles around turned at the sight of her. And when she had to rely on her natural feminine abilities, she had no difficulty doing so.

Her uncanny insight into a man's dulled thinking could be staggering. She enjoyed it and yet knew it could be a drawback to any lasting friendship. When men realized they had been out-thought or buffaloed, they seldom if ever wanted to be around her again.

She mumbled, "I suppose I do shake a man's confidence." She looked up, eyes blazing. "But why are they all such babies? Why can't they stand on their own two feet? I'm not trying to be their nurse, and I certainly do not intend to be their nanny."

Roberts looked her in the eye, allowing what she had said to sink in, turned again to stare into the blazing fire. "I don't know what I would do if I lost Irene and little Nikki. Irene is a wonderful mother and a fine wife to Bruce."

Elizabeth felt at a loss when her father talked about family. Somehow, her only place in the picture was her place in the railroad. Her business sense was what she brought to the family table — and her knowledge of people and things that women weren't generally supposed to think about. When her father spoke about Irene, her marriage, and his only grandchild, Elizabeth grew purposefully silent. Her youngest sister, Elsie, was still young enough to properly be single, but Elizabeth knew that she herself fell into the category of the odd.

"I'm proud of you too, Elizabeth," her father broke her reverie, "proud of your strength, your knowledge of business. This is the West, and like it or not, only the strong survive, not the gentle."

He caught himself. "Not that you have no gentle qualities, darling." Resting his hand on her shoulder and patting it, he added, "You can be the most gentle woman I know. But I think you've tried too hard — maybe to be the son I never had; the one you wanted to be."

"I only try to be strong because I have to, Father."

"I don't think so," he replied firmly. "You try to be strong because something inside of you needs to be. You have a need to be in control. You need the fastest horse — like that black stallion of yours. He'd kill anyone else that tried to ride him."

"It's just my way of finding excitement."

"No, I think it's your way of proving yourself, Elizabeth. You never take no for an answer. If there's something you can't have, it only makes you want it more. You want the railroad, and someday I suppose you will have it. I feel badly for you, though, darling, because if you're not careful you'll have the Denver and Rio Grande, but I fear you won't be happy with it."

"Because you think I need a man to make me happy?"

He took both her arms in his strong hands and looked into her hazel eyes. "Isn't that the way women were designed by God? To be happy with a man?"

The thought bothered her and she shook her head. "Well, I need to be myself, and when I am myself I seem to frighten every man I meet." Her flaming red curls bounced and sparkled in the light of the fire.

"Someday, I pray, you'll meet a man who is stronger than you are. I just hope, though, that you won't feel the need to control him, that you'll allow yourself to be vulnerable, just once in your life, sweetheart."

"Well, if that happens, Father, he'll have to be an exceptional man, someone like you, someone I can trust completely and feel safe with. A man I can respect, someone who won't back down when I am who I am. I'm looking for someone man enough to love Elizabeth Roberts, Daddy."

The big dogs moved suddenly, turning the general and Elizabeth's attention to the door. A loud creak preceded the opening of the door that led to the kitchen. A stoop-shouldered man looked around the corner at them. His hair, the color of moldy hay, was tousled. "I'm sorry, I didn't mean to interrupt you."

"Come in, Eric, come in."

He straightened his shoulders and sauntered into the room carrying a leather valise.

104

"Miss Elizabeth, I have the money right here. Ten thousand dollars in cash, just like you asked."

"Did you have any trouble at the bank?"

"Oh no, ma'am. I signed for it, and when I said it was for you, no one seem concerned."

Eric Torkelson, a stocky, Nordic-type, wore spectacles, but looked more like a blacksmith than an accountant. Elizabeth knew him to be utterly trustworthy, the essential element for his job. She had hand-picked him, considering herself a good judge of men.

"Are you armed, Eric?"

He opened his jacket to reveal a revolver in a shoulder holster. "Yes, Miss Elizabeth. I have a bulldog revolver. It ought to be quite adequate."

"I should think it would be," she shot back.

"Will you be coming with me, Miss Elizabeth?" His face brightened as he asked the question. "I would be delighted to have you along on the ride."

"I don't think so. I have too much work to do here."

The general looked her in the eye. "Now, Elizabeth, I'll need a good firsthand report, and I can't think of anyone better prepared to deliver judgment on the matter than you. Besides, you might have to make changes in the field, and I wouldn't want anything traveling over the wires that our friends on the Chicago Pacific might get word of. How do you think we learned of the missing train?"

She looked at Eric, then back to her father. "I'm afraid I'd slow you up . . . I would need to change into my traveling clothes and pack some things."

"You look fine, Miss Elizabeth, just as you are. It's only a train ride, and we can take the general's private car."

"That's right," the general broke in. "You have clothes in the car, don't you?" He took her by the arm and began moving her toward the door. "Go with Eric; go and enjoy the ride. Maybe you'll be able to hear more about the progress of the crew in the gorge from down Pueblo way."

Elizabeth turned to the accountant. "Eric, wait for me in the dining room. I'll be along directly. I have to have a few words with my father."

"Of course, ma'am. I'll wait right outside."

He turned and went out the door and Elizabeth closed it. She stood with her back pressed against it. "Stop doing this type of thing, Father."

"What do you mean? He seems like a very

nice young man, educated and all."

"That's beside the point. Eric is very efficient and trustworthy, but so is my fountain pen. I want you to stop arranging things for me. Let me pick my own men in my own way."

"I'm afraid that if you wait another five years, Mr. Torkelson will be your only choice; another ten years, and there will be no one."

"Let that be my worry, Father. I know you've been bitten by the grandfather bug and you've told me too many times what a fine childbearer I would be. But I have my own taste in men, and accountants just don't suit me."

"I suppose you want a drifter, a gambler, a soldier of fortune?"

She lifted her chin and reached out to straighten his tie. "You were a soldier, Daddy, and you've made a fortune."

"Very undependable types, child."

"Daddy, I don't care. When I find a man who moves me inside, then I'll do whatever I have to do to get him." She plumped the tie. "Don't I always get what I want?"

Chapter 9

The derelict sat on a spur just off the main track. The Irishman had pulled Number 9 as close as he could. Zac picked up a shovel and, along with the fireman, jumped down from the cab. Bruce Elliott swung down from the steps of the last car, his white shirt gleaming in the sun. "Why are we stopping?" he asked.

Zac had mounted the tender of the derelict and was beginning to shovel coal onto the ground beside Number 9. He raised his voice, "Got to get some fuel out of this here wreck. We ain't got much left ourselves."

"Well, here, let me help."

Zac looked around the tender and, finding another shovel, tossed it to the ground. "Why don't you get up in the cab and let the fireman there hand you up the stuff?" he suggested.

Elliott didn't say a word, he just mounted the cab and rolled up his white sleeves to work. Shovel by shovel, the three men passed coal between the two cars. Zac took it out of the wreck and passed the shovel to the fireman below, who in turn handed the shovel full of coal up to Bruce Elliott. The men constantly watched the track behind them and ahead of them for telltale smoke. With word out, Zac knew it was only a matter of time before the thugs from the Chicago Pacific arrived in force, and from where they sat they would be clear targets, nothing more.

After some time, even with the chill in the air, the sweat began to trickle down Zac's back. He stopped, removed his shirt, and after pausing to look at both horizons, started back to work.

"How long you figure it'll take 'em to get here?" the fireman asked.

Zac continued to pass the shovels down. "Don't know about what may be up ahead; your boys might have had somebody close. But I was kinda expectin' that Englishman to come into view sometime ago."

They continued to pass the coal over to Number 9, and then Zac looked up and saw the smoke. "That's him," he said. "Lord knows how I hate the English. They're never around when a body needs them and only show up to pester people."

He climbed down from the wreck. "Elliott, get your people forward and cut that last car loose, the express car." Zac knew the express car wasn't usually near the rear of the train; normally they were attached behind the tender, giving the smoke more time to get airborne before the passengers were hit with it. He could only guess that in a hurry, and with the large payroll they had been carrying, they had just violated procedure. Well, whoever had been responsible, Zac was thankful. For what he had in mind, that express car and its payroll were absolutely necessary.

As Bruce Elliott ran to bring the people forward, Zac took out several sticks of dynamite. He turned to the engineer. "Pull this thing up track about a hundred yards and sit."

The engineer pulled on the throttle slightly and rolled the big train forward, minus the express car, which Elliott had managed to uncouple. Zac took the blasting powder and tied it on to the rails near the juncture of the spur where the derelict had been pushed. "Keep your steam up and get ready to move out in a hurry," he yelled to the engineer.

He took his knife out and prepared the fuse, cramming one end of it into a stick of the powder. Taking out his pipe, he stuffed it with tobacco and stuck a match to it. He sucked deeply, watching the mixture glow inside the bowl.

Zac knew he had to time the fuse perfectly,

time it to blow in front of the abandoned car just before the Englishman's train reached it. He counted on their not being able to see the dynamite and on their not slowing down, assuming they could push the car forward on the front end. If he timed it right, he might be able to send the pursuing train off the rails right there. At least then he could take care of the problem behind them.

Running to the express car, he pounded on the door. "Crabbtree! Open up!"

"I'm sorry, Mr. Cobb," the voice inside sounded hesitant. "I can't open this door until we get to El Morro. You have your things. Please don't ask me to disobey my orders further."

"Crabbtree, it's your call. You can stay here and be sitting in a mess of splinters in a few minutes, or you can haul yerself outta there and stay in one piece. If you were working for me, I'd tell you to get out of here, but the man you are working for is about to split you wide open — that is, if my dynamite doesn't do the job first."

Without a word, Crabbtree slid the heavy door open. He peered out into the sunlight and gulped. "What do I do about all this?" he asked, waving his hand in the direction of the shipments. "Especially the payroll — that's a lot of money in there."

"Well, you can't leave it in there, 'cause it's gonna get plowed under."

"I'm the one who knows the combination, and they won't be able to carry a safe."

"Open 'er up, Crabbtree. Open 'er up and slide that thing out here onto the ground. You can stay around and make sure it gets handled properly if you like, but you better open 'er up first. The kinda damage a locomotive will do to the inner workings of that safe of yours might make gettin' 'er open durn near impossible in a few minutes."

The lights finally seemed to go on in Crabbtree's mind and he scurried toward the massive safe and spun the dials.

"Hurry up, Crabbtree, you ain't got much time."

Opening up the safe, the little man pushed the thing close to the open door.

"Better make sure it won't close by accident, Crabbtree, and dump 'er out. Take 'er over the side."

The man set the handle on the safe and pushed it over onto the ground. It landed beside the track with a thud and spilled some of the greenbacks onto the ground. Zac looked up to see the locomotive rounding the bend, heading their way.

"Better climb down, Crabbtree, and get yourself up that hill."

With that, Zac turned and ran for the end of the car. He waved his arm at the engineer. "Go ahead," he said, "pull 'er out!"

The engineer pulled on the throttle and Number 9 began to lumber forward. Zac reached behind his shoulders and pulled out the knife. It glinted in the sun as he held it to the fuse. He knew he had to judge the speed and time the thing just right. Dynamiting was something he didn't feel a great deal of confidence about; every fuse seemed different to him. He watched Crabbtree scurry up the hill. "Run, man, run!" he yelled.

The oncoming locomotive sped toward them, moving like a cat about to pounce on a cowering mouse, only Zac knew this mouse had some teeth. He puffed on his pipe, sending smoke into the air, and listened to the tobacco sizzle. Holding the fuse, he made his cut and stuck the end of the fuse into his pipe. Sucking hard, he watched the sparks fly off the end of his nose.

Pivoting on his heels, he ran for the departing engine. He'd done the best he could, now it all depended on that fuse and his guess about it. Looking back over his shoulder as he ran, he could see the approaching locomotive coming closer, and he could see the sparks continuing to fly from the fuse.

He grabbed on to the rail that led up the ladder to the parlor car and jumped. His boots scuffed on the iron landing, and he fell face first on the steps, but his legs kept spinning. Rolling over on the landing, he lay there and watched.

The train made contact with the abandoned car and a split second later the track underneath it erupted with an explosion that rattled the hills on either side of them. The express car shattered with the force of the blast and flew into the air in pieces.

"What in great . . . ?" The Englishman pitched into the engineer and both slammed into the throttle lever. The train ground to a twisted slide and kicked the safe up into the air, along with debris from the express car. Greenbacks flew everywhere as the train left the tracks and skidded to a leaning stop beside the hulking wreck on the spur. The cars behind them, filled with squealing horses and shouting men, slammed into the grounded engine and threw all aboard into a prone and bruised position.

For several moments everybody lay there. Smoke curled up from the open firebox door. Steam rose above the train, and the horses in the impacted cars behind them thrashed in their panic. Slowly, the pursuers began to get to their feet in the midst of the steam, smoke, and dust to survey the damage.

Peter Williams pulled himself to his feet and sent out a stream of curses: ". . . that . . . Zachary Cobb!" He looked at the slow-moving Number 9 and knew that he would never catch him now. Not today, anyway.

Turning around, Williams saw that the men who had scampered out of the cars were not tending to the horses or checking for further damage — they were running with the wind at their backs, chasing greenbacks along the length of the track.

From the crest of the hill on the side of the resting train, he saw Crabbtree rise up from where he had been hiding, then run down the hill, waving his arms and screaming at the top of his lungs as the bank notes fluttered in the breeze.

Williams glanced at the stunned engineer. "I should have assassinated that blasted Wells Fargo man myself. I should have shot him right at the restaurant." He paused and looked at the train making steam up ahead. "How I ever let this incident get this far is beyond my ability to comprehend."

Zac lay still on the platform, watching. His ribs hurt from the impact of his abrupt boarding of the train, but the pandemonium behind him brought a faint smile to his lips. Getting to his feet, he dusted himself off.

Bruce Elliott came out and stood beside him. "What a mess! I don't see how they intend to follow us now."

Zac held on to the rail and continued to watch the men scamper after the windblown bank notes. "They'll come after us all right, but not today." He turned to face Elliott. "Our main problem is ahead of us now."

"I don't understand," Elliott said.

"Well, they got through up the track, and I'm sure those men back there aren't the last of the Chicago Pacific people. There'll be more coming our way, and you can take that to the bank."

Turning back and entering the parlor car, Zac saw Irene and Nikki huddled on the floor. "It's all right for now," Elliott said. He put his hand on Zac's shoulder. "This is a man who seems to be prepared."

Zac felt his knees buckle, then he dropped to the floor. Everything went black.

After some time he felt a cool washcloth on his face. He blinked, opened his eyes, and saw that it was little Nikki with the cloth.

"You all right, young feller?" Sam questioned.

"I think so," Zac said.

116

The girl felt his face with her small hands. "Better?" she asked.

Zac took her hand and, placing it back on his cheek, he nodded. "Yes, honey, I feel better. Thank you."

The train was moving at a faster speed; Zac could tell the new coal was being used. They were making headway, but he knew they were heading into more trouble. He wearily got to his feet.

"I'd love a drink," he said.

"Here, let me get you one, feller."

Irene stayed his hand. "Nikki can do that, Sam." Stooping down beside the child, Irene raised her voice. "Can you get Mr. Cobb a drink of water, Nikki?" The little girl nodded and scooted to where a cup had been placed.

At the wreck of the chase train, Peter Williams took charge. "Get the horses out of there and saddle them up. Make sure they've had enough to drink first. We will take twenty of our best mounts and men and start after them. I don't know how far they'll get, but nothing will be served by all of us waiting here." He shouted out orders and pointed at the men still running after the money. "Get those men back here. That's the payroll. Make sure everybody has a rifle, side arms, and plenty of ammunition. You," he said, pointing to a man standing nearby. "Make sure we have enough provisions and water to last six days. Pack it on the spare animals. We pull out in twenty minutes."

"What about my train?" the engineer shouted from the cab above.

"Your train is not my problem, it's yours." Then he yelled at the man with the portable telegraph key. "Wire back to the last station and tell them what happened. Nobody's getting past this thing today. Tell them we are pursuing the criminals on horseback." The man appeared frozen in his tracks. Williams barked, "Do it now, man, do it now!"

Williams watched the man scale the nearby pole. Standing below, he continued to shout instructions: "This is very important! Tell them Cobb is going to Denver. He has a delivery to make, and he's not the kind of man who is given to dereliction of duty. He'll make that delivery at the Wells Fargo office in Denver, just like he's supposed to do. Tell them to make sure someone is there to intercept him, someone who is very good with a gun."

Chapter 10

The sky was dark overhead and in the distance Elizabeth could see the Sangre de Cristo Mountains. They were beautiful. She always loved the scrubby rolling hills of southern Colorado with the mountains standing behind them. The light gently filtered through the distant rain, making it a dark shadow on the land, a welcome shadow. The rain clouds appeared to be brush strokes of black in front of the sun.

The special train had only a coal car, a car for the horses and tack, and the special private car for the Robertses. She would have preferred to ride with the men and the horses, but here she was with the accountant.

"Eric, close the curtains. When we get to Pueblo, we'll have to go through the switching yard, and I'd rather people not see in here."

Without a word of protest he began closing all of the curtains, leaving hers for last. Turning up the wicks on the lamps, he sat down with the briefcase in his lap. "This is money I hope we get a chance to spend," he said.

Elizabeth paced back and forth. "I do too. If anything happened to Irene and her little girl, it would break my father's heart, and right now he couldn't take another heartache."

"Your mother's death was hard on him, wasn't it?"

"Yes, it was. It's been years now, but he still feels the grief. He did all he could for her, even traveled back and forth to England to be with her. The altitude here was just too much for her, so we were forced to stay in England while my father lived here. I hated England, but mother enjoyed the English countryside. I love Colorado."

Her thoughts drifted. "I think when someone loses someone they love, they inevitably feel they could have done more, seen the person more, said more. There are always words that go unspoken between people who love each other. People think they're saying all there is to say, when they are only thinking the words. That is never good enough."

"I'm sure the general did all he could."

"Yes, but he doesn't think so, and that's the point."

They felt the train slowing down and heard the whistle. "We must be coming into Pueblo," Eric said.

"Yes, we'll be in the rail yard soon. This

whole place is crawling with CP people, so we'll just sit tight until we move on. No getting out to smoke."

"I don't smoke, Miss Elizabeth."

"You men of the books are so proper around women. Sometimes I wonder if you don't have ice water flowing through your veins."

"No, ma'am, I for one can assure you that I don't. When I see you —"

Someone pounding on the car interrupted him. "Open up! Open up in there!"

"Just sit still, Eric. Let me handle this."

Elizabeth opened her purse and wrapped her fingers around a small derringer. When she opened the door to the private car, she saw two men standing outside. Both had prominent mustaches and wore white shirts. Detective badges decorated their dark suit coats. One of the gentlemen was bareheaded and emaciated-looking and clutched a handkerchief in his hand. The other was shorter, had twinkling brown eyes, and wore a bowler hat. "Step in, gentlemen; come in out of the wind."

They both came through the door, and the man with the bowler hat took it off as he stepped inside. He spoke first. "Excuse us for bothering you, ma'am. My name is Bat Masterson, and this here is Doctor John Holliday."

121

"Doc Holliday?" she asked.

The man stepped forward and bowed low. "Yes, miss, you are entirely correct. Doctor John Holliday, at your service, ma'am."

Elizabeth noticed the strong odor of whiskey. "Be seated, gentlemen, and make yourselves comfortable. This is my accountant, Mr. Eric Torkelson, and I —"

Masterson interrupted her. "We know who you are, ma'am. That's why we're here."

"Then sit down, gentlemen. What do you take? I have some good coffee on, and I also have port wine and whiskey, if you prefer."

"I'll take the coffee, if you don't mind," Masterson said. "Black."

"Miss, any whiskey you have here would be enormously appreciated," the doctor said. He broke out into sporadic coughing and put the handkerchief to his mouth.

"My friend here is a lunger," Masterson said. "The whiskey helps."

She released her grip on the derringer and, laying the bag aside, took the glass decanter and poured whiskey into a large glass. "Allow me to serve you, then, gentlemen. To what do I have the honor of a visit from two of the West's finest pistoleers?"

"Well, ma'am," Masterson said. "We work for the Chicago Pacific, as you undoubtedly have concluded. Our contacts told us you were headed this way to look for your sister."

"Have you found her? There is a nice reward posted for the man who does." She handed the drink to Holliday and poured the coffee.

"No, miss, I'm afraid we haven't. I'm also afraid we have to warn you not to go any farther in your search for her. We couldn't guarantee your safety." The deadpan manner in which he said the words made Elizabeth think there was more to what he was communicating than words alone.

"Are you two gentlemen threatening me? Because if you are, I want you to know that I have all the protection I need. I can take care of myself, and I didn't come alone."

"We are quite certain that's true, Miss Roberts," Holliday spoke up and sipped on his glass. "From what we hear about you, you seem to be always well prepared for any event." He lifted his glass with a toast in her direction. "You do appear to be a very capable woman."

"You may warrant that to be true, Doctor," she said.

"Miss Roberts," Masterson said. "We've heard the train your sister and her family is on has been hijacked by a very ruthless man, an agent who sometimes works for Wells Fargo."

She tried to remain calm. Showing her emotions to a man was irritating to her. "Why would he want my sister's family? All we've been hearing down in the Springs for months is how members of my family were soon to be taken captive by you men from the Chicago Pacific." Elizabeth felt her anger rise — fear always made her angry. "For all we know, you have my sister and her family yourself. We have nothing to do with Wells Fargo, we don't even have a contract with them. The D&RG does its own express shipments."

"We just think it would be best for all concerned if you turned around and went home, ma'am." Holliday spoke in a low drawl that revealed a Southern background. His eyes looked hollow. They were bright with dark circles around them.

Elizabeth knew both of these men were dangerous, and that Holliday was a killer, a man with a lightning temper and a draw that was even quicker. He began to cough violently and held the handkerchief to his mouth.

"Are you all right, Doctor? Can I get you some water?"

"No!" the man said, coughing through his

handkerchief. "That stuff is poison." He held out his empty glass. Sweat beaded up on his forehead. "I would be much obliged for more of that fine elixir of corn, however."

Elizabeth splashed him another full glass of whiskey, which he gulped down at once. She walked to the display case and, setting down the decanter, pushed back the curtain. "Gentlemen, thank you for your courtesy, but I think I'll go on. I've got to find my sister."

Masterson stood up and walked toward her. "Miss Roberts, this man Zac Cobb is considered dangerous. He has already wrecked one of the trains chasing the one he's on. He blew up the track while the engine was on it." He dropped his eyes slightly. "Our chief of detectives was on board that train. He's safe, however."

"Peter Williams?" she asked. "That snooty Englishman, Peter Williams?" Though worried about Irene and the family, she'd say or do anything to keep up the hard shell she carried now.

Masterson's head jerked up. "Yes. Yes, ma'am, Peter Williams."

Elizabeth smiled. "I think I'm starting to like this man Zac Cobb already. Tell me more." She could tell her interest in the man was pricking Masterson's hide, and it delighted her.

Masterson's jaw stiffened. "He's a killer, kills without warning, and seldom in a fair gunfight."

"Sounds like a smart man, too," she said. She loved needling these men — she knew what she was doing, and did it without embarrassment.

There was another knock at the door. Elizabeth reached over and opened it. It was a messenger. "Message for Mr. Masterson," he said.

Elizabeth took the envelope and, handing it to the detective, stood by the open door. She watched his eyes carefully as he read the note. He was cool and deliberate, this Masterson, someone she'd like to have working for her. He was obviously a gambler because she could see he tried hard not to display any emotion. She could read his expression, though, as he read the note, and knew that whatever the news was, it wasn't good news to him.

"Sorry, Miss Roberts. Doc and I have been asked to go to Denver. I do trust you'll find your sister and that she will be in good health, but my advice for you is to not continue east."

"Where did this train wreck occur?" she asked.

"In Kansas, I believe, just past Cimarron, near the Colorado border."

"And what do you believe this man's intentions are?"

"We can't say for sure, but it's very doubtful that he'll stay on the tracks. If Williams and the men who are chasing him don't find him, we have a mob of men from El Morro headed his way. They'll find him if he stays on the tracks, and if he doesn't, I think we have a good idea what he'll do."

"One lone man," Elizabeth mused, "and he has your whole army chasing him while he tears up your road, piece by piece. He sounds like quite a man. If you find him before I do, tell him I'd love to meet him." She smiled.

Holliday spoke up as he rose from his seat and put down his empty glass. "Miss Roberts, if we find him first, we'd be delighted to send you an invite to the wake, because that man will be stone cold dead before you see him."

"In some sense," Coruthers said, "I'll be happy to see that sun go down."

"Why is that?" Maxwell asked.

"Well, as it is now, we're coming at them boys from outta the sun. That don't 'zackly make us the easiest to see. I'd jest feel a durn sight better if that old mick could see who we are and try to stop hisself in time. With us both highballing right at each other, that ain't gonna give us much time to think, much less stop."

"Well, what can we do if he doesn't see us?"

"We can pray a lot."

"Is that it, just pray?"

"Well, I'm a telling you, mister detective man, there ain't no such thing as just pray. You been on these rails as long as I have, you got to have yerself a right fine prayer muscle. If we got to stop and they're red hot on us, then we got ourselves a situation."

"A situation?"

"Yeah, we do. We got to put that old mick's train on the ground, or ain't none of us gonna survive. I've seen wrecks where the cars were telescoped into the cars behind them, and I'm gonna tell you, that would kill ever' last one of them boys back there, to say nothing about what it would do to us. So if we see him coming, you and my fireman there are gonna have to put him right down on the ground, and in a hurry."

Zac and the Irish engineer had been staring into the setting sun for some time before it finally sank below the horizon. Both men were relieved not to be looking into it across the prairie land. They were in Colorado now and they knew they wouldn't be able to get much farther. Somebody would be coming up track to get them, and they had both strained their eyes to make sure they saw any oncoming locomotive first.

Zac pulled out his pipe, stuffed it with his mixture, and lit it. He then offered the mix to the Irishman. "Go ahead," he said, "help yourself."

"Glory, boy, I do appreciate it. That stuff of mine is old and dry." He filled his own bowl. "And this is, for certain, from Virginia."

"Yes, and the whiskey mixed with it is from Kentucky. I had my first pull of these makings when I captured a Yankee general. He wasn't going to need it in prison, and if I couldn't liberate him, I just figured to liberate his pipe tobacco."

"What made you fight in that war, son?"

Zac smiled. "Well, there were more than a few draft marshals roaming round to make sure every able-bodied man over sixteen was doing some fighting somewhere, but that's not why I joined up."

"You join to defend slavery?"

"Never! No man was ever meant to belong to another man."

"Then you were a secessionist?"

"No, can't say as I was that either." He took a pull on his pipe and sent sparks sizzling into the cold night air. "Aside from the necessity of the thing, I guess you could just say that I never liked the thought of a body being pushed around. I s'pose I just fought them because they were there, and not where they belonged." He looked up at the stars. "Seems like that was another world, that war, and my reasons now don't seem likely, but I was only fifteen, too young to be thoughtful or profound."

"And now you're doing this. Still haven't laid down your gun."

"No, I haven't, and it pains me some. But I do a job that somebody has to do, and I suppose I trust myself to do it better than anybody else."

"What do you mean, trust yourself to do it?"

"Well, I'm very good at what I do, and I'm proud of most of the results I get to see. But I guess I trust myself with it because I don't really care for it. I knew men in the war that loved it and I never trusted them, too much hatred they were carrying around inside themselves. I don't hate anybody, not even the people I go after. Hard to keep a level head when there's hatred in your heart."

"But you are like me, you don't much care for the English."

Zac laughed. "Well, I wouldn't call that hatred, though I would call it good taste."

They both laughed and turned back to look down the rails in the darkness. In the distance they could see what they had been dreading, the light of an oncoming train. "You better stop at the top of the rise," Zac said. "We'll have to get everybody off the train right up there. You and the crew can head back where we came from, and the rest of us will have to make it on foot."

"What about that train up there, bucko?"

"Just get 'er to a stop at the top of that hill and I'll take care of that."

The engineer was stone cold silent.

"What's wrong?" Zac asked.

The man shook his head. "Being an engineer myself, bucko, I know what happens when one of these things is hit, and it ain't a pretty picture. The engineer and the fireman are literally cooked, scalded by all that boiling water and steam up front." He applied the brakes to the rails.

"There ain't much I can do about that," Zac said. "I can't very well let them get here and chase us, us being on foot and all."

"Well, I know that. I s'pose I just hope that whoever is driving that rig has the presence of mind to put old Number Nine here on her side before it's too late. Somethin' about railroad men. We kinda like to stick together, 'cause it's either that, or we die together."

The train came to a screeching halt at the top of the hill and Zac hopped down from the cab. He jumped onto the ladder and opened the door to the parlor. "All right, folks, this is where we get off, and we have to do it right now. Take some water, food, and something warm, but we have to go, and I mean go right now."

He left the car and, standing beside the engine, called up. "Keep the steam up. Get as much coal in that as you can and then get down." Zac looked down the track. The oncoming train was closing the distance rapidly. "Okay, climb on down, fellers."

The others from the parlor car had gotten down and each was carrying a bundle. "All right, folks, this is as far as we go."

"I'm sorry, Mr. Cobb, I don't understand what you intend for us to do." Bruce Elliott sounded worried. "If those men arrive here they will find us as sure as the world turns."

"They won't be arriving here. Now I want to thank the three of you." Zac looked at the train crew, then took out a pouch of his tobacco and handed it to the engineer.

"Take this, and enjoy it."

The man stuffed it in his pocket and put his hand on Zac's shoulder. "Take care, me bucko, it's been a pleasure. You ain't half bad, fer a Johnny Reb."

"Thanks, Yank, you best get to walkin'. Don't stay around here, you won't like it."

As the three men moved down the track, Zac climbed into the cab. He pulled back on the Johnson bar and the big train began to move downhill. Standing on the edge of the cab as the train picked up speed, he watched the ground roll by. He jumped, then rolled along the ground several seconds before stopping himself. He lay for a moment, propped up on his elbows, watching the red lamps on the back of the parlor car disappear into the darkness.

He stood up and brushed himself off. "Come on, folks, we got to head north. We passed a bridge with a creek flowing nearby and we need to find it. It'll cover our tracks."

"Mr. Cobb," Irene spoke up, "when that train of ours finds its mark, many people will be killed or injured. What with my father's work and all, I've been around trains all of my life, and what will happen to the men in that cab . . . well. . . ."

Zac said nothing. He watched in the distance as Number 9 sped down the track. The hardness he had to have to do his job was the thing that bothered him the most about what he had become. "Let's go," he said. "We got a long walk ahead of us."

"Where's Nikki?" Irene looked around frantically. She saw the oncoming train in the distance and ran back to the rails.

Zac stepped back from the empty tracks and saw the little girl walking on top of the smooth steel rails, waving her arms for balance. He turned to Elliott. "Go get your wife, I'll get the child."

Racing forward, he scooped up the child in his arms and held her tightly. "Stay with us, honey," he said into her ear. "We don't want to lose you."

Chapter 11

They walked toward the bridge and started down the slope, the rocky ground crumbling under them as they skittered down the hill. Zac was in a hurry to get everyone below the level of the track.

He knew there would be an awful explosion any minute and that chaos would follow, and he wanted to make sure that at least Irene and the little girl were out of the way when it happened.

Always before, the people that he put to harm were people who were trying to kill him. While he knew the train was carrying men who had been sent to find and kill him, sent to kidnap the Elliott family, he was also fully aware that it had a crew on board that had nothing to do with that part of the business. They were doing a job. Zac admired men who were loyal to their work, men who asked no questions, men who could be trusted.

He motioned the people down the path beside the trestle and continued to look at the disappearing lights of Number 9 while he said a silent prayer. "Let's go, folks," he said. "We still got ourselves a very long walk before we can rest." Zac slung the heavy Sharps Creedmore over his shoulder and handed the shotgun to Elliott. "Why don't you hang on to this?"

The man looked at him, puzzled. "I don't use firearms, don't need them."

"Well, somehow I have a feeling that you're going to have to learn before we get you to where you're going. Been my experience that if a body carries a gun, he has far less occasion to use one."

"You've shown me just the opposite, Mr. Cobb."

Zac had no hankering for violence. He'd seen far too much of it in his lifetime, but his hatred for injustice was greater than his dislike for violence. He looked the man in the eye. They lived in two different worlds, Zac knew that. He lived in a world where a man had to make his own law more often than not, and he knew the professor here came from a civilized world; the world of the East Coast elite, a place of lecture, discussion, rhetoric, reason, and law. He knew Bruce Elliott was in for an education. He'd learn it, or he'd die. Zac wouldn't argue with him now, he'd just let him learn, and hopefully learn while there was still time. "Don't worry, I unloaded it," he said. "A body can't be too careful."

They began to follow the others down the hill. Sam Fisher was in the lead; Zac and Elliott brought up the rear. "You're pretty fair with those fists of yours, but these men are gonna come at us by the bunch. They ain't gonna stand in line to have fisticuffs with you. They're gonna come after us with everything they've got, especially after what I just did."

The men blinked at the distant lights. Trying to judge distance at night was sometimes hard, but they could see the train was moving at a fast clip toward them as it came down the steep grade.

Overhead, the stars burned brightly in the prairie skies. It was as if each light were a window on the scene with a witness standing behind it.

The train was still on a level plateau, but the engineer could see that ahead of him lay another downward slope that would put him up against the oncoming train in the valley below.

"Why doesn't he see us?" Coruthers continued to blink into the distance. He knew he was lucky to be in a position to see the oncoming train at so great a distance. Heading at each other, trains close fast, and once he started down that slope, he knew it would be too late. He had to think fast and do it now. He had to think about what had to happen to get people into action.

He pulled back on the throttle and began to sound out the sharp whistle signal to the brakeman — one long blast. He'd need the man to apply the hand brakes to the cars if they were to stop in time. Rapidly, he jerked on the handline. The whistle blast shook the night sky. He twisted the cock screws.

"We got to blow this steam!" Looking at his disheveled fireman, he shouted, "Get that derailer outta the tender. You and the detective here gotta get out there and put her down. We got to lay that mick and his train on its side or our goose is cooked. I'll whistle for the brakes."

The fireman scrambled over the coal and grabbed the derailer. It was painted silver so that it stood out from the blackness of the tender. He unhitched it and, turning back, collapsed onto the pile of coal. He knew every second was important and it made him nervous. He'd seen the derailer used before, but never when it had to be done right.

Behind them, the brakeman was screwing down the brakes on the car. He'd heard the blast of the engineer's whistle and knew exactly what it meant. Sparks flew from the rails behind the train, sending a shower of fire in all directions, hot iron erupting into the blackness of the night.

He remembered the stoves inside. In a situation like this, either he or the conductor had to put out all fires. Right now, though, he just hoped the conductor wasn't forgetting because he knew he'd never make it inside there to do the job himself. *I can't do it all,* he thought. He continued to tighten the wheel and watch the sparks fly.

Turning to the ladder, he climbed as fast as he could. He reached the top and ran forward. He had to get to the next wheel. Looking ahead, he saw the oncoming train. *That boy's not even slowing down. He'll be on us in no time.* He ran along the top of the coach. Finding the ladder, he took one last look ahead. *Why isn't he stopping?*

The train was slowing down but had begun the descent into the valley. Coruthers could see that the approaching train was continuing to pick up speed down below and was fast approaching the upward slope that would bring them together. The speed of the train in the darkness seemed to increase with each second.

"Don't wait fer me to stop all together," he shouted at the fireman. "You get yerself down there, you and the detective here. Get down there and lay that mick's engine down. Gimme a hundred yards 'er better. I don't want no house of iron laying down on toppa me. Is that clear? Ya hear me?"

The fireman nodded and stood beside the door, preparing to jump when they had slowed to a reasonable speed.

Coruthers turned to the detective. "This is where you earn your pay, Maxwell. You wanted this job. You, Williams — that blamed limey — and the diamond-studded Mr. Jim Ruby hisself, and all the other moneygrubbers who never have enough of their own, who always want what don't belong to them. You all make me sick. Now, get to that door and do exactly what my fireman tells you to do when you get out there. This ain't gonna require no guns or knives, but you gotta do it all the same. You understand?" He barked the last words into the man's face and glared into his eyes.

The man nodded.

"Then do it! Jump! Jump! Jump already!"

The burly engineer applied the brakes, and the locomotive and the trailing cars lurched on the tracks as sparks flew over the rails. He released steam from the boilers to further slow the train. He knew there would be no time to reverse the engine and try to stop the oncoming train by backing up in front of it. There was just no time, no time at all. The runaway was highballing toward them now. The uphill grade had slowed it some, he could see that, but it was coming on like a bad dream, a nightmare that you couldn't wake up from. All he could do was hope the fireman and his inexperienced assistant could get the derailer down in time.

"Everybody out! Everybody out now!" The conductor hurriedly made his way through the car, slapping the men in their seats. The whistle blast had warned him of the impending collision, and he knew full well what that meant. He had seen the results of telescoping railcars. The floors were all made out of wood with little or no undercarriage. The car closest to the point of impact would slice through the car in front of it, and each in turn would cram itself into the next car, cutting anybody who remained in the cars into pieces.

Startled, the men were slow to move. "Get out! Get out now! There's gonna be a wreck, and if you're in here when it happens, you'll die!"

He walked past the glowing coal stove. He knew he was responsible to put out the flames, but right now he just couldn't take the time. There was no time — he had to get these men out.

The men began to stumble toward the door, some trying to take time to gather their weapons and the little gear they were carrying. One stood up and shouted, "What about the horses?"

"The horses are dead," another man responded, "and we'll be dead too unless we haul ourselves on outta here."

The men at the front of the line stumbled and scrambled out the door. Some jumped from the platform, not bothering with the steps.

The fireman and Frank Maxwell had hit the ground, Maxwell taking a wicked spill. He shook it off and got to his feet. Sparks from the wheels of the 440 showered him, and hot steam spewed at him. He ducked low and raced forward.

"Come on! Come on! We got no time." The fireman waved at him, urging him forward. They could both see the oncoming train barreling toward them. The lamps on Number 9's cowcatcher glowed brightly, and the headlamp gleamed into the night sky. It was heading up the hill rapidly and both the fireman and Maxwell knew that when it cleared the crest of the hill, it would pick up more speed. It had a full head of steam and that steam would cook them all when it hit.

"This is far enough!" Maxwell screamed.

"It ain't either. We ain't come fifty yards yet."

"I said, this is far enough. We got to get this down and get outta here. I'm not about to watch that thing dump on top of me."

The fireman stopped and hesitated. He looked back at the suddenly still 440, the steam bellowing from its sides. "Okay, okay," he said. "Let's get 'er done."

They both stooped over the rails and began to tighten the derailer to the sides of the cold steel. The fireman kept his eye on the 440, expecting any moment to hear Coruthers bellowing, telling him how wrong he was to stop so close. He watched and worked furiously.

The beam from the lamp of the oncoming train dropped onto the two men as they tightened the derailer. It came up the hill with furious power, the cowcatcher seeming to shake from side to side, a wanton weapon on the rails, a dragon without eyes.

"Move! Move!" Maxwell shouted. "Get back, run!"

The two men sprinted from the track and ran toward the slope of the hill. The light from the oncoming train caught their coattails in its glare. They ran, and Maxwell looked back as he ran. He had forgotten everything now. He had no job; he didn't know who this man was he had been sent to corner. His mind raced as he ran. He had come down the rails like a cat sent to trap a mouse, and now he was running for his life. He chased the darkness and dove for the hillside.

Coruthers watched the runaway race past the spot he had dictated for the derailer. His eyes grew large, and in an instant he knew that he'd have to jump for his life. He had no desire to become another legend of railroad courage. There was nothing to be served by staying at the controls; there was no one left to save but himself. He ran for the cab door and jumped into the night.

Number 9 hit the derailer and lurched forward into the atmosphere, jumping from the rails like an antelope and sailing toward the hissing train. The trailing cars snaked behind it and began uncoupling, filling the air with the sound of snapping iron. Hitting the waiting engine, the boilers burst open, releasing the boiling water along with clouds of steam. The train exploded with an ear-splitting roar and the colliding metal monsters screeched and squealed plaintively at the starry sky.

Number 9 lay on top of the 440 like a beached whale, its cars scattered over the track and wrapped around the wreck. The explosion of the engine was soon followed by the mournful cries of dying horses and the few men who hadn't gotten off in time. The coal-fired stoves had ignited inside the splintered cars and fires erupted.

"Get those men out!" One of the CP men came racing back to the wreck. He rushed into the steam and flames and took the ax from behind the rear door of the car. Furiously, he began to chop at the smoking door.

Coruthers lay on the ground beside the track, his hair and beard singed. He tried to croak out orders to men who ran by him. Lifting his finger, he pointed to the flaming cars.

Zac slung the big rifle over his shoulder and took the little girl from Irene. "Here, let me carry her. We're gonna have to stay in the stream for a while." They watched the glow of the wreck shine in the night sky, lighting up the hillside. The explosion had been deafening and now they could hear the aftermath. No one said a word about it, but the reality of the disaster was not lost to anyone in the little party.

Irene looked up. "I'm glad we have this full moon to see by."

Zac didn't respond. He shifted the child

in his arms and sloshed into the stream. The water came down the rocks and spread north out toward the prairie. He spoke to the others. "Let's stay in the water awhile. They can't follow our tracks here."

The others stared at him. Zac took several steps and turned around. "Don't be fooled into thinking they won't come after us. They're gonna find every drifter with a gun and tell them to shoot first. Those people own this prairie and they intend to keep what they own, believe me." He turned again and continued to trudge through the stream, leading the way.

Trekking through water made it more difficult to move fast, but they continued for some hours. Zac, holding the child and forging ahead, seemed to give them the courage to follow on without complaint.

"Mister," the child spoke barely above a whisper. She touched his face with her fingers and felt his burly mustache. "Th . . . thaank . . . you, mister."

Zac leaned down and spoke into her ear. "Just sleep, Nikki. I'll take care of you. You just sleep."

She nodded her head and curled up in his arms as he continued to move through the stream.

Several hours later, Zac was startled by the

unexpected barking of a dog. Letting out a short whistle, he moved toward the edge of the water. A black-and-white dog appeared along the shore in a flash, moved downstream a stretch, then disappeared again in the line of trees along the creek.

Zac turned to the group. "Head for the shore. That was a border collie. There'll be a flock of sheep nearby."

Chapter 12

The long ride through the night had taken its toll on Eric Torkelson. Even though he was an accountant by trade and sat at a desk, he hated being cooped up, and train travel on one car, even if it was the Robertses' private car, was confining to him. It also had a way of reminding Eric about the world he knew so well but could never be a part of. He was an outsider and he knew it. And Elizabeth would make sure he remained one.

He tried to make himself comfortable, first in the overstuffed chairs and then on the sofa, but when dawn finally broke it was with great relief that he finally gave up trying to sleep and got up to busy himself making coffee. At least he knew how to do that, that and the other practical things that mattered.

His matted blond hair was in total disarray when Elizabeth emerged from her stateroom, looking as if she had slept like a baby. She always looked so perfect to Eric, every hair in place, neat as a pin. This morning the red highlights in her hair picked up the dawn light, making her appear more beautiful than ever. He straightened himself and tried to smooth out his wrinkled clothes.

"Good morning," he said.

She nodded her response and lifted the curtain to take a look outside. She wore a buckskin split skirt and a bright green blouse with puffy sleeves and a ruffled front. It made her hazel eyes dance.

Eric stood tall and patted down his hair as Elizabeth began to move around the car, drawing the curtains back. Her hair bounced beneath the large green-and-white ribbon she wore at the back. The graceful way she marched to each window made Eric nervous. "Would you like some coffee?" he asked. "I've made some fresh."

"Yes," she responded, barely looking in his direction, "but maybe you should shave and put yourself together first."

"Of course." The fact that she had noticed his appearance made him even more nervous.

"Looks like we're in Kansas," she said.

He walked toward the window and replied, "Just barely, I think."

Eric felt the train slow and heard the brakes squeal. "I wonder why we're stopping?" he asked.

She walked toward the polished cabinet and, taking out a revolver and holster, strapped them on. "There's no town out here, so I assume we've found the train we're looking for."

His eyes widened as he watched her check the loads in the gun. "I better get ready, then," he said.

Planting the weapon in its holster, she took down a lever-action Winchester from the cabinet and began to feed shells into it. "Yes, I think you'd better." Taking in his suit with a sweep of her eyes, she added, "And if I were you, I'd wear something I could ride in."

When the train had come to a complete stop, someone knocked on the door, and Elizabeth put down the rifle to open it. The conductor stood in the doorway. One glance at his ashen face told her something was wrong, terribly wrong.

"Ma'am . . . Miss Elizabeth, ma'am," he stuttered. "Y-y-y-you better come and see." He shook his head. "It's awful, ma'am. I can't explain it, you have to come see for yourself."

"Is it my sister?" she asked.

"I don't know, ma'am . . . but I ain't never seen a wreck this bad before."

When she swung down the stairs behind the car and looked up track, she gasped. The cars of the wrecked train were still burning, and columns of smoke rose into the clear blue sky. She stood speechless. Cars littered both sides of the track, but her eyes were drawn at once to the two engines, one sitting directly on top of the other. She stiffened, balling up her fists. On the side of the hill she could see covered corpses. Biting her lower lip, she moved forward, afraid of what she'd find.

A number of the Denver and Rio Grande men were talking to survivors, and Elizabeth walked toward them, almost too shocked to speak. Two men sat beside the tracks. One, appearing to be the fireman, had his head in his hands, and the other, dressed in a dark suit, stared off into the smoke-filled sky. Elizabeth spoke to him. "What happened?"

Not looking at her, he said simply, "It was murder."

"Murder? What do you mean, murder?"

He glanced in her direction and recognition dawned. "Murder, Miss Roberts. These men were murdered by that man who works for you . . . that Cobb feller."

"Were my sister and her family on the train? Are they here?"

He dropped his head and then looked back at the wreck. "No, they aren't here. They were supposed to be on the other train up there. But it's empty. We were to escort them back to El Morro, after we'd taken care of Cobb."

He breathed a heavy sigh. "I guess I'm the murderer here if the truth be known . . . the Englishman, myself, and Jim Ruby."

"I don't think I know you, sir."

"Maxwell, Frank Maxwell. I work for the Chicago Pacific."

"And they sent you to kidnap my sister and her family?"

"That wasn't my job. I was sent here to stop this train and to get Cobb. The fellow works for you, right?"

"He doesn't work for the Denver and Rio Grande. I wish he did. Looks to me like he was trying to protect my sister and her family." She studied the mangled wreckage. "Well, Mr. Maxwell, I'd say you succeeded in half your job. You certainly stopped this train."

The camp lay in a grassy draw, smoke curling from a stovepipe protruding from the top of the canvas-covered wagon. Two mules grazed near the wagon and a campfire burned. One of the wagon's wheels lay propped up against the wagon, broken in half. The axle sat on a stump.

More than a thousand sheep covered the hillside, and Zac's party paused to watch the dog work them. The animal circled the fringes of the flock, barking, driving them into place. The sheepherder below was sending out signals to the dog by a series of shrill whistles.

"What is it?" Nikki, still in Zac's arms, asked curiously.

He bent down and spoke into her ear. "It's a shepherd. He's using a dog to gather his sheep." Zac watched the thought register on Nikki's face, a picture forming in her mind, a picture she'd never physically seen.

"Is it Jesus?" she asked.

Zac looked at her and then at the sheepherder and his dog. He leaned down once again. "I don't think it's Jesus, Nikki, but I think Jesus sent him."

The little girl smiled and clapped her hands. "Good, good," she said. "Sss . . . somebody sent by Jesus."

The sound of the young girl's clapping and squeals carried into the valley, and the dog's head snapped around in their direction. The man directing the dog followed the animal's glance and stood like a stone, watching the spectators on the hill above.

Zac looked over his shoulder. "Guess we ought to go down and say our polites."

As they started down the hill, Zac kept his eyes on the dark-haired man below. He wore tattered trousers and a serape over a faded homespun shirt. He had sandals on his feet and a straw sombrero on his head. Gaining a better view of the camp as they approached, Zac caught sight of an older man with white hair.

He was hunched over the campfire stirring a pot over the low flame. The younger man called to him and he stood, turning toward the arriving party. Then he sat down beside the fire again and stirred the pot.

Zac walked up to the young man, still holding Nikki in his arms. "Howdy," he said. "Name's Zac Cobb. We come off of the train and we're on our way to Denver."

The man took off his large hat and held it in his hands. "I am called Pablo. Señor, Denver is a long way away." He held his hand out toward the north. "Days away in that direction, señor. We are going to market there, but it will be a long time before we get there. You can see our wheel is broken." He swiveled his head in the direction of the wagon. "We need to buy supplies in Denver," he continued, "and try to sell some of our sheep." The man glanced at the exhausted-looking group. "Your companions must be very tired, señor." He pointed to the fire. "Please warm yourselves by our fire."

"Don't mind if we do. We been tracking

through the creek, and I'm sure these folks would like to get dry and warm. Thank you."

As the group moved toward the fire, the old man with the shock of white hair stood up from his pot. He smiled.

"This is my father," Pablo said. "He is called Juan."

Zac perceived the man to be blind. His eyes were sunken and had a blank expression.

"Papa, these people are going to Denver. They have come to us from the train and want to share our fire."

"But of course." The old man waved his arms. "Come here, sit down. You may share our frijoles too, and our humble bread." He used a flat wooden spatula to take a piece of fry bread from a flat rock on the edge of the coals. "How many are you?"

"There are five of them, Papa, four adults and a little girl."

"A little girl? Where is the child?"

The younger man took his father's hand and laid it on Nikki's head as she lay in Zac's arms.

"Don't be frightened, child," the old man said. "I am old, and I am blind, but I love children." He turned his head toward Zac. "It's been such a long time for me to be with children."

Nikki looked unsure, and Zac could tell she hadn't quite heard all of the man's words. He leaned down to her. "He wants you to know that there's nothing to be afraid of, and that he's blind also."

"Also?" The old man said. "Is the little girl blind?"

"Yes," Zac said. "Nikki is blind and her hearing is bad."

"Ayee! Mary, mother of God. We are alike, child." The old man took the little girl's hands and placed them on his eyes. "I see from inside my heart too, little one."

Feeling Nikki's eyes, the old man ran both of his hands down the side of her face to her ears. "You, my dear one, have much music yet to hear, but we begin with the music of your own soul. You must start with that before you can hear anything else."

He lifted up his head while Nikki continued to run her fingers over his face and spoke louder for all to hear. "All have God's music in their souls, but most are too busy with the noise outside their hearts to hear it. This little one is blessed. She can listen to God alone." Taking the girl's hands from his wrinkled face, he held them and kissed them.

"Are you . . . the shepherd?" she asked, reaching up to his lips.

He slowly smiled. "Yes, I am a shepherd.

I care for the sheep."

She smiled. "You are . . . Jesus? Jesus cares for sheep. He . . . He loves us."

He nodded. "I am not Jesus, little one. But I care for the sheep, and I love you too." He lifted his head up to the others. "Sit down, sit down. You must be hungry. Share our bread and our fire. We have coffee. Pablo, get some cups and something to hold their food."

The young man hurried to the broken-down wagon while the old shepherd continued to make the group feel welcome. "We are very poor, but God supplies us with all we need."

"Thank you," Irene said. "You are most gracious."

"Yes." Bruce placed a stool on the ground closer to the fire and motioned for Irene to sit down. He put his feet near the hot rocks to try to dry off his boots. "We are quite tired and hungry. We've walked most of the night, and some of it through the water."

"Your dog found us," Irene said. "He was a welcome sight. Like a furry angel."

The old man smiled and began to chuckle. He snapped his fingers and the black-and-white dog ran to his side. He took Nikki's hands and placed them on the dog, and the child began to rub the animal with delight.

The old man patted the dog. "That is what we call him. He is an angel to us, sent from God, just as you have been sent by Him. You are God's messengers and we know we must be hospitable with the ones God sends."

Sam poured himself a cup of coffee and stood off to the side of the group, sipping the steaming brew. He stared back in the direction from which they had come. "I think we can just about count on some other people coming that we can't afford to show a lot of hospitality to," he grunted.

Zac poured a cup for himself. "I'm afraid he's right." He looked at everybody standing around the fire warming their hands. "It may not be today, but they will come."

"You have someone coming for you?" the old man asked.

"Yes," Bruce answered. He stood away from the fire for a moment. "Agents from the Chicago Pacific are trying to take our family prisoner."

"My father owns the Denver and Rio Grande Railroad," Irene explained, "and these men are trying to use us against my father. Sam here works for my father. He was sent to take us to him."

Sam mumbled into his cup as he lifted it to drink. "Didn't do a very good job of that, I reckon."

"Mr. Cobb," Bruce interjected, "saw it all happening. It was he who stepped in and saved us."

The white-haired man spoke to Zac. "Then you are the angel."

Zac sipped his coffee. "Not really. Not many would be inclined to call me anything like that."

The old man and the little girl continued to rub down the dog. "God has angels with swords," he said. "They are His messengers also, sent to protect us."

He placed his hand on Nikki's head. "The good shepherd has a staff in his hand to protect the lambs from the wolves." He stroked the child's head and spoke again to Zac. "Pablo and I are shepherds, and God may have sent you as His angel with the flaming sword."

Chapter 13

Elizabeth sifted through the remains of the collision. She saw the books scattered along part of the track and knew they must have been in Bruce's trunks. He never went anywhere without large quantities of books. It was one of the things she had always disliked about him. She saw him as an escapist, a man who fled from life in order to hide behind a college wall, a man who took shelter behind a book filled with words she didn't care much to hear about.

Elizabeth saw herself as a doer, not just a thinker, and if Bruce Elliott wanted to hide behind a book that was well and good, but Elizabeth deeply resented his taking her older sister with him. *Men can be a hindrance to a good woman,* she thought. *They take her away from what is truly hers to share in something that is foreign to her, taking away her womanhood and dignity in the process.*

She bent down and shifted some debris. A porcelain-faced doll stared back at her, its bright cheeks flush with paint and its curly yellow hair glowing like fresh-picked corn.

She held the doll to her breast and her eyes misted. Looking off to the north, she wondered about little Nikki and how she was faring without her doll. Nikki was exactly the opposite of what Elizabeth wanted to be, she thought. Handicapped and dependent. But she did have one thing that Elizabeth deeply desired, and that was innocence.

Elizabeth had seen too much of life — and people. And she trusted neither. People only wanted to get close to her for what they could get and men were the worst. What she wanted in a man, she knew full well, was a man who didn't want her at any price, and he certainly didn't want her railroad.

Elizabeth envied Nikki's blindness in a way. There were some things she wished she couldn't see, and at times she wanted very much to be a little girl again, safe and innocent. She stood up to her full height. She was who she was — Elizabeth Marie Roberts, and she ran a railroad.

"Miss Roberts, Miss Roberts."

Elizabeth turned to see Eric Torkelson striding toward her. He looked clumsy to her, out of place. His hat was pulled low around his ears, and he had stuffed his suit pants into boots that were obviously too big for him.

"Miss Roberts, I just heard the Elliotts

were not on board?"

"No, they must have all gotten off." She looked him up and down. "That suit won't fare very well in the saddle."

"In the saddle?"

"You don't expect me to sit around here, do you?"

"Well, no, ma'am. But I thought we might send for more help first."

"We are the help, and we're going after them. We've got to find them before Jim Ruby's gang does."

She waved her hand in the direction of the debris. "You think Ruby is going to excuse this?"

Torkelson blinked at her and swallowed.

"You think he won't do everything in his power to make sure he gets my sister and her family?"

"Yes, ma'am, I suppose he will. This sure is one big mess."

She walked up the slope away from the turmoil and watched the men from the Denver and Rio Grande continue to bandage the wounds of the survivors. Turning to look back, she saw that Torkelson was following her. Out of breath when he reached her, he tried to continue his thought: "And I'm sure whoever this Cobb man is, he's somebody Mr. Ruby would do anything to get."

A man called Yeager walked up to the two of them. Elizabeth had personally picked him as her ramrod. Her father depended on Sam Fisher, but she used Yeager as her muscle. He got things done. He wore his gun in a well-oiled holster and his rugged, lean look showed him to be a seasoned and capable man. His square pocket shirt was filled out, and judging from the wear on his shotgun chaps, he had spent a great deal of time in the saddle. He wore his flat-brimmed hat pulled low over his eyes.

"Miss Roberts, the men and the horses will be ready to go in twenty minutes," he said.

"Do we have all the supplies we need?" she asked. "We have to find these people, Yeager. We have to find them before Jim Ruby's men do."

"We'll find them, Miss Elizabeth. I follow sign real well."

Elizabeth wasn't the least bit worried about Yeager's ability. She watched the men beside the train and spoke in low tones, as if to herself. "We're going to have to send the train back toward Pueblo with the survivors of this thing. Some of these people are in bad shape. We're not going to be able to come back here and get supplies by rail."

"I understand that, ma'am. We've done everything you asked us to do and we're

163

ready. Every man has a hundred and fifty rounds of handgun shells and two hundred rounds of rifle ammunition. We're all carrying food for five days and oats for six. We're going light for hard riding — no tents, and no heavy cooking equipment."

"Thank you, Captain." Occasionally Elizabeth found herself using Yeager's army rank in addressing him. It made him seem more dignified when she introduced him to strangers, and at times like these it reassured her. She smiled. "Just like a cavalry scouting party," she observed. "And how about Torkelson here? You got a horse he can ride?"

Yeager smiled. "I think so. I got a wiry little paint saddled for him back there." He looked Torkelson up and down. "Won't be so far to fall."

Torkelson looked bewildered and squashed his hat farther down around his ears.

Yeager watched the men load the wounded and the corpses onto the steaming train, then lifted his eyes and squinted past the wreckage toward the east. "I think we got company, Miss Elizabeth."

Elizabeth looked in the direction of Yeager's gaze. She could see the line of riders heading their way.

"I'd say that would be the men of the CP, ma'am."

"Then we've got to hurry," she said.

"No reason to, ma'am," Yeager said. "Those horses look hard ridden already and the sun's barely up. If those boys get down for coffee after a hard ride through the dark, they won't be quick to light a shuck out of here for some time. Smartest thing we could do is make 'em feel at home while we ride outta here."

Elizabeth smiled. "You are cunning, Captain. You find so many ways to earn your pay." She straightened her buckskin riding skirt. "Well then, gentlemen, let's go greet our guests, but we better take care with them."

"We'll keep our right hands dangling free," Yeager said.

Peter Williams rode into the scene of the wreck at the head of the column. The horses were strung out and tired-looking. The men didn't look any better. They stared wide-eyed at the twisted steel and charred remains, shaking their heads at the sight of old Number 9 piled high on top of the 440.

Williams spotted Elizabeth and rode up to where she was standing alongside Yeager.

"Good morning, Mr. Williams. How nice to see you." Elizabeth could be ice cold when she wanted to be, and right now she wanted to be ice cold with sugar sprinkled on top.

Yeager had spread his men out, and several of them stood on the wreck with rifles at the ready.

Williams swept the hat off his head. "I say, Miss Roberts, how delighted I am to see you, and how surprised."

"Oh, I don't think you're that surprised, Williams. You must have known that I'd be trying to find my sister."

"And I see you've brought your own train and your own private army with you." The Englishman surveyed the armed men that faced him and grinned slyly.

"I always try to come prepared." She looked around. "You seem to have quite a bit of work to do hereabouts to clear your track. I guess there were some things you weren't quite prepared for."

"A situation we will expedite presently, Miss Roberts. We hadn't taken into account this Cobb man of yours."

"He's not mine, Williams. He's doing anything he's doing on his own."

"Well, I daresay all this destruction of Chicago Pacific property is something that you would have paid for if you had thought of the matter, am I correct?"

"Williams, you know as well as I do that any death and destruction you see here is something Jim Ruby has already paid for.

166

You people brought this all on yourselves. The CP is getting just what it deserves."

Elizabeth was rubbing salt into the man's wounds and she knew it. Normally she would have felt very good about doing just that, but right now she was anxious to move on and find her sister, ahead of the men from the Chicago Pacific. She was also concerned about Williams' reaction. He seemed too cool, almost as though he hadn't yet turned over his hold card.

Yeager spoke up. "Your men are welcome to what's left of our coffee. You look like you've had a long ride."

"I take it this Cobb fellow stopped your train, too." Elizabeth shot out the remark to draw a look from the Englishman, and she got it.

He squinted at her with a flash of anger but was quick to regain control. He looked around at the line of men bunched up behind them. "All right, gentlemen, dismount and see to your horses. Check your supplies as well. We have an invitation for coffee from the Denver and Rio Grande Railroad."

The men behind Williams swung down from their horses, but Williams remained seated on his mount. He leaned forward in his saddle and smiled at Elizabeth. "Allow me to introduce you to someone," he said.

Jake Rice stepped forward. Rice had tied his horse to the burned-out tender they had ridden up to, and now his hands swung free near the pearl-handled cross-draw revolvers he carried.

"Williams, if you think you can back me down with a hired gunny just because I'm a woman, then you've been misinformed. I don't back down, and I don't blink. I can shoot as straight as any man, and the men I have with me are the best — and unlike yours, they're fresh."

"Oh, I don't doubt your resolve, Miss Roberts. I have every confidence in you and especially in your common sense."

"We have to ride on, Miss Elizabeth," Yeager interjected. "We have a long ride ahead of us."

"Captain Yeager is right. I'd love to talk to you further, Williams, but we have to ride. We have the men from your train on board and will be happy to take them back to Pueblo. Some are severely injured. If I were you I'd wire back and alert your people to find medical help."

Williams smiled. "Oh that's quite all right, Miss Roberts. I wired Pueblo some time ago this morning." He lifted his eyes and looked west along the tracks behind Elizabeth's private train. "In fact, if I'm not mistaken, I believe that's our train behind you now. It will be filled with a group of our special detectives."

Elizabeth stepped back and looked down the track. She could see the smoke in the distance. Williams was not bluffing. He'd been smiling at her for a reason, and now, as Elizabeth looked at the train in the distance, she could feel his sickeningly sweet smile boring into her back.

Yeager seemed composed. He nudged Elizabeth's elbow. "Well, Williams," he said. "We'd sure love to stay for your friends, but we have to be moving along. We have business to attend to."

"I trust you're not planning on trespassing over Chicago Pacific property on this little business venture of yours. Because if you are, then it will be necessary for me to stop you, and I will have the full support of the law."

Elizabeth sneered at him. "Law! What would you know about the law?"

Williams was calm. "I know enough about the law, Miss Roberts, to know that the sections to either side of this rail you are now standing on belong to the Chicago Pacific Railroad Company. If you attempt to cross them without the approval of officials of the CP, you will be in violation of the law." He smiled once again. "And since I am the duly appointed official of the Chicago Pacific, I can guarantee you that the answer to that request will not be satisfactory to you."

Elizabeth stepped forward, but Yeager restrained her with his outstretched arm.

"Regardless of what crimes this Cobb fellow is guilty of, Miss Roberts, I do expect more respect for the law from General Sydney Roberts's daughter." Williams grinned. "I'm sure your father and the stockholders of the Denver and Rio Grande would expect no less from the lady who aspires to manage that ever-shrinking asset of theirs."

"You threatening us, Williams?" Yeager asked. "Because if you are, then I can practically guarantee that we're gonna empty your saddle here and now." He paused and looked the man square in the eye. "I'd say the men you're with are pretty outclassed as you stand, and if Miss Elizabeth here gives us the word, we can let the hoedown begin right now. You may have us outgunned when that train of yours pulls up, but I'd say you personally got a bit to sweat about."

"We're reasonable men here," Williams responded calmly. He looked down at Elizabeth. "Men and women, I should say. We can resolve this without further bloodshed. We wouldn't be so bold as to take your weapons or your horses — now, that would be illegal, wouldn't it," he smirked. "No, we will allow you to take the wounded back to Pueblo, just as you have so humanitarianly planned. The only difference is that we will require that you accompany them. Perhaps when you safely arrive at that fair city you will carefully reconsider this dangerous course of action you have initiated."

"That will never happen, Williams," Elizabeth shot back.

"Well, in that event, Miss Roberts, by the time you return here, I'm sure there will be no one to oppose your ill-considered adventure."

There was silence in the group, broken up only by the whistle of the approaching train. Elizabeth knew that what was about to happen would mean more death and dying, and that was something she wanted to avoid, if possible. It wasn't that she wasn't a fighter. But to give an order that would cause others to die when there was still no goal in sight and the prospects were for more to die when the trainload of fresh men arrived, that was something she found unconscionable. Yeager looked into Elizabeth's eyes. She nodded.

Yeager raised his hand to the men around the train to make sure he had their attention. "Nobody gets off of that train, Williams.

They put it in reverse and we both back up together."

"Fair enough, Mr. Yeager. We have enough here to accomplish what needs to be done."

"Okay, boys, get back on," Yeager shouted to the men around the train. Waving up at the engineer, he yelled, "Put it in reverse. We're backing up all the way to Pueblo." He turned to the Englishman. "You better send somebody to that train and tell 'em to back up to where they came from."

Williams looked over at Frank Maxwell, still sitting beside the track. "Maxwell, go make yourself useful and do as Captain Yeager here says. We have work to do and we wouldn't want to detain these good people."

Chapter 14

Zac was restless while the others slept most of the morning. He knew that the two mules grazing with the sheep wouldn't be enough to take them all to Denver, even if the sheepherders could have parted with them. The more he wrestled with the notion, the more restless he became. He was tired, dead tired, but he blinked his eyes against the sun for a time before deciding that he had to do something. He knew Williams and his men would be following them, it was only a matter of time, and he had to find some way to slow them down.

When he rolled to his feet from behind the broken-down wagon, he saw only the old man beside the fire, the old man and the dog. Reaching over beside the wagon, Zac picked up the Sharps and the belt that carried his special ammunition.

The dog spotted him at once, drawing the old man's awareness of him as well. Zac stepped quietly through the tall grass toward the fire, his rifle on his arm.

Sensing his approach even before Zac uttered a word, the old man patted the dog and began to speak. "You could not sleep, señor?"

"No." Zac walked up to the fire and picked up a cup. He liked his coffee strong, strong enough to float a horseshoe, and hot. Pouring only half a cup to keep it plenty hot, Zac drank it all down. It burned, and he liked it that way.

The man smiled. "God never sleeps. He always watches over us, even when we must sleep."

Propping up the rifle next to the tree, Zac took out his pipe. He stuffed the briar bowl. Pecking at the edges of the fire, he picked up a flaming piece of wood and ran it over the lip of the pipe. The flame danced as he sucked it onto the tobacco.

The old man sniffed the smoke and smiled. "Your smoke, señor, is like the incense that burns on the altar, a prayer to God." He circled his hands in the air. "We wave it before Him to remind ourselves that God has the same senses that are alive to us." He patted the dog. "And to remind us to be a prayer."

Zac puffed on his pipe and listened to the old man. He mused on the fact that something about the aged gave them greater wisdom. Not only that they had lived longer and therefore knew by trial and error the difference between right and wrong, but the fact that their own physical powers were limited, and when a man reached the limit of his own ability it was time he called on Someone greater than himself. It was time he called on everything he knew and pulled out the best he had.

The old man scratched his gray beard. "The Indians of the grass use the pipe to show their reverence to God also, señor. I think they see the smoke from the lips drifting up to heaven as something that speaks of prayer too."

The dog briefly left the old man's side and nuzzled Zac. "Never thought of pipe smoke as prayer," Zac said. "And I guess I've never used it to remind me to pray either, although I'm sure my mother would approve."

"Oh, I didn't say that, señor." The man smiled. "Like any other sweet smell, it should remind us that we are a prayer. Everything we do should remind us that God listens to us. He doesn't only hear our words, He hears everything about us. He hears the way we work. He hears the way we play. It all comes up to Him like incense from the burning altar, a sweet smell to His face."

"A sweet smell is something I never imagined myself to be, either," Zac said. "I splashed a little lilac water and some bay rum on myself one time when I had a night in Kansas City; felt silly doing it, but I was young then." He sipped the coffee and then puffed on his pipe.

The dog returned to the old man's side and laid his head on his lap. "Your mother was a spiritual woman," the old man said. "I can see her marks on your soul."

"Yes," Zac replied, "she was most definitely that."

"Mothers wait for God," the old man said. "They spend their lives waiting. They think they wait to grow up. They think they wait for a man. They think they wait for a child. They think they wait for the corn to grow, but all they really wait for is God — and the spiritual ones come to know that."

Zac puffed smoke from his pipe. "Well, that was something she knew, and after my father lost his leg in Mexico, he knew it too."

"Men often have to be wounded in order to pray and wait." The man shook his head. "Too much pride, too much self, men have."

"My father's last years were good," Zac said. "He depended on me and I liked that."

"But you depend on no one, señor?"

Zac quietly drew the smoke into his mouth and released it.

The old man smiled and then chuckled.

"I think you are too young yet, señor, young and with so much in your self that you cannot depend on other people yet."

He reached down and patted the dog. "Men have to lose something first in order to wait, and we have to lose something deep inside to make us need other people. We hate the loss. We brood over it, and some decide that God is to blame and hate Him for it, but it is a blessing." The man held his own coffee cup with both hands and smelled the aroma deeply. "Blindness is God's special blessing to me. It tells me I need others. It is God's way of freeing my mind to smell, to listen, to feel, to pray, and . . . to wait."

Zac saw Nikki crawl out from underneath the wagon. Her parents continued to sleep in the shade of the tree, but the child was restless. She felt the grass around her and then got to her feet and began to wander. Zac watched as she occasionally stopped and reached to the ground to feel the grass. "Nikki is up, I'd better go and get her."

"No," the old man said. "Let her find her way. She will come here on her own. The blind must wander for a while before they know where to walk."

Zac continued to smoke the pipe and watch the girl meander. Nikki stumbled first uphill and then in a slow circle, feeling her way in the air. Occasionally she would stop and reach down to touch a flower in the grass.

Zac threw several pieces of wood into the coals of the fire, and the crackle of the flames got the little girl's attention. She held her hands out and began to turn downhill, in the direction of the sound of the fire. She was quiet, and as she got closer Zac could see she sensed the warmth and began to smell the tobacco smoke mixed with the smell of burning wood. She took several steps and fell to the ground with a thud.

The dog ran to the little girl and snuggled up to her, licking her face. She laughed. The old man clapped his hands, and Nikki's head jerked in his direction. The dog ran back and she smiled as she walked toward him.

"Here, little one," the old man said. He held out his arms and Nikki crawled into his lap. She lifted her hands and felt the old man's face. Turning his head toward Zac, the man said, "You see, she comes without us. You will be wanting to use one of the mules, señor, and the wagon?"

Zac was startled by his sudden change of subject. "Why, yes, I would. How'd you know that?"

"Blindness," the man pointed to his eyes and smiled. "To look into people is better than to see them only."

"I just need the mule for a day or so, and I'll bring him back."

"The mule will come back to us if you let him go. He will not wander like the sheep."

"You must have been here for quite a while, then," Zac said. "I thought I would work on fixing that wheel of yours before I leave. We'll need to be moving on as soon as I get back."

"It is ready to go at anytime, señor. There is no need to fix the wheel."

"I don't understand," Zac said.

"We have the good wheel fixed to the bottom of the wagon. My son is young, he leans too much on his brain, so he uses trickery to allow us to stay and graze." The old man smiled. "The cattlemen do not like sheep, and they do not want us to stay in one place for very long. If anyone asks us to leave, Pablo shrugs his shoulders and points to the wheel." The old man chuckled. "Pablo is young, he will learn."

Zac eyed the man, and he envied him. He seemed so confident, so self-assured. He had nothing, yet he acted as if he had everything. Deep inside, Zac knew that was what he really wanted in life. Until now he believed contentment came from independence, to have the means to need no one, to do his job better than anyone else. But somehow he was coming to see how wrong that thinking was.

"Perhaps I talk too much," the old man went on. "Pablo says because I am old and blind I have nothing to do but think, pray, and talk." He took the hands of the little girl and guided them through the fur of the dog. "But thinking, praying, and talking are gifts that every man should have."

"Well, I'm long on thinking," Zac said, "but I'm kinda short on praying and talking."

"Well, thinking is not an easy thing to do, señor. Talking is easy," he laughed. "God spoke through a burro once, I seem to remember." The man paused and cocked his head upward in Zac's direction. "But the praying, ahí sí, the praying, that is the hardest work of all."

Zac watched the old man with the little girl. He wanted to help her and her family, but for the life of him he couldn't figure out why. Maybe it was because he saw himself as selfish at the core, and he felt the overwhelming need to put things right in the world. If he could bring justice to whatever he touched, then maybe he could sleep. He watched the old man sip his coffee and smile, contentment written on his lined face.

Zac tapped out his pipe and put the cup down. "I'll need a day's food and a canteen, and then I'll be going. I should be back this time tomorrow. Then we'll need to put the good wheel on the wagon and head north. Hopefully the tracks of the sheep will cover our trail. The people following us wouldn't hesitate to kill us."

"We will depend on the angel of the Lord, señor, and perhaps for today that angel will be you." He bounced the little girl on his knee and smiled. "Many times God puts His angel near us, the one with the sword of flame. You are such an angel, I think."

Zac drew smoke from the stem of his pipe. "First I'm a prayer, now I'm an angel." He smiled. "An angel who needs to wait."

"You are what God wants you to be, you can never be more, you can never be less. You have to do what you think is best, señor, but remember," he said as he placed the child back on the ground, "if you wait, what you are looking for will come."

Chapter 15

Williams smirked as he watched the train pull away. "I say, dear boy, how long do you think it will take them to discover the dynamite charge?"

Rice watched the fuse he had set sparkle. "I'd say they ought to get quite a surprise in about twenty minutes. It's a slow burner we got on there, and the boys kept them occupied real well while we laid it down. Ought to be a real humdinger."

"You don't actually expect they would attempt to keep their word and travel clear to Pueblo, do you?"

"Ain't likely. That Yeager is a determined cuss and the Roberts woman —"

"Yes, Miss Roberts, what a pity! I do so love a woman with fire."

Jake Rice smiled. "She's got plenty of that, all right, and in about half an hour she's gonna get all the fire she can handle."

Williams took out his gold watch and pried it open. Watching the train continue to back up over the hill, he snapped it shut. "We have work to do, Jake, let's get cracking."

Williams moved down the line of horses and began to check the cinches. "Are you quite certain you brought enough oats?" he asked one of the men.

The man looked up at him and nodded.

"These animals have to be ready for a long, hard journey, and I won't tolerate any man falling behind because of his horse."

Peter Williams was efficient, but he was more than just efficient, he was a driven man when it came to doing a job. He personally checked all the details and trusted no one who worked with him, which was why the fiasco with Zac Cobb had struck him a terrible blow. Above all, he had to appear to be wiser than anyone around him. He was the rising star of the Chicago Pacific, and that was a position he wanted to maintain at all cost, no matter whose body he had to step over, friend or foe. A person corrected him at their own peril.

Peter walked through the line of horses, gruffly asking each man about his ammunition, food, and horse. "I won't tolerate failure!" he shouted. "We have to find those people and find them today; now get ready to mount up."

"Mr. Williams," one of the men interrupted his tirade, "these horses are played out, they've been ridden all night. If we don't give them a rest, they'll be spent before the morning's over."

He let out a stream of curses, backing the man up with his fury. "Blast you! You'll do exactly as I say!" Williams shouted, "and so will the horses, for that matter. We will keep this mission on course until I have this Cobb fellow in my hand, do you understand?"

The man nodded, his concern for the horses lost in the face of Peter Williams' need for success. The Englishman had made mistakes but no one ever dared speak about them. His errors in judgment were the best kept secret of the Chicago Pacific Railroad.

The men turned their heads and exchanged glances as Jake Rice silently pulled the cinch on his saddle tight. It wasn't that Williams didn't care what people thought. He cared very much. It just depended on who those people were. He always did whatever he could to give the appearance of confidence and invincibility to anyone who was a superior. Bowing and scraping to Jim Ruby had become a way of life to him. No, he cared about people, but they had to be people who could reward him. Other people were simply tools, something to be used and then cast aside.

He marched up and down the line of horses, shouting at the men and waving his arms. "Zac Cobb, do you hear me? Zac Cobb! We have to get that man and we have to finish our job. If it kills every horse and rider here, we have to get that man." To the railroad, Cobb had become a stunning wake-up call that Peter Williams was not invincible — a wake-up call to the officials of the Chicago Pacific and perhaps to Peter Williams himself, but certainly not to any of the men who worked for him.

Yeager had posted himself in the cab of the locomotive. He'd let Elizabeth Roberts and that accountant of hers ride in the private car, but it wasn't for him. As the train picked up speed, he watched the men gathered at the wreck. There was something about the deal they had struck that bothered him — bothered him a lot.

He had fought Indians in his day, and one thing he appreciated about the Indian was the fact that he could be trusted. If a person knew the Indian, he knew what he did was always predictable. An Indian was unreliable only to the white man who was ignorant of his ways. It was the white man who couldn't be trusted, and watching Williams and Rice as the train backed up underscored the point for Yeager. The smiles on their faces may have been because they had forced the Denver and Rio Grande to back down, but then again they may have known something that he didn't. Yeager had spent his whole life being a fighter, a fighter and a good judge of men. "I don't like it," he said to the engineer.

"Don't like what? We got plenty of steam. We'll make it just fine."

Anger rose in Yeager as he watched the men in the distance prepare to leave the wreck. They were going to his party, and he wasn't invited — and there was something wrong, something very wrong.

Zac had fashioned a halter and he sat the mule bareback. He smiled as he thought about it, thought about what friends would say if they saw him astride a jackass. Men always said, "Mules get you there steady like, but when you get there, you're still riding a mule." He smiled and kicked the animal's sides. He had to figure out some way to lay down a false trail, and that wouldn't be easy. Failing that, he had to be ready to set up an ambush.

He kicked the animal to move it along faster. Mules weren't known for their quickness, but they were surefooted and they had plenty of bottom to them. They could go all day, and then some.

Zac moved up the slope from where the creek emptied into the valley. He knew the creek was headed to the Arkansas River, and if he could, he'd find a way to get the bunch from the CP turned that way before they came onto the grassy valley. Even if they eventually discovered they were headed down a dry trail, and they surely would, by then the tracks of the sheep herd might cover their escape and allow them to put some good distance between them and the mob of railroaders.

The light of day showed the damage that had been done by a recent prairie fire. Lightning played a big part in what lived and died in this area of the country, and whatever had caused this had devastated the ground. It made it easier for him to understand why the shepherds had left the flock to feed in the still-green valley below. Evidently, the fire had stopped before it reached the grassy low ground. The bare terrain would make covering up his tracks even more difficult. It made him nervous, but he had remembered to bring a few empty burlap bags. They would help.

He wove his way through the trees and into the creek bed, moving upstream. He'd also used a knife to cut off part of Nikki's dress and had the material stuffed into his pocket. He was sure they'd recognize the bright blue fabric. *A drunk couldn't miss it,* he thought, *especially on this ground.*

The creek was shallow. It was what had made walking through it the night before bearable. It was shallow, but the sudden drop of the land to the valley below made walking through it hazardous. The water bubbled and rushed past him, making him thankful for the mule. A horse might easily stumble. The marks on the boulders on either side of the creek showed that the shallowness of the water was unusual. The boulders rose up from the creek bed like large shoulders for the water, dry and bare shoulders. The scrub oak that normally would have grown along the water's edge peeked out at him from above and beyond the huge rocks.

Zac kept his eyes focused on the lay of the stream bed, picking his way through the shallows. Occasionally, he saw small fish that darted among the rocks. He thought how good they would taste laid out over hot coals, but he had no time to fish now. He didn't need a fishing line; he'd tickled many a fish onto the bank of a stream in his time, sometimes in fast-moving, icy waters. The temperature of the water was what made it hard to lie down beside a hole and wait for the fish to get near enough to place his hand slowly underneath it, wait for just the right moment. To do it, a man had to be patient — and hungry. He was hungry and the water was ideal, but he couldn't take the time. Had he lifted up his eyes, he would have seen that he, too, was being watched by something that was as hungry as he was.

"Last tracks here." Clay Boy, the Cherokee tracker that Williams had brought with them, had been surveying the north side of the roadbed. The wreck had made picking up specific tracks difficult, but it helped them to know which direction Cobb and the little group he was with were heading. The Indian squatted just off the track and looked down at the moving stream. "They go down here," he said.

"Spread out!" Williams shouted. "Get on both sides of the stream and we'll find them directly. They're on foot, so they can't be very far ahead."

The men fanned out and began to pick their way down the hill. Several of them dismounted and began to follow the banks of the creek, keeping an eye out for any sign they might come across. They led their horses around the large boulders and kept their eyes on the ground. They knew that even if the group had taken to the water, they had to come out somewhere. This was an area and a route that wasn't well traveled, so any sign they could find would be what they were looking for.

The CP men grumbled as they rode. Some had slept in the saddle during the night for brief snatches of time, but others had ridden through the darkness, blinking their eyes and complaining to each other. They hadn't eaten since the day before, so hunger topped off their fatigue. Jake Rice watched them and listened. He knew they would say nothing to Williams. The man was driven. His ambition fed him, but for the rest of the men this was just a job. They had no hatred for Cobb. They had no pride that had been broken, and they weren't trying to impress Jim Ruby. They just had a job to do and right now they were tired and hungry.

"Peter." Jake drew rein and got Williams' attention. "If we don't give these boys something to eat and let 'em shut their eyes a mite, they're likely as not to ride right over any sign they find."

"We have to keep moving," Williams said. "We can't depend on that charge we placed. We don't know how far ahead of that Roberts woman we can stay and I won't be stopped. I won't be stopped and the men will go on when I say. When I stop, they can stop."

Rice moved his horse on. He didn't respond. He was a hired gun and only that. And he knew that when push came to shove he wanted men who could back him up, and ones who were able to shoot straight.

Yeager climbed to the top of the tender and watched the lead train they followed climb a rise. "Get ready!" he shouted to the engineer. "I want this thing stopped cold when I give the word. I don't like this. That man was just too confident." When he saw the train behind them disappear over the crest of the hill, he scooted back down the tender and into the cab of the engine. "Now!" he said "Stop it now! No whistle, just stop it!"

The engineer applied the brakes and began to let out steam. The train skidded and screeched, sending sparks along the rails. As it slowed, Yeager jumped to the ground.

Elizabeth and Eric were thrown against the wall of the car and wound up in each other's arms, to Eric's embarrassment and excitement.

"What now?" Elizabeth shouted. She ran to the door and jumped to the ground. Yeager stood beside the car that carried the horses. As Elizabeth ran up to him he reached underneath it. "What's happening?" she asked.

He pulled out the bundled dynamite and held it up for her to see. "A farewell gift from the Englishman. Their fuse was defective, otherwise —"

"My Lord," she said.

"It would have killed all the horses at a minimum."

"And us too," she said. "That settles it. There's only one thing these people respect and that's brute force."

Yeager nodded his head.

"We've got to get back there and unload."

"Wouldn't do that, ma'am. We want those people on that train back of us to think we're still following them. We'll get the men and horses off now and be out of sight in five minutes. It'll take us a while to catch those folks, but it'll be a lot safer. The engineer can keep following them after we get every-thing off. The people back there on that train may be worried right now, but by the time they stop and head back here, we'll be gone and this thing will be coming their direc-tion."

"All right, let's move then. We don't have a second to lose."

The big cat strode slowly above the stream. He hadn't eaten in more than a week, not since the fire that had consumed or driven away the game. Not a rabbit, antelope, or deer was in sight. He watched the man on the mule below. All natural fear of man dissolved in the face of hunger. Surviving the wall of fire outside his den, the animal was slow to leave the only home he knew. But hunger made him desperate enough to leave it to search farther afield for food. Every ounce of attention was focused on the man on the mule.

Zac had ridden upstream for three or four hours. By the time the sun hung high in the sky, he had rambled over what it had taken them all night to cover on foot. He swung the mule to the shore and dismounted. Taking out the burlap, he tied the material around the mule's hooves. The rough cloth would cut the imprints of the animal's tracks to something that only the best of trackers could follow and he doubted if the men from the Chicago Pacific had the best of trackers with them. He hung on to the homemade halter and wound his way through the boulders to the burned-out trees above him.

The big cat watched the man from the other side of the stream. As hungry as he was, instinct told him surprise was his best weapon. He would carefully follow and make sure of his kill before he showed himself.

Zac found a likely spot on the burned-out

bank above the stream. He scuffed his feet slightly and walked back and forth in front of the mule. He knew he couldn't afford to look too obvious, create too many questions in the minds of the men who would follow — but still, the tracks of five people would be hard to duplicate. Tearing off a piece of the blue dress, he snared it on a sharp but burned branch.

Chapter 16

Zac moved toward the hills that bordered the creek. The brush was burned and the terrain bare. He knew that somewhere he would have to come to the end of the fire's damage. He just wasn't sure if he could wait till then to double back, which he would do only after he had laid down a believable enough trail in the more direct route to the Arkansas.

If he could get the men who were following them to believe that was the direction they were traveling, then he might make it back to camp and head north before nightfall. The darkness would stop the pursuers, unless they merely continued in the direction of the Arkansas. He knew from enough chases of his own that if you know where someone is going, you can find them without following their trail. All a body had to do was deadhead and pick up sign later, pick up sign or spot smoke. He just wanted to leave a trail convincing enough to keep the pursuit going in the wrong direction.

He broke several branches along the way, just enough to show a fresh-snapped twig.

Anybody ought to see that, he reasoned. Meandering back and forth in front of the mule, he kicked a few stones loose from the ground. Stones that had become embedded in the earth and then been kicked loose showed a color on the surface that was also easy to spot. The trail he was leaving would not have been believed if it were only him the men from the CP were following, but a woman, a professor, an old man, and a child, that was a different matter. Such a group could be expected to trace their route, even while trying hard not to.

Zac stopped and took a drink from the canteen as he looked over the land. The grassland was normally a place of beauty. It had a different quality to it and it was never treeless. The trees chose their own spots, and generally one could tell where to find water by spotting where the trees grew, but even the prairie itself was a thing of beauty. The openness made a body feel all alone, and that was a feeling that Zac enjoyed. He stared into the distance and shook his head. That was his problem. Jenny would have told him as much. He carried his solitude around with him like a badge of honor.

The big cat stopped at the edge of the rocky outcropping along the creek's high banks, eyeing Zac's movement, and the sight of the man and mule only increased his desperate hunger. Instinct kept the animal from venturing into the open. Innate fear of man kept him at bay. Winding his way through the boulders, the lion watched the man move into the distance. When he was out of sight, he crept to the crest of the next hill, waiting. Lowering his nose to the ground he picked up the scent of the man and mule and fixed them in his brain. He wouldn't lose them.

Zac moved up the hill and then skirted around it. The last thing he wanted to do was to skylight himself against the Colorado prairie sky. The contrast would be seen for miles. He snapped several branches and moved around the hill. It was there that he spotted the running water. That was the place to stop. From there he could double back and further accent the trail. Perhaps if the CP men got that far, they'd think the group had again gone into the stream; after all, it was a pattern. Turning the mule at the stream, he laid out another piece of the blue material and headed back to the creek.

Pablo had positioned the wagon perfectly. The broken wheel sat beside the axle that he had rested on a large rock. It made it easy for them to use a lever to boost the wagon just enough to slip on the good wheel. Even the old man could manage enough pressure to do that. The old man had cooked fry bread and wrapped it around dried lamb.

"When do you think he will be back?" Irene shielded her eyes from the high sun and squinted. She was feeling very vulnerable without Zac. Looking over at the wagon, she spotted Nikki immediately. The little girl was attempting to walk up the wagon tongue, swinging her arms to balance herself.

"She is all right, señora," Pablo said. "She will hurt nothing."

Irene got to her feet. "She will hurt herself," she said.

The old man patted the dog. "To live with great pain, a person has to be hurt," he said. "Your daughter will live with some pain, it's only right that you allow her to be hurt."

The little girl suddenly lost her balance and fell from the wagon tongue. She began to cry.

Without another word, Irene ran toward the wagon.

"Pain is somethin' the Robertses have always been able to shuck light of." Sam Fisher had a fresh cigar clamped down between his teeth, only this time it was lit. "Guess it comes from always having what you need. Of course, the general lived with not having things in his younger years." He blew smoke and bit down on the oversized stogie. "Pshaw! He went through the war." He took the cigar out of his mouth and, holding it in his fingers, blew another pillar of smoke into the air. "But them girls of his, now that's another story. They're all brave, but they're all babied, too."

"See here!" Bruce Elliott spoke up. "I resent that suggestion."

"I didn't say they weren't tough. I just said they've always gotten what they wanted. The little ones were given what they wanted, but that Elizabeth, whew! She tended to take what she wanted and woe be unto you if you and she wanted the same thing." He laughed. "I've played checkers with that woman enough when she was little to know that. She'd whip me good and proper."

Irene returned with Nikki in her arms. She held the girl close and sat back down beside the fire.

"Will she live?" the old man asked, smiling.

"She'll live," Irene said. "She just fell." The woman held Nikki close and spoke into her good ear. "Why do you insist on taking chances, darling? You scare your mother."

The old man spoke up. "It is because she wants to live that she takes the chances, señora. She does not like the walls inside of her head."

"I suppose you're right," Irene said.

"I like to climb," Nikki said. "Can I climb again?"

"We had better put the wheel on and pack our things. I think we should be ready to go when Señor Cobb returns," Pablo said.

"We have no right to put you at risk," Irene said. "These people are after us, not you."

"You are human beings in need," the old man responded simply.

Zac retraced his steps to the creek and began to wind around the large rocks that shaded the bank. Above him the mountain lion waited, muscles tensed. Watching the man returning to the creek, he scrambled to the top of the rocks that shadowed the path.

Without warning the lion leaped, launching himself with a growl on top of Zac, sending him tumbling to the ground. Rolling over, Zac scooted toward the rocks, placing his back to the boulder that towered over him. The lion became distracted by the mule, which was kicking into the air to defend itself. One of the kicks landed a solid blow to the big cat, sending him flying. Without any further delay, the mule scampered down the bank and through the creek to the other side.

Zac turned to face the lion and slowly got to his feet. His rifle lay a few feet away, out of reach. His revolver was still in place, but he knew that if he fired a weapon the sound would carry down the creek, something he wanted to avoid at all cost. He needed something between him and the lion. Shucking his jacket, he wrapped it around his left arm.

The lion circled. Zac could see the animal was weak, but very large all the same, large and menacing. Reaching his hand to the back of his shirt, Zac drew his large Green River knife. He kept his back to the rock and watched the cat circle. The lion swished his tail and began to scream. Zac knew the big cat was waiting for him to run. Tackling prey from behind was what a beast like this did best. Whether the animal would attack him head on depended on one thing — how hungry the lion was. Zac could see the cat's ribs. He was facing a very hungry lion.

The beast snarled and slapped at Zac, ripping into the jacket on his arm. Zac struck back with the knife. Backing up, the animal screamed and prepared once again to rush. He began a dash in Zac's direction and then suddenly stopped short and snarled. Once again, Zac had refused to turn and run; he would not show the beast his backside. The animal stood in front of him and snarled. It screamed and snapped its claws at him while Zac fended off the blows with his carefully wrapped arm, flashing the blade in the animal's direction.

In the distance the scream of the lion could be heard by the CP men. It was the sound of a large cat with cornered prey.

"What do we do now?" Rice asked.

"We continue our search," Williams responded. "We just have to move more carefully."

The men held their horses only with great difficulty; the noise had spooked them.

"We can't get any closer," Rice said. "Not with these horses, we can't."

"All right," Williams said. "Let's have some men move forward on foot and have their horses held back. We'll drive the animal out, or shoot the beast. Who wants to go?"

The men all held on to their horses, and no one volunteered. The big cat screamed again.

One of the men snapped his animal's reins. The man was tired and hungry, and now he was irritated. He pulled his saddle gun from the scabbard and jacked a shell into the chamber. Holding the rifle into the air, he fired a shot. "There," he shouted. "That ought to do it."

Williams ran toward the man and, skidding to a stop, knocked the man to the ground. "You fool!" he shouted.

The man sprawled on the ground and his horse, now free, ran wildly back toward the creek. Grabbing for his gun, the man found himself staring directly at the muzzle of Williams' Colt.

"Go on!" Williams shouted. "You've already shown yourself to be a fool. Draw that gun and I'll kill you." He leaned down into the man's face. "You don't know who is out there. What if those people heard that shot?" Williams sent a hard kick into the man's ribs. "Get up! Get up and find that horse."

The man slowly got to his feet and dusted himself off. He walked off in the direction his horse had run, looking at each man in the group he passed.

"What are you looking at?" Williams shouted. He snatched the reins of his horse from the hand of the man who held them and quickly mounted. "Let's go!" he shouted. "Our companion here has taken care to alert the lion of our presence and, more than that, he has told the people we are pursuing how close we are!"

The lion's head turned at the sound of the

shot and Zac slashed at the beast in the same instant with his knife, catching the animal on the face. That was all it took — the cat sprang backward and ran.

Watching the cat's retreat, Zac unwound the jacket from his arm and put it on. Aside from a few tears, the buckskin was intact. He picked up his Sharps Creedmore and slung it over his shoulder. He wouldn't be far behind the lion. He had to be gone by the time the CP men arrived, and he had to watch what sign he laid down.

Snapping off a branch, he stirred the dust and dirt around where he, the mule, and the big cat had scuffled. Backing toward the creek as he wiped out his tracks, he stepped into the water and threw the branch into the stream. Then he turned and ran through the water. He had to find cover and find it fast.

Chapter 17

Hours later, when Zac walked into the valley, he saw that the mule had already returned to camp. Everyone was gathered around the fire and Zac knew they must be worried. Heads rose as he walked down the grassy slope.

Irene ran to greet him. "Thank God! Thank God you're here. We thought we heard a shot. We were worried, especially after seeing the marks on the mule. Pablo thought it looked like a mountain lion attack."

Zac nodded his head, and the two of them walked into the fire circle. "We've got to go," he said. "We've got to light outta here right now. Those men could ride in here anytime. If there's a tracker with them, they'll be here real soon. Without a tracker, they'll be here by morning."

"Well then, let's get." Sam Fisher chomped down on his cigar, brushed aside his white walrus mustache, and pulled his derby down tight.

"We won't be able to fit everybody inside that wagon," Zac said. "And we got to get everyone out of sight. Sam, I'll take you with me on foot and we'll get gone out in front of this bunch. Elliott, you take my shotgun and get in that wagon with Irene and Nikki. Stay out of sight. I don't care how you do it, under a blanket, anything."

"Señor, we put the top up, and everybody will be okay. If those men see us, they see only the sheep and our little shepherd here." Pablo patted the dog.

Zac and Sam moved ahead of the others. Zac kept an eye on the herd from the crest of the hills to the north of the moving sheep and wagon. He knew it was late in the day. It was late enough that by reason, they should be looking for a place to camp, not breaking camp and moving on. They had to put some miles between the family and the CP men though, and any distance would help.

As he watched the sheep fan out walking north around the wagon and saw the black-and-white dog keep them moving, he had no worry about the men from the CP finding their trail. If they suspected the group might be with the shepherds, it would be just a guess, and if they had tried to follow the false trail he had laid down, then their tracks would be even more nonexistent.

"So you've worked with these Roberts

people for a while?" Zac tried to make small talk as he walked with the older man.

"Ever since the war."

"Looks to me like you're still in the war," Zac said.

"Guess so. I looked forward to this job soze I could put drunks and deadbeats off of the train. Don't really mind chasing outlaws neither, but we're at war here and I thought I retired from that."

"Then why do you do it?"

"The man."

"Roberts?"

"Yeah, General Roberts. Been with him for a while. He's a thinker and normally I don't relate to men like that, but the general's a doer too, and I like that in a man."

"Sounds like this daughter of his is cut from the same bolt of cloth."

"You got that right. And if there's ever anything that woman wants from you, you best just give it to her and walk away. Oh, don't get me wrong, she's quite a looker, that one, and she's a nice enough woman, it's just that she's a woman who makes me nervous."

"Why?"

"Because she ought to just settle down and start a family, not build railroads. But she's headstrong, that woman is. She ain't never found a man that matches up to her, I guess, and if she ever does, he ain't got a snowball's chance in hell." The old man stopped and looked him up and down. "Boy, looks to me like you may be in more trouble than you know."

Zac smiled as they started back to walking. "Well, it's hard enough for me to settle down with the one woman I want, and it'd be danged near impossible with a woman I don't."

The older man limped along. He wanted to change the subject. Women made him nervous. "Guess I've gotten too soft. Used to walk all over creation in the army, but now I'm just used to planting my behind in a railroad car."

"Can't say as I'm all that accustomed to being afoot either," Zac said. He turned and walked back to the crest of the hill, getting down low as he approached it. He saw the men riding up to the rear of the herd. Signaling to Fisher, he laid low and counted the men in the group.

"What is it?" The older man lay on the ground and crawled forward.

"They must have a tracker with them," Zac said. "Keep your head down. A tracker will be looking at these hills; he won't be looking at the people."

★ ★ ★

As the men from the CP rode through the sheep and up to the back of the wagon, Peter Williams rode to the front of the group and spoke to the man handling the mule's traces. "We are looking for a group of people that may have passed this way."

The old man pulled back on the reins. "I am sorry, señor, but I have seen no one." He smiled. "But as you can see, I have seen no one for many years."

Inside the wagon, Bruce Elliott huddled under a blanket with Irene and Nikki. Supplies and canvas were piled on top of them, the sawed-off shotgun in Elliott's hand as a last resort.

"You're blind," Williams said. "I can see I'm talking to the wrong person. We'll search your wagon and be on our way."

"Ho!" Pablo yelled from the edge of the herd, wading through the sheep toward the mounted men. "What is it you want, señores? We are not staying on your land, we are moving on."

"We're just looking for some information," Jake Rice spoke up.

"We are looking for a group of criminals and a little girl," Williams said.

"I am sorry, señor, you are looking in the wrong place."

"Our tracker here, the Cherokee" — he motioned to the dark-haired man in the saddle — "says the people we are seeking came down to the valley. We are simply going to search your wagon and then we will be off to look elsewhere."

"We can't let you do that, señor. It is our only property and we have nothing for you in there."

Jake Rice was getting impatient. "We don't exactly need leave from the likes of you two. I don't see how you can stop us. You gonna sic your dog on us?"

The black-and-white dog snarled at the man and Rice drew his revolver.

"Señor, don't! Stop!" Pablo moved between Rice and his line of fire. Turning to the dog, he shooed the animal away. "Vamanos! Go! Go take care of the sheep!"

Zac scooted the Sharps Creedmore forward. Sliding open the chamber, he dropped a shell into the housing. Quietly, he rammed it into place. Lifting up the sight, he adjusted it. He rested his cheek on the smooth butt of the rifle and stared straight down its barrel.

"I can't even see that far," Fisher whispered.

Zac pulled the set trigger and froze in place.

Rice maneuvered his horse and, knocking Pablo to the ground, once again took aim at the dog. The reins in his hand seemed to explode, cut cleanly by a force he hadn't seen. Only then, after the sudden jerking of the leather and the movement of the horse, did they hear the explosion of the Sharps.

The men's heads all swung to the sound of the big rifle, and they maneuvered their horses into position.

"Leave the dog and those people be!" Zac shouted.

Williams moved his horse forward. "Cobb? Is that you up there?"

"No," Zac shouted with sarcasm. "It's the United States Cavalry. Now, don't that make you feel a lot safer?"

"Cobb, come on down and we can talk."

"No, Williams, that's not the way it works. The way it works is you and your men down there ride them ponies of yours up this hill, while me and my friend here try to see how many saddles we can empty. One thing I gotta tell you, though, your saddle's gonna be the first one to see daylight. That's a promise I can durn sure make."

Williams jumped into the wagon behind the old man and drew his revolver. He aimed his gun at the man's temple. "Cobb, I refuse to play the game by your rules any longer, is that understood? If you and those people with you don't start walking down here right now, this innocent man is going to pay the ultimate price for your brazenness and bravado."

There was a pause. "Spread out, men. Make some space between yourselves. If he starts shooting, I want you to ride up that hill and take him! Got that?"

One of the men spoke up. "Us? You want us to ride up there while you stay in the wagon?"

"You will do as I say," Williams shouted to the men. "Do what I say the first time, and we will make it through this. There is to be no dissension in the ranks. We act as one body here, all responding to one brain — mine. Understand?" He raised his voice and shouted over the old man's shoulder. "Unless you start down that hill, Cobb, I will kill this man here and now."

"You go down that hill," Fisher said to Zac, "and they'll kill you. Then they'll come up here and shoot me. Next it'll be the Elliotts and the Mexican sheepherders." He lay close to the ground next to Zac. "I don't know how you made that first shot, but do you think you could plant another one in that Englishman's noggin down there?"

Zac had jacked another round into the

chamber and now squinted down the barrel. He looked intently into the sights and then pulled up his head. Without saying a word, he took another look through the sights.

"Cobb!" The Englishman shouted. "We will kill them all and start with these two greasers first if you don't surrender, and surrender right now." He maintained his revolver against the old man's temple.

The old man spoke up loud and clear. "Señor, I am ready to die. No man is prepared to live, until he is ready to die."

"I'll kill him, Cobb. You have my word on that."

Zac lifted his head up from the rifle. "I don't think I can get a clean shot." He got to his feet and stood on the hill. "All right, limey, I'm coming down. Let the old man go."

"What are you doing?" Fisher asked. "How you figure on gettin' out of that down there?"

"I ain't exactly sure," he said. He looked down at the group of men on horseback. "I guess the old man's right, though. A feller who's scared of dying can't rightly live." He handed the rifle and the ammunition belt to Fisher. "Hang on to this, Sam. Wouldn't want it in the wrong hands, now would I?"

"I'll do the best I can."

Zac hitched up his gun belt and began to stride down the hill.

"Here he comes," Williams said. "Do not shoot. I want that man myself. He's to be my trophy."

Then to Rice, who had dismounted his horse and was trying to refashion his severed reins, Williams said, "When our man gets down here, you disarm him." He signaled with his head toward the back of the wagon. "Then we will further explore what cargo our friends are carrying."

Zac walked to the edge of the sheep. "These people had nothing but kindness for us. Let them go."

"Why certainly, Mr. Cobb. We wish harm to no one. We only want to bring you to justice, swift justice."

Zac pulled back the edge of his jacket, exposing his low-slung Colt. "I await your pleasure, Williams."

"Oh now, Cobb, surely you do not think me foolish enough to duel with you, a man of your reputation."

Rice stepped forward. "I'd be happy to oblige you, Cobb."

"No, Jake. I shouldn't think that would be necessary," Williams quickly responded. "I can attest to his prowess with a rifle, but not with a Colt .45. I can't spare you, Jake."

Rice stepped toward Cobb. "No risk involved." He looked Zac over. "I've heard all about this man. Man in my line of work, it pays to know who you might face some day, and I know all the short-trigger men. The word I hear is that he's good, very good at what he takes aim at, but that somebody like me can expect to get off the first shot. He's a shootist all right, but he ain't no leather-slappin' pronto bug."

"I do generally get off the last shot," Zac countered.

"If there is any shooting whatsoever, Cobb, we will be forced to take the lives of these two shepherds." He smiled. "Now, you wouldn't want that, would you?"

Zac held up his left hand as if to silence the man, and then deliberately reached across his waist and unbuckled his gun belt, allowing the Colt and holster to fall to the ground. The old man felt Williams' grip slip on him, and tying the reins, got off the wagon seat.

"There you are, Rice. We have a Southern gentleman here, the type of man who protects the innocent at all cost." He grinned. "You have to understand American chivalry, dear fellow. People like our Mr. Cobb are lost in the wrong century. Now take his gun."

When Jake Rice stepped forward, he saw horses coming over the hill to the west of them. The group of riders fanned out as they rode down the hill. Jake recognized the red-head who led the group. Elizabeth Roberts had caught his eye at the site of the wreck, and here she was again.

Elizabeth and the men from the Denver and Rio Grande rode up to the edge of the herd. "Afternoon, Williams. I didn't expect to find you riding in a shepherd's wagon."

"We members of Her Majesty's great nation take our riding pleasure in many ways. I had not expected to see you so soon either, Miss Roberts."

"Somehow, Williams, I don't think you expected to see me at all."

"Well, in any event, we do seem to be in quite a dilemma here. It seems to be what you Americans so quaintly describe as a 'Mexican standoff.' The only thing is" — he laughed — "we have two Mexicans here that your friend over there wants to protect."

Elizabeth's face reddened. "Williams, you are a snake, and if I were a man I'd personally climb down from here and pull your fangs out one by one."

Zac watched the young woman. Even if Williams hadn't identified her, he'd have known who she was right away. Her reddish blond hair glowed in the low-slung sun, and her eyes shone with rage. She was plenty angry. Zac liked that in a woman.

"What I'd like to do is plant you and these killers of yours in the ground, but I want you to skeedaddle back to whatever hole you crawled out of instead."

"If you insist on displaying that type of temperament, my dear, I'm afraid there will be bloodshed, and I know you don't want that." Zac could read the man's mind. He was going to play his last card in the hope of backing her down. She was a woman, wasn't she? It was obvious to all that Williams' men were not up to a fight.

"Oh yes I do!" Elizabeth shot back. "I want *your* blood spilt. With what you tried to do to our train, I ought to take you back to that tree and leave you swinging on a length of rope."

"Well, it does appear that blood will be spilt, Miss Roberts. I detest that, but unless you leave and allow us to do our job of bringing this man to justice, we will have no choice but to start shooting."

Chapter 18

Williams heard the sharp snap of the hammers on the shotgun. From behind his back came the words, "Sir, you have no idea how much you would regret the decision to pull that trigger."

The Englishman froze. *If I thought that cargo contained the Elliotts, why did I think they wouldn't be armed?*

"Just lower your weapon and put it down. Do not make me kill you."

Williams stared straight ahead. Defeat was not something common to his thinking. He could tolerate a setback. He could be patient and even appear calm, but deep within his soul the anger raged, the anger and the empty feelings of doubt. Not having things within his power to control was seldom the case with him. Williams lowered the hammer on his revolver and laid it down on the wooden seat of the wagon.

"There you are," Elliott said. "I could see you were an intelligent man."

Zac walked down the slope and through the gathered riders. He watched Williams silently climb down from the wagon, mount his horse, and motion for the men to ride. To speak would be to admit defeat, and defeat was something that Peter Williams had never allowed himself to tolerate.

They all watched the men from the Chicago Pacific ride off to the west. Sam Fisher hobbled down the hill and stood beside Irene and Nikki Elliott. "I hope you don't think that's the last we'll see of him," Fisher said.

"I hope it isn't," Elizabeth shot back. "I want to see that man dead. That will be the last I'd like to see of him."

The old man climbed down from the wagon, edged his way into the herd, and whistled for his dog. The rest of them talked about how they would get back to the special train.

Out of the corner of his eye, Zac watched Elizabeth carefully. She was full of fire, fire and ice.

Her hazel eyes turned to meet his. She fastened her gaze on him. "You must be this Zachary Cobb I've heard so much about." She grabbed the riding glove on her right hand and pulled it off. Reaching out to him with her bare hand, she smiled.

The woman's hair bounced and her eyes seemed to dance when she looked at him. She was almost too perfect. Her skin was the color of pure cream, and her lips had the hue of strawberry preserves. Her chin was strong. The most unnerving thing about the woman was the confidence she wore like a badge. She seemed to be the type who took life by the scruff of the neck and shook it. Zac detected an inner beauty as well in Elizabeth, beauty that went beyond her natural pleasing features — the flaming red hair, smart figure, perfect skin. It said she liked who she was — loud and clear — shouted it to anyone, even those who didn't want to listen.

Zac stared at her outstretched hand for a moment. He didn't want to listen to her, didn't want to see her beauty, but that was all he could hear, all he could see. He knew his hesitation must appear awkward, but he couldn't help himself.

Elizabeth broke the silence. "This is the West, Mr. Cobb. You can shake it. You don't have to kiss it."

He smiled and shook her hand.

"There you are," she said. "I don't bite. At least I don't bite the hand that feeds me, or the one that protects my big sister and her family."

From the corner of his eye, Zac picked up a knowing look from Sam Fisher. Apparently the uneasiness he felt in the presence of this woman he'd heard so much about was obvious to others as well.

Fisher pushed up the back of his derby, lowering the hat over his eyes, and stuck out his lower lip.

Irene joined her sister, placing her arm around Elizabeth's slim waist. It was then that Zac realized he was still holding on to Elizabeth's hand. He dropped it suddenly, tried to regain his composure.

"It's so wonderful to see you," Irene said. After they hugged, she looked up at Zac. "And I must tell you, Elizabeth. We would never have made it if it hadn't been for this man. I don't necessarily approve of his methods, but I do appreciate the way he kept us from harm."

Zac's discomfort deepened as Elizabeth's eyes bore straight into his. He knew women seldom maintained a steady gaze at a man for no reason, that modesty prevented them the risk of being thought easy, cheap. But this woman did not turn her eyes away from Zac's face.

He didn't pretend to know what a woman thought, what went on behind their eyes. It was a total mystery to him. And he didn't know this woman at all, but he knew one thing — she wasn't cheap. Any man who got involved with Elizabeth Roberts was going to pay a dear price — everything he was, and everything he ever hoped to become without her.

"Did you know there's a reward waiting for you, Cobb," Elizabeth said. "A sizable one, I might add."

Zac cleared his throat. He was flustered and he wondered if his warm face meant that it was red. "I need to get to Denver directly. Got Wells Fargo business to finish there. After that, I'll be heading on back to California." He walked toward the little girl standing by her mother's side and, stooping down in front of her, put his hands on her shoulders. He leaned forward, close to the child's good ear. "Goodbye, Nikki. I need to go."

"You'll have to come to Glen Eyrie — that's my home — to collect your reward first, Mr. Cobb." Elizabeth walked toward him.

"Zac, ma'am." He looked up at her. "Just call me Zac."

"All right, Zac, and please call me Elizabeth. That's what my friends call me."

"Well, fine." Zac swallowed. "Elizabeth. I'd sure appreciate the loan of a good horse. Like I said, I need to get to Denver as soon as possible." Looking down at the little girl gave him good reason to avoid looking into the woman's eyes. He'd go to collect the reward. He'd go, conduct his business, do his job for Wells Fargo, but he'd watch himself with this woman. Somehow it was comforting to have Jenny's letters in his pocket.

Nikki reached up and felt Zac's face, running her fingers over his mustache. "Goodbye, Mr. Cobb," she said. "Can you come see me?"

"Yes, Nikki, I'll come and see you, and maybe, just maybe, I'll give you another ride on my back like I did last night."

Nikki smiled and nodded her head.

"I'm afeared" — Zac looked up now at Elizabeth — "that I'm gonna have a bit of explaining to do to Wells Fargo, me being late and all."

"I wouldn't worry about that," Elizabeth spoke confidently. "In fact, they may be very grateful. We're negotiating with them to provide for the Denver and Rio Grande's express service. I think they're going to appreciate the courtesy you've shown us, perhaps even in a substantial way. You're going to go home from this trip with quite a tidy sum."

She took the reins of a large red roan and brought the animal forward. The gelding stood over sixteen hands high. "Here," she said. "We brought extra horses for all of you.

This one will go all day if you ask him, and still have some left in him." She patted the horse's neck. "This gelding's a favorite. You'll have to make sure you come back with him."

Zac stood up and took the roan's reins from Elizabeth. "Don't worry, miss." He looked down at the child. "Me and Nikki here have gotten to be friends. I'll need to pay her a visit like I said I would. 'Sides, what I do doesn't come cheap and that reward money will help a great deal." He thought maybe the promise of a visit would put the woman's mind at ease, even if it did make him feel nervous. He did need the money. And he'd taken enough risk on this trip — he deserved some recompense.

"What does he want?" Zac looked past Elizabeth and watched Peter Williams ride back down the hill. Williams brought his horse to a dead stop in front of them.

"Sorry," he said, "found this animal hurt and we had to put him out of his misery." He dropped the body of the black-and-white sheep dog from the pommel of his saddle onto the ground, dead from an obvious gunshot wound. "It seemed the only humane thing to do."

Pablo ran forward and scooped the dog up from the ground. "Oh, Holy Mother! What have you done? What have you done?" The old man moved feebly past the gathered people and, taking the dog in his arms, held him close. He stood silently, tears streaking down his dusty cheeks.

"I suppose the moral of this terrible accident is not to become entangled in other people's affairs," Williams said. "I hope you learn the lesson someday, Cobb. Perhaps you will have someone instruct you when you finally arrive in Denver."

Zac looked up at the Englishman, aware that the man was making the problem between the railroads a problem between the two of them, and it made him angry. Rarely did personal feelings cloud his head at work. Passion and anger only displaced good judgment. But the obvious threat, combined with the death of the dog, made him flashpowder angry. He moved his hand to his holster.

Williams tipped his hat to the silent but boiling Elizabeth Roberts. "Good evening, madam." Next he stared directly into Zac's eyes. There was a challenge in the look. "Cheerio, Mr. Cobb." Tugging on the brim of his hat, he clapped his spurs to his horse's sides.

The group watched the lanky Englishman gallop his horse back up the hill. "He seems to know all about your business, Cobb,"

Bruce Elliott said.

"People like that," Fisher interjected, "with the kind of job I'm in, are supposed to know everything about everybody they face. He knows about everybody here. Knows where we live, where we drink, and what we smoke." He grunted. "You can count on him knowing anything he thinks will give him an edge."

Irene turned to the still silent Zac Cobb. "But you aren't planning on facing him again, are you?"

"No, he isn't. He'll be in California and we'll be facing him," Elizabeth said. Elizabeth always made it a point to appeal to any area in a man where she thought him to be vulnerable, and she knew enough about Zac Cobb to know he didn't like unfinished business, didn't like to leave a job undone, leave an enemy feeling they had bested him. And she counted on Zac being the kind of man who could command her respect. She drove her point home. She'd do anything to keep from losing this man to the first westbound train out of Denver.

Zac was reading her mind again.

"Williams will be standing in the Grand Canyon of the Arkansas just waiting for us when we get there," Elizabeth said. She looked up the hill and watched as Williams cleared its crest, but out of the corner of her eye she watched the still silent Zac Cobb. "He's not beaten," she said, "not yet, not as long as he has breath and Jim Ruby has another dollar."

Zac took the big roan that one of the men was handling and tightened up the cinch. He didn't say another word. He'd said all he needed to say, and he didn't like being read, not by anyone.

"Here, I'm goin' with Cobb," Fisher said. He took the reins from one of the men in the Rio Grande company.

Zac stopped and looked at him.

"Well, I am." Fisher shot the words in Zac's direction and looked over the saddle and canteen of the horse he'd just taken. "You done enough here for two lifetimes, soze the least I can do is come along and make sure you don't get yourself back-shot." He took up his stirrups on the horse. "I know you don't want me, figure I'm too old. Well, I ain't!"

He lowered his voice and moved next to Zac. "Can't say as I look forward to going back with this group, no ways. My job's done here and that woman makes me nervous." He smiled. " 'Sides, I know your type, all fiery and stuffy and li'ble for trouble."

Zac mounted up, then watched Fisher try

to mount. The old man made several attempts to get on the horse, but without success. "Try puttin' that horse downhill from you," Zac suggested, cracking a slight smile. Even in his worst of moods and situations, he could see the humor in things — a trait that had always been a strong suit for him. It helped him to clear his mind and to think straight. He watched Fisher swing the horse around. "Works better that way," Zac said.

The man muttered. "Like I said, I marched in the army and been on trains ever since. Never did like these things."

Heaving himself up, the man launched himself off the ground and into the saddle. Successfully astride, he straightened himself to his stubby length and cocked the derby to the side of his head.

Zac walked his horse to the wagon where the old man sat, still holding the lifeless sheepdog. He reached out and put his hand on the man's shoulder. "Sorry about the dog," he said.

The old man wiped his cheeks with the back of his hand and smiled. "It is part of why God has given us a heart, señor, to feel pain and to know love. If we cannot feel the pain, we cannot know the love. Love and pain are friends, not strangers."

PART II

THE CASTLE

Chapter 19

The rain was heavy when Zac and Sam Fisher rode into Denver. It rolled off the wide brim of Zac's gray hat, but splattered into the older man's face. The derby Fisher wore offered little protection from the elements. He spotted the livery stable first and ran his horse down the street toward the large, open doors. Zac smiled and trotted his horse behind the man and into the stable.

The gray-haired man had stepped to the ground and was shaking the rain from his overcoat. It was soaked, and so was he. "That's it for me. Never could stand these things. Don't sit right with me," he said, walking around unlimbering his legs, "and I don't sit right on them." He massaged the seat of his trousers.

Zac unsaddled his own horse and then, opening up a stall, slapped the rump of the big roan. He began to unsaddle the older man's horse. "Why don't you pay the man. I'll give these animals a rubdown and then we can find a bed."

"Ummph. My bones need it."

"Just pay him for the one night, and a little bit of oats to go with the hay. I got to finish my delivery to Wells Fargo, but tomorrow we ride out of here."

"We ride out of here on the train." The old man stuck his lower lip out.

"Have it your way. You buy the tickets and get the space for these animals." Zac led the second horse to the stall. Picking up a brush, he ran it over its withers. "When I get back from the office, I'll meet you in the hotel lobby across the street. If we can't get rooms to ourselves, I'm coming back to sleep with the horses."

The old man grunted. "Ain't enuff you ride 'em, now you want to sleep with 'em."

When Zac walked into the Wells Fargo office, it was almost closing time. The clerk was a young, lean man with dark mutton-chop whiskers. His sleeves were rolled and the shaded cap he wore was tilted upward, showing a balding forehead. Zac dropped the carefully wrapped package and the heavily weighted money belt he'd been carrying onto the man's desk. "Delivery from Chicago. It's late. Just write my receipt, and I'll be on my way."

"Are you Zachary Cobb?"

Zac leaned the big rifle in its case on the side of the man's desk and laid his shotgun on its heavily scratched surface. He reached into one of the large pockets of his buckskin jacket and pulled out his pipe. "I am." He filled the pipe while the man wrote out the receipt.

"Well then, here you are. Yeah, you are late, but everybody knew you'd get here."

Zac took a match from a cup on the man's desk and struck it.

"Got a wire here for you from the home office and another money belt they want you to take to Colorado Springs."

Zac made a sour face as he lit his pipe.

"Guess they figure it's important," the man said.

Zac opened the wire and puffed the pipe to life. He sighed deeply as he read, then stuck the wire along with the receipt into his pocket and strapped on the money belt. Picking up his weapons, he walked to the door.

"Uh," the young man scrambled around the desk. "One more thing you ought to know. Some men have been in here looking for you." Zac whirled to look at him. "Three gunslingers have been asking for you. Two of them I recognized — Bat Masterson and Doc Holliday. The other one, though, I've never seen before."

Zac turned and left, closed the door without responding to the clerk. He walked through the rain across the street. He noticed the door to the livery stable was ajar, and just inside a man watched him. The stocky man lit a cigarette and took measure of him.

When Zac was past the door, the man opened up his gun and dropped a round into the empty chamber. He could wait. He'd sit in the dark stable and wait for Zac to return. If it took too long, he'd go to the hotel when the lights upstairs went out.

Zac strode down the walkway and into the hotel. Sam Fisher was at the desk in the lobby. "I got us a room. Place is full, but there's space we can share with a few cowboys upstairs."

Zac motioned to the adjoining saloon. "I'll be with the horses. Let's go get a steak."

"Sounds fine to me, but there's a bed for you upstairs."

"Horses don't snore."

The table they sat down at was quickly attended by a man wearing a bloody apron. "We'll be needing a couple of steaks," Zac said, "and I'd like some buttermilk."

"Whiskey for me," Sam added.

Zac laid the shotgun down on the table and propped the Creedmore on an empty chair. Then he pushed his hat back and surveyed the room. Only a few men looked their way; the room was busy with gambling and drinking. The rain outside had filled the place with wet customers trying to escape the downpour. Puddles had formed in the sawdust on the floor and the potbelly stoves glowed.

The waiter returned with a bottle and glass for Sam and sat a large glass of buttermilk in front of Zac.

"How can you drink that stuff?" Sam asked.

"More men been killed in the West by bad whiskey than by bullets," Zac responded. He sipped the buttermilk and smiled. "I doubt that stuff of yours there is more'n an hour old."

Fisher drank down a glass of the amber liquid and coughed. "Burns bad," he said, "jes' the way I like it."

The huge, juicy steaks came, overlapping their plates. Zac began to cut into his just as two distinguished-looking men walked into the saloon and up to the bar. After talking to the bartender, they turned on their heels and eyeballed Zac and Sam. Zac knew the cut of the men, even without a formal introduction, and when they walked toward him he wasn't the least bit surprised.

"You Zac Cobb?" It was the shorter of the two who spoke. He had dark eyes and an imposing mustache. The frail-looking one who stood beside him gazed at Zac with cold blue bloodshot eyes. Both wore black suits and ties and had their guns tied low.

Zac placed a piece of meat into his mouth and fixed his concentration on cutting the steak in front of him.

The two men stood awkwardly beside the table.

Sam spoke up. "We haven't had a decent meal in a while, so why don't you boys state your business and let us eat."

"My name is Masterson and my friend goes by the handle of Dr. John Holliday, and if your friend there is Zachary Cobb, then it's our business to make this his last meal."

"I know who you are," Sam spit out the words. "And if I do say so, you've rolled a long way down the hill, working as expensive killers and helping the Chicago Pacific steal track that don't belong to them. I knew your brother Ed in Dodge City. Shame the way they kilt him."

Masterson appeared struck by the back-handed nicety, and Zac continued to eat his steak.

"And if you're here to kill this man," Fisher went on, "you won't fare any better than the men who kilt Ed, and you won't be the first to try, either. This here," he said pointing to Zac, "is a man made outta spring steel and rawhide, and I'd advise you to haul yourselves back out into that rain and stay healthy."

Masterson leaned on to the table. "This doesn't concern you, old-timer. It's between us and Mr. Cobb, here."

"Well, it's my dinner you're interrupting, so it does concern me. You start slapping leather, and it'll be the *two* of us you'll have to kill."

Zac finished his steak and pushed the plate back. "I don't have any quarrel with either of y'all. I work for Wells Fargo. I don't work for the Denver and Rio Grande, and frankly, I don't give shucks who wins this railroad war of yours. I'm just here to do my job."

"Appears to me, Cobb," Masterson continued, "that you're into this thing pretty deep."

"I lent a hand to some folks 'cause your bunch had some people trying to do harm to a family with a child. Where I come from, no man would do less."

Zac laid his knife beside his plate and scooted his chair back slightly. "This thing has become something personal, something personal between me and that Englishman you're working for. If he's the sort you want to kill or die for, then I guess we better have

237

at it. Otherwise, I'll just get on about my business, and I reckon you ought to do the same."

The frail gunman, Holliday, who had been content to remain in the background, stepped forward. He coughed loudly and then cleared his throat. "I wake up every morning looking at death in the mirror, Mr. Cobb. How it comes, though, I'd prefer to be my choice, not this disease I carry with me."

"A man has to be ready to die before he can live," Zac said.

"You are right there, sir," Holliday replied. "And I can assure you, I am ready. When the grim reaper looks back at me when I shave, he seems to beckon me to the other side. He crooks his finger and says, 'Come over here, John, it ain't that bad,' and I for one am inclined to follow him." The man coughed loudly and struggled to stifle the gags with the palm of his bed sheet white hand. "Where are you from, Cobb?"

"North Georgia. My folks are dead, but that's where I hail from."

"I thought as much. Your speech and that gray officer's hat give you away. Combined with the fact that you use your eating utensils like a gentleman." He looked at Masterson. "I do declare, I find that rare in the West.

But you show some obvious culture and up-bringing. From what I've heard of your courage, the fact that you rode with the boys in gray does not surprise me in the least."

"Well, all that is part of my back trail. Now, I just work for the Wells Fargo company."

Masterson pushed his dark suit coat behind his low-slung revolver, but Holliday lifted his hand slightly in front of him, then signaled the bartender. "May we sit with you for a moment?" he asked.

Zac nodded as the bartender came forward. "Bring us the smooth liquor you have back there," Holliday croaked, "and four glasses." He smiled. "I like my whiskey from Kentucky, when I can get it."

Zac could see the tension in Masterson's eyes as the two of them sat down at the table. Masterson cast a look in the direction of Holliday, who had taken out a white handkerchief and dabbed it to his mouth.

"This miserable lung disease brought me West, but my home is Georgia, just like you — Valdosta, Georgia — a place I'm afeared I'll never see again."

"Know the place," Zac said. "Prettiest azaleas I ever saw."

"Yes, that's Valdosta." Holliday poured four glasses from the new bottle and pushed one of them toward Zac. "I drink with crackers from Georgia, but I don't particularly enjoy shooting them." He sipped the drink and began once again to cough into his handkerchief. Wiping his mouth, he fixed his gaze on Zac. "You have gone and made yourself some powerful enemies hereabouts, Cobb, but I won't shoot a son of the South, especially one who wears the gray hat of a cavalry officer." He coughed again and began a series of wracking deep gags. Sputtering, he continued, "Can't speak for Masterson here, he's a company man too, and it's a company that wants you dead."

Most of the men seated at the bar had turned to watch their table, and Masterson swung his head around, noticing the attention of the crowd.

"Guess everybody round here knows everybody's business," Zac said.

Masterson pushed his derby back and, picking up the drink that had been poured, smiled. "I suppose so. Looks like they enjoy watching somebody die." He held the glass up to the light and looked through the liquid. "And I suppose if somebody wants to die, a glass of this stuff is the best way to start." He gulped the liquor down and grinned.

Avoiding the glass of whiskey, Zac picked up his buttermilk. "Nobody takes the job that I have without being ready to kill or be killed, but a body still has a choice. I don't wrong people who stay clear of me and I expect others to do the same."

He drank down what was left of the buttermilk and wiped his mustache. "Killing somebody is a choice — for me, it means choosing right from wrong." He ran his hand over his shirt. "But I'd say if someone has to make a choice, then it ought to be one that means something — it shouldn't be for a railroad, and it shouldn't be for somebody else."

"Exactly right," Holliday shot back. "Appears to me if Peter Williams wants you dead, then he needs to call you out his ownself." He rose from his seat. "We were paid to kill you, Cobb, but now I'm going to make some real money at those tables over there." His eyes twinkled. "Some easy money."

They watched him walk away and Masterson leaned in. "All right, Cobb, you win, at least for now. Doc, there, won't raise a hand against you." He looked up at Zac's hat. "That gray hat of yours came in handy. I've never seen a man quicker or more deadly than Doc. Most men he'd kill as soon as he would a snake."

"I'm not sayin' he couldn't, but I'm not quite as easy to kill as a snake," Zac returned.

"So I've heard!" Masterson laughed. He got up from the table. "You watch yourself, though. There are others who don't care what color you wear. In fact, some would *prefer* to blow the lights out on a Rebel."

Zac watched Masterson walk away, and Sam wiped his forehead. "Boy, you are dangerous. You make people plumb hate you. I don't expect you have many friends in these parts, but things will be different in the Springs."

"A man nobody hates ain't worth spit," Zac said. He reached into his shirt pocket and pulled out a month-old letter from Jenny. As Fisher ate, Zac reread the letter by the light of the dim overhead lamp. Folding it up, he fished in his pocket for the stub of a pencil and pulled out a piece of paper and an envelope. Fisher looked on as he scribbled a letter.

"Somebody special?" Fisher asked.

"Somebody very special," Zac said. "Figure the way things are going here, she may get this before I get back home. Can you do me a favor?"

" 'Course."

"Mail this for me back at the lobby desk. Maybe it'll explain where I am and why I'm not home yet."

Zac got to his feet and picked up the shotgun. "I'll be with the horses, and I'll see you at daybreak." He could see the look of bewilderment written all over the old man's face. "I'll durn sure get better sleep than you will. Don't worry about me. It's getting to where I wouldn't know what to do with a bed."

Zac walked easily toward the livery. The rain had stopped and he noticed that the man who worked the stables had blown out his lamp. It was a little too early for most townspeople to be in bed, but Zac figured the man must be out drinking, or whatever else a man in Denver did at night.

He walked through the livery door, and the lamp that hung directly over it bathed him in a soft light, leaving the rest of the stable in darkness. He turned to find another lamp, when suddenly a man stepped out of one of the stalls. Zac could see the man's faint outline, shielded by the shadows. "You still here?" Zac asked, assuming the figure to be the livery man. "Thought you might be out drinking."

Zac dropped the rifle in his hand when he heard the cock of a revolver and then saw the flame blossom from the end of the gun. The bullet struck him firmly in the midsection and toppled him backward. Rolling to the side, Zac drew out the Shopkeeper special from behind his back and fired. As the man lurched forward out of the shadows, Zac fired several more shots in rapid succession.

Chapter 20

The ornate railcar sat at the end of the line in Pueblo. The lights outside its door glowed through the red lenses of the lamps that peered into the night sky. Jim Ruby was in town, and men on the tracks were careful to talk in hushed tones as they walked past his car. There wasn't a man among them who hadn't heard about the court ruling and, above all, no one wanted to give the impression of business as usual.

Peter Williams stepped quickly over the tracks. Conflicting feelings battled deep in his gut. He didn't like to be beat. Each time he passed one of the workers on the track, he could see that they knew what had happened. They knew that the courts had given the Royal Gorge to the Denver and Rio Grande, and they knew that he and his men had come limping back into town empty-handed. He had always enjoyed the looks of awe from the men that had accompanied his rise to power, and now he read a look of amused contempt on their faces. He knew what they thought without their saying it.

They saw him as an uppity foreigner, an uppity foreigner who had lost.

The anger inside him was mixed with other feelings, feelings that perhaps he had joined his future to a falling star. He knew enough about America to know that nothing was more powerful in this growing country than the railroad, and perhaps he had chosen the wrong one. He had not failed the Chicago Pacific — maybe it had failed him. The special train hissed as he walked by. As he passed, he could see Ruby sitting at his desk through the windows. He mounted the stairs and knocked on the door.

"Who is it?"

Williams knew that Jim Ruby knew exactly who was knocking on his door. The very thought of standing outside in the dark and having to knock bothered him in the first place, but to have to call out like a child at his mother's bedroom door made his blood boil. "It's Peter Williams, Mr. Ruby."

A moment of silence followed, making him even angrier. "Come in, Williams." Ruby's voice boomed even in normal conversation. Williams knew that when he lowered it, it was for special effect, for which other men raised their voices. When he opened the door, his heart sank even further. Jake Rice sat on the couch beside Ruby's

246

desk. Williams nodded at him, and his jaws tightened.

Ruby folded his hands on his desk. For a man who had just received bad news from the courts, he seemed relaxed. It was one of the qualities about Jim Ruby that Peter Williams most admired. But it unnerved him. The large, bearded man wore a white shirt and tie with a blue silk smoking jacket of Chinese design.

"I sent for Rice, here," Ruby said, nodding at the gunman on the couch.

"Of course," Williams smiled. "I thought perhaps I would find you working on a large piece of meat about this time, Jake." The fact that Jim Ruby had sent for Jake Rice before Williams had a chance to give his report was telling Williams all he needed to know.

Ruby didn't bother to explain. "I'm sending Rice into the canyon to dislodge those people from my track."

Williams blinked and Jim Ruby seemed to read his mind. "I don't care what the courts say!" he stated flatly. "I didn't get where I am today by listening to a bunch of old men in long robes."

Williams' mind raced. *If he's sending Rice down the line into the canyon, I must be out of a job.* He cleared his throat and tried once again to demonstrate to Ruby that he had been thinking about how to deal with the railroad's problems. "Well, sir, you won't have to worry about that meddlesome man from Wells Fargo. I have three very good men in Denver who are dealing with him right now. They won't —"

Ruby interrupted him. "I don't care one iota about Cobb!" He stood up behind his desk. "You dealt that man a hand yourself. I've lost two locomotives, one water tower, miles of track, and a number of good men, all because you decided this Cobb fellow was worth the trouble."

Williams was speechless, hands at his side. Every passerby near the train would overhear Ruby's words to him, and inside Peter Williams died a little.

"When that man," Ruby continued, "took those people out of your hands in Kansas, you should have cut our losses and let them go. When a plan doesn't work, you figure out a plan that will." Ruby stood up and strutted around the desk toward Williams. "But you wouldn't let go, Williams, and you drove your men so hard that when you finally did catch up with those people, not a one of them wanted to fight for you. I can't have that."

"Sir, I only did what I thought I had to do."

Ruby moved closer to him and lowered his voice. "You did what you did, Williams, because you let that Cobb fellow get under your skin. He showed you up; he kicked you off that train into the dirt in front of every one. Face it, Williams, you let your dirty britches get the best of you."

Williams struggled to maintain his composure, especially in front of the man who had been taking orders from him, but he knew that everything Ruby said was true. And he knew that if he wanted to keep what he had, he'd have to swallow his pride and do something spectacular.

"Williams, I like your style. I like the way you thoroughly look after the details. But when you let personal feelings cloud your judgment, then you become the problem. You let our whole operation become a personal war between you and this man, Zac Cobb, and I suspect you've managed to get him riled up to the point that he's willing to work for our enemies."

"Sir, I hope he decides to do exactly as you suggest."

"You want him that bad, do you?"

Ruby sat back on top of his desk and eyeballed the lanky Englishman. "Personally, Williams," he went on, "while I admire the work you've done for me in the past, with you matched up against this Zac Cobb, I wouldn't give a hoot in hell for your chances. Now don't get me wrong, I've seen you draw and you're fast, one of the fastest men around. If you weren't you wouldn't be in my employ. You'd rival Rice here, I'd wager."

He pushed his hands into the large pockets of his ornate silk jacket. "But there's more to it than speed. I'm not sure you've ever been up against a man like this Cobb, a man who's capable and ready to face death. From what I hear, he's not a gunfighter, but he's the kind of man gunfighters do their best to avoid."

Peter Williams hated being lectured. He was angry at Jim Ruby for delivering it, but he was madder still at Zac Cobb. That man and what he did was the cause of it all.

Ruby turned and picked out a long, thick cigar from his humidor. He bit off the end and spit it on the floor. "Some of those men won't fight for you, so I have to send Rice here down track with the men to try to dislodge those gandy dancers and send them back home. I will, too, and you can count on that. And until those judges are man enough to strap on guns and ride down here to take it from me, then the Chicago Pacific Railroad will have possession of the Royal Gorge."

Striking a match, Ruby puffed a flame on the end of the cigar and smoke began to rise. "Of course, what I'd like is for that almighty General Roberts to deed me the right of way. I'm going to that man's castle for dinner." He picked up a printed card and fingered it. He smiled. "You see, Williams, in our circles, mortal enemies have dinner together and talk about court rulings. The old man invited me, and I intend to go."

His face hardened. "I had hoped to go with an ace up my sleeve, but now all I have is my arm."

"Sir, let me have one more try at the plan. I believe I can get that ace for your sleeve. I may not have it by the time you take supper and exchange pleasantries with General Roberts, but I *will* get it for you."

Ruby blew smoke. "And how do you purpose to do that?"

"I will get several good men that I trust" — he shot a glance at Jake Rice — "and I will find a way to get one of the general's little darlings."

"You can't get in there, that castle is a fortress."

For the first time Williams smiled. He, too, liked to have an ace up his sleeve and he had one, one that only he knew about. "I have someone inside who is working for me, someone who will help me do whatever I need to do." Williams knew that was only partially true, but he also knew that it made him look indispensable at the moment, and he knew that if he could pull it off, he could make himself shine again. He would become the rising star of the railroad yet.

Ruby smoked his cigar and looked the lanky Englishman up and down. "The thing I like about you, Englishman, is the thing everybody else hates about you. It's also the thing that makes you the most susceptible to making mistakes." He bit down on his cigar.

"What's that, sir?"

"You have such a hatred for being beaten you'd step on your own mother to avoid it if you had to. You have no loyalty. Your only allegiance is to Peter Williams."

Williams started to open his mouth, but Ruby cut him off. He held up his hand.

"Don't bother, Williams. It's true. I admire a man who operates from total self-interest. But I warn you, it does cloud your thinking, this hatred of losing, and it may get you killed in the end." He blew a stream of heavy smoke from the end of the cigar. "But it's what I like about you. I like men around me that I can know inside out, and you never surprise me, Williams. I know what you'll do at any given time. A rattler can always be expected to strike an out-stretched hand, and you can always be expected to make yourself look good at all cost." He smiled broadly. "It reminds me of myself, twenty years ago."

Yeager rode down the canyon with the twenty men who had ridden with him on the rescue operation. They were good men, men to be trusted, and now they had to make good time. He knew enough about Ruby's operation to know that a court order wouldn't stop the man, and everyone knew the men in the canyon had to be relieved and supplied in the meantime. Twenty men, and the two dozen mules they were towing with supplies, wouldn't slip into the canyon easily. There was just no easy way, but the long ride down Phantom Canyon seemed the best. They picked their way along the side of the creek and rode along the tree line. The bare slope on the hillside was covered with Indian Paintbrush. The blanket of small red flowers made the tall green grass bleed.

Overhead, he could see the clouds bloom-ing, and they could all feel the wind begin-ning to pick up. Yeager had been in Colorado long enough to know that any kind of weather could be expected in the moun-tains, with little or no notice given.

"I don't like it." The man rode up beside Yeager and put into words what everyone was feeling.

Suddenly, thunder boomed and lightning cracked overhead. Hail began to fall. The icy balls were small, but they rattled on the rain slickers the men wore, the tops of their hats, and the tarps that covered the mules' backs.

Yeager turned to the group. "Let's get down there into the trees and get offa this hill."

They ran the horses as fast as the mules could keep up. Yeager didn't like being under trees during a lightning storm, but he liked the open hillside even less. There was something about the notion of riding over a slope on a horse during a lightning storm that made the toughest rider feel exposed.

The hailstorm intensified as they rode, hail pelting their faces and thunder crashing, punctuated by rips of lightning. One bolt flew into a stand of aspen nearby and seemed to explode the trees with the fury of a direct artillery assault.

The men rode down the hill and slowed up at the bottom, picking their way through fallen aspen that littered the ground like a broken train trestle. The horses and mules picked their way over the downed branches and broken trunks of the trees. The caravan was slowed to a trickle while all around them the fury of perdition was breaking loose.

Moving under the trees, the men sat on their horses and watched the storm pass overhead, much of the hail being dissipated by the leafy branches above them. Clouds of steam rising from the sweaty horses and mules gave them a ghostlike quality, and Yeager thought it looked like a phantom cavalry brigade suddenly appearing out of the mists of time.

The lightning cracked overhead and the men ducked their heads. Had the bolt struck them no instinct would have been fast enough to make any difference, but the reasoning of it didn't stop them from flinching.

"How long you 'peck it'll take us?"

The man's question served to break the tension in Yeager's mind. "I was countin' on two days. Now" — he looked up at the sky between the trees — "we better figure on three."

"You think them boys'll hold on down there?"

"They don't have much choice. When we get to the grand canyon of the Arkansas River" — the two men ducked as the lightning and thunder rattled overhead — "if it don't sound a whole lot like this, we better hightail it back to Glen Eyrie."

"You reckon we're li'ble to meet up with CP men afore we get there?"

Yeager looked at the man and then stared off into space.

The man broke Yeager's concentration again. "Well, if'n we do, I don't 'speck we'll just swap howdys with 'em."

Chapter 21

Zac had his hat pulled down over his eyes. The ride to the castle was uphill from the depot, and Sam kept talking about the sights there were to see and the hot springs that were over the hill. Perhaps it was the embarrassment of riding in the buggy that made Zac ride with his face half-covered, or maybe it was the ongoing monologue of the man next to him, but for whatever the reason, he was merely enduring this ride in the surrey with the fringe on top.

The mares that pulled them were a pair of the most expensive-looking carriage-pullers he'd ever seen. Zac could tell a lot about a man from the horseflesh he rode, and from the looks of these animals and the horses he and Sam had been loaned on the prairie, he knew this General Roberts of the Denver and Rio Grande must be a man who didn't have to worry about money. The men who had shown up to take the horses back to town rode ahead of them, and he thought to himself, *What a pretty penny one of those hired men's horses would fetch at auction. Whoever this Roberts is, he knows good horseflesh.*

"I better light up a cigar while I still got the chance." Fisher reached into his suit coat pocket and produced one of his large, dark, special cigars. "The general don't take too kindly to these being smoked in the house." The man leaned toward Zac while he struck a match to the end of the cigar. "So I guess I'll smoke it while I can." Puffing it to life, he grunted, "Another one of the reasons I don't like staying in that place."

Zac didn't exactly care why the man had lit the cigar, he was just happy to have him puffing on the thing rather than talking. It was one of the reasons Zac liked his pipe. It gave him an excuse not to talk.

The gatehouse was set back on a large, expansive lawn. Iron gates rose from the high wall on either side of the road, and the horses up ahead and the carriage with its team came to a stop. A short, squatty man ambled out of the stone structure and, unbolting the gate, swung it open. He grabbed the reins of the horses that pulled the carriage.

"What's kept you?" he asked. "I was expecting you over an hour ago."

Sam gave an aside to Zac. "Henry knows about everybody's business round here; when they go, when they come, who they're with. He's a pester 'bout that."

"I had to give the guest a tour of the town," Sam yelled at the man. "You wouldn't want me to be a bad host, now, would you?"

"Of course not."

The striking thing about the hidden valley was not the creek that flowed through the middle of it and out near the gatehouse, but the cottonwoods that were losing their airborne fluff this time of year. It looked like a snowstorm in sunshine that would have puzzled any newcomer. As the carriage rolled on down the roadway and into the valley, Zac could see the guards stationed on the hillsides, their rifles glinting in the afternoon sunshine.

"That there is the eagle's nest the place was named for," Sam explained. "Glen Eyrie, the valley of the eagle. The general's gardener is a Scotsman. He named the place and it stuck."

Zac looked to where Sam pointed and saw the massive eagle's nest clinging to the side of the rocky hillside, but what really caught his eye were the sandstone spires that rose from the floor of the valley and overshadowed everything around them. He pushed his hat back and stared. They were something to behold.

"I reckon a body never gets used to seeing

them things," Fisher said.

"I reckon not."

Fisher spoke to the driver as they rounded one of the massive rose-colored rocks. "Go on up to the house; we'll unload up there. Miss Elizabeth is waitin' for us, I 'speck." He turned to Zac. "Elizabeth Roberts will put you up in the castle. She won't allow you to sleep with the horses tonight, and that's for durn sure."

When the surrey rounded the massive walls of what Zac could only guess to be servants' quarters, and the largest stable and carriage house he had ever seen, he saw the castle. The structure was massive. The stone walls were covered with moss, and the parapet rose into the blue Colorado sky like something out of a fairy tale.

"Takes a body back, don't it?" Sam said.

Zac nodded.

"The general built the place for Mrs. Roberts, but I don't think she lived in it long."

Zac watched a goat meander around the buildings. On the lawn, a small schoolhouse stood in contrast to the castle, and four children in the doorway watched them pass.

"Them's two of the general's youngest along with their cousins." Sam puffed vigorously on the cigar. "He had the school built here soze to keep a watch on the children till this trouble blows over. Can't take a chance sending 'em into town."

The surrey rolled over the bridge and two men stood by the posts to take the horses and bags. When Zac got down, Elizabeth came down the walkway from the castle. "Welcome to Glen Eyrie," she said.

"Thank you." He looked up at the house. "Don't think I've ever seen anything like it."

"And you won't, either," she said. "Not for a thousand miles in any direction. Come on inside, we have some iced cider waiting for you."

Zac walked up the path, and Elizabeth stopped him beside the moss-covered walls. Several men were spraying the walls down with water. "I'm afraid Daddy has this mossy dream for the castle. The air is so dry around here, though, that I don't hold much promise for it. You can see the wires holding it on. We grow all of our own vegetables here on the Glen, and if these men can't get the moss to take root, nobody can."

The entrance was huge and the heavy oak doors swung open to a room filled with leather-covered chairs and sofas and a sweeping oak staircase hand-carved with ornate designs. Irene brought Zac and Sam each a cut crystal glass of cider. "How wonderful to see you both. Please have some refreshment. I hope everything went well with your business, Mr. Cobb, and that you had no further difficulty."

Fisher laughed as they took the glasses. "No difficulty, unless you call being shot at a difficulty."

Elizabeth's and Irene's eyes widened. "You were shot?" Irene asked.

Zac took the glass. "Somebody took a shot at me in Denver."

"Woulda got him too, if it hadn't been for the money belt he had strapped on." Sam chuckled and put his hand with the cigar on Zac's shoulder. "Zac here had a difficulty, but the other fella had a fatality."

The women blanched. "I'll take that cigar, Sam," Elizabeth said. She took it from his hand with two fingers and dropped it into a polished brass spittoon against the wall. "You know we don't allow smoking in the house." Looking at Zac, she smiled. "And, Mr. Cobb, if you'd care to smoke your pipe, there's a terrace, and I believe your room has a balcony. Sorry. Daddy doesn't approve of the habit. At least not in the house."

Zac's hands dropped to his sides as he continued to gawk at the high ceiling with its intricate plaster designs. He had never felt more in awe — or more out of place — in his life.

"There you are, good fellow." Zac looked up to see a tall, elegantly dressed man walk into the sitting room. He was followed by three of the biggest dogs Zac had ever seen. The man extended his hand. "Welcome to Glen Eyrie. I am Sydney Roberts. You are a most honored guest, Mr. Cobb, and I hope," he said, shaking Zac's hand, "that your stay with us will be a pleasant experience for you."

Zac wasn't quite sure what to say next. "Well, it won't be long. I need to get home to California."

"We can keep you quite comfortable here, Mr. Cobb."

"I can see that," Zac said. "Your place looks like the kind my mother read to us about when we were kids."

"Yes," Roberts said, "King Arthur, I imagine. Well, we do have all the amenities here, more than enough to make you never want to go back to California. Didn't you get the Wells Fargo wire?"

Zac's jaw tightened slightly. "That I did, Mr. Roberts. But I have an understanding with the company. I take a job when I choose to, not necessarily when they ask me to."

"Then you work for yourself?"

"No," he said. "I work for Wells Fargo, but only after I agree to."

"Splendid, then when I tell you what the job pays, you can work for the Denver and Rio Grande."

Zac frowned. "I won't do that. As I said, I only work at what I want to, and your war with the Chicago Pacific is something I'd just as soon stay as far away from as possible. I've already been shot at, stomped on, threatened, and generally inconvenienced 'cause people just *thought* I worked for your railroad. Makes me downright nervous to think 'bout what might happen if I actually did."

Elizabeth stepped forward and placed her hand on Zac's arm. "Mr. Cobb here is a man of principle, Father. What he did for Bruce, Irene, and Nikki was something that he thought needed to be done."

"And, Cobb, I am deeply in your debt for that," Roberts added.

"Ten thousand dollars reward money in debt, General, from what your daughter here has led me to believe." Zac once again looked around the room. "And from the looks of things, I wouldn't exactly call that deeply."

Irene broke the tension. "Father, let me take Mr. Cobb to his room. He'll need to freshen up and change before dinner."

"Yes," Elizabeth added. "We do have a special evening prepared in your honor, complete with wild game for supper, dancing, and an orchestra."

Zac swallowed. It was the most uncomfortable feeling he'd had in years. Sam hung his head when Zac looked at him, staring straight into the red carpet.

Moments later, Zac was looking at the fanciest room he had ever seen. Green drapes hung over the large windows that led to the balcony, and a red bedspread set off the hand-carved wooden canopy bed. Zac stood on the bearskin rug in front of the fireplace and felt lost. A suit of clothes lay across the bed, complete with white shirt and tie.

Elizabeth walked across the room and pulled open the curtains. "This is your room, Zac. It has a wonderful view and the bed is quite comfortable." She walked back toward him as Irene stood at the door. "We only guessed at your size. We do dress for dinner here at the Glen, and tonight will be especially formal. You will want to be at your best. Mr. Jim Ruby of the Chicago Pacific will be a guest as well."

Zac watched her move about the room and make modifications in the flowers on the dresser. Then she opened the closet. "You can hang your old clothes in here. The servants have prepared a hot bath for you down the hall."

"It's very important to you that you're in charge of things here, isn't it?" Zac's question caught the woman by surprise. She stopped where she stood and looked at him. He returned her look, eye to eye.

"I'm sorry," she said. "I didn't realize."

"I may have been reared in the South, but I'm not a field hand," he said.

She edged her way to the door and stood beside Irene. "I never imagined that of you." Her eyes went down. Zac could see her embarrassment. "I suppose I'm much too used to filling in for mother. Irene's been back East, and . . . I guess I've gotten too familiar with the role of hostess and supervisor at the same time. I'm sorry."

"Apology accepted."

Elizabeth moved quickly out the door and down the hall, and from the sound Zac could tell that she was running. Irene looked down the hall after her, then looking in the other direction she smiled. "Here, darling, he's in here."

Nikki stood in the open door and then began to walk toward Zac, arms outstretched. Zac scooped up the child in his arms and hugged her.

He spoke into her ear. "I've missed you, sweetness."

The little girl kissed him. "I missed you," she said. "Will you give me a horsey ride?"

"Of course I will."

Irene walked toward him. "There have been two women in this house that have talked about nothing else but you for days."

Zac smiled at the little girl, and then lifted his eyes to Irene.

"Nikki has been talking about the horsey ride you gave her and the fun she wants to have with you, and that sister of mine you just sent down the hall crying has talked about everything else that is knowable about Zachary Taylor Cobb for the past three days."

Zac's face flushed. "I didn't mean to hurt her feelings."

Irene smiled. "Oh, don't worry about her. Worry about yourself. Elizabeth Roberts has gotten back up on every horse that's ever thrown her."

Peter Williams disembarked the train from Pueblo and was met by two men at the depot. They recognized him at once. "Mr. Williams? We have an extra horse for you. It's only a short ride to Manitou Springs and we got the two other men you asked for. We hafta meet the man you want at a shack near there. He ain't got much time, so we hafta move fast. Is that your gun there?"

Williams nodded.

"Mind if we take a look at it? We ain't never seen one of them things."

Williams slid the rifle from the scabbard. The gun was mounted with a bright copper telescopic sight.

"Whew-ee!" the man said. "Bet you can hit a silver dollar with that thing."

"At over three hundred yards."

It was after dark when the three of them drew rein outside the old shanty. Three other horses were tied outside. They pushed on the door. Williams was not about to make any more mistakes. He felt like a man living on borrowed time, a wounded mountain lion cornered in a box canyon. He glared at the men. "Is everything ready?" he asked.

"First, where's my money?" The small man stood by the potbelly stove warming himself. "I ain't about to lose my job if'n I don't see the money."

Williams reached into the saddlebags he carried and pulled out a leather bag. He tossed it at the man. "You may count it if you like. Three hundred dollars, just as we agreed."

The man looked at him and then opened the bag. He poured the gold coins onto the table beside the stove and began to stack them. "This ain't gonna be enough, Mr. Williams. My price has gone up."

Williams raged inside, but controlling himself he walked toward one of the few chairs in the shack. He sat down and, trying not to look at the man, began to pull off his boots. "We agreed on three hundred dollars," he said.

"I know what we said." The man carefully dropped the coins back into the bag. "But this is dangerous business. My price is five hundred now."

Williams could see the other men nervously shift about the room. Loyalty was something Peter Williams knew little about. He wrestled the boots off his feet and stretched his legs out. "I am a hard man to deal with, Mr. Clement. But I always treat the men who work for me fairly."

He knew how ridiculous it sounded. He'd already lost control of the men who had been under him once in this operation, and he knew that the other men listening were well aware of his reputation. Fear and power had always been the method he'd used in the past, but now he had to make a special effort to communicate that he would reward the men who worked for him. It galled him to have to do it, but once again he reached for the saddlebags.

"You think your information is that vital?"

The man beamed at the prospect of more gold. "Old Henry knows it all. I knows who comes and goes on the place and I can tell you everything you want to know. Otherwise you'll be warming yourself by this stove, or getting cold out there in the grass for days." The man grinned, showing a mouthful of missing teeth.

Williams opened the saddlebags and produced another bag. Opening it up, he carefully counted out ten more twenty-dollar gold pieces. He held the money out for the man, who walked forward to claim it. As the man reached out for the coins, Williams clinched his fingers around them. He gritted his teeth and spoke in a low tone. "If what you inform me turns out to be unworthy of five hundred dollars, you can be sure that I will personally kill you."

The man held out his hands, and Williams dropped the coins into them. "Oh don't you fret none about that. I know where that gal is riding to in the morning and I know she plans on taking with her the man you're looking for. You can get her and kill him to boot."

Chapter 22

Yeager had driven the men and the animals far too hard that day. They had passed the cabin he had planned to stop at several hours ago. He'd made up for the time lost in the storm and then some. Now, with darkness settling in over the mountains, he rode on ahead to find another likely spot for the men to bed down for the night, someplace with water and grass for the horses and mules. Already the mules were straining under the load they'd carried all day, and he knew that unless he found a spot and found one quickly, there would be trouble. He peered through the gloom and then spotted the campfire. In the valley below him he saw the fire glowing through the blue spruce trees.

Reining up his horse, he turned the animal around and rode back to the staggering column. "Hold up," he whispered. "You can shuck your packs under them trees but keep the animals quiet. I think we got trouble up ahead."

The men quietly dismounted, and Yeager sifted through the bunch, choosing three

271

men. "I want you with me, and bring your saddle guns."

It was only a matter of minutes until the four men stalked down the valley grass and into the trees. They moved quietly, listening for anything that might indicate who the men were around the campfire. The evening stars and moon had begun to cast a soft light over the valley floor, but Yeager and the men kept to the trees.

Signaling with his hand, he spaced the men around the line of trees that sheltered the glowing fire. Then he gestured that he would circle the camp and approach it from the other side. Moving uphill he stepped carefully over the ground. He knew full well how sound carried at night and, stopping, he pulled off his boots and tied a rawhide loop through the top straps, slinging them over his shoulder. He'd make it the rest of the way in his stocking feet. Damp feet would be far less dangerous than stepping on a twig in the dark, announcing his presence.

Circling to the hill above the group, he already spotted two men crouching near the fire. If this was a sentry group for the CP, he had to know it before he took his men any farther. He'd know it and he'd act.

He kept his eyes away from the fire below,

searching through the gathering darkness for anyone who might be stationed away from the camp. If it was a group of cowboys passing through, or hunters, they wouldn't have a guard stationed nearby. If it was men from the CP, he knew the situation would dictate they take extra precaution.

Moments later, he was glad he'd taken off his boots. There above him stood a man with a rifle silhouetted against the twilight. Slowly he slung his own rifle over his shoulder and pulled out the long knife from his belt. Crouching low, he moved like a crab over the rocks and grass. He'd lie low when he got to the man, wait for him to turn his back. There would be no alarm, no scream, only swift and silent death.

More than an hour later he returned to the men who waited in the trees. He motioned them forward, and they slowly approached the glowing campfire. Signaling two of the men around the other side, he unslung his rife and stepped into the light.

"Howdy, boys," he said. "You looking for us?"

Both the men sat upright in their bedrolls.

"Now don't do anything foolish; I'm not alone. You reach for anything and we'll leave you out here in shallow graves like your friend up there."

★ ★ ★

Uncomfortable in the formal clothing, Zac felt stiff and strange as he descended the staircase. He always tried his best to adapt to anything that was demanded of him, however, and even though he'd rather be on a fast horse heading out of town, he was determined to be whatever it took to fit in. He'd fit in and he'd go one better, he'd set aside his feelings and have a good time. He didn't know how he'd fare in the bed upstairs; he might just curl up on the rug in front of the fire for the night. If a bear had been snug in the skin, he sure could be.

"Mr. Cobb," the general called when he spotted Zac at the foot of the stairs. "You look splendid."

The stately man rose from the table and walked over to greet him. "I believe the cook has prepared a meal for us tonight that you'll long remember. We have lobster sent in on ice from Maine, fresh oysters, and medallions of elk."

As Zac strode into the room, the men at the table rose to greet him. "This is Mr. Torkelson, our accountant and attorney, and I believe you know my son-in-law."

Zac nodded.

"And the distinguished gentleman over

there is Mr. Jim Ruby of the Chicago Pacific Railroad."

Zac took his seat. "Mr. Ruby and I have met."

Ruby smiled. "Yes, Roberts, that's right. I offered your man here a job with the CP, and he turned me down flat."

"Well, good, Ruby," Roberts laughed. "Then you are in good company. Cobb refused to work for the Denver and Rio Grande only this afternoon. I would guess our pay scale doesn't meet up to his high standards."

Zac's place was beside Elizabeth and they exchanged glances. The dinner was memorable for many reasons. The idea of eating something that looked like an overgrown insect was certainly brand new to him. He watched carefully as each person at the table pulled the creatures apart and dipped them into the butter bowls at each plate. Exchanging pleasant conversation with a man who had been trying to kill him for the past week was also a new experience.

"I trust you are enjoying your stay in Colorado, Mr. Cobb," Ruby said.

Zac forked the strange white meat into his mouth and then patted his napkin on his mustache. "I believe I'll enjoy it better than my time in Kansas," he said.

"You certainly have chosen a fine place for

your visit." Ruby gestured with his fork at their ornate surroundings. "There isn't a better spot in the wilderness than this one."

Elizabeth looked at Zac sympathetically, sensing how uncomfortable he felt at the very notion of making small talk with Jim Ruby. Elizabeth hated the man and what he had tried to do more than Zac ever could, and yet she kept her feelings beneath a cool exterior. Tonight she was General Roberts's daughter, a hostess to the man who had been threatening her family. If she found him in her gunsights tomorrow she'd pull the trigger, but tonight she'd pass him the potatoes and smile.

Zac took in the dinner serving arrangement with some amusement. The general's dislike for servants standing beside the table had prompted him to adopt an unusual procedure. Behind a glass window above the dining room, a servant quietly stood, signaling to an accomplice below for replacement servings. From the ornate paneling in the dining room wall a conveyor belt ran to a location beside the table. It would open and a heaping bowl or platter of the needed food dish would appear to replace the empty receptacle on the table. Zac continued to eat without so much as raising an eyebrow, but he thought the ingenious orchestration better entertainment than any tableside singer in San Francisco.

After dinner, the women rose from the table and moved into the adjoining music room. Zac watched Elizabeth as she excused herself and walked away. He couldn't help but admire the woman. Her white gown was stunning and the blue sash around her waist accentuated her remarkable figure. She was more than the beautiful woman he'd seen in buckskin, and she carried herself as though she knew it.

The men pushed back their chairs and listened as the sound of the piano carried into the dining room. "Elizabeth plays well, doesn't she, Mr. Cobb?"

"General, it appears to me your daughter does well at most anything she tries."

Ruby broke the pleasantries with the first sign of his intentions for the evening. "General Roberts, what would you take for that track your men are laying?"

The general cleared his throat. "I'm afraid the Denver and Rio Grande isn't for sale at any price, and the courts have already seen to it that we will continue to lay track."

"Now, now, we're men of the world, Roberts. Everything has a price." He glanced over at Zac. "Everything and everybody. My men are eager for that road, and I don't think a piece of paper in Washington City will be enough to stop them from getting it. Your gandy dancers are all bottled up in that canyon. They can't be resupplied and they'll soon be out of ammunition."

"I assume you intend to obey the law, you and your men," Roberts said.

"If that's what you assume, General, then you don't know me or my men."

Zac rose from the table. "You'll pardon me, gentlemen, but I think I'll have a smoke on the terrace. The music and the night air are too good to miss and, frankly — no offense — this conversation is something I'd rather not stomach on top of those seagoing insects."

He left the men to their exchange and, walking out to the terrace, felt for the pipe and tobacco he'd stored in the fancy coat pocket. Stuffing tobacco into his pipe, he struck a match and lit it. The smoke rose as he walked the length of the terrace, listening to the piano music and the sound of the water in the moat below.

"I think you carried yourself very well at the table tonight."

The piano music had stopped and Zac turned to see Elizabeth. She stood there quietly, her bare shoulders shining in the moonlight.

"Can't say as I cared much for all of the conversation, though."

"I could tell," she said. "That's why I thought I might join you out here. I'm sorry about the way I handled myself this afternoon. Would you forgive me?"

"Of course." He knocked the dottle out of his smoldering pipe and stuck it back into his pocket. "Women get used to the way things should be. It's hard to have that interrupted by some cowboy."

She lowered her gaze slightly. "Well, and I seem to frighten away any man that I would rather impress. My father has tried to push gentlemen callers that I don't care for on me for so long that I suppose I've developed a knack for being offensive. Maybe I'm just too strong a woman."

"I wouldn't worry about that," Zac said. "I kinda like someone who knows who they are and what they want. Makes things plain that way and easier to deal with. You'll make some man a wonderful wife. Any man would be proud to have you."

"I don't think I could be satisfied with just any man." She stopped and looked up into the night sky. "Do you see that star?" Elizabeth's face seemed to shine. Zac followed her gaze.

"Which one?" he asked.

She pointed. "That one, the bright one. Look just to the right of it. See the one that's just a little dimmer?" She continued to stare into the sky as if she were watching a friend. "I like to think that it only appears dimmer because it's higher up in the heavens."

Zac watched her eyes sparkle, and the look on her face seemed more childlike than he had seen it before. The peek at the child beneath this woman put a soft smile on his face. "Yes, I see it." He looked up at the star, but he couldn't take his eyes off Elizabeth for long. He watched her. Women were such mysterious creatures, and the more Zac had been able to see into the hearts of the women he had known, the less he thought he really knew about them.

"That's my star," she said. "My father used to take me out here when I was little. He would point to my little star and tell me how it first appeared on the night that I was born." She took hold of his arm and looked into his eyes. "He told me how it was sent by God to remind me of where I came from and where I was going."

"And where are you going?"

"Don't you know?" She looked at him. There was a fire in her eyes that he had seen in Elizabeth every time he looked at her, a passion for life. Zac knew instinctively that this moment in time had been set aside for him and Elizabeth, a time he had feared from the instant he first saw her and yet perhaps a time that he needed as much as she, a time to show him what he really wanted.

"No, Elizabeth," he lied, "I don't know. I don't know where you're going." Looking at her now, he knew her to be a woman driven by a deep sense of what she wanted out of life. This was a woman to be reckoned with, and at that moment he felt like a coon only slightly ahead of the hounds. He looked back up at the night sky. Try as he might, this was a conversation he could not stop. If he kept looking up, away from her, maybe she would let it pass.

"I think you know, Zac. I think you've known from the very first day we met out on that prairie. I'm afraid I don't have time to be the coy country girl and I wouldn't know how if I did. When I see something I want I try to get it as quickly as I know how." She gently turned and, placing her hand on his shoulder, leaned toward him. Standing slightly on her toes, she kissed him softly.

Placing his hands on her arms, he edged her back. "Elizabeth, your star is not mine." He looked deeply into her shining eyes. "Your star is about the most beautiful thing I've ever laid my eyes on. It burns very brightly, but it's not my star, Elizabeth."

She backed away from him and leaned against the edge of the wall. "It's the woman you write to, isn't it? Sam told me."

"Yes it is, and it's me."

Reaching out, once again she took his hand.

"Then why aren't you married to this woman? What holds you back?"

"I'm not so sure she wants me."

Elizabeth moved closer. "Not sure she wants you, Zac Cobb? I can't imagine a woman not wanting you. Maybe you mean you're not sure she wants you as you are, doesn't want your way of living."

"I suppose so. Feller like me is mighty hard to put up with, given what I do and all."

"If you weren't the man that you are, Zac Cobb, my sister and her family would be prisoners now, or worse. And as for what you do, everything you do comes from what you are, from deep inside."

Zac could feel himself being pried opened by this woman, opened like an oyster at the dinner table. He didn't like it, and to allow it to happen from a woman who desired him, one whom he found so attractive, frightened him. He was a man who was always in control and now he could feel that control slipping away.

She moved closer to him, not taking her eyes from his. "Zac, I could love you — the real you on the inside, love you for what you are, what you do. I know enough about men to know that a woman has to love everything there is about the man she marries; love his ambitions, love his dreams, even his faults. All these things about a man are what make him what he is."

She reached out and took his arms, drawing him closer. "I could love everything about you, Zachary Cobb. I could love you and allow you to be whatever it is you want to be. My deepest delight would be to simply share that with you. That's all I want."

"No, Elizabeth. I think you've always gotten what you wanted. I 'speck as a little girl, anything you wanted — from a pony to that star up yonder — your daddy would see that you got it. Then when you had it, you'd want something else. Right now you think you want me. . . ."

She blinked back the tears that had formed in her eyes. She stared right through them and at him. "Everything I've ever wanted in life was to be loved for who I am. In that way I'm just like you, Zac. Everybody has always wanted to change me. When I was little they wanted me to be more ladylike, to practice the piano. What I wanted was to ride fast horses and climb the rocks around here. Now they want me to settle down, marry a stable man and have children, but what I want is to run a railroad and make my mark. I want that and a strong man who's a man in his own right . . . a man like you."

She moved her hand up his shoulder and placed it on his neck. Her fingers were gentle and warm in the cool night air. "I feel safe with you, Zac, safe and content. Somehow I feel that if I could know what it means to be loved by you, then I would know what it means to be what I was made to be."

Zac reached up and, taking her hand, brought it down to his side. He held her back. "But, Elizabeth, this is about you, it isn't about me."

"But it could be, it could be." She looked up at the castle. "All this could be yours, all this . . . and me."

Zac looked into her eyes. He knew that in some sense what he was being offered was all that he, too, had ever wanted — to have his own place on the earth, his own place and a name that stood for something. Now Elizabeth was offering it to him — no strings attached. No strings now, but Zac knew enough to know there would be steel cables later on.

He was a simple man. His tastes were simple. He liked it that way. Everything about the place smelled of complications, complications he could never live with. And then there was Jenny, the woman whose letters he carried with him everywhere. If he couldn't bring himself to have her, then there would be no other.

"It's your star, Elizabeth Roberts, but it's not mine."

Chapter 23

Peter Williams rode out of Manitou Springs at daybreak. Too well-known to risk going to a hotel, he spent a sleepless night in the shanty. The sleeplessness combined with the pot of coffee he downed put his nerves on edge, but he managed to remain outwardly calm. He had been struggling for the last few days to keep what he was feeling under wraps. It wasn't fear of the fight — facing Cobb through the scope of his rifle didn't take a great deal of bravery. But he was nervous about appearances. He was to be in charge of a success, after all. What fear he did have was based on past failures. To fail at this point would be worse than death.

The men rode silently at his side. The horses snorted, their breath creating puffs of steam in the early morning air. Williams' animal pranced from side to side, eager to stretch out and run, but he held the reins tight. The large boulders on either side of the trail blossomed into house-sized rocks and then into spires that reached into the sky. The beauty of the rock garden was seldom lost on anyone, but today Williams had only one thought on his mind, to find a place with good visibility, a place with a long shot.

"How 'bout that up there?" The man pointed toward the large overhanging rock that shadowed the trail. "They got to come this way, and you got yerself a pretty good shot from up there."

Williams stopped and blinked at the stone structure, shielding his eyes from the rising sun.

"The sun'll be at your back up there," the man smiled. "But it'll be dag nab in their eyes. Won't even see you."

Williams dismounted his horse and drew the scoped rifle out of its scabbard. He looked down the rocky trail. Turning to the man who had suggested the sight, he handed him the reins. "Hold the horse here," he said. "We know the two of them will be riding, but we have little idea who might accompany them. We may have to ride out of here quickly after I shoot."

Looking at the others, he pointed out several locations farther along the trail. "I want you men to separate yourselves along the way here. If there are others with them, you can ride back to Manitou Springs, but if it's just the girl, take her."

"What do you want us to do with her?"

The man sounded overly eager.

Williams shot him a hard look. "Keep your hands off of her. Do you understand? I will not be far behind, and I want the girl unmolested. I have plans for her myself."

The men smiled.

Williams countered their thinking. "You've got it wrong. That young woman is invaluable to the CP. If we have her in our hands we can dictate the terms for the surrender of the Royal Gorge. We will get that general to sign an agreement that no court in the land can overturn," he said confidently.

The men nodded and rode off. He watched them take positions and then checked the spare ammunition he carried for the rifle. He had more than enough. If he didn't kill the man with one shot, he knew there would be more sleepless nights in store for him in the future.

Zac was awake early. The sound of servants bustling past his door made sleeping past dawn undoable. He didn't like cities and he didn't care to sleep in hotels, and the castle was one of the fanciest hotels he had ever been in. The only thing missing was the sound of drunks stumbling in the hallway late into the night. He got up from the bearskin rug and sat on the bed, pulling on his trousers.

He still had a sick feeling in his stomach from the night before. He didn't know if it was the strange food or the uncomfortable conversation with Elizabeth, but his stomach was turning, nonetheless. He unrolled his green drover shirt, slid it on, and tucked it into his pants. Cinching on his leather conch-studded belt, he picked up his holster and strapped it on. He checked the loads in his Peacemaker and slid it into the holster. Breaking open the little Shopkeeper special, he spun the cylinder and stuck it in his belt, behind his back. Sloughing on his buckskin jacket, he picked up his hat and walked out the door and down the stairs.

"Good morning, Mr. Cobb." The general poured a cup of coffee from the sideboard beside the dining room table and handed the steaming cup to Zac. "Do you take cream or sugar?"

"Only if the coffee is bad," Zac said.

The general smiled. "My daughter tells me you will be riding with her today."

Zac sipped the steaming brew. "I promised your granddaughter a ride, but I don't recall any promise to your daughter."

The general smiled and poured himself a cup. "I've learned over the years, Cobb, to let the women make all the plans that don't involve my work. It keeps them happy, and when they're happy so am I."

"Well, General, you've obviously done very well with the part of your life that you do control."

"Yes, I suppose I have. But my family is what gives me good reason for success."

Zac sipped his coffee. The man was impressive and Zac admired him. He had beaten back the wilderness and built things that would last. A man could hope for no more than that. "I suppose I'm too used to making my own way in life. I'm beholden to no one, and I guess that makes me antsy about having to bend my life to satisfy folks."

"In a way, I admire you deeply, Cobb. You remind me of a gladiator, a medieval warrior lost in time. You enter the ring of life and you compete, only you don't do what you do just for the money. You seem to believe in things."

"My folks brought me up to believe," Zac said. "It's the thing I can never seem to shuck free of."

"You are a Christian man, then?"

Zac pondered the thought. "Can't call what I do Christian, but I s'pose it is in a way. I punish lawbreakers, anybody who would steal from the company I work for."

He sipped the coffee and thought. "I suppose one could say, General, that the roots of my life are Christian, but the branches are definitely in doubt."

"Can a man drift away from his roots?" The general studied the man.

Zac walked toward the glass doors that opened onto the terrace. He looked through them toward the east, toward home, to another time, another world. "There are things no man can drift away from — things that will outlast everything." He spoke to the general with his face turned toward the blossoming sunrise.

Wheeling suddenly, he peered at the general. "I have listened to prayers from my mother's and father's lips, the words of which I believe will go on in time long after this castle has crumbled." Watching the man's eyes, he let the statement settle. Perhaps at any other time such thinking would have embarrassed him, but he knew the general to be an educated man, a man who loved good thought, and the notion stimulated him. He continued, "When the last wave has settled on the ocean's shore, my mother's prayers will be in the thinking of God, and when the last sunrise back there has come up across those Kansas plains, my father's good name will still stand."

Roberts looked at him with a mixture of amazement and intrigue. This man wasn't the simple man he appeared to be and Roberts's appreciation of him grew by the moment. "But you haven't answered my question. Can a man drift far away from his roots?"

"I s'pose only time can answer that, General. As I said, my roots are strong, the branches are in doubt from time to time."

"Mr. Cobb, I don't believe I would be so concerned about the branches in your life. But the buds — the tender buds that bloom — that is where the newness of your life will come. That is where I would place my hope if I were you."

Roberts put down his cup of coffee. "There is much more to your actions, sir, than simply a desire to bring your company's vengeance on thieves. That motive alone doesn't explain why you would concern yourself with protecting my family on that train. The men who wanted them had taken nothing from Wells Fargo."

Elizabeth suddenly appeared in her riding clothes. She moved to the sideboard, taking a fresh muffin and pouring herself a glass of juice. Then she sat at the table and listened to the two men.

"That's a question I ask myself, too," Zac

said. "I reckon I can't abide the weak being wronged by people who ought to know better."

"But you can't change all the cruelty in the world," the general replied.

"No, I can't. But I don't have to sit by and watch it, either. My daddy wouldn't tolerate that, and I'm his son."

Roberts looked over at Elizabeth, who was unusually quiet. "Don't let our talk keep you two from that morning ride of yours. Mr. Cobb and I can continue this later."

He walked with the two to the door. Halfway across the room, he pulled Zac aside. "Just like you are a son of your father, Elizabeth is my daughter. I've competed for everything I've ever earned and I do not give up easily. Don't let the way I appear at the peak of my success fool you. I have wrestled with the devil for every nickel, and that daughter of mine is just like me."

Elizabeth waited across the room beside the door. When Zac and the general reached her, she took Zac's arm and led him out the door. "I'm riding the big roan and I'm letting you ride Storm today. Go take a look at him. He has fire." She smiled slyly. "We'll see what kind of a rider you truly are."

"Be careful there, Cobb. That stallion of Elizabeth's is like the wind. I've never seen her let anyone else ride him." The man scratched his chin. "Probably reflects her concern for the rider more than the horse. He will beat you to death."

"See for yourself, Zac," Elizabeth said.

Zac put on his hat and walked out toward where the two horses were tied while Elizabeth turned back to her father. "You've always said I was woman enough to get anything I wanted."

The general nodded.

"What I want is him."

"You may have met your match there, my dear."

"I don't think so. I don't think he knows yet what he wants in a woman, but what he needs . . . is me. He needs a woman who frightens him, scares him to death, someone he can never turn his back on and feel safe."

The two of them rode slowly out of the grounds, nodding to Henry as they passed the gatehouse. "That's an English riding saddle," Elizabeth said. "You have to hang on with your legs; no saddle horn," she laughed.

"I don't hang on when I ride anyway; I just ride."

"Well then, you will ride today. You seem infatuated with the notion of controlling everything and everybody; we'll see how you handle Storm." With that, she slapped her reins to the withers of the big roan and galloped off.

Zac hunched low on the stallion and the animal exploded down the trail, sending billows of dust up behind him. Catching the roan in short order, Zac determined to put some distance between himself and the redhead. Galloping ahead, he began to weave the stallion through the towering rocks, the horse's hooves sounding like the echo of Chinese firecrackers.

From his overhanging rock perch, Williams could hear the approach of the galloping horse. He readied his rifle, steadying it on his open hand as he lay on top of the rock. Looking through the sight, he lay the cross hairs on the trail below and waited.

Zac skidded the stallion to a halt and turned the animal around to wait for Elizabeth. He smiled as she rode up.

Williams could see the two of them around the corner from a large rock. He sighted through the brass telescope on top of the rifle and tightened his finger slightly on the trigger. There was no clear target yet. He would keep his finger on the trigger until they came into better view.

"You had enough racing?" Zac asked. "Want to just ride now and enjoy the view?"

"You do sit a horse well, Zac Cobb." She laughed. "I expected you to ride like an ordinary cowboy."

"I've been on many a chase," Zac said, "and I'd prefer a good horse to any of those trains you build. Those things can be dangerous."

"So I've heard," she laughed, "especially the trains that you're on."

Grinning, he patted the big stallion's neck. "Only when I'm feeling especially irritated. Normally, I just sleep on them."

"And did you feel in control of Storm?" she asked.

"Elizabeth, I think this animal is a far sight easier to control than you would be."

The young woman rode up next to him and smiled slyly. "You're right about that. No man can take his eyes off of me or turn his back on me, as you appear capable of doing to that woman of yours. But you seem to be a man of daring. I'm not sure how well you'd deal with comfort." Patting the stallion's head, she quickly slipped off the bridle. Jerking it free, she used the reins to slap the horse's rump. The big animal bolted and ran back down the trail. She yelled at Zac, "Let's see you control him now!"

Zac hung on tight and slouched low, his legs clinging to the sides of the horse. He was too panicked to be angry. The stallion ran wildly through the rocks, back in the direction of Glen Eyrie.

The last thing Zac wanted to do was jump from the animal. Reaching around his waist, he unbuckled his belt, sliding it free with one hand as he clung to the horse's neck and mane with the other. Inching the belt around the stallion's neck, Zac pulled it tight and buckled it. At least he had something to hang on to. Now he hoped the horse would run into a box canyon or into the creek so he could regain some control.

Storming past the entrance to Glen Eyrie, the horse showed no sign of slowing down. Zac had hoped the draw of the stables would turn him into the closed iron gates, but the stallion was feeling the freedom of life without the bit and now seemed determined to lose its rider.

Now on the open road, Zac began to ease out of his buckskin jacket, keeping one hand or the other on the belt. When the animal still kept its frantic pace, Zac struggled free of the jacket and slapped it over the horse's eyes, pulling back on its head. The beast came to a sudden halt.

Zac's heart was still racing when he got down from the stallion. The animal continued to prance as the two of them stood by the side of the dirt road. Zac took hold of the end of his belt and, leaving the jacket tied around the animal's face, began the long walk back to the castle. "You sure are something else, big boy," Zac spoke softly to the horse as they walked.

It was over an hour later when Zac and the stallion walked up to the gatehouse. Henry ran to open the gate. A look of surprise registered on his face. "What are you doing here?" he asked.

"The stud here decided to take me on a tour," Zac said, "a rather hurried tour. You seen Miss Roberts?"

"Nah, I ain't; she ain't been back."

"That's funny. I'da thought she'd be back here laughing her fool head off."

Henry held the open gate and took off his hat, wiping his head. "She ain't here. If'n she'd a ridden back in I'da knowed it."

Zac hardened his jaw. He was worried. "Go get me another bridle. I better go look for her."

Chapter 24

Yeager and the men from the Denver and Rio Grande tugged the mules laden with their desperately needed supplies up the ridge that overlooked the Arkansas River. The rimrock was steep. It would be impassable here from any direction. The water below them swirled in fitful whirlpools of white water, each eddy leading onto a restless drop or pounding slap of the water to the edge of the sharp rocks.

Looking across the swirling river no boat had been foolish enough to dare, Yeager spotted the words written in bold white letters on the rimrock: "The way of the transgressor is hard."

"Tarnation!" Boots MacKenzie was a hardened, bearded gandy dancer who had driven rails halfway across America. He'd seen it all, but the sight of the swirling water and the words written high on the rocky wall made him stop and take note. "Now why you reckon they done gone and wrote them words?"

Yeager had busied himself unstrapping the

packs from the sides of the mules. "See that redwood pipe beneath that rock shelf over there?"

"Sure."

"Well, convicts put that pipe in to bring water to Cañon City. I suppose whoever wrote that wanted to make sure those boys never forgot why it was them doing all the work."

Boots and the other men began to pitch in with the packs. "Been my experience that all of life is hard," Boots said.

"You got that right," Yeager shot back. "It's just that it gets so much harder when you're swimming upstream against it all."

"Or they wind up like them two we left back there in the valley," Boots chuckled. "No horses and no boots is mighty tough on a man."

"Some people never learn. They violate the law and wrong every man they meet, then they wind up working on a thing like that over there" — Yeager pointed toward the pipeline across the river — "and in a place like this."

Yeager pulled the block and tackle out of the packs. "Let's scout out the top of the rock here. We got to find a place to lower the supplies down. Also, we got to make sure we're behind the Rio Grande lines. We wouldn't want to drop all this stuff to them CP boys, now, would we?"

All heads went up when the gunfire erupted below them. "Sounds like they're just below us and a little downstream," Boots said.

"Reckon so," Yeager replied. "You men just stick by the stuff here, while I go down and make sure we can lower the supplies." He picked up a case of rifle ammunition and slung his Winchester over his arm. "Grab the end of that rope. I'm going down with this. Then set up that block and tackle. When I get below, you better start sending that stuff down." He called to the men waiting beside their horses. "Sounds like they may need all of us down there. When we start lowering supplies, I need about a dozen of you boys to come down quick."

The men nodded and Yeager put on his gloves, then grabbed the rope and began to lower himself down the face of the canyon. As he skidded down the side of the hills, he kicked up a cloud of dust and sent a shower of rocks and debris down in front of him.

As Yeager hit the bottom of the rocky shelf, he landed hard, sprawling onto the railway roadbed. Getting to his knees, he could see at once why the fighting was taking place. There was no space between the canyon wall and the swiftly moving torrent except for the shelf that was being used as the narrow gauge passageway. The gandy dancers had been blasting into the mountainside and clearing the way for a bed for track. For the railroad, any railroad that had that narrow passage, it would mean high freight fees for the shipments to Leadville and the high mountain towns beyond.

The gunfire was coming from around the bend and track lay in front of him. Yeager got to his feet and cautiously ambled down the track in the direction of the firing. Rounding the bend, he could see the barricade. Fifteen to twenty men were pinned down behind a number of railroad ties and rocks. Several of them were returning fire around the edges of the barrier, while the rest were taking shelter and huddling behind the wooden beams.

One of the men spotted him and nudged another man, who was firing. Yeager removed his hat and waved. Crouched low, he ran for the rear of the wall and then to the men, who were obviously worn out, but happy to see him.

Three-fingers Kelly, a man who had lost part of his left hand in a blasting accident, reached out and grabbed Yeager by the sleeve. The man was dirty, unshaven, and gaunt-looking, none of which was unusual for Kelly, but the others in the group were equally pitiful looking. "The saints be praised, Yeager. We were beginning to believe you'd get here only in time for the buryin'. We're almost out of something to shoot back with, we are, and we haven't put a morsel of food in our mouths for nigh on to three days."

Yeager broke open the box. "Well, I can take care of the ammunition problem for you men, and Boots and the boys will be coming down that hillside soon with more ammo and food."

"Hallelujah!" Kelly yelled.

The men scrambled for the munitions. After thumbing rounds into their rifles, each of them grabbed handfuls and crammed their pockets full. In a matter of moments, having found new vigor in their ability to return fire, the men sent a new hail of gunfire from the wall of ties.

"Those boys over there thought they had us for sure, Yeager." Kelly had turned to fire at the people behind the rocks, but then came back and squatted beside Yeager. "It was like they were lions smelling blood." He smiled broadly underneath the red stubble of a beard. "But now they'll think twice, by golly, they will think once again."

★ ★ ★

Jake Rice had ridden in from Cañon City with twelve men. All the way in, he had been afraid that the shooting would be over by the time he got there. The word in Cañon City had been that the men of the Denver and Rio Grande couldn't last much longer. They had no way to get supplies or help, and each passing day put them closer to starvation. Several CP men in a bar where Rice had stopped had told him to take his time, that everything was over. The sound of the gunfire had surprised him, and now, only minutes after his arrival, the renewed vigorous fire from beyond the wooden wall turned his eyebrows up.

"I thought you said they were finished!" he shouted. Rice was clean in comparison to the men who had formed the bulk of the CP band, and his white hat, dark suit, and tie made him stand out even more. Everybody knew, however, who he was and why he was there. No one questioned his ability. The two guns he carried, slung low, made the case for him. He was said to be able to shoot the eyes out of a bumblebee at fifty feet, and anyone who had ever seen him work knew the truth of it.

The men around him pulled their heads back from the rocks and makeshift fort they had erected. "Thought they were," one of them replied. "Maybe they squirreled something away, but it can't last much longer. When they're through, we'll just walk over there and take their guns. We'll take their guns and send them home."

"Home, nothin'," another man replied. "We'll bury 'em. Use their bodies for part of that there roadway."

"You sure there's no way out of there?" Rice asked.

"Nah, not unless you're a crow."

"And there's no way to supply those men?"

"Ain't likely. Them walls are steep back there and b'sides, we got us some scouts all along the sides of them hills and back into the valleys up there too. Ain't nobody getting in without us knowing it, and fer durn sure nobody's getting out."

"That's got to be the last of 'em," another man chipped in. "They're all having a last hurrah."

Rice took off his hat and peeked around the rock fortress. He'd learned never to die on somebody else's say-so. What people thought was often as not something that had grown root in their mind. It might be right, but then again it might be just hope, and hope was not something for which a man shoved all his chips into the middle of the table.

Peering around the rock, he could see at once that any frontal assault was useless. The piles of railroad ties were riddled with gun ports, and it looked to him as if more than twenty guns bristled out in their direction. If the men over there had enough ammunition, then nobody was going to rush them and win.

His heart pounded. The men he had ridden in with had begun to scatter and find places to shoot from. Rice watched them take position. He had over forty guns now, more than enough to hold their own. It was a real Mexican standoff, but that would never do. He knew something the men around him didn't know: the courts had already made sure that time was an ally of the Denver and Rio Grande. If something was going to happen, he'd have to make it happen, and soon. The longer they sat, the more the wheels of the law had a chance to turn — he knew that full well.

Ruby hadn't quit. Ruby was a man who would never quit, and a man who couldn't abide failure. He wasn't about to die in this thing, either — no, who died would be up to him and the crew that squatted with him behind those rocks. That's what he was paid for, that's what he knew how to do — make sure the opposition did the dying. And he'd do his job, too. If they didn't get this pass, it wouldn't be because he didn't do his job.

He moved back behind the rocks and went to the other side of the fortress. Peering around the edge of the rocks, he surveyed the river as it rushed past him. Close to him, a rifle round crashed, splintering rock and sending shards flying that stung his cheek. He jerked his head back. "Now that's enough, that's far enough." He was shocked at the close call.

He looked over the river and could see the white words clearly printed on the canyon wall: "The way of the transgressor is hard." He could see the narrow ledge that wound its way underneath the pipeline. It was a place the men who had worked on the pipeline stood to put the redwood tubing in place. It would never do for a railroad bed, but a group of men could pass by on it, and there was cover, too. Large boulders were strewn along the pathway, pock-marking the area with places a person could remain concealed.

"Is there some way a body could get across that river?" he asked.

"Shore," one of the men drawled. "We got one of them suspension bridges across this here river, and some track on it. They'ze layin' track on the other side to the south. It's back quite a ways, but a body could get to it in a few hours."

"All right." Rice motioned with his hand, gathering the men around him. "We've got to get over there and pour some heat on those boys from the other side. All we need is a few; I need ten good riflemen. Who wants the job?"

Several men raised their hands. "Beats sitting here," one of them said. Other men nodded and scooted forward until the full ten were selected.

Rice gave his instructions. "You men get back to that bridge and make your way down to that ledge. When you work your way across from those boys, you open up." His face lit up and a slight smile crossed it. "I want you in position by early tomorrow morning. Everybody ready at sunup. When you start pouring lead down their line, they'll run like rabbits. When that happens, you signal us and the rest of us here will rush 'em. We'll catch 'em running back for cover and kill 'em like a bunch of quail. Is that clear?"

Everyone nodded.

Rice looked up at the sun and squinted. "We've only got a few hours till it gets dark, but if you do what I say, it'll be over this time tomorrow. We will have a complete day to hunt them down without their cover. Then we'll get on to some serious drinking."

The men smiled.

Yeager made a small fire while the men continued to shoot around and through the railroad ties at the men from the CP. They heard the thumps from the sound of return fire as the shots hit the thick wooden barricade. Yeager poured water into a cook pot and hung it on the irons over the growing fire. Lifting an ax, he remained on his knees and began splitting firewood.

"Glory be, Yeager, what you doing there?" Three-fingers Kelly slid back toward him and positioned himself near the fire.

"You men are hungry," Yeager said. "Don't see how a man can fight for long on an empty stomach."

"We are powerful hungry, I have to admit. We've been sitting around the fire for days now dreaming of beefsteak."

"Well, I can't promise you that," Yeager said, "but I s'pose by now the elk jerky we've got will taste a lot like it." He poured boiling water from the large kettle into a coffeepot and, reaching into his jacket pocket, dumped a sackful of fresh coffee grounds into the steaming water.

"But you don't have to bother yourself with being our scullery maid here," Kelly said. "We have some boys who can do that."

"You boys have done enough," Yeager said. "I only wish I could cut you loose and send you into town for some rotgut and dancing."

"Sleep would be enough."

Yeager smiled. "I can see that clear enough just by looking at your eyes. Well, maybe when we get the fresh men in here, we can send you boys down the track a mite. You can rest tonight while we hold them off."

"That will be music to the men's ears. Like a sweet lullaby from the land of the green."

"Why don't you go back and pass the word," Yeager said. "Then pick a few at a time to come back for coffee. The rest of the men ought to be here directly."

In a matter of minutes, several of the men Yeager had brought with him began to straggle in, each bringing boxes of supplies and ammunition. They mixed with the men who were coming back for coffee, and then took their places at the barricade. The hungry men who squatted beside Yeager at the fire were full of questions.

"How much longer?"

"When we gonna hit those people?"

Yeager had been under fire before. He had commanded men in the War Between the States and ridden with them during the Sioux uprising. He knew the men here were all tired and battle-weary. He'd seen it all before. He also knew the best way for a leader to get the confidence of his men was to serve them. He poured the coffee and only wished he had answers for them. He had no confidence in the courts or in the sheriff's office, but his trust was in the man in the castle — General Sydney Roberts. General Roberts and that firebrand daughter of his who was calling the shots.

Chapter 25

Zac spent almost an hour walking through the rocky terrain, stooping low and studying the tracks. He'd seen enough of the big roan that Elizabeth rode to recognize its hoof-prints immediately. The other tracks came from several directions. He followed them a short distance before he spotted the place where two other horses had been tied. Looking up at the towering flat rock, he spotted the position that commanded a view of the trail below, the place near where he and Elizabeth had stopped. He didn't need anyone to tell him what had happened.

He mounted the stallion and pulled the reins around. Clapping the spurs to the animal's sides, he galloped back toward the castle. Everything inside him wanted to follow the tracks immediately while there was still plenty of daylight, but he knew that would be the height of folly. He'd need a different horse to follow them, one that could be depended on. He'd trade speed for dependability any day. He'd also need some supplies, ammunition, a different saddle, and his

Sharps Creedmore. When he found the men who'd taken Elizabeth, he had to be able to do whatever it took to bring the girl back.

Riding back through the gate, he spotted Henry in the shadows of the gatehouse. He didn't stop to speak to him, but continued riding through the grounds toward the castle. He didn't want to be the one to tell Sydney Roberts about his daughter but he'd have to. His stomach turned. He didn't want to be here at all. He just wanted the promised reward paid to his bank and to be on the next train to California, back to Jenny and Skip, but he knew now that would not happen anytime soon.

He reined the stallion up outside of the castle and, dismounting, loosened the cinch on the horse's saddle. After patting the animal down, he turned and walked toward the door. He dreaded the look in Roberts's eyes when he told him the news of Elizabeth. But there was no way to avoid it. He'd come close to feelings of loss himself, concerning a child, with Skip. The youngster wasn't even his son, only a boy in California who looked on him as a father, but Zac knew how he would feel if Skip were missing at the hands of evil men.

As he walked through the door of the castle, he saw the general standing talking to someone he never thought he'd see again, yet right now probably the man he needed to see most.

"Señor Zac, señor Zac, how good to see you again! My father and I thought we would be too late to wish you *vaya con Dios*." The young shepherd rose quickly from his chair while the old man tilted his head up in the direction of the door. Zac hurriedly shook the young Mexican's hand.

"Miss Roberts promised us a job here caring for the animals after we sold our sheep."

"How was your ride, Mr. Cobb?" The general smiled as he patted one of the large dogs.

"General, I don't have much time to explain. I need another horse and some supplies, a pair of binoculars too. Elizabeth's been taken, I'm afraid . . . by that dinner guest of yours, or the men who work for him. They apparently had an ambush set for us, knew where we were going to be and when."

Sam Fisher and Bruce Elliott had walked into the room and stood in disbelief as Zac continued. "I know where their trail is and I need to get back there before I lose too much light."

"How could this have happened?" The general was crestfallen.

"I don't know, but they were ready for us,

and if I were you I'd start looking into who passed the word about our whereabouts, and I'd start with that man who works at your gate."

"Henry? He's worked for me for years."

"I don't know, but it had to be somebody who knew what we were about. When there's money in the picture, men can go bad, sir."

The general put his hand on Zac's arm. "Mr. Cobb, realistically speaking, I have plenty of help here."

Zac could see the man's eyes misting, and he knew the general didn't really mean what he was saying.

Roberts went on, "This isn't something you have to do, Cobb. I've already wired the reward you were promised to your bank in San Francisco. This is family business, it's no longer your concern."

Zac looked the man in the eye. "Like I said, General, most men can go bad when there's money to be had, but I'm not most men. When I rode out that gate with your daughter, her safety became my responsibility. I will get her back, and you can take my word on that."

"Thank you. I know I'll feel much better knowing you're looking, and I'm sure Elizabeth would take comfort if she knew."

Zac moved toward the stairs, stopping for

a moment to lay a hand on the old man's shoulder. "It's good to see you. I'm sorry I don't have time to talk."

The white-haired man nodded. "I understand, señor. You must do what you do best. I will pray for you. That is what I do best."

"That's the thing I need most right now," Zac said.

Minutes later Zac came back down the stairs with his rifle, ammunition belt, and saddlebags. Bruce Elliott and Sam Fisher met him at the bottom of the stairs. "We're going with you," Elliott said.

Fisher pushed Elliott gently aside. "Look, Cobb, I know how you feel. You no more want a greenhorn and a fat old man riding along with you than you want a bunch of them hounds of the general's baying at your heels, but we're going anyway. Now, you can have us riding with you or yapping along behind you on our own, but we're going."

The general and Eric Torkelson emerged from his office, the general with a six-gun strapped on his hip. He caught Zac's look of desperation. "Don't worry about me, Cobb. Torkelson and I are going to Denver. The court has ruled in our favor, and I'm going to get a sheriff's posse and try to end this thing. If we can get the shooting stopped and force those men in the canyon out of our way, then whatever reason the CP may have had for taking Elizabeth will be a nonissue."

"Well, at least one of you people knows what you ought to be doing," Zac said. He glared at Elliott and Fisher. "You men can come if you're bound and determined, but I won't be looking after you."

Nikki felt her way to Zac's side and, reaching up, took his hand. "My daddy is a man too," she said. "He can go with you, Mr. Cobb."

Zac stooped down and tenderly spoke into her ear. "A person doesn't have to do what I do, honey, to be a man. Your daddy is a real man. He loves you and your mother and is the kind of man who can be depended on. A man like me can't be counted on for much, but you can trust your father."

"Will you come back, Mr. Cobb?"

"Yes, sweetheart, I'll be back and I'll bring your Aunt Liz with me. 'Sides, I promised you that horsey ride, didn't I?"

The little girl nodded her head and smiled.

"Well, I have to come back and give you that ride, now, don't I? I'm a man of my word, I mean what I say. My pledge is my bond, honey."

Zac got to his feet and looked at Elliott. "If I had that wife of yours and this little girl here, I'd no more think about walking out that door with a gun strapped on than I'd think about swimming up the Mississippi, but if you're determined, then we better get."

The men from the stables had tied three fresh horses outside the castle. Bedrolls and provisions were cinched to the saddles. Zac adjusted the stirrups on a lanky blood bay gelding with three white stockings. He tightened the reins and mounted. He noticed Elliott eyeing the stallion that was still tied up beside the other three horses. "Don't even let the thought cross your mind — you climb on that puddin'-footed horse," he said. "We need animals that won't spook and that black shadow jumper would have you in Wyoming by morning." Zac clapped his spurs to the bay. "And we ain't goin' that way!" he shouted back over his shoulder.

When Elliott and Fisher caught up with Zac, he was on the ground, studying tracks. Remounting, he headed south. "Five of 'em," he said. "And the woman."

Minutes later they came over the hill and looked on the town of Manitou Springs. "We'll stop here just to make sure they're not still in town, but they'd be foolish if they were."

"How can we track them through busy streets like that?" Elliott asked.

"Professor, you don't have to track a man by following every step he takes. A body follows somebody by knowing where the water holes are, that and the best passes." They rode down into town. "And it always helps to know where the person you're following is headed."

"Do we know that?"

" 'Course we do," Fisher shot back. "Those CP people will take her to Cañon City. They'll more'n likely get as close to the fightin' in the canyon as they can. That way when they try to make the swap, she'll be handy."

"You got more than muscle to speak for you, Sam," Zac smiled. "There's a brain under that derby."

"Ummph," the man grunted. "I'm a detective. That word speaks for more than a little bit of thinking."

"So it does. Fisher's right, Elliott. If they're not in town, we'll pick up their trail south of town. Six horses all bunched up are hard to cover up, and I can recognize the stompin's of that big roan Elizabeth's on without even getting down off my horse."

The street stretched out in front of them and wound its way up to the foot of Pike's Peak. Zac pointed. "We'll spread out and ask around. Elliott, you start here. Fisher and I will go on down. We'll meet at the hotel over yonder in an hour. Even if they've done skedaddled, that'll leave us about two hours of sun. I want to be sure we pick up their trail afore dark if they're not in town. I've seen enough of Colorado already to know that sky could go from robin's egg blue to rain, thunder, and hail in a matter of an hour."

After only twenty minutes, Zac found himself talking to a bartender who remembered the men who had hurriedly downed several drinks and purchased a number of bottles of whiskey. They had not waited to try the tables and left before the shots they poured down had managed to warm their guts. He walked out and mounted the bay.

Checking his watch, he could see he had a forty-minute wait for Elliott and Fisher, and he didn't much want to weave in and out of every jug joint in Manitou Springs looking for the two of them. He had to find a way to draw them out into the street. Drawing out his Peacemaker and the little belly gun, he put the reins of the horse in his mouth and kicked the spurs into the animal.

The horse bolted from a dead stop and Zac began to fire rounds of lead into the air. He galloped up the street, and then grabbing the reins, he skidded the horse to a stop. Wheeling around, he rode back as he continued to puncture the sky over Manitou Springs with smoke and flame.

Men poured out of the saloons and peeked out the windows and doors. Manitou had never been a place that hosted celebrating cowboys, and the sound of one man fandangoing the town was a rare thing indeed. Zac spotted Elliott first and signaled him toward the end of town, and then running his horse forward, he spotted Fisher. "Let's go. They're gone by an hour or better and we're burnin' daylight."

The three men rode quickly out of town amid the ogles of people who had sauntered out of the buildings to see the cause of all the shooting. Sam Fisher lifted his derby and tipped it to the people who lined the wooden walkway as he awkwardly rode past them. Zac kept his eyes on the ground, watching for signs of the group, and in a matter of minutes, he pulled up the bay. Climbing down from the horse, he squatted near a patch of ground close to the road.

"What is it?" Elliott asked. "Did you find something?"

Zac motioned for them with his hand. "This is where Elizabeth sat while they waited for the men who rode into town." He pointed toward the fresh horse droppings scattered over a wide area. "The horses were here for a spell."

"How do you know Miss Elizabeth was here?" Fisher asked.

Zac pointed to a large rock beside the road, a convenient place for someone to sit. "Take a look at this," he said.

The men leaned closer. There on the side of the rock was a freshly scratched sign . . . a star.

"What does that mean?" Elliott asked.

Zac looked down the trail that led to the south. He spoke to the men in a low tone. "The star is a kind of sign between the two of us. She knows I would recognize it. She knew I'd be trying to find her and she wants me to follow her star."

The three of them remounted and slowly moved down the trail. Zac was in no hurry now. He had no desire to come within eyesight of the group that rode ahead, at least not in daylight. The men could see lightning strikes on Cheyenne Mountain against the storm-darkening sky. The electric fingers seemed to walk the distance of the mountain. The mountain was dark and rose ominously into the sky. Years before, it had been thought to be a place of evil spirits by the Arapaho and Utes that lived in the area.

The rain began to sweep down the trail and through the trees that were scattered on either side. The three men could hear it before they could see it, but then it fell on them. Zac had already pulled the piggin' string off his pommel slicker and wrapped the oil cloth around him. Quickly, the other two men followed suit.

He wasn't worried about losing their trail now. The men who held Elizabeth were going in the direction he knew they would go. They were riding at a pace that would be steady, and more than likely they were drinking to keep their insides warm. He knew enough about the type of men who would be hired to perform this kind of work to know they wouldn't ride far in the cold rain, not with the liquor swimming in their insides. They'd camp soon.

Darkness came without warning in the midst of the sudden rain. Below them, the men could see the glowing lights of Colorado Springs, and in the distance a moving train lit the tracks with its lamps. The whole problem was about the coming of the railroad, and as Zac watched the train move toward the Springs, he thought about the passing of the days of the stagecoach as a means of public travel. There were still plenty of places locomotives wouldn't yet reach, but he knew it was only a matter of time before the company he worked for would have to change with the times.

The thought crossed his mind briefly that the men they were chasing might rendezvous with a waiting train. If that happened, then Elizabeth might be taken to a place that would be harder to reach, at least right away. The thought troubled him a bit. It held risk for them. The Chicago Pacific didn't own these tracks, however, and they couldn't safely meet up with a train until they reached Pueblo. He tumbled the thought inside his head and continued to ride, his hat pulled down against the rain. Over an hour later, when they rounded a bend, his eyes were drawn immediately to a welcome sight a couple hundred yards ahead. A fire was blazing behind a stand of trees.

Chapter 26

Zac got off of the big bay and loosened the cinch. "Ground hitch your horses here," he said. "We'll wait here a spell and let 'em finish those bottles of theirs. With the rain and the liquor, I think they'll be plenty dazed by the time we come up on 'em."

"What about Elizabeth?" Elliott asked.

Zac looked off at the fire in the distance. "I don't think they'll lay a hand on her. She's what they got to bargain with. We'll let 'em relax a bit and then split up and come on 'em from three sides. I don't want any shootin', though, not unless somebody goes for an iron. That understood?"

The men nodded in agreement.

"Open up a coupla cans of them peaches," Fisher said. "My ribs are startin' to rub on my backbone."

"All right," Zac smiled at the man. "But I think you got a ways to go, Sam, before you starve." They all grinned, and Fisher pulled his derby down around his ears.

They sat down on the rocks in the cold rain and passed the peaches around. "Check your loads," he said. "Make sure you got a sixth round under the hammer; you just might need it."

"I haven't used a revolver since the war," Elliott said. "I'm afraid I might be of more danger to you with one than I could ever be to them." He picked up the Winchester beside him. "But I believe myself to be somewhat proficient with one of these."

"Let me tell you, Cobb," Fisher interrupted. "When this boy says he can do something, you better believe him. I've seen him work with those hands of his, and he's a terror. He may be an East Coast dandy, but he can flick those fists of his like a rattler's tongue."

Zac looked into Elliott's eyes. "And you can shoot one of those? I'm gonna have enough on my mind without having to worry about returning your body to that family of yours."

"Mr. Cobb, I wouldn't trust myself with a revolver and the thought of pulling the trigger on that shotgun of yours would terrify me, but with a rifle I can kill a running deer with a single shot."

"Those people aren't deer, professor, they're men. When you kill a man you take away from him everything he is and everything he's gonna be. It's serious business.

One pause, one blink of the eye, one thought about what you're doing, and you're the one who loses everything."

Elliott picked up the rifle. He pushed open the lever and began to load it. Looking up at the two men, he stiffened his jaw. "Elizabeth is part of my family. A man must be prepared to defend his family no matter what the cost to his own feelings. I won't like it, but if we can free her, I am thoroughly prepared to do whatever is required."

"Then that's good enough for me," Zac said.

"I've wondered," Elliott went on pensively. "Can a man do what you do on a daily basis and not lose his soul and his sensitivity in the process?"

Zac had both revolvers in his lap. He checked the action on the guns and slid a shell into each cylinder. "I suppose that's a question I can't rightly answer. I have no idea what I'd be like if I hadn't started this job. I only know what I am now. I know when I went into the war I was just an average farm boy from Georgia, but that war had a way of changing anybody who it ever touched, even people who didn't fight in it."

"It sure changed me," Fisher said. "I was a career soldier when it started, stationed in California. But there's something about shooting a man who looks like you, speaks the same language, and comes from a home just like yours that makes anybody pause a mite. You think. You think about it a lot. But when the shooting starts, you stop thinking."

"You think you're able to stop your thinking if the shooting starts?" Zac asked.

Elliott slid the action shut on the rifle. "I can," he replied, "and I will. I will kill those men if I have to, but I will hate it."

"Good," Zac said. "It's hating it that makes us different from those men up the trail. They do what they do for the money, and there are some men who do it for the pleasure. That's the type of man who stops being a man. When a man starts down the road of making his only living with a gun, he's already owned up to the fact that he hasn't got the guts to build something. Whether he knows it or not, life has already got him whipped. That's why I got that ranch of mine in California. I got to build things. I got to watch things being born. That's why calving time at the ranch is the best time of all for me. There's a time to be born and a time to die, but I'd rather be around when it's time to be born."

Fisher reached into his inside pocket and took out a cigar.

Zac stopped him. "Just chew on that," he said. "Up here, the smell of tobacco can carry quite a ways." He stood up and planted his Peacemaker back into his holster. Sticking the little belly gun into his waistband, he took the sawed-off shotgun out of a saddlebag, broke it open, and dropped two loads of the ten-gauge shells into the open chambers. "This is something that tends to end a gunfight before it starts." He paused. "Makes 'em think real hard before they pull iron."

He motioned to Fisher. "You circle down below and come up from that way real easylike. Keep your distance for a spell. Professor, you stay along this here trail and move in. Just come up to the trees and go to ground. I'll go up the hill there and circle in from the south. When the moon hits the top of the mountain, both of you come in close and wait for my call."

Zac reached into his saddlebags and took out the moccasins he carried. Taking off his boots, he slipped them on. He wanted to be as quiet as possible when he got in close, and he would try to work his way into the camp. If he could spot Elizabeth's location, then he could stand over her before any action began. He knew the sound of a snapping twig could bring the men to guns even if they were half drunk, and he didn't want to run the risk of that. The moccasins would allow him to feel the ground he was on before he put his weight down on it.

He watched Fisher move downhill and, taking a last look at Bruce Elliott, Zac began the trek uphill. Climbing over the rocks, he slipped the thong over the hammer of the Peacemaker. He could see the fire burning brightly and it worried him. He knew the men were probably drinking and talking about their plans, but the camp looked too easy to spot to make him feel right about it. It was more of an ambush camp than men who had stopped to cook dinner. Of course, he was used to chasing men on the dodge, but these men seemed too confident to suit him.

He moved steadily uphill, away from the glowing fire. He was used to working alone, depending on no one but himself; that was the way he liked to work and it suited him. He knew Fisher could be counted on not to be hotheaded. *The man may have white hair and a rounded girth,* he thought, *but at least he can shoot straight and be counted on. Elliott is another question.*

Zac continued up the hillside, over the downed scrub and through the trees. *At least they are people who care about what they are doing,* he thought. But sometimes that was the most dangerous part of a job like this. Zac knew that people who cared might let their passions get the better part of their judgment. To be cold inside when you had to kill was what made the thing tolerable. It made facing down the men you were up against something that could be done, even when you were outnumbered. If a man couldn't tell what you would do, couldn't tell what was on your mind, the doubt alone put fear inside of a man.

He moved quickly over the grass that lay between the trees. The moon hung full in the sky, bright enough for a man who was looking to see. If the men below were smart, they'd have at least one lookout, and that was the man he had to find first. He had to find him and take him out quietly before he edged his way into the camp.

He crouched behind the rock and watched the moon. It hung over the mountain and seemed to stand still. Zac looked the ground over carefully. The open ground between him and the trees worried him a mite. The spot was a good one for anyone who might be looking in his direction, but that was why he had chosen to circle around and come in from the south. If they had a lookout, it was only fitting that he'd be positioned between the camp and Manitou Springs. There was no reason for them to think of someone approaching them from the south. That was his edge, and that was what he counted on. He'd circle the camp and come in searching for a lone man positioned a ways from the camp, a man standing uphill and looking back to the north.

He watched the clouds move overhead. Moments later, when they passed in front of the moon, he moved quickly and silently over the grass. Hunched down behind a deadfall, he studied the glowing fire. There was no sound, no movement. Quietly, he inched around the logs and, moving one foot slowly in front of the other, he edged himself into the trees.

Turning his face away from the glow of the fire, he studied the moonlight filtering through the trees. His eyes strained to see any movement or the glow of a cigarette. Men who stood watch all too often tried to keep warm in the worst way.

The moon hung low over the mountain now. Time was short. If he hadn't found the lookout before it touched the mountain, then Fisher and Elliott would be coming close. They'd be close and maybe, just maybe, there would be a man behind them. Zac used his eyes to search through the trees. He saw nothing, no movement at all. He heard no sound, no talking, not even a man clearing his throat. Moving closer now to the fire, he saw why. The camp was empty.

He quietly got to his feet and moved through the trees, careful to take each step on solid ground. If this was an ambush, he wasn't going to walk into it. He quietly cocked the hammers of the shotgun, and lifting the thong off the hammer of the Peacemaker, he drew it out of his holster. With the .45 in one hand and the ten-gauge in the other, he quietly moved into the camp. Lifting his voice, he called out. "Sam, Elliott, come on in. They're gone."

He saw the two men as they cautiously approached the camp. "They're gone?" Fisher seemed puzzled as he walked into the light from the still glowing embers of the fire.

Zac picked up an empty whiskey bottle and tossed it to the man. "Yeah, they're gone, but they were here."

"Why?" Elliott asked. "Where are they?"

Zac stooped down and stirred the coals of the fire. Reaching into his pocket, he took out his pipe and stuffed it with tobacco. He took out a still flaming stick and lit the pipe.

"We didn't figure on them buying time," Zac said. "It's an old trick. They know where they're going, they just wanted to slow us down a bit. They built a big fire, hoping to hold us up while we moved in to take them, and we did just that. There's some drinkers in that bunch, but whoever's leading 'em has some smarts."

"How far ahead you figure they are?" Fisher asked.

Zac stood up and moved through the hasty camp. "I figure they're about four hours ahead of us now. From the look of that fire, that'd be about right."

"It was pretty bright when we first spotted it," Fisher said.

Zac scuffed the ground with his moccasin. "Yeah, my fault. I should have seen it right off."

"Should we wait and go after them in the morning?" Elliott asked.

"No sense in turning a four-hour lead into eight. They'll be moving fast now. They know where they're going and so do we. Cañon City. If we ride on, we ought to get there about daybreak."

Zac found a rock and, holding it up, struck a match. It bore the same sign as the boulder in town — Elizabeth's star. "No," he said, "you can wait here and come on in the morning, but I'm lighting out now."

"If you're going, Cobb, then we're all going," Fisher said.

PART III

THE CANYON

Chapter 27

Eric Torkelson stood at the station, his right hand in his coat pocket and his left hand firmly gripping the battered briefcase. His jaw stuck out against the wind as he stared at the empty rails. His rumpled suit and uncovered blond head stood in stark contrast to the crowd of heavily armed men surrounding him. This was his first time as a member of a posse. He quietly clutched the leather satchel as if it were a lethal weapon. No one ever knew exactly what he carried in the bag, each man assuming something different about him. Many viewed him only as the general's secretary, some knew he was a lawyer and an accountant, but few men ever tried to nudge him into a tussle. The powerful build beneath his wrinkled clothes made them think twice. His silence caught most men unawares. He had a look of quiet confidence, even out of his element, and standing at the station with the armed detectives from the Denver and Rio Grande made him look particularly out of place. No one would have guessed he carried a pearl-handled revolver in a shoulder holster or that he was lugging fifteen thousand dollars in the beaten briefcase and not a bunch of the general's papers.

"You do have the court order with you?" the general asked. That Torkelson would be unprepared would be the last thing Roberts would have thought of him. Preparation and painstaking detail were the things that marked the man. But the general was nervous.

Torkelson didn't say a word. He simply lifted the papers from his breast pocket with his right hand and then slid them back out of sight. The general's appearance on that night did more to trouble Torkelson, however, than the event itself. Roberts was dressed in his high-top English riding boots with his hat pulled down over his eyes, and he carried a rifle, something Torkelson had never seen him do before. There was a look in Roberts's eyes that also unsettled him — a look of defiance, a steely-eyed determination that he had only heard about and that had seemed to disappear when the general's wife died.

Roberts took out his gold watch and pried open the lid. "Horace said he'd be pulling into the station at nine with a dozen deputies. The tracks from Denver are cleared and

I shouldn't expect him to be late."

Torkelson cleared his throat, something he was wont to do when nervous. "Will we have enough men? The Chicago Pacific has the roundhouse in Pueblo bottled up. I understand they have scores of detectives there, led by Bat Masterson."

Roberts's fingers tightened around the rifle. "I don't think gunplay will be necessary tonight, Torkelson. We have the law on our side. Whatever else those men in Pueblo may be, they are men who still have to live under the rule of law. The days of men doing as they please are over in Colorado."

Thoughts raced through Torkelson's mind, thoughts he wanted to speak. These were the same men who had kidnapped Elizabeth. They had chased the Elliotts through most of Kansas and Colorado, and somehow Torkelson knew that it would take more than a court document to stop them.

He knew all of that, but he didn't want to say any of it to Roberts's face. The general had too much respect for the law, too much belief in the wisdom of convention, and there was little need to tell him otherwise.

Roberts seemed to second-guess his own reasoning as he looked down at the weapon he carried. "Of course, should force become necessary, I have every confidence in the men here, the men and Sheriff Whitehead. Horace and I have known each other for years. I trust him and his judgment implicitly." He looked over the thirty-odd men standing on the platform with them. "I asked Horace to deputize these men when he arrived and I think our numbers, combined with the moral force of law, ought to be enough to carry the day." He paused, looking down the track. "We will go through Pueblo and then on to Cañon City and the Royal Gorge. If we can break the siege there and send those men who oppose us on their way, there will be no further need for the men who have Elizabeth to keep her."

Torkelson cleared his throat. "It seems reasonable, General, but those men I've seen from the CP don't strike me as reasonable people. They have too much at stake here, too much money already invested, and too much pride."

Roberts seemed to ignore the comment. He turned his back to Torkelson and paced the empty track. Nearby, on a flaming grate, a coffeepot was bubbling and several of the men proceeded to fill their cups with the scalding liquid. One of the men held out a cup to the general, but he waved it off and stepped back to Torkelson. He spoke in a soft, low voice, his eyes fastened on Torkelson.

"I know you're concerned, son, but you needn't be. I have no intention of getting you men killed here tonight. I will not risk one more human life for another section of track."

"I don't understand, sir," Torkelson said. "You're carrying a rifle."

"Leadership by example, son. My intention is to make a show of force, a show of force combined with the persuasion of the law, but my faith is not in that. My faith is in the Lord." He smiled and drew himself erect. "Eric, if we do His will, God will not allow His servants to suffer shame."

In spite of the general's expression of confidence, Torkelson could tell he was worried — worried about Elizabeth, and more than a little worried about the reliability of the men who were trying to find her.

"I am not like this Zac Cobb fellow," the general continued. "I went through the same war as he did, but in doing so, I swore never again to take another man's life. God's will for me is to build, not to kill and destroy."

"But, sir, there are times when it seems necessary to kill."

"I agree. But that is a burden I no longer will permit myself to carry. I will leave that to the men for whom God has intended it, men who must do such a thing because it is part of their nature. This man who stayed with us, this Zachary Cobb, he is such a man, but I am not. When I look into his eyes I see a troubled soul, a man who is not at peace with what he knows he must do, but a man who is being used by the Lord, nonetheless."

"How can a man be troubled when he's doing what he must do?" Torkelson asked the question knowing he would receive an answer. For him, working for Sydney Roberts had become more than a job, it was an education about life itself, and one that he valued.

"He is like an angel with a flaming sword," the general went on, "but a sword that will pierce his own heart if he is not careful. He is driven to do what is right. Something deep within him makes him use that gun of his. He fears no man. But somehow, Torkelson — and I do not know exactly why I feel this so strongly, save for my knowledge of men — I believe the only man he truly fears is himself."

"How can a man fear himself?"

"Cobb is a remarkably sensitive man, and also one who thinks deeply. I believe him to be a man who suspects what he is becoming and is afraid of the hardness that is developing in his own heart. That is something, my dear Torkelson, that I refuse for myself. No railroad is so dear that it warrants a trade for a hard heart."

Torkelson's face wrinkled as his heavy blond eyebrows and his mouth turned down.

"Does that confuse you, Torkelson?"

"Only in one sense, General. You see, I thought you had plans for this man."

"What sort of plans would I have for him?"

"Well, not business plans, sir . . . family plans, I suppose."

The general smiled. "Elizabeth has plans for him. But then, you know my daughter. She has her own mind, and I've found over the years that when a woman has her own mind about a matter it always remains unsettled if you solve it for them."

Torkelson nodded.

"No, Eric, my choice for Elizabeth has always been you from the first day I laid eyes on you. You offer the calm resolve in life that she so desperately needs. You have a determination that is not showy or flashy but deliberate and steady."

The shrill whistle of the train snapped their heads to the north. It sent fear up Torkelson's back. He wouldn't know what to do if it came to shooting. He didn't have the general's scruples. There was no resolve rooted inside him about solving a problem without gunplay. He had never been good with a gun and he didn't know what he would do if he had to use one, but one thing he did know, when it came to finding out, he wouldn't let fear control him.

Elizabeth's roan picked its way across the rocks on the trail. For some time she had been able to see the lights of the town and the tracks that ran through the valley below. It gave her some degree of confidence to know the direction her captors were taking her, but confidence was something she had never been known to lack.

"These ropes are too tight. They are making my fingers numb."

The tall Englishman rode up to her and, reaching over, tested the ropes. He loosened them slightly. "It wouldn't do to have those dainty hands of yours damaged, Miss Roberts." He smiled. "I would find it difficult to live with myself if you should suffer."

"I find it hard to believe you have any degree of conscience whatsoever, Williams."

He rode along beside her as she bounced with her hands behind her back. "Oh, many things would surprise you about me, Miss Roberts. I am a man of letters, quite educated, and very aware."

The bearded thug that rode ahead of her,

holding the reins of the roan, laughed. "You wants I should untie her, Mr. Williams? I could hold her hand, if you like."

"Would that be preferable to you, Miss Roberts?" the Englishman asked.

She lowered her voice and spoke through clenched teeth. "I think you know the answer to that, Williams. If one of you dares to lay a hand on me, my father would not rest while any of you still has breath in him."

"Oh, you'd like me, little lady," the bearded man went on. "The womenfolk all find me handsome to look on." He turned his head back toward her and smiled, gaps in his teeth visible through the heavy black beard.

She lifted her chin and looked forward, past him.

"I think we will find your father quite agreeable to our demands when we reach the canyon." The Englishman's words poked at her. "When he sees you there and realizes the hopelessness of his situation, we can concur on a settlement that will satisfy everyone."

"I don't think you'll ever make it to the canyon," she shot back.

"Oh, we will get there, Miss Roberts, rest assured of that."

Elizabeth was the type of woman who had

always interested Williams. She knew her own mind, thought herself to be the equal of any man — the woman was dangerous. Ordinarily, Williams viewed women as something used for momentary diversion. This one could hold his attention for a long time. Right now what he wanted most of all was the satisfaction of breaking her spirit.

"You don't actually believe that Wells Fargo agent has any interest in what happens to you, do you? I know his type. He and I are professionals, that's how we stay alive. He wants to go home. He wants the reward you have already paid him, and he wants to free himself from being involved in someone else's fight. No, he's been living on borrowed time for a week now. Why would he want to do anything other than pocket your money and take the next westward bound train? You are living a delusion, Elizabeth Roberts."

"Who is living the delusion here?" She spat out the words. "Who are you trying to convince, me or you?" She looked at him and smiled slyly. "You know good and well that he's behind us, and when he finds you, he will kill you. That's what I want to see, Williams, the look of fear in your face when you see him."

The bravado of the woman stung him, but

he maintained his composure. "Even if he were behind us, he would be far too cautious to plunge headlong into the darkness and try to follow our trail. He may be impetuous, but he is not foolish, and by now he is too far behind us to attempt any sort of rescue."

Elizabeth didn't respond. She looked ahead in the direction of the rocky trail. She knew one thing: anything she could do to slow these men down would be worth the risk. Riding a horse through the darkness at full speed with her hands at her back was something she might attempt in spite of the risk, but the man in front of her held the reins too tightly. Any attempt to break free wouldn't get very far. But maybe she could orchestrate a fall. A delay would be worth the bumps and bruises.

She watched the roan pick his way over the trail. She'd find her spot to fall. In the darkness, she might even be able to roll free and slip away. But she couldn't fall on the rocks; a broken arm or leg would be disastrous. If she could manage to panic two of the men into doing something foolish, something that might reduce their guard over her, there might be a chance.

"I think you're overconfident, Williams. Maybe he didn't fall for the notion of your making camp so early. I know I wouldn't have. I would have drawn my gun and ridden right into that camp, and if that's what he did he could be overhearing us right now."

She could see that the remark hit a bull's-eye, even though the Englishman tried to maintain a poker face. She'd played poker with the men of the railroad enough to know when a man doubted his hand, and right now Williams was doubting his. He drew up his reins.

"Stay on the trail," he said to the man leading the roan. "We will heed Miss Roberts's advice and double back a short distance. Then we will catch up with you."

He jerked the reins and signaled two of the men to follow him. Elizabeth listened to the three of them ride back into the darkness. She had won. Even if nothing more happened, she took great satisfaction in the fact.

It was only a matter of minutes until the two of them rounded a bend with enough moonlight for her to see the ground ahead. To her side they were approaching a slope of clear ground, one that offered her a chance to roll down the hill and into the rocks. The full moon peeked through the clouds.

Elizabeth looked up at it. "That's a china moon," she said. "My mother used to say that when the moon was full like that, it looked like a china plate."

The man stopped the horses and looked up. "Guess it does at that."

"Mother said people do strange things in the light of a china moon."

As the man moved the horses forward, she slipped her right foot from the stirrup and hung it loosely for a few seconds. Then she jumped.

Chapter 28

The men from the Denver and Rio Grande had all been sworn in as deputies. The entire contingent of suddenly official lawmen were crammed into two passenger cars of the special train tighter than nails in a penny keg. Torkelson sat at the back of the car, near the door, clutching his satchel and watching the men try to check their firearms and struggle for more space at the same time. He'd agreed to ride in the car, but just now he envied the general riding up in the locomotive with the engineer, fireman, Governor Hunt, and the sheriff. Just a puff of cool Colorado air, free from the sweat and tobacco that filled the car would have been a welcome relief.

He watched the men carefully. Many of them were new to the D&RG, but Roberts felt they could all be trusted to do their duty. It was one of the things that Torkelson was most concerned about. The general simply trusted too many people to do the right thing, just on their say-so. Many times Eric had heard the man say, "Men won't always do what you tell them to do, but they generally do what you expect them to do." The general would smile and then add, "The trick is to expect them to do the best work possible." Eric only wished his nature allowed him that kind of confidence. Maybe it was the lawyer in him that made him see the worst in men, or the accountant side that required exactness and detail, but whatever it was, he'd never have the general's trust in men. He knew that.

The ride to Pueblo would be a short one. Eric only hoped that when they got there, the general's view of men would be the accurate one. Somehow, though, looking at this mob of men in the car with him, Eric was unconvinced that the people they were going up against would see the moral force of the law in these men's unshaved faces. He grunted. Those men who worked for the CP were like any other hired guns. They were more than likely the spitting image of the men in the car with him. They respected guns and they positively revered money, but they didn't give a hoot for the law.

The brakes grabbed the rails and the wheels squealed. The huddle of men squeezed forward as the train slowed to a halt. Eric stood up and held on to the seat to keep from being pitched headlong into the men seated in front of him. He straightened up, opened the door, and stepped onto the rear landing of the car.

Swinging himself down to the ground, he could see the lights of Pueblo in the distance. He ran forward to the locomotive. When he reached it, he shouted into the darkened cab. "General? General Roberts? Is there a problem?"

The engineer leaned his head out the door of the cab. "The general, the governor, and the sheriff have gone down the track. There's a feller with a signal lamp up ahead."

Eric ran to catch up with whatever decision was being made. He knew it wasn't his to make, but advice was what Roberts paid him for, and Eric was going to see to it that the man got his money's worth.

Eric ran up to the four men standing on the tracks and stopped to listen. Roberts made no introductions, so Eric just stood beside him as the man with the now-darkened signal lamp made his report.

"Them rail yards won't be no problem fer ya. Mosta them boys done cleared out and gone to the canyon. There's a few of 'em though, and they might take a snap shot at ya, but ya still sure nuff got to get yerself through that there roundhouse, and unless you got some kinda army back there, y'all jes' ain't agonna make it."

"Well, we do have an army back there and, by Jupiter, we intend to use it." The governor had always been known to use his mouth first in anything that required thinking, and even though he was now the former governor, Eric saw that little had changed with the man.

The general looked at Sheriff Whitehead. "That roundhouse will be a formidable obstacle to our passage, Horace. It's solid, and easily defended."

"Worse 'en dat, General," the man went on. "Them boys gots themselves a Gatling gun in there. I watched 'em shoot it off tonight. It's a fearful sight to see in the dark, like some kinda fire-breathing dragon, only worse, lots worse."

The general and Sheriff Whitehead took the news in stunned silence and stood there, absorbing what they had heard.

"These men of ours are courageous," the governor said. "They will not be stopped by a revolving cannon."

"How many men are in there?" Eric asked, patently ignoring the governor's comment.

"Near fifty, I'd say, maybe more."

"Fifty? Are you sure of that?" The sheriff's nervousness was apparent. He swallowed. "General Roberts, this man's right. It will take the army to get them boys outta there.

We'll have to wire for them."

"We'll have the army," the governor said. "Cavalry can be here tomorrow, tomorrow night at the latest."

Roberts's head dropped. "Horace, I cannot expect you to allow your men to be put to such great risk." He fell silent. Lifting his head, he looked off in the direction of the lights of Pueblo. "I'm afraid I'm beaten. In spite of what you say, Governor, I know the army. By the time it responds to this, my men in the gorge will have been dead and gone for a week. Plus, my daughter is in those people's hands."

"Do you know," Eric asked, "if Masterson is leading those men in the roundhouse?"

Roberts, the governor, and Sheriff Whitehead stared at him, but the man in the shadows nodded. "You durn betcha he is. He's a slick one, that man is."

"Is the man they call Doc Holliday with them in there as well?"

"Nah, don't believe so. I'da known it, if'n he wuz."

"Why do you ask, Torkelson? Is there something you know?" The general usually called him by his last name in the presence of others. Eric knew it was so other men would sense no favoritism in the way he was treated. He never viewed the formality as a slam when it happened. He understood perfectly well. Besides, when the two of them were alone, he knew there was an affection that passed between them that would have been hard for others to understand. It was as if he were the man's son, the son he never had.

"Well, General, I hope you won't hold this against me, but I do play poker from time to time. When I play, however, I try never to make it a game of chance. It's a game whereby one learns to depend on the laws of probability. There is a probability in the cards, and when you get to know the men you're playing against you learn there's a probability in them as well."

The sound of the steam escaping from the locomotive behind them momentarily diverted the men, but then Eric continued. "I've played poker with both Masterson and Holliday before. If the good dentist were in there, then I'd say that what I've got in mind would never work. You see, Doc Holliday is rarely motivated by money. For him, it's the thrill, the risk, the chance. He loves to watch you sweat."

"You have a plan, then?" the general asked.

"Yes, General, I have a plan. We'll have to get close to the roundhouse. But when we do, I think I can take care of the problem there." Eric knew this might be his only chance to show the men with guns how a businessman could work and he was going to take it.

"By yourself?" the sheriff asked.

"That's the only way it will work."

Elizabeth wrestled with the ropes behind her. She crouched low behind the rocks and then moved ever so slightly down the hill. Each time she moved she felt as if she were a blind person stumbling through the darkness.

Without her hands, she couldn't feel for the best place to put her feet and, to her, the sound of the sliding rocks and snapping twigs resulting from her movement were deafening. She watched the man up on the trail continue to look for her, but he was looking at where she had been only moments before, not where she was now. The sound of his horse walking through the brush had covered the sound of her movement. Her heart pounded. If he stopped for a moment and listened carefully, she knew she would be heard. The man had no light. In some ways, he was as crippled by blindness as she was by the ropes that held her hands fast. The farther away from the trail she could get herself, the better off she would be.

She slid down the hill a bit farther and, crouching next to a large rock, felt for a rough edge. She didn't care about any damage to her hands. She simply had to get the ropes off. Continuing to watch the man frantically search the trail, she groped the rock with her fingers.

There! She had found it. A sharp edge! She turned her back to it and began to rub the rope against it with great vigor. Scooting her wrists up and down over the rock, she could feel the sharp edge bite into her skin. She rubbed on, digging deeper into the ropes as well as her wrists.

The man uphill from her had now remounted and was beating the brush on horseback. He had taken his rope off the pommel of his saddle and was using it to whip at the tops of the scrub oak that dotted the hillside. He swung his horse from side to side and walked it down the hill slightly. Pulling up, he looked carefully over the rocks.

Elizabeth continued to bite at the ropes with the sharp rock edge. She watched the man on horseback silhouetted against the dark sky. When the man moved his horse again, she knew she'd have to move. With or without her wrists being free, she couldn't chance staying where she was any longer. She only hoped the sound of the man's horse moving through the brush would continue to cover the noise of her movement.

She watched as the man once again dropped his glance toward the ground and beat at the brush. She could tell he was panic-stricken. From what little she knew of Peter Williams, she knew he was a man who didn't suffer fools well. This man had reason to be unnerved.

She edged her way around the rock and moved her feet over the ground. The snap of a twig beneath her feet horrified her. She froze. She could tell the man on horseback had heard it too. He spurred his horse downhill, in her direction. She stooped down beside the rock as he veered off to her right.

Only the rock stood between her and the man now. She could see him looking over its edge, but he wasn't looking in her direction. She felt helpless. She didn't want to have to depend on Zac Cobb or on any man who might be following her. She'd always been able to kill her own snakes, and she didn't want to start now with the idea that men would be the ones to rescue her when she got into trouble. The man would find her if he kept exploring the rock, but she couldn't move, not now. To move and risk the chance of another noise with the man so close to her would mean certain capture. To stay where she was would mean the man would probably find her as well. She prayed.

Suddenly, she heard the sound of horses' hooves on the trail above them. The man towering above her on horseback jerked his head around in the direction of the noise. "Down here!" he yelled.

Elizabeth watched the man move his horse up the hill, toward the riders on the trail. This was the only chance she had. Unless she got some distance on the men now, she would once again become their prisoner, or worse. She moved around the rock, putting it between her and the men. She listened as the man approached the others.

"She's down here," he called out. "She jumped off'n her horse and she's down here."

Elizabeth heard the horses making their way down the hill and took the opportunity to move away from the rock and into the brush. She stumbled, but she was sure the sound of the approaching horses had covered the noise of her fall. Scooting her feet back under her, she got up and continued to move down the hill. She could hear the men talking as she moved through the brush. She could make out the shrill sound of the Englishman now. He was angry. She began to run, moving between the rocks and the junipers.

The men on horseback fanned out and moved down the hill in her direction, carefully picking their way through the rocks and brush. She kept watching them as she moved. If only they would move to the side. But they seemed determined to follow her path through the darkness and down the hill.

She squatted down beside a rock and once again rubbed the ropes that held her. Desperate, she scraped them hard; suddenly, they snapped. She reached for her wrists and held them. Then putting them to her mouth, she wet the chafed area with her spittle. Her wrists burned.

She moved off toward the north. The men seemed determined to move down the hill, and she figured if she could make her way around them, she might have a chance to get away. If she could get back up to the trail, behind the men who were searching for her, then maybe she could run toward the men who had been following them. She skirted around the brush, keeping low and still focusing her attention on the men uphill.

The moon hung low, but clouds had turned the night into semiblackness. While they muted the moonlight from the landscape, Elizabeth moved north with deliberation. With her hands free, she felt a growing confidence. She stepped lightly over and around the rocks, momentarily snagging her blouse on some mesquite. Pulling it free, she crept on.

She lost sight of the men and knew she had managed to get around them and above them. She alternately jogged and walked briskly until the sight of the trail brought a great sense of relief. The clouds momentarily moved off the moon and the light showed her the direction she needed to go. It seemed to her that God had smiled on her efforts and was making it easier for her to move quickly in the direction of her rescuers. She was determined to put as much distance between her and the men looking for her as she could.

She began to run. The excitement and tension had suppressed her fatigue, but now she was feeling tired. She ran up the trail and spotted the creek the horses had stepped over some time ago. Reaching it, she dropped to her knees. Leaning down to the rippling water, she drank deeply from the stream. Sitting up, she splashed her face, then dipped her swollen wrists into the cold water, feeling the sting on the burns and cuts. The momentary pain was soothing.

Once again she leaned over the stream and drank.

"I wondered how long it would take you to come back here."

The words of the Englishman jerked her head up, the water dripping from her face. The man had stepped out of the trees and stood over her, his hands on his hips.

"You are quite the ambitious one, Elizabeth Roberts, but oh, so predictable."

Elizabeth slowly got to her feet. Her heart sank. Everything inside of her seemed to die.

"I was not about to search the bushes for you. I simply surmised that you'd find your way back to the trail and be here taking refreshment." Williams took her arm. His fingers bit into the muscle. "I brought your horse. You've cost us some precious time, so we'll have to travel with great haste."

She pulled her arm free. "You'll regret this," she said.

"Oh no, Miss Roberts. You are the one who will regret what you've done." He smiled. "I have a very special place in mind for you, a place those who are searching for you will never find. The men following us could look for years and never discover your whereabouts."

Chapter 29

The juniper valley that lay along the path to Cañon City stretched before Zac and his companions. They had followed the trail left by the men who had taken Elizabeth. The markings were so clear in the moonlight that Zac could easily distinguish the tracks left by the roan that Elizabeth rode. When he came to the spot on the trail where she had dismounted, he stooped down and looked at the trail.

"Looks like she left 'em here," he said. He walked up the trail a little farther and crouched low over the beaten path. " 'Pears to me, they all mounted up here. There was some scuffle and the like." He stood up and looked down the trail into the valley. Holding his hand straight out, he signaled down the trail. He saw the marks of deep digs in the soil, marks that would only be left by horses on the run. "They all lit outta here like the devil himself was on to 'em. They're not covering their tracks very well." He mounted the bay. "Seems like they ain't hardly tryin'."

Bruce Elliott seemed puzzled. "I'm afraid I don't understand. Why wouldn't they try to conceal their tracks?"

"They wouldn't need to hide where they're goin' if'n they was going straight on to Cañon City," Fisher said. "Them well-traveled streets there would cover most any tracks. Does make things a little queer, though."

"How's that?" Elliott asked.

"Elizabeth Roberts is not 'zackly somebody you could confuse with anybody else on the street. If they take her into Cañon City, somebody's bound to recognize her. And that's got to be where they're bound for. Anyplace else, they'd be more careful."

Zac clapped his spurs to the sides of the bay and the animal lurched forward, followed by Fisher and Elliott. Tracking men was what he did for a living, and tracking their minds first is what made it easier. If he knew the men, he'd know where they were going. They needed food, shelter, water, protection, to conceal their stolen loot, or to set up an ambush to rake off their pursuers. There just weren't that many options for hunted men. If he could figure what the men they were following needed, he'd know where to find them. Right now, he knew what these men needed most of all . . . a place to safely store Elizabeth Roberts, a place out of sight, a place she could not run away from.

Zac slowed the bay down to a canter. He thought they'd take her to some abandoned mine, or some other safehouse near the disputed canyon. They'd need to have her close enough to produce her when it came time for the showdown. A man had to show his chips in any poker game, and Elizabeth was the ultimate chip in this high-stakes game. It was a puzzle, but one he'd think on as they rode. He didn't want them to get too far ahead. Elizabeth had done her best to slow them down. That was just like her. She'd done her part, and Zac was going to make sure that whoever it was who had her wouldn't have any rest or food before they got to Cañon City. He'd stay on their tails all the way into town.

Elliott rode up next to him. "I do hope they haven't hurt her," he said.

"Well, I'm sure as the world she's given 'em plenty of cause."

"You don't think —"

Zac stopped him midsentence. "No, I don't think they've hurt her. Whatever trouble she is, she's still Elizabeth Roberts. Anybody who lays a hand on her, providing she doesn't turn it into a bloody stump, is gonna be looking through the cottonwood leaves on the end of a rope." He held his hand to his mouth and spoke in a low tone. "Sound carries out here."

The train pulled into the rail yard in Pueblo and several men leaped from it, scrambling into the darkness. Eric watched from the window as one of the men climbed over baggage and onto the top of the station while the other men crouched beside the door. He watched the man on top cut the telegraph wires and signal to the men below. Two men kicked in the door. He heard the gunfire explode from inside, flashes of it coming through the window. The thought that men inside the building were probably dying sent a shiver up his spine.

The gunfire stopped and the train, now at a dead stop, hissed steam in the sudden silence. Eric rubbed his hands in a circular motion on the window. The night air had combined with the breath of the men on board to fog up the windows.

The man on the top of the station had now slithered his way to the platform itself, and the two men who had gone inside emerged from the station and stood on the platform, ejecting empty shells from their chambers. Eric heard the holler from the engine, a voice shouting at the three men. All heads turned in the direction of the voice. As one, they jostled in the direction of the train. The engine began to lurch forward. The men caught the passing platform and jumped aboard. Eric watched all three men come through the doors and take their seats as they continued the process of reloading their weapons.

Eric got up from his seat and walked to the rear platform, his heart pounding. With all the shooting he had just witnessed, what he had in mind might make him a convenient target. The men from the CP might even consider his death a means to partially settle the score. He swallowed and clutched the briefcase under his arm. Something had to happen soon to settle this. In his mind, business and only business could end the war. As it was, everybody was losing money, lots of it. This stretch of track was fast becoming the most expensive steel ever laid, and there wasn't a man working for either railroad who didn't know that for a fact.

Eric knew he had to do something to stop it even if it meant risking his own neck. There would be enough congratulations, promotions, bonuses, and handshakes to go around if this nonsense came to a halt. On the other hand, certain factors could make it so that the war would never end. Certainly any harm to Elizabeth Roberts would bring the house down around everybody's head, but short of that everything was forgivable where there was enough money involved.

Once again, Eric felt the train's brakes take hold. He knew this would be his chance. There was nothing gained by waiting. The roundhouse was out there in the darkness, bristling with gunslingers and an engine of mass death, a Gatling gun. He stepped out onto the platform and watched the train pull to a halt. He could see the strange building in the darkness. Trains seemed to peek out of tunnels at the table and on it sat the 444. He could see several barricades erected in front of the table and strung out on either side of the 444. He couldn't see any of the men of the CP but he knew they were there, looking out at him right now. He could sense the smell of death in the night air. He swung down from the platform stairs and stepped to the ground.

Eric walked slowly to the engine. He knew very well what an inviting target he was. He was no hero, but he was ambitious. That was why he'd studied law and accounting. He knew out West, working for the railroads, that the combination of both would be indispensable. It wasn't that he loved money, although the things it could buy were pleasurable. What he really loved was the ability to prove himself. And proving himself meant using his considerable business skills to overcome any obstacle in his path.

He stood beside the darkened engine cab. "I guess I'll go on in there," he said.

"We'll cover you, boy." The governor shoved a rifle out the window of the cab.

"Please, Governor," Eric said, "put that thing away. I can't see that it will do me any good, and it might just get me killed if they see it."

"Torkelson's right," Roberts interjected. "He's out there taking all the risk right now. It's his decision, and he's on his own." The general stooped down and, staying low in the engine, spoke to Eric. "Are you sure you want to do this, Eric? We have enough men here to take those people — they're not to be trusted."

Eric swallowed. "When it comes to the high freight rates to Leadville, I'm not sure anyone is to be trusted, General. No, I've made up my mind. This can only be solved by the use of good business sense. I will make a deal with those men in there, a deal too good for them to turn down."

With that, he turned and walked in the direction of the turntable with its bristling battlements. He held both arms directly away from his body. The briefcase was light, but with his arms extended it seemed to be made of lead. He could see that several men behind the barricade had poked rifle muzzles from behind the piles of railroad ties. There was also some talking going on.

"Bat! Bat Masterson!" He called out to the battlement with some hope that the man he had gambled with on several occasions might recognize his voice. "It's me, Masterson . . . Eric Torkelson."

From behind the barrier Eric heard a slight laugh. "Torkelson? That really you out there?"

"Yes, it's me, and I want to talk."

"Are you armed?"

Eric had forgotten about the revolver under his coat. The oversight now made him a little nervous. "I have a pistol in a holster under my left arm. Can I take it out?"

"Best to do that, Torkelson, but do it slowly."

Eric set the briefcase down on the ground and carefully used two fingers to remove the nickel-plated pistol from under his arm. Holding the weapon away from him, he stooped down and set it deliberately on the ground. Behind him, the locomotive spouted steam out its sides.

"All right, Mr. Attorney, walk toward us, but do it slow and easy."

Eric bent down to pick up his briefcase and suddenly several rifles were leveled in his direction. "It's okay!" he shouted at them. "I just need to get my papers here."

"It's all right, boys," Eric heard Masterson give instructions. "He's a lawyer and a paper pusher. He more'n likely couldn't shoot a dying dog."

Eric slowly picked up the bag and stood tall. He knew what Masterson said was probably true, but it galled him, nevertheless. He walked slowly toward the wall of railroad timber and stopped within ten feet of it. He could clearly see Masterson now. "Bat, I need to speak to you privately. Can you come out to me? I can vouch for your safety."

Masterson swung his head from side to side, looking at the men on either side of him. Eric sensed his hesitancy. "I can make this all worth your while, if you just trust me," he said.

Masterson blinked his eyes in Eric's direction. "All right." With that he walked around the stack of railroad ties and out to where Eric was standing.

"Listen, Bat, this is bad business, but I know you to be a reasonable man. We have a court order turning all of this track and property back over to the Denver and Rio Grande, and we have the sheriff and two hundred deputies to back it up."

"I don't care if you have the spirits of the Seventh Cavalry behind you. My orders say no one is to pass."

"I'm afraid we will have the cavalry here in a matter of days."

"You have that Cobb fella in there with you?"

Eric shook his head. "No."

Masterson smiled. "For a minute you had me worried."

"You should be worried. He's out tracking the men from your railroad who have kidnapped General Roberts's daughter."

"That's bad," Masterson said.

"There won't be a man in the territory who will offer you any help when word of this gets out, and if anything happens to that woman, there will be hangings."

Masterson crossed his arms over his chest. "None of that was my doing."

"I know that, Bat, but I'm not sure anybody else does. I do want to make things worth your while, however."

"How's that?"

"Well, you and I both know that long after men like you have done your fighting, dying, and hanging. . . ." Eric threw the notion in of hanging because he had plainly seen on Masterson's face how the thought of Elizabeth's kidnapping and the hysteria that might spread to a lynch mob had worried the man. "Anyway, after the fighting is over, men who are behind a desk and riding in private cars will exchange money, sign papers, and smoke cigars. Nothing will change. They'll have their railroad, and you'll have six feet of fresh dirt."

"What are you suggesting?"

Eric held up the briefcase. "In here, I've got fifteen thousand dollars. Five thousand in gold and currency for you, and ten thousand to be divided among the men you have in there with you. Of course, you can feel free to distribute it in any way you desire."

Masterson's eyes twinkled. "You think you can bribe me, Torkelson?"

"This isn't a bribe," Eric shot back. "This is simply payment for services rendered. I rather doubt that either you or the men in there are stockholders in the Chicago Pacific Railroad. You have no personal stake in this thing one way or the other. You are simply a businessman, trying to make a living in the manner in which you choose. Now, if you tried to offer some remuneration to the sheriff on board our train, or his deputies, or the judge that signed the legal order instructing us to take back this building and track, that would be bribery."

"You are the lawyer, aren't you?"

"That's what I was trained to be, Bat, a lawyer. And a rather good one, I might add."

"Well, if I ever get in a jam with the law, you're the man I want sitting at the table with me, Torkelson. I can handle you with cards in both our hands, but this way you've got me in your own game and with your own deck."

Eric was silent. Long ago he had learned the simple truth that when you lay a proposal before someone and call the question, the next person who speaks loses. There was a brief moment of silence.

"All right, Torkelson. You just walk away. Sit the bag down and walk away. I'll handle everything inside. I'll pay the men and give them a running start while you and those people you call deputies just stay on that train. Is that understood?"

Eric nodded and set down the bag. He paused beside the revolver on the ground and looked at Masterson.

"Go on. Pick it up and put it away. Just do yourself a favor, Torkelson, never try to use it. You stick to pencils, it's the thing you do best."

Eric picked up the revolver and shoved it back into his holster. Turning away, he walked back to the train and stood below the darkened cab door. He spoke to Roberts, who was standing in the door. "All right, it's over. We'll have to wait for them to clear out, but they will."

"How did you ever do it, Torkelson?"

"I used the money I was carrying, the reward money."

"You mean to say you bought those men off?" the governor blustered.

"I just made it worth their while to leave, and in the process saved a few lives."

"How will we get that much cash in hand again if those men try to make a deal for Elizabeth?"

"General, that's what I'm counting on Mr. Cobb to do. With him involved, I doubt we will need cash. His methods are much different than mine."

Chapter 30

Williams called a halt to the fast pace as they rounded the bend on the trail that over-looked Cañon City. He signaled to the men and they moved down the hill. Barricades had been erected along the railroad tracks snaking into town, and Elizabeth realized that Cañon City was fast becoming an armed camp for the CP.

The streets were quiet in the predawn hours. No music poured out of the saloon doors, and the people of the night had crawled back into their daytime habitats. As they rode through one of the side streets, Elizabeth could see that the traffic in the town and the busyness of the coming day would do much to confuse anyone who was trying to follow them.

A swamper stood at the door of one of the brightly lit saloons and leaned on his mop, watching the riders pass by and turn up the street in front of him. Williams, who had lagged behind the others, glared at the man, then turned his face away from him and slowly walked his horse up the street.

Ahead were the walls of the prison. The structure was ominous-looking, its walls dark and forbidding. Williams signaled to a man on the wall and then led the way around the structure. They circled the walls of the prison, stopping at a white house that stood next to the rear wall. Williams swung his leg off his horse and got to the ground. He walked up to Elizabeth.

"Welcome to your new home, Miss Roberts. It may not be the castle you have grown accustomed to, but you will find it is much safer." He reached up and took her by the arm, gently pulling her off the horse.

She straightened her riding dress. "This is lower than I thought even you would be capable of, Williams." She held out her hands. "Untie me."

He grinned. "Oh, I am an exceptionally capable man, Miss Roberts, and an inventive one as well." He took out his knife to cleanly slice the rope around her wrists. "I think you may be shocked to discover that your father is not the beloved hero of southern Colorado that you thought. There are many citizens who are willing to do whatever it takes to stop that railroad of yours. One of them just happens to be the new warden here."

"You will pay for this." Elizabeth sat down on the rocky curb in front of the house and, lifting her dress, began to gently massage her ankles. As the men uncinched their horses, she picked up a sharp rock. She kept an eye on them as she scrawled a star on the boardwalk. Leaving the sign had become the only way she could attempt to affect the circumstances of her life now. It was a small effort, but it was important to her. Elizabeth had always taken charge of her own life. She never viewed herself as a passive shrinking violet who merely allowed men to move her around at will. Whatever she could do now to help maintain her view of herself as someone to be reckoned with was all-important. She watched Williams loosen his saddle and then she scooted over to cover the star.

"Miss Roberts, when we deliver the ultimatum to your father, he will be so overjoyed at having you back at his side that he will be willing to overlook what we have done."

He walked over to her as she positioned herself firmly over her sign. She braced herself as he took her arm and pulled her up. "I'll see you hanged for kidnapping," she said. She looked around at the other men. "You and every low-life mixed up with you."

The group mounted the stairs that led to the porch of the attractive white house. The door opened as they approached, and a dapper man in a suit and tie stepped outside the door and closed it. The man was thin. He wore a heavily waxed mustache, and streaks of hair were plastered over the top of his otherwise bald head. He looked nervous.

"I have a place for her," he said, "but you'll have to be very quiet. No talking when you go through the house. My wife's asleep and you mustn't wake her." The man anxiously surveyed Elizabeth. "If my missus knew what I was doing, I'd never get another night's sleep."

Williams nodded his head and the man hesitantly opened the door and let them in. The lamps were turned low and flickered over the overstuffed red velvet furniture. They quietly shuffled their way through the house.

"Brave man you have here," Elizabeth said.

Williams dug his fingers into her arm. She ground her teeth slightly and glared at him.

Walking out the back door, the warden signaled to the guard on the wall. They made their way around the prison as the first hints of dawn began to color the peaks to the west. The splash of pink that painted the far rocks caused the men to pick up their pace. Darkness had been their cover, the early hour virtually guaranteeing that no one would be stirring about. The warden placed a hefty key into a steel door at the back of the prison and turned the lock.

They moved into a long corridor. Lamps shone faintly on the surface of the rough rock, barely lighting the passageway toward a darkened corner of the cellblock. Other lamps were apparently left unlit for the purpose of creating a black hole in the deepest part of the prison. The warden fumbled with the keys until he found the right one. Twisting it into the massive lock, he pushed open the heavy, windowless door. Williams led Elizabeth in as the warden struck a match to light the lamp on the wall inside the cell.

He blew out the match and turned to Williams. "I will need more money for the guard on the wall. He's the one who will be bringing Miss Roberts her meals." He glanced sheepishly at her. "Of course, I will look in on her myself from time to time."

Williams reached inside his inner jacket pocket and produced a roll of bills. Counting out a number of large ones, he planted them in the warden's hand. "That ought to satisfy your needs," he said. Turning to Elizabeth, he smiled. "This ought to keep you out of harm's way."

Elizabeth frowned. "From harming you, you mean?"

"Be that as it may, Miss Roberts, you are

best advised to keep quiet. The men who are housed down the hall would like nothing better than to know that a fine figure of womanhood is living within reach. If one of them should find a key . . . well, none of us could claim any responsibility. . . ."

"They can't be any worse than you," Elizabeth shot back.

Williams removed his hat and raked his hand through his hair. He sighed deeply. "I won't see you again, my dear, at least not until a deal has been struck. In the meantime, save your insults for the rats." Williams tipped his hat to her, and the warden quietly slipped out of the cell, slamming the door shut behind him and turning the key.

Zac rode down the hill as the sun was beginning to rise. Sam Fisher and Bruce Elliott had been riding hard, trying to keep up. They reined their horses in as Zac stepped down from his.

"They're down in Cañon City, then," Sam said.

Zac looked at the trail that led toward the town. He crouched down to study it more closely.

"We better get down there and see if we can catch 'em." Fisher was anxious to move on. "They're more'n likely curled up nexta some eggs and hot coffee right now."

"Shouldn't we go on, Cobb?" Elliott prodded.

Zac got up from his squatting position, stepped to his saddlebags, and pulled out a handful of oats. Putting his hand to the big bay's mouth, he watched the animal lap up the grain.

"We don't wanna lose 'em, Cobb," Fisher said.

Zac brushed off the few loose oats remaining in his hand and mounted the bay. "Those people have been in an awful hurry to get here. It had to be for a good reason. I don't hanker to ride into some ambush. Plus, if I was them and didn't plan on staying, I'd be on my way to the livery to swap those played out animals for something fresh."

Fisher and Elliott looked at each other, and Sam bit his lower lip. Thinking was a big part of what it meant to be a good detective, and apparently that was what Zac was doing now. Even though they'd been chasing the people who had Elizabeth, he knew the mind was a good way to catch people too. He wanted to charge into town like a man after a fire, but thinking first was important right now.

"You want Elliott and me to check the

stables whilst you circle round to the west? If they've lit out you'll find the trail, and if we spot them horses of theirs we'll come a runnin'. Don't suppose those horses will be hard to pick out."

"Reckon not," Zac said.

It made Sam feel good that he'd been able to contribute in the thinking department, even if his plan was something Zac would have said anyway. The three of them split up and Sam and Bruce watched Zac circle the town to the west.

As Fisher and Elliott rode into the dawn-lit street of town, they heard the usual sounds of a new day — barking dogs and the sweeping of stiff brooms on the boardwalks.

Sam nodded at the men, who received his greeting with silent stares. The railroad war had put everybody on edge, and any stranger who rode in was sized up by anyone who saw him. Sam could tell by the looks of the men with the brooms that they all wondered which side Bruce and he were on. He sat his horse like a toad on a wet rock, and anybody who knew anything about men could easily decipher that he was no passing cowboy, not the way he looked on horseback, not the way his derby hat was tilted on his head. He was out of place and he knew it, and the college professor who rode at his side looked equally odd.

Only a few shops and a couple of cafes showed any signs of life, and there was only one buggy tied at a hitching rail. As they passed one of the saloons, Sam spotted the swamper leaning on his mop. Beside the man sat a drunk sobering up from a long night of bad whiskey. Sam looked the two men up and down as he and Bruce continued to ride up the street toward the stable.

The two gingerly dismounted their horses in front of the livery. Sam knew that if the men they were after had exchanged horses, tracking them would be difficult. Fresh horses would be harder to catch, too. They might be able to get three more, but then again, if they were at all suspect, getting three horses would not be easy. Cañon City was, after all, a CP town, and the horses they were on carried a brand any stableman would recognize. "We better tie the horses up out here," Sam said.

The two of them pushed the big door open and walked into the stables. Inside, a small, skinny man was forking hay into several stalls. The man was still in his red long johns and stopped his work when he saw them.

"Can I help you fellers?" he asked.

"All depends," Sam said. "Got some good horses to rent out?"

"Tarnation! Sure is mighty early to be doing such business. Just sold one to a foreign feller."

Sam didn't need to know any more to be sure who the man was talking about and didn't want to arouse suspicion by asking too many questions. He creased his mouth with a forced smile. "He musta been in a hurry like we are."

"Guess so. Mighty early to be in such a hurry if'n you ask me." The man forked the hay he was holding into the stall. "You boys let me finish with these horses and then I'll show you what I got." He pitched more hay. "Got a few good ones left that ain't been spoken for. Got some for sale and some for rent."

Sam walked over to the horses in the stalls the man was attending to and looked them over. He could see they were the animals they had been chasing all night. They were played out and badly in need of washing. There was also no mistaking the big roan. It was a Glen Eyrie horse, the one Elizabeth had ridden. "You say you only sold one?" he asked.

"That be what I said. Only one horse, a fine buckskin gelding to boot."

"Five rode in and only one rode out."

The man continued the feeding and then stopped, leaning on his pitchfork. "Yeah, queer, ain't it. Comin' in here so early, wakin' me up and all, and then just swapping for one horse."

"An Englishman, you say."

The man looked at Sam and cocked his head to the side. "I didn't say. I said he was a foreigner. You lookin' for him or somethin'? You the law?"

Bruce Elliott stepped forward, clearing his throat. "Mercy no, we are not peace officers by any means. We only had some friends we were going to meet here, four men and a woman."

"Well, I ain't seen no woman." He pulled on the top of his red long johns. "Not me standing here and lookin' this a way. I did see four men though and sold the foreigner my gelding." He paused. "Couldn't rightly say if'n he was an Englishman or no. Sent 'em on over to the Rusty Meatplow fer some vittles though, so I reckon you can ask 'em yer ownself."

"Might just go on over and do just that," Sam said. "Where would we find it?"

"It's over yonder, 'cross the street. Tell 'em Charlie sent ya."

"All right, Charlie, we'll do that. Meanwhile, if you could lay three horses by for us, we'd sure appreciate it."

Sam and Bruce turned and walked out into

the street, stopping by their horses. Bruce watched as Sam checked the loads in his revolver. Opening the door to the cylinder, he dropped a sixth round beneath the hammer. "You up to this, professor?" he asked.

"Shouldn't we wait for Cobb?"

Sam looked across the street at the dimly lit cafe. "Don't think so. Can't never tell when he might get here. He might have run into Williams on his way out of town. Besides, those boys might finish and be gone long before he gets here."

"I'd feel a lot better if Cobb were here," Elliott said.

The comment only made Sam more determined than ever. Fisher raised himself to his full height and cocked the derby down over his eyes. Planting the revolver back into his shoulder holster, he frowned and straightened his suit coat. "Cobb's good at tracking, but I've been in this business since afore he was born. You're as safe with me as a baby in his mother's arms." He started walking across the street, but then turned and glared back at him. Pointing at the rifle in Bruce's saddle, he said, "You up to using that thing, or am I gonna have to go it alone?"

Bruce didn't reply. He slowly drew the rifle out of the leather boot and walked behind Sam to the front door of the restaurant.

Chapter 31

Zac was trotting the bay back up the street when he heard the gunfire. Spurring the animal forward, he stepped out of the saddle in front of the restaurant where several men had scurried out. Desperate panic was on the men's faces, like the look of a cat being thrown into a swirling river. Zac drew his Peacemaker and stepped through the door.

Sam Fisher lay on the floor, propped up against the wall, and Bruce Elliott was squatted over him, pressing a wad of napkins into the man's chest. Three other men were on the floor. One was as dead as last year's news, another was out cold, while the third man was leaving a trail of blood as he crawled toward the door. His hand groped for a six-gun near Zac's feet. Zac stepped on the man's wrist hard, pinning it to the floor.

Zac's brown eyes locked on to the old man. They were like deep and troubled waters as his thoughts raced. This was the last place and the last town they needed to pick a fight in. He looked at Bruce Elliott as he hovered over Sam. "What the blazes happened here?" he asked.

Sam coughed. A deep rumble came from his chest as he spoke. "Don't go to blaming the professor here." Sam's words came out in a smoky whisper. "My own fault. He wanted to wait for you, but I wouldn't let him."

Elliott lifted the napkins and Zac saw the crimson pool spread across the old man's chest. Sam spoke again. "I got two of 'em after they shot me. The boy here did well. Cold cocked the man who shot me."

Zac lifted his boot from the wounded man's wrist and, in the same motion, slid the revolver across the floor. Grabbing the man by the shirt, he slid him against the wall. His lips moved but he didn't speak.

"These people ain't got Elizabeth," Sam croaked, "and she didn't ride out with the Englishman."

"Try not to talk," Elliott said. "We've sent for the doctor."

Zac turned his gaze again on the wounded gunman. Holding him by the collar he stared into his eyes. "You're gut shot, mister. Bad way to die. You won't live for the hanging. So tell me, where's Elizabeth Roberts?"

The man's eyes rolled back in his head with a groan.

Outside, they could hear the sound of

boots on the boardwalk. Seconds later, the door flew open and a man with a drawn gun stepped cautiously inside. His nightshirt was half tucked into his pants and his boots were on the wrong feet. Between red suspenders, a big star was stapled. "What's goin' on here?" Then his attention focused on Sam. "Sam . . . Sam Fisher, what in heaven's name!"

Sam gave a slight smile, then he looked at Zac. "You boys get yourselves outta here now and go about your business. I've know'd old Tom Mahorn here plenty a years. He and his missus can see to my dying."

Zac started to get to his feet, but Sam reached out and grabbed his sleeve. "Tell the general I done all I could," he whispered. "Tell him I was old and slow, but I did my job."

"You did just fine," Zac said. "You did as much as any man, and I'm proud to know you." He forced a smile. "You ain't half bad for a Yankee."

Sam coughed, gave a pained smile. "You just tell him, Johnny Reb, what I done told you, you understand? Tell him straight."

Zac nodded.

The sheriff knelt down beside Sam as Zac got to his feet. Looking back at the people crowding around the door and the windows, the lawman shouted, "Don't just stand there! Somebody get that sawbones! Tell him to get here right now, ya hear? We need to get this man moved." Then he spotted the cook who had been hovering behind the serving counter. "Will somebody tell me what happened here?"

Zac motioned Elliott toward the door, and reluctantly Bruce got to his feet. Taking him by the arm, Zac pushed him through the growing crowd. Bruce was dazed. Moving into the street, his eyes filled with tears. "It happened so fast. I just can't believe it. We were just asking questions when one of them drew his pistol and fired. I did all I could, but it just happened too fast." He gulped. "I've never seen a man die before my very eyes."

Suddenly Bruce caught a glimpse of the swamper who had been standing outside the saloon when they rode into town. The man averted his eyes, and Bruce stomped up to the man. "You saw us ride into town," he said.

The man looked passively at the swarm of people who were still gathering in front of the cafe. "I seen ya."

"Did you see those men in there ride in before us?"

Sheepishly, the man looked down at his

worn-out brogans and bit his lower lip.

"For heaven's sake, man, a woman's been kidnapped. If you know anything, tell us now."

The man turned his head from side to side as though looking for someone, then looked down again without a word.

Zac forced himself up against the man, crowding him chest to chest. He spoke in a low, menacing tone. "If you know anything you're not saying, we'll see you hang, same as them."

Yeager had been up before the sun, which now slid reluctantly into the dusky canyon. The tops of the peaks turned pink first and then glowed ever so slightly with a color that reminded him of salmon. The morning sky was cloudless, often the case in Colorado. But the same sky could produce rain, thunder, hail, or snow before supper.

The wind that ripped down the canyon rippled the flames on the fire like a thousand flags flying in battle. On top of the fire, Yeager had placed a large pot of water that was now rumbling with a steady boil. He reached his hand into the sack of ground coffee and, pulling out a handful, added it to the pot. It turned the churning water into a murky brew. He set the pot slightly aside on the grate to allow a low boil.

The past night had been the longest in recent memory for Yeager. He knew the dawn would come, but sometimes he had his doubts. Time was on their side, however. If he could keep the CP wolves away from the door long enough for the promised help to arrive, then they just might get what they'd been fighting for. Otherwise, it was anybody's guess what might happen.

The river was up from the run-off of the snow in the mountains, and it surged past the craggy rock on the other side — the jutting stone finger called Pinnacle Peak. The craggy structure pointed a crooked probe in the direction of the towering canyon walls, not the sky. Twisted trees dotted the sides of the slopes, looking for all the world like survivors of a great catastrophe. Each of them seemed to struggle for light among the fallen rocky remnants of repeated slides. They remained frozen against the toppled wall of rock, like dancers left after the band had ceased to play.

The peaks shadowed everything, each one a powerful giant of the earth, silent testimony to the fact that anything man could build — even a railroad — couldn't come close to the marvel they were. They were stone sentinels, holding up the sky.

Yeager dipped a cup of cold water and poured it into the pot to settle the grounds. It was a trick he'd learned from his grandfather. He couldn't keep his eyes off the cliffs. They had seen all, heard all. Bullets had nicked their feet, yet they stood silent, watching. *No railroad is more powerful than the hands that made these,* Yeager thought. *When all is said and done, these things will still be here. After all,* he thought, *the One who made them will still be here; the men who built the railroad will all be dead and gone.*

"Yeager, you better come up here and have a look."

He kept himself low to the ground and moved quickly from the fire to the wooden barricade. Edging his glance around the sides of the tar-soaked railroad ties, he followed the man's pointing finger. In the distance, across the river, he could see a number of figures slowly moving from rock to rock. "Mighta known," he said. "Don't reckon we can expect them to just sit there and wait. Now that you've gotten supplies and some more men to back your play up."

"Don't s'pose so." The man grunted and continued to stare into the distance at the men filtering among the rocks.

"I don't reckon they've seen us," Yeager said. "Maybe we can give them a mite of a surprise." He looked the man over. "Go find me your best rifle shots and get the rest of the boys up here too."

The man returned several minutes later with three men in tow and the rest of the men rolling out of their blankets and moving toward them. Yeager pointed out the approaching men in the distance to the marksmen who sat near him. The three of them took their rifles, studied the men.

Yeager turned to the group. "All right, boys, they're coming up on us. They'll go all or nothing today. We got some help coming in from the law, but those boys'll blast us outta here before it arrives."

The men blinked at one another.

"Now, I figure we got to put some men across that river. Otherwise, those men will have us in a crossfire when they get up here. Who'd like to volunteer? We'll lay down some good fire for you."

The men remained silent. Some looked at the raging swollen river, others peered at the men approaching. The ice cold waters of the Arkansas were tumbling with fury.

"Listen, Mr. Yeager," one of the men spoke up, "ain't none of us here anxious to drown or get shot fulla holes this morning. Now don't take this personal, but crossing that river would be a pure fool thing to do.

That water's moving mighty swift, and if'n a body ain't careful, he could float right up on them boys' camp and their guns to boot." He swallowed. "That is, if'n he don't drown first." He went on. "And even if a feller was to get to the other side, chances are his cartridges would be wet and useless." The man shook his head. "No sir, only a fool would do such a thing."

Yeager slowly unbuckled his gun belt. Rolling it up and laying it on the ground, he tightened the rawhide strap that held the knife sheath to his leg. He sat his hat on top of the gun belt. "Well then, boys, I s'pose you're seeing a fool standing before you."

The men looked at each other, then back at Yeager, incredulous. Their lack of faith in his ability to pull this off was written all over their faces.

"Now, I'm gonna wait till them boys get into rifle range, and then I want you three to cut loose. Maybe if you can keep their heads down, they won't be able to see what I'm doing."

Kelly pushed his hat forward. "Yeager, these men won't say it, they respect you too much. But you are a durn fool. You'll be deader than a steak a minute after you hit that water. And even if you manage to crawl up across there, what the blazes do you intend to do with a knife?"

"You just watch me," he smiled. "And give me cover."

One of the men brought him a steaming cup of coffee, and the three sharpshooters spread themselves over and around the barrier, trying to get themselves into a flat shooting position. They waited.

Yeager lay low next to the swiftly moving, tossing river and watched the men on the other side continue to edge closer. When the shots from the marksmen rang out, he watched two of the men in the distance jerk and pitch forward. The rest of the men went for cover just as he hit the water.

The ice cold waters of the Arkansas grabbed him and spun him around like a rag doll in the midst of an arctic hell. It sucked the breath right out of him, but he struck the water furiously with his hands. His splashes were moving him, but the current carried him farther away from the men who were all shooting, desperately trying to keep the heads of their opponents out of sight.

He could hear the roar of the guns as he lurched with all his might for the opposite rocky bank. He was a fool and he knew it, a fool for ever allowing himself to think he could possibly affect the outcome of the battle all by himself.

The men were yelling now and continuing to shoot without regard to a target. Some fired at the places where they thought the men were hiding, others laid down a steady rhythm of lead at the barricade that faced them in the distance.

Yeager struggled against the freezing tide that was filling his face. His hands surged forward and he kicked for all he was worth. Swimming had never been his strong suit, but now he knew that if he was to survive, he'd have to be the best he could be. He choked on the bubbling torrent and groped his arms forward . . . through the worst nightmare he'd ever known.

As he reached the slippery rocks, he felt his meager grip slide across their surface. The river tore him loose from the cold boulders and bounced him farther downstream, down the frigid waters and toward the men who might see him and take aim. He scrambled with his feet against the churning mass. He knew that no matter how exhausted he felt from the tortuous swim, he had to wedge himself against the tide, search for some foothold. Jamming his leg into a crack, he held fast. The water was now moving over him, but he lunged forward.

Pulling with all of his might, he heaved himself onto the cold shore. Lying on the ground, he inched forward. To lie there was to die. Somehow, it didn't seem a bad alternative.

Panting on the ground, he felt the heat surge from deep within his soul. In his deepest being he longed to be the best he could be on this earth. He inched forward, craving the air. Getting to his knees, he writhed toward the boulders that spotted the trail. He lay beside them, still gasping for breath.

Minutes later, his mind snapped free. He could clearly hear the gunfire from the other side of the river. He began the slow and painstaking climb up the side of the massive cliff above him. He doubted he'd been seen. No shots were coming at him. He grimaced as he crawled hand over hand up the sharp rocks. He knew full well this could be the most arduous part of his mission. Blanking the pain from his mind, he continued to climb the rocks. He wasn't sure how long it had taken him, but the look of the redwood pipe that carried water to Cañon City was a wonderful sight. Flopping his body down on the overhanging ledge, he craned his head around to look for a trail. There it was!

He ambled for the cut in the rocks and once again climbed for the crest of the high rimrock. Banging his knees and shins, he scrambled for the top. As he reached the crown of the high cliff, he could clearly hear the withering fire from across the river. Scrambling along its surface, he reached the point where he thought he could make out return fire below.

Sliding down the surface of the rocks, he could see the men under him. They crouched behind boulders and were returning the fire of the men he had left. Now he could put his plan into play. He moved himself into position behind large rocks that dotted the surface of the cliff and placed his water-soaked boots on them. Groaning with all of his might, he tried to push the rocks from their position.

The first rock moved slightly, and he strained to free it. Scooting closer, he pushed with both legs. The large boulder came free and began bouncing down the side of the craggy rock face. As it rolled along the rimrock it gathered momentum and picked up other rocks that tumbled with it toward the bottom, toward the men below him. Paralyzed by the sight of the sudden rockslide hurtling toward them while all around them flew the shots of the marksmen, the men froze . . . until it was too late.

Chapter 32

The fresh buckskin horse that Williams rode flew along the cinder road that lined the tracks. He lashed at the animal with the rawhide quirt and slapped its sides with his spurs. Time had been lost during the night, and he was going to make sure that he made up for it, even if it meant the death of a horse. He just didn't care. Peter Williams had never been one to be cautious, certainly not with a goal firmly in view. The buckskin's shoes beat a steady staccato of wild cracks.

Time was precious to Peter Williams and he had little patience for people who acted as if it weren't. For him, it was one of the most difficult things about living in the West, and America in general, for that matter. Everyone in this country seemed to have no room in their system for driving themselves in daily life. They seemed too slovenly to suit his taste. Laziness seemed to be an American virtue, he'd often thought. Perhaps it was what made him think he'd be successful here. After all, if he couldn't compete with and best people in America, then where could he?

He swatted the horse's rump as the animal continued to gallop down the road. Peter Williams was creating a cloud of dust along the road out of Cañon City, but he didn't care. Since he was traveling alone, there was little chance of someone connecting his tracks with the ones they had followed the night before. Besides, the buckskin was fresh. Even if the men had decided to follow him, they'd never be able to catch him in time. The thought of beating those men gave him satisfaction.

He looked at the empty tracks that ran beside the road. This was what it was all about. Roberts would be coming his way with a trainload of deputies, and he would be ready. He no longer felt the long leash from Jim Ruby that he'd been used to, but he still had enough power with the railroad to do whatever it took to get control of the canyon. Everything could and would be forgiven, everything except failure.

He knew enough about operations to know that the CP had two locomotives near the canyon — one was on the other side of the hanging bridge, and the other was near the men who were holding the Denver and Rio Grande men at bay. The faster he could get to that one, the faster he could turn it around and take care of Roberts. He'd seen the devastation that Cobb had caused with a runaway train, seen it up close, and it wasn't very pretty. The twisted mass of steel was a picture that he found hard to get out of his mind. He didn't find it repulsive, however; quite the contrary, he found it fascinating. A runaway locomotive could cause a great deal of damage. His time with the railroad had shown him that. It had convinced him what a weapon a train could be.

He studied the tracks as he rode. He'd race to pick a good spot, somewhere around a curve, someplace that would make it impossible for a train to back up and avoid a collision. If he could wipe out Roberts and the deputies who were with him, then the delay would give him enough time to root those men out of the canyon. By the time the public found out what had happened, the Royal Gorge would belong to the Chicago Pacific.

He galloped past several gandy dancers. The men were on a handcar slowly meandering down the track. They looked up and stopped pumping on the handles as he raced by. The grime was already caked on their faces and their day hadn't yet started. These weren't his men. These were people who would just as soon lay track for the CP in the morning and the Denver and Rio Grande on the same afternoon. They worked for whoever was paying them at the moment, and in that respect they were no different than he was. The only difference was pride.

Peter Williams knew that money was important to him, but there were other things that persuaded him more. Power and all that went with it was the thing that made him do what he did. The ability to control the men around him, to tell them what to do and to watch the fear in their eyes, that was what gave him the greatest satisfaction.

The humiliation of failing to get Roberts's granddaughter had grated on him. The thought of the night when Jim Ruby dressed him down in the railcar still made him angry. And the worst part of the experience was the fact that Ruby did it in front of a man who had been reporting to him. He would never forget the smug look on Jake Rice's face. Peter Williams knew he had been riding high before that time, riding high with everyone afraid to cross him. Zac Cobb had changed all that. The man had interfered and had made him look the fool. For some time to come, Peter Williams knew he would be laboring hard to rub that out of people's minds, but he would — he certainly would.

He continued to whip the horse forward. He would tolerate no slowing down now.

Nothing would impede his climb back up the ladder. Once again the men would fear him. Once again he would talk and people would jump. Once again he would know power.

His mind was alive as he rode, swirling with what he had planned. Details, details were all important. He would not be caught off guard again by a failure to tend to the details. He had laid the trap that brought Elizabeth Roberts into his hands, surely he'd get credit for that. The woman was trouble, she'd shown him that during the night. Everything she thought and everything she did was trouble, but now he could forget her. He'd forget her until he was ready to use her, and he would use her. He'd stop the men from the Denver and Rio Grande and then he'd play his trump card — Elizabeth Roberts.

The Roberts girl would be safe where she was. He'd seen to that. Enough money had changed hands to keep her put away until he needed her. What he had done gave him some sense of satisfaction. And he wouldn't have her to worry about, which was even better. Elizabeth Roberts was unpredictable, but now she was out of his hair.

The one loose cannon that he couldn't account for was Zac Cobb. The man had been a burr under his saddle since the first time he'd laid eyes on him. Williams gritted his teeth. Everything he knew about Cobb had shown him how dangerous the man was. Cobb was treacherous, but he was no gunslinger. When it came down to it, Peter Williams was fully convinced that if it came to a shoot-out with the man, he would be the one standing when the smoke had cleared. He was plenty fast, not as quick as Jake Rice, but fast enough for Cobb. Besides, he had no intention of letting Rice get the credit for anything. He had to kill Cobb himself. He'd tried to ambush the man, and only fate had saved him. Next time, he'd make sure he confronted Cobb face-to-face. He'd tried everything else, but the next time the two of them met would be their last.

The buckskin was breathing hard. Williams had been running the animal for some time now, but it didn't matter. He'd get there and he'd get there in a hurry, with or without a breathing horse. He whipped the animal with increased fury.

Elizabeth's lamp flickered softly. She could hear the man coming up the dark hallway. His voice and the song that he sang grated on her.

"Nellie Bly, Nellie Bly, bring the broom

along, we'll sweep the kitchen clean, my love, and have a little song. Hi Nellie, Ho Nellie, listen here to me. . . ."

The man was outside her cell now. He lifted the cover to the outside peephole, and Elizabeth could feel his eyes on her. She took one last look at the position of the spiders that had been crawling on the wall and the rat cowering in the corner and then, reaching over from her cot, turned down the wick on the lamp, extinguishing the flame. Elizabeth had no fear of critters, but she couldn't stand the thought of being a spectacle. The darkness enveloped her. There was a strangeness about being in total darkness, but it was better than what stood outside her cell door.

"Now, missy, why you want to go and do that for? There's creepy things in there. Put 'em there my ownself, just to keep you company." He laughed.

The sound of the man's laugh reminded her of a shovel raking fresh gravel. Elizabeth had never been a source of amusement for anyone, not since she was a child. She was trying hard to be the son her father never had and respect was something she craved.

Elizabeth reached down and pulled the moth-eaten blanket up over her. Even though she knew the man couldn't see her in the dark, she felt more secure covered.

She stared up into the totally black room. She had no match. There would be only darkness now, but she felt safer. She wouldn't give them the satisfaction of her leaving things the way she had found them.

"Missy, you can't be cuttin' old Johnny outta your life," he whispered. "I'm s'pose to bring you your vittles, and then you and me can have a good ol' time." His soft chuckle was like a pebble tolling down a washboard. "I'll be seein' you soon now, hear? You and me is gonna be real close."

She listened to the man's irritating laugh as he walked down the hallway. His laughter increased the farther he walked and its sound echoed down the corridor, followed by the noise of the heavy steel doors slamming shut.

Hours crawled by before she heard the sound of the doors again. There was no song, but she knew by his shuffle that the guard was coming back. She boiled inside. Long before, she had learned to shift her fears into feelings of anger. If she could be angry enough, any trial she faced could be attacked, not run away from. She would battle this man for all she was worth. But she knew that right now he simply represented everything she had been going through.

He slid the key into the lock and turned it. As he cracked the door open, she could see a faint light filtering in. "You been waitin' fer me, missy?"

She cringed. Sitting up, she scooted away from the door and pressed her back to the wall.

The man stood in the opening and struck a match. He grinned broadly and, lifting up the globe on the lamp, lit it. "Thought you might want some company with your meal." The man's teeth shone brightly through his heavy brown beard. His blue guard's jacket was open, the brass buttons hanging loose. He was a large man, but not well built. He looked like a bear staring at a hive of fresh honey.

"I am not hungry," she said.

He reached back to a table outside the door, producing a covered pail and a tin spoon. "You better eat," he said. "You're li'ble to be here fer some time. I gots some good stew here."

He set the pail on the table and uncovered it. Elizabeth could see steam rising from the tin bucket. "The warden is letting you have some of his dinner, and I hurried to get it to you whilst it was still somewhat hot. Believe me, it beats anything the rest of the folks in here is gettin'."

Elizabeth swung her legs around, putting her feet on the floor. The man's eyes brightened at the sight of her legs.

"I ain't seen nothin' like you in my whole life," he said.

Elizabeth felt sick inside. The man's looks made her angry. She bit her lip. She'd always been in control of her life and she knew men could be brutal. She'd heard stories that made her skin crawl, but she paused to think of what to do next.

"You know keeping me here is kidnapping and false imprisonment," she said.

He took off his hat and scratched his head. "I reckon so, but this here is a CP town, and we can protect ourselves."

"The law is the law everywhere, even in Cañon City, and kidnapping a woman is an offense punishable by hanging."

He tossed his hat onto the chair. "Then if I'm about to get myself hung, I might as well enjoy myself a little first." He grinned broadly and blinked his eyes. "I can't hang myself no higher by watchin' you eat."

Elizabeth Roberts knew how to be coy when she wanted to be. She'd never been one to lead a man on, she never had to. They always knew where they stood with her. But this was different. This man wasn't a servant, a beau seeking her hand, or somebody her father had in the palm of his hand. "Why don't you hang your coat on the peg back there," she said. "Then you can watch me eat."

The man turned his back to her and began to wrestle free of his jacket. Silently getting to her feet, Elizabeth picked up the cane-backed chair beside the table. Raising it above her head, she brought it down on the man with force. It shattered, sending pieces flying in all directions. The guard staggered and sank to his knees.

Swinging his leg around with surprising speed, he swept Elizabeth's feet out from under her. She fell back on the cot. Struggling, the man staggered to his feet.

"You stay back!" she screamed. "I won't have you touching me."

"You ain't got no more choice in that, missy." The man began to move toward her.

Elizabeth's eyes darted back and forth, looking for anything that might protect her. She held up her hand. "Stop right where you are."

The man continued to inch toward her as she took the lamp and held it up. "Stay right there!" she yelled.

As the man took another step, Elizabeth flung the burning lamp toward him. The oil from the lamp burst into flames, spreading onto the guard's pants and across the floor in a liquid sheet of fire.

The man began to viciously beat at his clothes. He cursed her as he stumbled backward into the dim hallway.

Elizabeth picked up the blanket and tossed it on the burning oil. She knew that if she could keep the man away from her, other guards might respond to the smoke. Listening to the guard roar outside her cell, she began to scream. Other inmates began a chorus of chants, punctuated by yells. Moments later, Elizabeth heard the sound of men running toward her end of the hall.

"Here, here! What's happening here?" The warden and two guards began to smother the flames on the floor of her cell.

"You keep that ape away from me!" Elizabeth screamed.

"Get out of here!" the warden barked. He swept his arms back at the men. "I'll handle this." Pushing the two surprised guards outside the door, he took a lamp from one of them and stood in Elizabeth's cell. "You're only bringing more trouble on yourself, Miss Roberts."

Even in the dim light, Elizabeth could see the veins in the man's neck bulging. There was more panic in his look than anger. She clinched her fists and pinned her arms to her sides. She felt a strange surge of power.

"No," she said. "You're the one who's bringing the trouble." She began to jab her finger in the air at the man. "You might think your political friends can get you out of this, but that won't happen if I am touched."

He nervously clinched his hands. "I'm sorry about that. I had no idea. Anything that man tried to do was his idea alone."

"He works for you," she shot back, once again sticking her finger out at him, "and you're responsible. You'll hang just as high as he will. I'll see you swing from your own gallows. Don't lie to yourself about that. You will hang and I'll see that you do."

Elizabeth dropped her hands and shook her fists as they hung stiffly by her side. She was angry, and her fear had disappeared. She felt like a wounded lion snarling in a corner. No matter what happened to her now, she was going to take these people down with her.

The man held up his hands apologetically. "I'll see that you won't come to harm. I can promise you that."

"You'd do better just to let me go."

"I can't do that. Peter Williams would kill me."

Elizabeth lifted her chin defiantly. "I can promise you this. There's a man who's looking for me right now, and if he finds me here, he'll kill you. Don't think these walls can keep you safe from him."

Chapter 33

Zac and Bruce mounted their fresh horses and rode up the street.

"There appears to be a fire in that building up there," Bruce said.

The stone structure of the prison that stood at the end of the street sat behind trees that showed a small column of smoke feathering out of one of the upper windows. They could see a guard running along the wall.

"I doubt there's much danger of that thing burning down," Zac replied. "It's built like a rock."

They reached the end of the street and turned to the road leading out to the Royal Gorge. Zac knew Cañon City would be the perfect place to stash Elizabeth. It was close enough to the fighting to produce her if needed, and the place was filled with men working for the CP. Besides, Elizabeth Roberts was a tough woman to control, he knew that full well. She was bound to give the people who had her no end of trouble. He smirked inside. Those people deserved everything they got. They'd be finding the tables turned on them every step of the way.

The bay had picked up a stone and Zac noticed the hobble. "Hold up a bit," he said. He put his feet on either side of the leg the bay was favoring, and feeling his way along the horse's leg, he squeezed it and pulled it up. There it was, close to the frog. Reaching into his pocket, he pulled out a bent nail he carried for just such a purpose. He raked at the caked mud from around the tender, meaty frog that padded the bottom of the animal's hoof and pried out the stone.

"There," he said, patting the animal. "That'll feel a whole lot better."

"We better hurry on," Bruce said. "They'll be gaining on us, and some of those people back there might be trying to find and question us."

Zac had never been a man who delayed when it came time to do what had to be done, but long ago he'd learned not to hurry off in the wrong direction, and some things were unsettled in his mind. He stood beside the bay, checking the cinch on his saddle to give himself time to think.

Only one horse had been let loose at the stable, yet there were the five horses they'd been following. One of them was the roan, so Zac knew she'd been brought into town. He knew perfectly well where three of the men were. One was at the undertaker's with another on the way, and another had a man-size headache from the butt of Bruce's rifle. There was no way the man could be interrogated, not with the place crawling with CP men. The less said the better. Elizabeth had to be somewhere here in town. The only question was where.

"We had best be moving along," Bruce Elliott said impatiently. Zac admired a little bit of that in a man. It showed a good work ethic. But not at the expense of thinking.

"We're finding Elizabeth Roberts," Zac said. "There'll be time a plenty for the limey. His kind always shows up."

"You think she's here in town?" Elliott asked. "Why would they leave her here?"

"She's here, all right. I can feel it in my bones." He turned his head back down the street and watched the continued bedlam in front of the restaurant. "Somebody has her here, somebody those fellers had all lined up to watch her."

"It could take us days to find her."

Zac mounted the bay. "It could at that."

"Well, Cobb, we don't have days. Besides, no one here is about to cooperate with us, certainly not after what just happened."

"All we know is the man with the mop saw them riding down the street here."

"That's what he said."

"And yet there are horses in the stable back yonder."

"What are you getting at, Cobb?"

Zac lifted his eyes and continued to watch the ever-thinning whisper of smoke from inside the prison. Now he heard a number of the guards shouting.

"You ever seen a jailbreak, Elliott?"

"No, I can't say as I have."

"Well, I was just wondering. Most of the time fellers try to break out of one." He lifted his hat, running his fingers through his dark hair. "What do you think would happen if somebody tried to break *into* one?"

"That's crazy! You think those men put Elizabeth in there?"

"I ain't thinkin' nothin', I'm just supposin'. Let's us take a ride around this thing and see what we can see."

Elliott grunted. Zac could see the look of hostile disbelief in his face. "I think we're wasting valuable time here doing that."

Zac turned the bay around and started up the street. "I've learned something over the years, Elliott. I've learned to trust my hunches. Now, you go on ahead if you're determined, but right now my hunch says to look around this here thing."

Elliott followed. He wasn't happy about it,

but he'd hitched himself to this ride and he was determined to follow through with it. As the two of them rounded the stone wall, they spotted the white house with the red trim. A sign swung from a post nearby proclaiming, "Warden."

Zac pulled up to the hitching post. "She's here!"

"How do you know that?"

Zac motioned with his head and, jerking the reins on the bay, rode on. Elliott watched his sudden departure and hurried to catch up. Riding up to him at the back street shanties, he reached out and pulled on his jacket sleeve. "How do you know? What makes you think she's in there?"

"Elizabeth's star. She's been leaving that sign all along the way. It was etched in the walkway outside the warden's house."

Elliott blinked.

"We'll wait out here somewheres till it gets dark, then I'm gonna break in."

"You're sure?"

"Just as sure as I am the sun's gonna set tonight. You saw all that commotion in there."

Elliott nodded.

"I'm a bettin' our little redheaded wildcat had somethin' to do with that." He smiled. "Those boys in there handle some of the roughest men in the territory, but they've never had to deal with Elizabeth Roberts."

The two of them rode up a large rise that overlooked the town. From the top, they could easily observe anything that happened in town and, more importantly, they could see anything that happened in the prison.

They stretched out beneath a scrub oak, and after eating some of the grub packed for them, Zac took out his volume of Tennyson and lit his pipe.

"You care about that sister-in-law of mine, don't you?"

Zac took the stem out of his mouth and blew smoke. "Yes, I suppose I do."

"Are you in love with her?"

Zac looked down at the walls of the prison. "A man would sooner saddle up to a barrel cactus than love that sister-in-law of yours."

"The way you take life on a dare, you strike me as such a man, Cobb. But you didn't answer my question. Do you love her?"

"She is fetchin'." He once again began to smoke. The silence between them was uncomfortable. Zac knew full well that he hadn't answered Bruce's question, and he turned it over in his mind. Pulling the pipe from his lips, he looked Elliott in the eye. "I like her, I like her a lot. Maybe it's her way that I love best, but I love someone else."

"Someone else?"

"It might not appear so, but I do have a life in California."

Elliott seemed flustered. "Yes, I would suppose you do, I just thought there might be something else going on inside of you involving Elizabeth."

"Any man who ever laid eyes on that woman would have something going on inside of him, I reckon. It's just that" — he paused, stumbling over his words — "I got this attachment back home."

"Attachment?"

"Somebody loves me, and that's mighty important to a man."

"Don't you know that Elizabeth loves you? I've seen it in the way she looks at you."

"No, she wants me but that don't mean she loves me. When a woman loves a man she has to know everything that's going on inside of him, not just what she sees on the outside. Real love ain't no 'buyer beware' thing."

"And this woman of yours back home, can she see all of that?"

"I think she sees more of me than I do."

"You are a complicated man," Elliott replied. "Not many men would risk their life for a woman they don't love, in a battle that isn't theirs."

Zac continued to smoke his pipe. He knew full well that he wasn't like many men, never had been, never intended to be. It had always been his desire to rise above the level of the men around him, to rise above them not in the money he had or in the position he rose to, but in the way his mind and soul worked. If a body couldn't be the best at what he was on the inside, then there was no reason to go on breathing.

"I guess I just don't like to see folks stepped on."

The dusk had settled on Cañon City and lights were beginning to twinkle when he got to his feet and saddled the bay. "I want you to go on down to the stable back there and get the roan," he said. "Elizabeth's gonna need something to ride."

Elliott cleared his throat and shuffled his feet. "Those people know who we are. How do you propose I do that?"

"I don't rightly care, professor. You can buy it, borrow it, or steal it for all I mind."

"I'm not sure if I can do that."

Zac turned from his saddle and looked the man up and down. "Listen here. You wanted to come on this ride. You made yourself a part of what was to happen out here. You might not have known what that would mean, but you dealt yourself this hand all the same. It's time you carried your end of the log." He wasn't angry, even though the thought of a man claiming he couldn't do something irritated him. He just wanted Elliott to do more than his scruples had ever allowed him to do before. There was an element in this man of the East that had always wanted to be an observer, without getting his hands dirty in the doing of a thing. The man was capable, he just didn't know it. Zac knew that when there was something a man wanted bad enough, he had to part with whatever it was inside of him that was keeping him from it. Zac knew this to be true. Now he just wanted Bruce Elliott to find out on his own. "You just have the roan by those trees outside near that white house in an hour."

Williams arrived at the camp along the Arkansas. The buckskin had been ridden hard. The sight of the animal made the men mumble. They had already taken most of the day recovering the bodies from the other side of the river left by the landslide. They still didn't know what had caused the catastrophe, but Rice had his suspicions.

"What in the blazes has gone on here?" Williams asked.

Rice wasn't feeling much in the mood for conversation, especially one that involved Peter Williams. He sat at the fire drinking coffee.

"A landslide," he grunted.

"A landslide?"

"Yes, you know, something that happens when rocks tumble down off of a mountain," he scowled.

Williams could tell that he was treading on dangerous ground with Jake Rice. He'd have to be careful. He'd already been shown up in front of the man, and he didn't want any part of having to back down again. But he didn't want any part of a fight with him either. It was one he would lose and he knew it. He changed the subject. "I'm going to need that locomotive back there and two of your men."

"Why?"

"Because unless we stop him, Roberts will be here shortly with a court order, along with a small army. If that happens, then we will have lost."

Rice looked around at the eight bodies that lay covered side by side. "Seems to me, we've done lost already."

The notion of Jake Rice so discouraged and seemingly beaten heartened Williams. Just days ago their places had been reversed.

He had been the beaten one. He wouldn't gloat now. He still needed the man too much. But it did give him a great deal of satisfaction.

"No, we have not lost. I have Elizabeth Roberts."

The snap of Rice's head and the man's wide-eyed look made Williams smile on the inside.

"You got her? The she-devil?"

Williams smugly nodded his head.

"Where?"

"I have her safely put away in Cañon City. She is going to stay exactly where she is until we need her. When the occasion arises and the people from the Denver and Rio Grande are negotiating a new deal, we will have her as part of it. But first, I need to stop that train Roberts is on."

Rice motioned to two men standing around the fire, and they sauntered over to them. "Peter Williams here's got a plan. You two will help him."

Williams took the two men to the locomotive and called up to the cab. "Get the boiler hot, we are leaving." He motioned to several men standing nearby and began to bark out orders. They weren't his men to order around, but it was in his nature to do just that. "See here, you'll all need to lend a hand. We need more of that fuel."

It took some time for the locomotive to get up steam and find a spur track that would allow them to reverse their direction. Williams had not failed to notice several places where he could keep the train under steam while they waited for Roberts. The darkness had settled into the canyon when Williams saw the spot he had in mind. He motioned to the engineer. "Stop right there."

"I'll stop fer ye, but I ain't about to cause no wreck." The old engineer brought the locomotive to a skidding stop, Williams and the other men bracing themselves against the cab. The old man puffed on his corncob pipe, his steel blue eyes seeming to shine in the darkness. "Yer on yer own from here," he said.

"You are an employee of the Chicago Pacific, and you will do as I say."

The old man took his gloves off and dropped them on the floor of the cab. Removing his cap, he ran his fingers through his white hair and dropped the cap on top of the gloves. "I can get myself another job. What I can't get myself is another soul."

Williams grimaced. "Pick up your things, and do as I say."

"Mister, fer a man from England, you shore don't understand English very well. I won't do it, and that's that! I seen myself a train wreck before. I wuz drivin' when one happened during the war. Happened along the Delaware River in 1864. We wuz haulin' Rebel prisoners. We run ourselves head-on into a coal train."

Williams was impatient. He didn't like to be opposed by anyone, especially an old man who was a common employee. But there was something about these old engineers that set them apart. They may have been working for a specific railroad, but they were a breed apart, and they thought of themselves that way. There weren't many of them by comparison, either, and they tended to know each other.

The old man went on, "I took 171 into King and Fuller's cut with full steam and had to jump clear of it. I don't think there's ever been a noise like that, hundreds a tons of twisted metal all bustin' into each other. Them engines was raised up in the air like two giants fightin' it out. By the time I gimped myself over to it, I wanted to puke out my innards. Had a friend a mine drivin' that coaler. His fireman, Tuttle, was killed right off, but my friend was still alive."

The old man's eyes blazed. "Ingram had himself pinned up next to a split boilerplate with scaldin' steam roastin' him alive. With his last breath, that man was warning me off, afraid it was gonna 'splode all over me."

The old man quickly smeared a tear out of one eye. "I'm tellin' you, you don't know what you're about here. Floors buckle and open. Timbers snap like matchsticks. Driving rods bend like little wires. Wheels and axles get broke and scatter all over creation. I jes' ain't agonna do it. This is where I get off."

The old man climbed out of the cab, and Williams reached down and took out a lantern from the fireman's box. He pointed into the darkening sky at the faint outline of a hill.

"There, that's where I want you. When you see a train emerge from that mountain behind you, then you signal down here. Light the lamp and swing it back and forth."

He reached down again into the fireman's box and took out two signal flags. He stuck them in the faces of the two men he had brought along. "If it has not come by the time the sun rises, you will need to wave these. Do not fail me, gentlemen."

Chapter 34

Zac tethered the bay near the trees and slid his sawed-off shotgun out from inside his bedroll. Just looking down the barrels of the thing was often more than enough to make most men back down. He had no desire to pull the trigger on any man. Most of these people were just doing a job. Long ago he had learned if you wanted to stop a fight before one started, you had to be well-armed and have the deliberation to use what you carried.

It was dark now, and Zac walked briskly toward the house. Through the kitchen window, he could see the people sitting in the dining room. He walked to the front door and, without making a sound, he twisted the doorknob and walked in. The overstuffed furniture was red velvet. White lace cloths covered the tables, and Tiffany lamps flickered.

Immediately he noticed the door leading to the grounds of the prison; it was heavy oak. A large ring of keys lay beside the door on a table. Picking up the keys, he silently tried several until he found one that turned the lock. Closing the door behind him, he locked it. Having a locked door between him and the people eating dinner might give him time.

Looking up, his eyes fastened immediately on the guard stationed on the wall. The guard carried a rifle and had his back to him. The street would be far more interesting at this time of night with the lights on and the music coming from the honkytonks. Zac counted on this. This was the man he'd have to kill if it came down to it. He'd have to do it quick, and he'd have to get off one of his better shots with a side arm. He moved around the inside of the wall, all the while keeping his eyes on the man's backside.

Reaching the cellblock, he looked inside. He could see a guard sitting reading by lamplight. To call out might mean that the man would ask for some kind of identification. It would also mean that the man on the wall would, at the very least, turn and see him. The only thing he could count on would be for the man to discount anyone coming into the cellblock area. After all, the man was paid to shoot people breaking out, not somebody breaking in. He wouldn't chance using his voice. Zac tried the keys.

"Yeah, who is it?" The man inside looked up from his paper.

"The marshal," Zac mumbled.

The man grumbled, putting down his paper. "Marshal who?"

Zac didn't respond. He'd been heard. He stuffed the keys back into his pocket.

"Who in heaven's name gave you keys?" Standing up from his table, the guard ambled around it. "Nobody told me about expectin' anybody." Mumbling, he limped toward the door. "Carn sarn people can't ever leave a body be. Can't even read a paper or eat a meal round here." He peered out the window. "Marshal who?"

Zac took out his Wells Fargo badge and flashed it briefly. Just enough for the man to know it was a badge, but not enough for him to know what kind of badge it was. "Just open up," he said. "I've come for one of your prisoners." Zac looked back at the guard on the wall, now staring at him. He waved.

"I don't know you. You got papers?"

"You don't have to know me," Zac said. "You just have to turn those keys. I can show you my papers in the light."

The man was grumpy. His reading had been interrupted and his meal disturbed. "Hand your papers over to me through the window."

Zac glowered back at the man. "Now listen," he barked. "This ain't no army camp and I'm on important business. You just open this thing up. I'll have to shift through the rest of what I'm carryin' in the light and then show you what to look for." Zac had always run a bluff well at the poker table.

The man fumbled for his keys and continued his barrage of murmurs. Slipping the key into the lock, he turned it and growled, "Can't you do your business by the light of day? What's so all-fired important?"

Zac walked through the door and stood while the man shut it and turned the key. He swung the shotgun out from under his coat while the man continued to murmur with his back to him. Turning around from the door, the man's mouth fell open.

"I've come for the woman."

The man gulped. "What woman? We ain't got ourselves no women in here."

"You take me to Elizabeth Roberts right now, or I'll go through this place and turn everybody loose till I find her."

"You wouldn't."

"Don't you bet on it."

"Listen here, mister, I don't know nothin' 'bout no woman."

"You had a fire here today. Where was it?"

The man backed up. "Just put that thang

down. Don't get yerself all het up."

"Fella, you don't want to see me all bothered and I don't want to have to put the lights out on you. Now, you just show me where the fire was, and I'll take it from there."

The man stammered. "The f-f-f-fire was in the far corner . . . upstairs. But I don't know nothin' 'bout no woman."

Zac looked up at the dimly lit, gray-painted stairs.

"Horace is up there, and he's mighty conscientious."

Zac looked behind the man at the unlit storage closet. "Pick up your chair and put it down in there."

"What ya gonna do?"

With the barrel of the shotgun Zac pushed the man into the room and sat him down. Looking around, he found a length of rope.

"What ya gonna do?"

Pulling the man's hands stiffly behind the chair, Zac looped the rope around his wrists and cinched it tight. He spun the rope around the man and the chair and then looped it around his legs. "Where's the keys to the cellblock?"

The man stuck his chin toward the table where he had dropped the keys. "What ya gonna do?"

Ripping a handkerchief into strips, he

wound it around the guard's mouth, tying it tight. "You just sit real still here. If anything happens before I get back with the woman, you may be the first to die. I'll just turn these cons loose and give 'em my knife."

The man's eyes were wide and he nodded his head.

Zac made his way to the stairway. The walls were low and he ducked his head as he went up. He heard the sounds from the cellblock above him, the sound of the prisoners, singing mixed with loud chatter. The solid steel door had a barred window that allowed him to see inside.

Peeping into the semidarkness of the cellblock, he saw the empty tin plates of the inmates pushed outside into the hallway and, at the end of the hall, the guard seated by a light. Trying the keys, he found the one that fit the lock. Gently, he turned the key. He shoved the shotgun inside his jacket and swung open the door.

The guard lifted his head as Zac marched down the darkened corridor. The sight of someone unescorted and walking through the prison at night was something that obviously surprised him, and Zac continued to walk toward him, like a man who knew what he was doing and where he was going.

The man tilted his chair forward and

banged it to the floor, getting to his feet. "Who are you?" He paused and stared at Zac while Zac continued his brisk walk toward him without saying a word. "I said, who are you, and what are you doing here?" Much of the chatter on the cellblock quieted down. The guard reached under his jacket for his six-gun, fumbling with the flap. The fumble cost him.

Zac swung the shotgun out from his jacket and rapped the man's forehead with its butt. It thumped like a ripe melon, sending the man to the floor in a heap. Zac pulled the man's revolver out from its clumsy holster and stuck it in his pants.

Feeling around his belt, he found the key. He set the shotgun down on the table and took off the man's boots. Rolling the man over, Zac proceeded to strip the man of his jacket, shirt, and pants.

A murmur had started throughout the nearest cells, and several men pushed their faces up to the bars. Ignoring them, Zac turned the key.

The light filtered into the cell, and Zac could see Elizabeth. She was standing on her cot, armed with a table leg.

"Elizabeth." He breathed her name softly.

She blinked at the light. "Zac!" She started to cry.

Zac put down the shotgun and clothing and, walking over to the cot, took her in his arms and lifted her to the floor.

She crumpled like a sack of oats in his arms and continued to sob. "I knew you would come, I just knew it. I prayed you would."

Brushing back her hair, he gently kissed her forehead. "I'm here, Elizabeth, I'm here. But we have to go . . . now."

"Yes." Her lips quivered. "I'm so sorry, Zac. I should never have done to you what I did on our ride. I've kicked myself a thousand times since for doing it."

He traced his fingers down the trail of her tears and kissed her cheek. "Somehow, you always seem to be apologizing to me. Now why is that?"

She bit her lower lip. "Because, I guess where you are concerned, I make a fool out of myself. I try to be the businesswoman in control of her life and others, but I never seem to pull that off with you."

He didn't like being delayed, every second counted. But he knew that if they were to follow his plan and get out of this place, Elizabeth was going to have to be in control. Zac kissed her cheek again. "Now, you put these clothes on, you hear?"

She silently nodded her head and wiped her tears.

At her slight hesitation, Zac held her firmly by the shoulders and shook her gently. "Elizabeth, you've got to hunker down and do what I say." He brushed back her hair again and wiped her face. "Look, I'm gonna step outside while you change. I want you in this guard suit, then we're gonna walk right outta here, comprende?"

The guard was still out cold when Zac walked out of the cell. He hadn't moved a muscle. It was only moments until Elizabeth slipped outside the door, and Zac picked up the man's heels and dragged him inside the cell. Tossing her the guard's cap, he said, "Stick your hair under that."

He watched as she crammed the waves of red hair under the blue cap. She was beautiful even when she was miserable and dirty, but she had more than beauty, she had grit and fire. It was the quality Zac had always admired in Jenny, and he could see that Elizabeth had it too.

He handed her the shotgun. "Hold this under your arm and we're gonna step out of here in a hurry. Don't make eye contact with anybody. These boys are gonna be hootin' shore nuff if they get wind that somethin's up. And if they can tell you're a woman, we're done for."

The prisoners that lined the dark hallway

continued to murmur, more loudly now. Some were shouting. Zac and Elizabeth walked past them briskly, creating more noise as they passed by each cell. This uproar might be the only thing that gave them up, and time was of the utmost importance.

They moved through the open cellblock door, closing it but not bothering to lock it. Winding back down the stairway, Zac stopped at the bottom and peered around the corner. The noise was getting louder now. His heartbeat was rising with it. No one seemed to be there. The empty chair and table still stood by the door. Passing by, he saw the guard straining against his bonds.

Zac took off his hat and crammed it under his jacket. "Just hold the shotgun under your arm and walk behind me. If the guard on the wall sees you, give him a wave."

The two of them walked through the door and into the darkened yard of the prison. Immediately, Zac could see the guard on the wall. The noise coming from the cellblock had obviously gotten his attention. Zac watched the man carefully, keeping his hands by his sides, ready to draw his .45 if he saw the man raise his rifle.

"Is everything okay?" the man yelled down to the two of them.

Elizabeth held up her hand and waved it

over her head. The man paused. Standing in front of the warden's house, Zac remembered he still had the keys to the door with him. If the man on the wall had any sense at all, he might be a little troubled by the idea of him pulling the key out and using it.

He felt for the key, put it in the lock. "Why don't you turn the key," he said to Elizabeth.

Elizabeth moved around him as Zac stood aside and allowed her to open the door, all in an effort to appease the guard with the rifle.

Opening the door, they both walked directly into the warden's living room. The warden and his wife were seated by the fireplace. She dropped her knitting and the warden got to his feet. "What's the meaning of this?" he asked.

"Just checking out one of your prisoners, Warden."

Elizabeth stepped around Zac and took off her cap, shaking out her hair. "This is the man I told you would come for me."

"What is she doing here?" the woman asked, turning to her husband.

Elizabeth moved toward her. "Your husband has been involved in my kidnapping."

"Samuel, is it true?" The woman had gotten to her feet and was clinging to the warden's arm. "Did you have anything to do with this woman being here?"

"I can explain." He edged toward a desk beside the sofa.

Zac took the shotgun out of Elizabeth's hands. "You better practice your explaining with her because the judge you stand in front of when this thing is over won't be as sympathetic. Step back."

Zac pointed the ten-gauge at him and walked toward the desk. Opening the drawer, he pulled out a nickel-plated revolver.

"Listen," the man said. "This woman and her family will be of little importance in a short while. Colorado will move on without them."

Zac was getting angry. There was something about politicians and political appointees that made him angry normally, but one that couldn't bring himself to apologize when caught at dirty dealing was lower yet.

The man held out his hands. "Now just hold on, I have something for you, something I can divide with you." He reached into another drawer and slowly brought out a stack of bills. "There is five thousand dollars here. I'll give you half to leave the girl."

Zac cracked the nickel-plated pistol on the side of the man's jaw with a suddenness that was startling. The man's head snapped back, and the bills went flying. With a fluid motion, Zac reached around and grabbed the hair on the back of the warden's head, putting his face down on the tabletop. He held him there, pressing his nose against the hardwood. "You owe this lady an apology."

The man grunted as Zac pressed down harder. "I'm sorry . . . Miss Roberts . . . I apologize," he muttered in muffled tones.

Zac released his grip on him and stuck the revolver into his own pants. "I'm doing you a favor by taking this, otherwise the lady here will be a widow. I'd suggest if you want to busy yourself that you do it by packing. The sooner you get out of the state of Colorado, the sooner you can shun the law you were sworn to uphold."

Zac and Elizabeth walked quickly out of the house and toward the trees. He could see Bruce waiting; Bruce, his horse, and Elizabeth's roan. Bruce took her into his arms.

"I'm so glad to see you," he said. "I honestly didn't think you were in there, and I've been standing out here praying for the longest time. I didn't know what to do next."

Zac mounted the bay. "I see you got the roan," he said.

"Yes, but we won't discuss it."

"Professor, as long as you do what you're supposed to do, there ain't no need to discuss anything."

Both Bruce and Elizabeth mounted. "Did Sam come with you?" she asked.

Zac motioned them away from the prison. "We're riding out that way. I'd like to stay outta sight of the wall up there, just in case that warden decides not to pack."

They rode out quickly, meandering through the back streets of Cañon City. It was then that Bruce told Elizabeth about Sam. She drew up her reins.

"Where is he?" she asked.

"We are not sure," Bruce said. "I believe the doctor took him in, but it looked like a serious wound."

"I've got to go and find him."

"He's not going to make it," Zac said.

"All the more reason for me to find him. No man should die alone, not without someone beside him that loves him."

"You're only alone before you die," Zac said.

"I don't care what you say, I've got to find him."

The sound of the train pulling into the station and the gunfire that erupted around it put an end to the discussion. "That will be your father," Zac said.

The three of them slapped their horses and rode toward the sound of the shooting.

Chapter 35

The Denver and Rio Grande engine sat at the station house spewing steam. The place was swarming with badged men as they rode up. Several of them drew down on Zac, Elizabeth, and Bruce. "Here, here! Stop! That's Miss Roberts herself!" one of the men shouted.

The men lowered their weapons and several ran toward the front of the locomotive, where a group of others were standing. Zac and his party dismounted and were almost immediately surrounded.

"Elizabeth!" Roberts moved briskly toward his daughter, arms outstretched. "Thank God, you're alive!"

Elizabeth ran to him. Embracing him, she murmured, "Daddy, Daddy, you're a wonderful sight."

"I never thought any of this affair would come to this. I had no business putting you at such grave risk."

Zac stood beside the big bay, along with Elliott, and lit his pipe.

The former governor, ever the politician,

elbowed his way to the front and grabbed Elizabeth's hand. "Miss Roberts, you are a brave woman indeed, the kind of woman who has made our great state what it is."

Elizabeth looked past him at all the men mixing on the platform. "Where did you get all these men, Father?"

"These men are deputies," the governor answered. "Special deputies from four counties, more than two hundred strong." He stuck out his chest. "We are here for a show of force."

"I have a court order here," Roberts interjected, "and these men are here to see that it's enforced." He looked back at Torkelson and motioned for him to come forward. "This brave attorney of ours is solely responsible for saving us from a great loss of life last night. We'd have been here this morning, but it took such an infernally long time to clear the tracks from Chicago Pacific interference."

"Father, I have so much to tell you, but first I need to say that I'm alive because of Zac."

"I am deeply indebted to you, Cobb. I don't think I can ever repay what I truly owe you."

Zac brushed the gesture aside and continued to enjoy his pipe.

"And Sam has been mortally wounded, I fear," she added. "I want to go to him."

"It's true, sir." Elliott stepped forward. "I was with him this morning when he was shot. He may be gone."

"I'll assign some deputies to go with you, Elizabeth. We don't plan to move out until daylight. The men are tired and they need something to eat. Besides, the light of day will show our opposition how futile it is to resist us. Will you come with us in the morning, Cobb?"

"I don't believe so, General. I've had my fill of crowded trains."

"Of course." Roberts looked over at Elizabeth. "You'll be wanting to move on. Your mission is more than done here. I have a special train with workers due in here tomorrow. Your shepherd friend will be on it. He and his son wanted to come. It can take you to Denver where it unloads its supplies and then you can be on your way home."

Elizabeth's face was drawn with sadness. She knew the time would come for Zac to leave, but she wanted to do everything she could to delay it. She clutched at her father's arm. "Daddy, I think we should have a special gala at the Glen when this is over. It wouldn't be right to have it without Zac."

"We will have to see what the man wishes,

my dear," he said quietly to her. "In the meantime, I'd suggest you go and find Sam. Will you be staying, Cobb, or returning with the special train in the morning?"

"General, by the looks of things, you're going to have men stepping all over each other before the night's through. But I would like to see the thing settled and over with." He pulled off his hat and ran his fingers through his hair. "If you don't mind, I think I'll just take the bay on down the road. The night air is the best for sleeping, and I'll join you in the canyon in the morning."

"Splendid! Capital!" the governor interrupted. Zac could see the man had been anxious to get a word into the conversation.

The night air and the open skies was something Zac had been craving for days. He said his goodbyes to Elizabeth and Elliott and took very little time to begin trotting the bay down the road and out of town. He rode easylike, and the quietness of the valley that snaked itself beside the tracks was something he could enjoy now — no loud noises, no gunfire, no people bustling around him. The cold steel of the railroad lay like a coiled serpent in the moonlight. Overhead, scattered clouds matted the moon.

Zac rode on for several hours. Town noise and lights were fading in the distance. There was something inside of him that functioned best when he was alone. To depend on no one, worry about no one, was a feeling his soul craved.

He heard the yapping of coyotes in the hills, and an occasional rabbit darted across his path. The bay had been well-rested during the day, which was more than Zac could say for himself. The sight of the mob at the railroad station had served to remind him how tired he was. When he reached the edge of the Arkansas River, he pulled rein and stopped for the night. It would be a cold, dark camp, but he didn't care. He just wanted to sleep.

The morning sun was still a ways off when he awoke. The horse had been hobbled but still had managed to wander a bit. He took the halter and some oats and made his way over the rocks toward the animal. "Here, boy, some breakfast for one of us."

From the bottom of the draw beside the river, he could see the hanging bridge. It was a wonder, stretching over the chilly waters. A few birds ventured out, circling overhead, and he could make out the form of a hawk. He figured it would be some time before the train from Cañon City arrived. All those people were like ants — only thing was, ants were more organized, had more purpose.

446

For a man who mixed with people a lot, Zac knew he'd never mixed well. He was a solitary man, and that's the way he liked it. As he saddled the bay, he thought about it and decided he'd been born a hundred years too late.

This place would have been a fine spot a hundred years ago, before the people came, before the railroad. Often he had longed to put his foot down where no man had been before, to carve out a place from the fresh raw land that God had left only the day before. The thought made him smile.

Where he rode, the valley had been invaded by the river. Its mist rose into the morning air, washing the earth with a cold cloud that shone in the breaking sun. It was as if the valley held a dark mystery, a secret that it would share with only a few. But now, the men from the railroad wanted to open its riddles to everybody who could buy a ticket. There was something bittersweet about that. Progress was a sad thing. *This ain't the plains of God no more,* he pondered. *It's only real estate.*

The track crooked its way around several curves and deeper into the valley. Several elk lifted their heads from the stream and scampered away as he rode on. *No prettier sight in all the earth,* he thought, *red elk standing in green grass, beside blue water.*

A long, low train whistle shattered the silence of the morning. It was a mournful sound, reminding him of a funeral, a funeral for the earth. He pulled up the reins of the bay and sat still, listening to the whistle and swinging himself around in the saddle to watch the empty tracks behind him. It would be storming past him in a matter of minutes, roaring by and crammed with gunmen. It would grind its way past him, and it would be good riddance. If it weren't for seeing the shepherd again, he'd just as soon ride on.

As he swung back around, something caught the corner of his eye. High overhead, he saw a red flag beating a signal in the morning air. He couldn't see the man waving it, only the flag. Suddenly he knew. Something was wrong. Something terrible was going to happen.

He heard the other oncoming train before he saw it, the sound of the wheels grinding across the silent steel. Then he saw the smoke from the locomotive. It puffed a column of steam into the air from behind the ridge in front of him, and it was heading right toward him.

He moved the big bay to the side and watched as it chugged into view from around the sharp bend. The wheels were churning and the driving rods pumped as the engine picked up speed. He watched carefully as it roared by. The cab was not empty. Zac could see the man at the controls, but the man was looking out toward the right side of the cab and did not see him. It was the Englishman, Peter Williams!

Zac put his spurs to the bay's sides and the horse lurched forward, running along the side of the tender. He held his head down and ran, galloping now and picking up speed. The rhythm of the horse was smooth. It flew along the side of the cinder track bed. There would be no stopping now. Zac's hat flew off, and he and the bay kept pace with the quickening train.

Moving closer to the tender, Zac took his left foot from the stirrup. He leaned toward the handrail that swept down from the top of the coal box and ended next to a small platform near the large black ball of steel. He jumped.

His hands fastened onto the rail, and his feet were skimming the ground. The steel platform had connected solidly with his rib cage, and he felt the piercing pain of the impact. It shot through him like a live wire charged with a strike of lightning. Gripping the rail, he pulled, hoisting himself onto the narrow platform. He lay there for only a moment, the shock of the landing unbearable. He clutched his chest and sucked for air.

As he got to his feet, every movement surged the pain deeper into his body. Blinking from the agony, he climbed for the top of the tender.

In front of him, he could see the lanky Englishman continue to look down the track ahead. Zac scampered onto the coal and scooted forward on his belly. Every movement was excruciating, but still he inched forward. Time was short. He heard the whistle again from the oncoming train. How far off it was, he could only guess. He only knew he had to blank every thought of pain out of his mind and move now as if his life depended on it, because it did.

He turned and sat himself down on top of the coal and then slipped forward, sliding down the pile of coal toward the man who drove the death train. Panic surged through him as he felt his revolver and the belly gun he carried jar loose during the slide. Landing in a heap in front of the tender, he hit hard.

Williams turned and saw him. "Cobb!"

Zac launched himself toward the man as Williams drew his revolver. He hammered the man's body hard with his head, separating him from the shucked pistol. Zac lay at

Williams' feet as the man began to kick at him.

Grabbing one of Williams' boots, Zac twisted it, tumbling the Englishman back onto the pile of coal.

Williams bounced up and swung, landing a solid punch in Zac's middle that sent the breath right out of him. He staggered, fell against the side of the cab. Turning to his right, Zac could see the steam rising from the approaching train as it drew closer to the blind curve.

The Englishman followed the blow up with several jabs to Zac's stomach and then launched a jolt at his chin, snapping his head backward.

Zac was in trouble. He wasn't fighting, he was just hanging on to consciousness. Things were spinning inside his head. The cab itself seemed like a whirling merry-go-round of delirium. He didn't have much left and he knew it.

Williams moved forward for the kill. Many times in the last days he had dreamed of this. Cobb had cost him everything, but most importantly, he'd cost him his self-respect. No matter what happened now, the Englishman had to kill him. The railroad meant little if he couldn't face himself in the mirror. He would pick Cobb up and stick his head into the burning boiler. Nothing would give him greater pleasure than to feel Zac Cobb die in his hands. He opened the door to the boiler and, reaching down, took Zac by his jacket and lifted him up.

Zac was still conscious but his strength was spent. The pain that raced through him robbed him of the ability to think. The only thing left was to die. But not without a fight.

Zac could feel the heat on the back of his neck as Williams moved him toward the boiler. The sound of the approaching train whistle was closer now. Reaching his hand behind him, Zac pressed it up against the hot metal. The searing sound of his own flesh quickened his mind. He gave a last desperate kick, setting Williams off-balance and onto the floor of the cab.

Zac wobbled to his feet.

Quick as a cat, Williams grabbed the shovel that lay beside him and swung it. It landed on Zac's shoulder, spinning him toward the open cab door. "You've come to me once too often, Cobb. Now I'm going to kill you." Williams was livid, onto Zac with blinding speed, continuing to hammer him with the shovel.

Zac grabbed the shovel and spun Williams around, bashing him against the solid steel of the cab in an attempt to loosen his grip.

452

Looking forward, he could see the blind curve now. Only moments and the approaching train would come into view, and by then it would be too late. Zac jerked on the shovel, but the tall Englishman held firm. Pressing backward, the man slammed Zac up against the hot boiler, sizzling his flesh once again.

Zac hit the floor, holding on to the shovel with a viselike grip and jerking Williams forward. The Englishman banged his head on the boiler. Below him, Zac launched a kick in the man's groin, loosening the Englishman's grip on the shovel.

He bellowed like a cow caught in barbed wire and stumbled backward toward the open door. Grabbing for the handrail, he fell. Holding on in a death-grip, he lost his footing and his feet went out from under him and over the edge of the car.

Zac got to his knees and watched as the man hung on helplessly. The whistle blew once more, and Zac reached for the Johnson bar, shoving it into place. He applied the brakes and heard the screeching sound of steel on steel. Hoping against hope that he'd acted in time, he watched as sparks flew up from beneath the wheels and around the dangling Englishman.

Ignoring his pain and against his better

judgment, Zac reached for Williams. Grabbing the man's jacket, he hauled him up onto the cab floor. Unexpectedly, the effort and the resulting pain that shot through him sunk him to his knees. The agony he felt made his head swim. In a few seconds everything had gone from black to white. When he lifted his head, he could see Williams had his revolver pointed directly at him.

"This is where you die, Cobb."

From the corner of his eye, Zac could see the short-barreled belly gun not two feet away. He slowly palmed a handful of coal dust from the floor.

"You have cost me success for the last time, you bloody Yank."

The man cocked the revolver, and Zac threw the dust in the Englishman's face, then grabbed for his belly gun. Flame shot from Williams' misguided gun.

Zac held the trigger down on the Shopkeeper Special and began to fan the hammer. One by one, the .45 slugs found their mark, jerking the Englishman's body like sledgehammers against a tin street sign. The man pitched backward and fell through the open cabin door of the slowing locomotive.

On the ground beside the track, his eyes blinked back the last signs of life.

Chapter 36

"Señor, señor, you are a praise that has breath."

Zac blinked his eyes open. He lay on a cot in the open air, saw the old Mexican shepherd, a wrinkled hand over his heart.

The old man's hands moved up Zac's body, felt his face. "This is what I have prayed to Jesus for, señor. I prayed that when I came to you again, I might feel your good heart beating inside of you and hear the breath of your life once more."

Elizabeth was kneeling beside him now. She placed a cold cloth on his forehead. "You haven't been moving much since yesterday, and I wouldn't let them take you away by train. I was afraid the travel would be too hard on you."

"Where am I?"

"We're camped beside the suspension bridge, next to the river. The plans are to be here for several days to look things over. We have lots of men laying track. And we're going to have a big picnic. My Aunt Liz shaved you."

Nikki crowded her way under the old man's arm and patted Zac's cheek. "You are smooth now, except for your mustache. Can you give me a horsey ride?"

"I don't think Mr. Cobb will be giving anyone a ride for a while yet, Nikki," Elizabeth said. "He needs to rest."

"And then can he give me one?"

"Yes, hon, I will. I can't see myself rustin' away here too much longer." Zac could feel the bandages tightly wound around his chest. The slight breaths he managed hurt.

"Here, sweetheart, let me take you back to your mommy and daddy. You need to play, and I have something to show Mr. Cobb."

The old shepherd sat still beside him as Elizabeth led Nikki away. "Dis woman," he said. "You know she loves you very much."

Zac lay still. The thought made him feel heavy inside. To have another woman care about him was a responsibility he didn't want to stomach.

"I already got one woman who loves me, and sometimes I think that's one more than I need."

The old man laughed. "Señor, a man like you works best alone on this earth, but a man lives best when someone loves him." The man ran his hand through his white beard. "Sometimes, I think, it takes a match, a hot spark, to light the lantern. The lantern burns slow and long. The match, it is very hot, but it does not burn for long."

"And you think Elizabeth is that match?"

"I think she may be part of God's plan for you, señor. Apart from that, I cannot say."

Zac turned his head and watched as Elizabeth gave Nikki back to Irene. She was a beautiful woman, the kind of woman most men would die for. She turned and made her way back to him.

"Do you think you can get to your feet?" she asked.

"I'd like nothing better."

He swung his legs off the cot, and Elizabeth helped him as he stood up. He felt the rust melt with each step. The pain was still there, but having his feet under him felt wonderful. Elizabeth steered him over toward a nearby tent. "There's someone in here that's been the biggest baby I've ever seen. He's been asking for you all day."

Zac ducked his head as he cleared the flap on the tent.

"Look at who I have for you," Elizabeth said.

"Reb? Is that you, Reb?" Sam Fisher lay on a cot, propped up by pillows. He had his hand wrapped around a glass of whiskey and

457

was smoking a cigar.

"Fisher! Why ain't you dead?"

"Durned if I know. I did my best to die, but I guess I failed at that too." The old man squinted at Zac. "I took three Minié balls from you Rebs during the war, so how am I gonna up and let some tinhorn from the Chicago Pacific kill me with a little old .32? Thing don't do nothing but spit out tiny pills, and I reckon it'll take a whole shovelful a them to dish out one dose a death for a fella like me." He lifted his glass.

Zac laughed, then winced and clutched his side. "My momma used to say, only the good die young. But I reckon that don't qualify you for any miracle. You ain't good, and God only knows how old you are. Musta been that little girl's prayers out there."

"Yeah, I reckon so. Hers or the old Mexican's. He's been in here a bunch, spoutin' Scripture at me whilst I was trying to sleep. Guess he's got so much of the stuff in his head, he don't need them eyes to read it."

Several days passed and the day of the picnic arrived. The camp continued to be busy with inspecting and laying track. The cooks had been roasting lamb and steers all day. Sam was sitting up now. He sat next to Zac and watched the cooks turn the meat.

A gruff grin spread over his face. "Time was a few days ago when I'da whacked one of those in the head and settled down to eat it right then and there."

Zac was moving around much better. He stretched his muscles and did some light exercise, just to make sure everything was working. Bruce Elliott and General Roberts walked over and joined the two wounded men. "This day seems like it's been a long time coming," Elliott said. "And it's such a beautiful day too, no wind and not a cloud in the sky."

Roberts brushed the salt and pepper mustache under his lip. "It is a wonderful day. I had some men go over the bridge. They will be bringing back the locomotive the Chicago Pacific had over there. We will need to return it, along with the rest of their equipment."

"I don't think you'd catch me riding over that bridge on a train," Zac said.

"Oh, it's perfectly safe. I must say, I think those people did an excellent job building it."

The women joined them and they began to talk about everything imaginable, everything except the struggle for the place they were all now enjoying.

The whistle from the train turned their

heads and Irene screamed. Nikki had wandered out onto the railroad bridge, balancing herself on the steel rails, waving her arms like a bird in flight.

Everyone froze. Several men stood on the edge of the low-slung railroad bridge, calling for her.

Zac, Bruce, and Elizabeth ran for the bridge, followed by the rest.

Elizabeth screamed, "She can't hear them. She can't even hear the train."

The locomotive had begun crossing the steel span, and all who stood beside the structure could clearly see that there was no way possible for someone to run onto the bridge, grab the girl, and make it back in time. The men standing beside the structure continued to yell at Nikki without moving.

"I've got to get her," Bruce yelled.

Zac grabbed his shirt. "Don't be a fool."

Elliott struggled and Zac threw a punch into his chin, knocking the man to the ground. Without hesitating, he reached for a horse tied nearby, grabbing a rope and a rifle from the saddle. He began sprinting across the bridge.

Nikki had felt the movement of the train and froze in place. She turned and began to walk back between the rails, but the engine was fast overtaking her.

460

Zac continued to run. As he ran, he tied a knot onto the end of the rope and cinched a slip knot into it. Looping it under his arms, he continued to run toward the little girl.

The train was now moving at a pace that left them only moments to spare.

Zac tied the other end of the rope onto the action of the rifle. He tightened the knot securely as he ran. Scooping up the child in his arms, he looked up. The engine was now only yards away. There was no more time.

Laying the rifle beside the rail and running the rope between the ties, he clutched Nikki close to him and jumped. The two of them swung out above the river. Swinging beneath the bridge with Nikki screaming in his arms, he watched the locomotive pass overhead. The swaying motion worried him. The rifle and its position between the rails was the only thing holding them above the roaring river, and he felt the movement of the rope tug at the wedged rifle. It was slipping.

The rope bit into his underarms and he could feel the pain once again shooting through his ribs. He bit down hard, and then began to talk to the child. "It'll be fine, Nikki. Your mother's coming now, and they'll pull us up."

The child continued to cry and Zac began to worry. No one would come for them until the train passed, and the rifle continued to slip. He had to stop the swaying motion of the rope, but how?

"Honey," he asked, "can you help?"

Nikki cried more softly. "Yes."

"I'm going to put your legs through my belt and I want you to hang on to me so I can use both hands. Can you do that?"

The girl nodded.

Zac stuffed the little girl's legs through his belt. He didn't want any mishap. The last thing he wanted was for Nikki's arms to slip off him and have her plummet to the raging river below.

Feeling her legs safely inside his belt, he spoke calmly to the child as the rope continued to swing. "Now, Nikki, you hang on around my neck. I'm going to pull us up this rope and try to stop it from swinging. Can you do that?"

"Yes." The girl was sniffing bravely. She laced her fingers around the back of his neck and clung closely to him.

Zac pulled on the rope as the rifle continued to slip. With each heave, his ribs ached. He gritted his teeth as the intense pain shot through his upper body. Hand over hand, he pulled the two of them up the rope. Looping the coils of hemp created by the climb around his elbow, he continued to climb.

The upward movement of the two of them slowed the oscillating of the rope. Beads of sweat formed ridges of moisture on his forehead as he struggled against the pain.

Overhead, he could see the crowd forming on the bridge. At last, he felt a tug on the line as men pulled on the rope. "Hang on, honey," he said, relieved. "They've got us now. We'll be all right. Are you okay?"

The girl mumbled. "Y-yes . . . I'mmm okay."

Slowly he let the line slide through his hands. It burned his skin, and he started to uncoil the line from around his elbow. The ascent toward the bridge was steady.

In a matter of minutes, the men on the bridge were pulling the two of them over the edge. "Get the girl," Zac said.

Irene took her daughter from the men's arms. The men grabbed Zac by the jacket and hoisted him up. His arms hung loosely by his sides as Elizabeth and Bruce elbowed their way to him.

Zac grinned through the pain and ran his fingers through his black hair. "Trains! I hate trains."

Chapter 37

Zac stood beside the depot. He never carried much in the way of baggage. Never needed much. Things only got in his way.

"I trust you will find my car comfortable," General Roberts said. "There will be someone aboard to tend to your needs. I've made arrangements for you all the way to San Luis Obispo."

Zac was embarrassed by all the fuss. He studied the exterior of the ornate special coach. The gilded windows and stained glass were quite impressive. Brass lamps hung along the side.

"And I'll be along to protect you from any hooligans we're apt to meet up with along the way," Sam Fisher grinned. "My rear'll be a sight more comfortable in there than on one of them four-legged devils you ride." Fisher had been up and around for a few days. He picked up his bags and marched to the rear platform.

Roberts cleared his throat. "Sam insisted," he said. "He's always wanted to see that part of California, and he thought you could do with some company."

"Normally, I'm most comfortable all by myself, but I've been with that old man for so long now that he's growing on me. I'll try to send him back to you in one piece."

Zac stooped down and took Nikki by the shoulders. "Sweetheart, I have something for you." Reaching into his pocket, he pulled out a hand-carved horse. "I whittled this out for you, hon. When you feel it, you can think of me."

"Oh, I w-w-will," she said. "I will think of you all the time, and I'll pray for you, too. When I grow up I want to marry you."

Zac glanced up at the general and smiled. "Folks in your family are mighty smitten with the idea of weddings."

"Mr. Cobb, I think you will find as you get older that family is the most important thing. It's the only thing you can count on — love, love that lasts a lifetime. We've been holding to that principle in the Roberts family for years."

Zac stood upright and laid his hand on the girl's head. "You're gonna be some kind of a woman too, sweetheart."

"Zac Cobb, we will never forget what you've done for us." Irene blinked back the tears from her eyes. "I don't think we ever realize how fragile life is, how completely vulnerable we are, and especially how dependent we can become on a total stranger. You had no official responsibility for us, and yet you risked your life time and again."

Zac removed his hat. "Ma'am, the West is where people look out for one another. I was just in a place to do what any man ought to have done."

"You were in a position to do what no other man could have done," Bruce said. He rubbed his jaw and cocked a smile. "You certainly delivered the kind of blow to me that no one has been able to do in some time."

Zac smiled and put his hat on. "Well, professor, even an educated man learns sometimes. Besides, you held your own pretty well. You'll do."

He could see Elizabeth standing behind them, like a forlorn calf waiting for the barbecue.

Irene tugged on Bruce's arm. "We have a carriage waiting, darling. Let's allow Mr. Cobb to be on his way."

Zac watched the family walk back to the carriage. Elizabeth hung back. She looked especially beautiful in a bright green dress that made her red hair look even more radiant. Her natural curls glinted in the morning sun. She stepped forward and took Zac's hand.

"I suppose there's nothing more I can say."

"No, I don't suppose so," he said.

"You know how I feel about you."

Zac stood with his hand in hers. In a way, this was as bittersweet a moment for him as it was for her. Saying goodbye was something he never liked to do. The niceties of the thing always grated on him. To promise things he never intended to deliver went against his principles, and goodbyes always lent themselves to just that kind of thing.

"Can I write you?" she asked.

"I don't think that would be a good thing." He could see the tears begin to form in her eyes, but he wanted no doubts left in her mind. If Elizabeth Roberts was ever to have a moment of loneliness, he didn't want to be the one she turned her thoughts to. "There's just no sense keeping a fire going that will only bring you pain."

She straightened up. "All I can say to you, Zac, is that woman in California is someone I deeply envy, and I don't even know her. It's a feeling I've never had before, and I guess I don't yet know how to deal with it."

"You'll handle it, Elizabeth. I think you can handle just about anything that comes your way."

She swallowed and gripped his hand tighter.

"Let me tell you something, Zachary Cobb. Before I met and came to know you, the only thing I ever thought I could love was what I could do for myself. I never let anyone get close to my heart, never let a man other than my father gain my respect. If you've taught me anything, you've taught me what love feels like. If I meet anyone that remotely makes me feel like I do when I am near you, I will never let that man out of my sight."

Zac wasn't quite accustomed to talking to a woman about his feelings. Women and feelings were two subjects that he believed himself to be a stranger to. "Elizabeth, when this train leaves, you'll have your whole life ahead of you. You're the kind of woman that can do anything you choose to do. You have a great strength inside of you, strength that has nothing to do with your father, or this railroad. It comes from deep inside. I'm proud to know you, and I'm proud to call you a friend."

"Then there can be nothing else?"

"Nothing's better than being called a friend, Elizabeth. We live in different worlds. You have all of this. I have my ranch, my job, and whatever I can put a saddle on. You have your star, but it's not my star, Elizabeth."

She held his hand tightly. Leaning up, she kissed him. "Then goodbye, friend."

The employees of Thorndike Press hope you have enjoyed this Large Print book. All our Large Print titles are designed for easy reading, and all our books are made to last. Other Thorndike Press Large Print books are available at your library, through selected bookstores, or directly from us.

For information about titles, please call:

(800) 257-5157

To share your comments, please write:

Publisher
Thorndike Press
P.O. Box 159
Thorndike, Maine 04986